Praise for Louise Bagshawe:

KU-512-122

'Jam-packed with edgy, sophisticated women and sexy, powerful men, you'll be hooked by the racy, romantic intrigues, and the twists and turns of the plot' *Woman*

'If you like your novels fast-paced and full of characters you'd love to call a friend (or indeed an enemy) then you'll really enjoy the latest one from Louise Bagshawe' *OK!* magazine

'Intelligent and lively' *Daily Mirror*

'One of the most charming and lively romances I've read in a decade . . . I couldn't stop reading it, or cheering on the heroine' *Australian Women's Weekly*

'A great book. A classic story of life, love and ambition' *Woman's Own*

'A fat sexy book that throbs with vitality from the first page . . . Bagshawe has produced a classic of the genre' *Daily Express*

'A gloriously glossy blend of glitzy women, handsome men, and the power of friendship' *Living Edge*

Also by Louise Bagshawe

Career Girls
The Movie
Tall Poppies
Venus Envy
A Kept Woman
When She Was Bad . . .
The Devil You Know
Monday's Child
Tuesday's Child
Sparkles

Louise
Bagshawe

Glamour

headline
review

First published in Great Britain in 2007 by HEADLINE REVIEW
An imprint of HEADLINE PUBLISHING GROUP

First published in paperback in 2007 by HEADLINE REVIEW
An imprint of HEADLINE PUBLISHING GROUP

1

978 0 7553 0434 9 (A-format)
978 0 7553 3669 2 (B-format)

Typeset in Meridien Roman by Avon DataSet Ltd,
Bidford-on-Avon, Warwickshire

Printed and bound in Great Britain by Clays Ltd, St Ives plc

Headline's policy is to use papers that are natural, renewable and
recyclable products and made from wood grown in sustainable forests.
The logging and manufacturing processes are expected to conform to
the environmental regulations of the country of origin.

HEADLINE PUBLISHING GROUP
An Hachette Livre UK Company
338 Euston Road
London NW1 3BH

www.reviewbooks.co.uk
www.headline.co.uk

Acknowledgements

Firstly, I would like to thank my wonderful agent Michael Sissons, and secondly, my brilliant editor Harrie Evans, who had her patience stretched to the limit with *Glamour* – she obviously works well under pressure as she has shaped this into a wonderful book. The entire team at Headline and PFD also get all my thanks. It has been a fantastic experience growing with Headline and I am very grateful for the wonderful sales, marketing and press teams. A special vote of thanks to the Board.

Glamour would never have been written without my husband Anthony. Since I am never going to write that ten-volume history of the New York Yankees, this book is dedicated to him. PS. Darling, I am looking forward to the Balrog.

Prologue

GLAMOUR

The name was written in brass letters, each one sixteen feet high, polished like a mirror. They glittered on the front of the store like solid gold, sparkling in the California sun, like a permanent firework.

What a store! In Hollywood, the city of the stars, GLAMOUR said it all. A landmark attraction since the day it first opened, the new building was a must-see on every tourist itinerary. All-American razzmatazz; a monument to luxury, money, and power.

The flagship store was ten storeys high. Dwarfing Harrods in London or Saks in New York, LA's GLAMOUR was the ultimate shopping temple. Sleek and modern, it had been fronted with glossy black granite, so that the golden letters shone even more brilliantly. The trademark uniformed doormen and valets, both men and women, who attended to shoppers' every whim, stood to attention behind the huge glass front doors, waiting for opening time. At GLAMOUR, shopping was an exquisite pleasure. Once you entered those doors, the cares of the day fell away. You were in another world; soft carpeting underfoot, exquisite fresh flowers at every corner, assistants to wait on your every need. Every shopping trip was a vacation, and around the world, women with money just couldn't get enough. If you bought so much as a hairband in GLAMOUR, somebody would wrap it in the iconic triple G tissue paper, tie it with mint-green ribbons, and carry it to your car – should you so desire.

The clothes were fabulous. The scents adorable. The shoes haute couture. The jewels must-have.

They loved it. And the women who had founded it were set to become amongst the richest in the world. Everybody knew their story.

Three women. Beautiful, powerful and rich.

And, it seemed, absolutely ruthless.

Once they had been the closest of friends. Once, they had all suffered. And, together, they had triumphed.

So how had it gone so wrong?

'It's the Princess!' The little girl tugged on her mother's coat sleeve, jumping up and down with excitement. 'Look! Momma. It's her. There she is!'

'You're right, baby!'

Her mother, Coco, a bank teller in her mid-thirties, leaned over the thick velvet rope that flanked the long red carpet that swept across Rodeo Drive. Keisha's childish enthusiasm was infectious. She hoisted her daughter up on her shoulders, so the girl could get a better look.

Across the street, forced back by security, was a gaggle of media reporters, cameramen and boom mike holders, all talking intently to camera. Two local TV news choppers whirred overhead.

Normally you only got this sort of turnout for the biggest stars. A-list actresses, the First Lady, the Lakers. But these three young women were legendary. America – and the world – was watching this meeting.

Coco felt her stomach knot with anticipation. She was going to be late taking Keisha to school, late for work. But it was worth it. She'd pushed her baby into the crowd, determined to show her three of the most sizzling, famous businesswomen in the world.

The American dream. Anyone could make it. It could be

you in that limo. Never mind school – *that* was a lesson Keisha should learn. Coco turned towards the car as the LAPD shouted, motioning for everybody to get back. Keisha squealed in delight.

The security men swarmed around the gleaming black vehicle. There were olive-skinned soldiers, lean and dangerous looking, the palm tree of Ghada emblazoned on the chest of their uniforms. Mingling with them brawny Americans with dark suits, shades and earpieces – the Secret Service.

A man stepped forward and opened the back door of the limo.

The Arab security men snapped to the salute.

A slippered foot emerged from the limo, swathed in gorgeously embroidered gold thread. It was followed by the swish of a long dress, a floor-length robe in butterscotch silk, well cut and covered with ornate stitched designs; modest, self-assured, and beautiful. The woman stood up; she wore a simple veil across her hair, secured with a solid semi-circle of polished gold; her aquiline face was calm and confident.

'She's so beautiful,' Keisha gasped. 'Can I get a dress like that, Mom?'

'I don't think it would fit you, baby,' Coco replied.

The crowd recovered from its fit of awe.

'Princess! Princess!'

'Princess Haya!'

'Haya, over here! Highness!'

The gold-robed vision smiled and waved; to the dismay of her handlers, she strode up to the barriers, shaking hands and greeting the crowd. They cheered and shouted; Haya chatted graciously.

'I want to meet her!' Keisha squealed.

'There are hundreds of people here, honey,' Coco said, not wanting her daughter to get disappointed.

But then four black-suited men brushed past her – and all

of a sudden, there was the Princess, standing before them, resplendent in her traditional gown; gleaming, as golden as the sun, like something out of Coco's childhood fairy stories.

Keisha clapped her hands.

'You're a real live princess!' she shouted.

And as Coco watched, Princess Haya laughed, reached forward, and gave the little girl a big hug.

'And so are you,' she replied. Then she looked at Coco.

'Ma'am, you have a beautiful daughter.'

'Th-thank you – Highness . . .' Coco stuttered.

Haya grinned and winked at the amazed mother. Then she turned smartly, and walked up the red carpet, past her bowing security men, silken robe fluttering in the light breeze.

'Oh my gosh!' Keisha was saying. 'She hugged me! Oh my gosh!'

'Come on,' Coco said. 'We got to get you to school, honey.'

Normally this would have provoked instant moaning. But Keisha allowed herself to be drawn along, meekly, lost in her own little world.

To be honest, Coco had a buzz as well. That was cool – *way* cool. When they reopened the store, after the big meeting, she would pop in – buy herself a little something. Not that she could afford much. But just entering GLAMOUR made you feel like you were living the dream.

As she hustled her happy daughter towards the car, Coco stole a glance backwards over her shoulder. The crowd was still there, adrenaline up, chattering as they awaited the other two.

'Miz Nelson.'

'Yes?' Sally shouted back. She had to shout – the whirring of the chopper blades was just too loud.

'If you look to your left, ma'am,' the pilot bellowed, 'you can see the store. We'll be landing in just a second.'

4

'Great!'

Sally gave him a thumbs up, and the pilot smiled at her momentarily before turning back to the controls. Like all men, he was flirting with her.

Sally shook her long blond hair smoothly down her back. It was a shimmering curtain of platinum, expensively and expertly coiffed on Fifth Avenue by Rolande himself, owner of the famous line that she had discovered. She snapped open her Hermès Kelly bag and removed a compact mirror. Too fabulous for words! No wonder it had been the hit of spring's accessory line. She ran through the numbers in her head – $500 times, how many? Ten thousand? Why, she'd made millions just from this *one* product. Customers couldn't get enough of that Sally, GLAMOUR magic. And whatever the other two said, *she* was the one that knew how to give it to them.

Sally examined her beautiful face critically, looking for flaws. But there were none. Her skin, helped along by the very best facials and professionally applied Lassiter make-up, was glowing. She looked fantastic. Her body was buff and lithe – a personal trainer worked it out daily – and her dress was French Riviera chic – a Pucci print with a white silk jacket over the top, designed just for Sally. Sassy, cool and irreverent, she carried it with her Kelly bag and trademark Manolos. Throw in a large pair of tortoiseshell glasses and she was the living spirit of summer.

Sally knew she looked like a star. But then again, she *was* one. She leaned across the soft leather seats of her personal helicopter and looked down on the seething crowd milling outside the GLAMOUR red carpet. They were her fans – the fans of the dream. The other two girls, well; she shrugged to herself, still angry – they'd just helped with the mechanics.

Sally Nelson was the star here. She was Barbie. She was Lady Liberty. The all-American icon, blond hair, tanned skin, healthy Cali lifestyle, and oh yes, the small matter of a billion dollars or two to boot. She had appeared in more ad campaigns than she could count, and the public ate her up. GLAMOUR. That was her, wasn't it? Not cold, bookish Jane, or regal Haya – who, let's face it, had taken herself out of the game.

When they thought glamorous, they thought Sally. She smiled triumphantly. It was her store, her dream. They had named it after Sally!

Of *course* GLAMOUR should be hers.

'Please remain seated until the airplane has ground to a complete halt,' said the steward.

Jane Morgan didn't even look at him. She had already unbuckled her belt and jumped to her feet.

'Ma'am, please take your seat,' he said uncomfortably. Wow. That Limey broad was something. His boyfriend was tough, but even he'd be scared of her.

'Please get out of my way.' She turned to him, her famous black eyes cool. 'This flight was delayed for four hours.'

She snapped open the overhead locker and retrieved her laptop bag, oblivious of the other first-class passengers' stares.

'You're defying FAA regulations.'

'Correct.' She shrugged. 'I don't pay ten thousand dollars for a first-class ticket in order to be prevented from doing my job.'

'We tried to make you as comfortable as possible, ma'am,' he began.

'I don't need to be comfortable. I need to be in Beverly Hills. I have a meeting. And I'm *late*.'

She made it sound like a terminal condition.

Every fancy businessman, society wife and ruddy-cheeked CEO in the first-class cabin was now watching the show.

He heard himself remonstrate with her, almost pleading. 'It'll just be a minute . . .'

There was a small shudder, and the plane docked with the exit tunnel. The pilot, perhaps sensing the steward's trouble, switched off the seatbelt signs, and with that little ping, all the suits were up, fumbling around their laps, trying to get their bags.

Jane Morgan was already standing by the exit door. First in line.

The steward smiled weakly at the passengers shoving past him. He sure wouldn't like to be on the opposite side of the table at that lady's meeting. She should come with a government safety warning.

'Highness, I must advise against it.'

Ahmed al-Jamir, the Embassy's special adviser, leaned across the table, his dark eyes intent on Haya's. 'Your position—'

'I am a member of the board,' Haya said mildly.

'I meant your *royal* position,' al-Jamir persisted. 'This business stuff can be left to others. You should simply sell your stake. What is the point?'

Her dark eyes raced across the figures in front of her; finally they lifted and regarded him.

'The point is that GLAMOUR is *my* company. It's *my* store. And I haven't forgotten that.'

Even if the others had.

He was ready to weep. The Princess would be Queen one day, maybe one day soon. Her husband controlled countless billions, a major army. Even before the inheritance, Haya had her pick of no less than sixteen separate palaces, more jewels than she could wear.

For all its high-profile branding, this company was nothing. Nothing!

He lowered his voice and said as much. They both knew

what he really meant. It was unseemly for a princess of Ghada to be playing around in American business! Look at the Englishwoman, Jane Morgan. Famous across the world, although al-Jamir did not dare voice the thought, as one *hell* of a ball-breaking bitch.

He did not want *Siti* Haya mentioned in the same breath as Jane Morgan! It demeaned her, it demeaned Prince Jaber. It lowered the very royal house!

Haya closed the company report and turned her gaze to the security men and civil servants.

'Leave us.'

'But Princess—'

'You can wait outside the door.'

There were a lot of reluctant bows, and then they all trooped meekly out. Haya gazed at al-Jamir.

'When I married His Highness, I told him I had no intention of surrendering my past life.'

'But events—'

'Yes. We all know what happened.' She would not refer to the change in their circumstances. 'Nonetheless, Ahmed, I founded this company. I began its spirit. I began its ethos. Something Sally and Jane apparently want eliminated. You need not fear; today will be the very last day I spend engaged in the world of business. I know my duty.'

She tugged her silken robes a little tighter around her shoulders, and the diplomat was impressed. Indeed, whatever her origins, Haya al-Jaber bore herself as though the crown were on her dark head already.

'But you and everyone else needs to understand something. *I will not let them destroy this place.* Today is the last meeting. And I'm going to make it count.'

He was silent in the face of her anger.

'You may call them back in,' Haya told him, regally, dismissively.

She turned back to the report.

*

Sally blew one last kiss to the cheering crowds, waving just the tips of her manicured fingers at them. 'Thank you all *so much*!'

She crossed the red carpet to where the hungry media were waiting. Flashbulbs popped like fireworks; a forest of boom mikes jostled forwards towards Sally's face. The Arabian princess had cut them dead, and that was lame, but so what? Sally was the real golden girl, America's sweetheart! The reporters shoved forwards, yelling questions at the star.

'Sally! Is it time to get your revenge?'

'Who owns GLAMOUR?'

'Are you here to take control?'

'Is this an American company?'

'What do you have to say to the fans?'

That last one was a perfect softball. Sally stopped smiling for the photographers and turned to camera.

'I want to thank them for their love and support! I couldn't do it without you guys!' she purred.

'What're your plans, Sally?'

'You know how much I love GLAMOUR! I'm just here to set things straight.' She gave America that famous wink. 'Now don't y'all worry, because I'm here to see everything works out *just fine*.'

'But Princess Haya! Jane Morgan!'

'I looooove those ladies,' Sally said brightly. 'But everyone knows that GLAMOUR *is* Sally Nelson! Now, if you'll excuse me, I have to get to work.'

She blew another kiss, direct to TV land, pirouetted on her Manolos, and sashayed up the red carpet while the doormen saluted.

The reporters buzzed. Sally Nelson knew how to give good coverage. They got what they needed; Sally was a star.

She was gonna kick those other girls' asses. None of the paparazzi had any doubt.

*

'It's coming up ahead, Miz Morgan.'

'I know where the store is,' Jane said shortly. She examined the letters from her bankers. Every word of the legal document mattered. Sometimes, lawyers let things slip; she didn't trust them.

'Shall I take you out front?' Her driver peered ahead. 'There sure is a big crowd. Look at that turnout!'

'No. Make a left here.'

'A left?'

Was he deaf? 'Yes,' she snapped.

'But GLAMOUR—'

'We're not going to GLAMOUR. We're going to the storage warehouse. There's a closed parking lot between the warehouse and the offices.'

'You don't want anybody to see you,' he said, slowly clocking on.

That's right.

'I can't stand fuss.'

In the rear-view mirror he watched the chestnut hair, wound tight into a neat bob, as tight as she was. Damn! He'd seen porcupines with less prickles.

But Jane Morgan paid good, real good, and at Christmas his bonus could run into thousands of dollars. His colleague's son, the one with the gimpy leg, had gotten bullied at school and Miz Morgan had paid for private Catholic college. Now the kid was maxing out his SATs, Rafael thought he might be going to make a scholarship to the Ivy League.

He swallowed and shut up. So she didn't fraternize. That was OK. Everybody that worked for Morgana Inc. knew who the boss was.

'Yes, ma'am, you got it,' he said.

Two minutes later he had dropped America's toughest new businesswoman, queen of the Dow Jones, at the back of the warehouse. He watched as she swung her neat legs in their court shoes out the back of his car and marched off, between the enormous trucks full of GLAMOUR goodies, through the parking lot.

So she was arriving on the down low. Jason figured she had some calls to make, last-minute deals, something like that.

Most thought this was her last stand. That it was all over. Not him.

He'd never bet against Jane Morgan.

The boardroom crackled with energy.

The long, glossy mahogany table was packed. Rows of men and women in dark suits, high-priced lawyers, investment bankers and M&A sharks, all toying with their pads and Mont Blanc pens, or pretending to read their figures.

Behind them, the view was fabulous. High over Beverly Hills, the floor-to-ceiling glass walls showed every billboard, every limo, the smog haze hanging over the city. But nobody was distracted.

Around the head of the table, on the left, sat Princess Haya, her security men hanging back behind her chair, cradling their guns.

Directly opposite her, Sally Nelson. The famous blond hair cascading glossily down her back. Those baby-blue eyes steely and hard, revealing the businesswoman behind the star. She was more than a figurehead, and she was here to let them know it.

And, insisting on her right to sit in the chairman's seat, Jane Morgan, all in black. Dressed for her own funeral?

Three powerful women. Once best friends. Now deadly rivals. Each of them determined to control the world's most famous store. A global icon.

Its fate, and theirs, would be determined today.

Jane Morgan stared down the length of the table; she nodded coldly at Haya and Sally. Most people in this room thought all her plans were about to be ruined, but her voice, that famously cool English voice, betrayed no fear.

'Good morning. The meeting will come to order.'

Chapter One
Los Angeles – 1987

'You gotta FIGHT for your RIGHT to PAAAARRRTTYYY . . .'

The boombox radio in the corner of the playground was pumping out rap, the Beastie Boys blasting into the still air of a muggy fall day in Beverly Hills. It was the start of the new term, and the teachers smiled to each other and looked the other way. Already the over-privileged girls of Miss Milton's Academy were settling back into their tight little cliques. Julie Manners, the queen of tenth grade, had her new toy out and she was showing off. Julie and her friends wore their white socks around their ankles, hitched up their skirts, pinned their hair back with Ray-Bans and wore badges proclaiming heavy metal bands. They banged their heads, long hair flying, to show just how tough they were.

The teachers, milling around the registration booths outside, pretended to be deep in conversation, ignoring Julie and her clique. Her dad was a movie director, and that made her powerful. This was the eighties; fame and celebrity counted for a lot in this town. And everywhere else, come to that.

Most of the girls, younger and older, were already forming knots around the queen bee, pretending to like the music, complimenting her on her hair, her Lee Press-On nails, the cloud of Dior Poison she liked to swan around in. Julie eyed them all with a nasty sneer, her hair tossing, as though deciding where to dispense her favours. It was social

13

death to be disliked by the most powerful clique in school.

And the staff had learned to fear her too. Teachers Julie's dad didn't like tended to have short tenures at Miss Milton's. They shut their ears to the deafening music, pretending it was no big deal. Heavy metal and rap were *in*. So was Julie. And everybody wanted to be just like her.

Well – almost everybody.

A dark, slender girl sat in the opposite corner of the playground, next to the oh-so-hip Zen garden the school board had planted over the vacation: raked lines of gravel, flat stepping stones, square pools, bonsai trees and flourishing patches of bamboo. She sat on the lawn, reading a book, her neat leather satchel beside her.

Unconcerned with Julie's court. Waiting for someone.

'Limey,' hissed Melissa Smith, kicking at her as she passed.

'Do sod off, Melissa,' the girl replied equitably. She wasn't much to look at; neat hair in a severe ponytail, black-rimmed glasses, no make-up. But there was a certain resilience to her.

Melissa Smith was one of Julie's cronies.

'The bookworm's at it again. What's this?' She snatched up the slim volume. '*Ariel* by Sylvia Plath. Studying up on laundry detergent?' Melissa snickered. Jane Morgan didn't suck up. And she didn't fear bullying. Two reasons to hate her. The girl wasn't pretty, yet she didn't seem to care. She was all round *weird*.

'It's poetry. Course, you'd have to actually be able to read to know that. How was summer school?' Jane asked coolly.

Melissa flushed; she had been forced to take summer school to catch up on her grades. Everybody knew Jane was a superbrain.

'Great,' she lied. 'And you know, there were *boys* there. Not something you'd know a lot about.'

'Not interested,' Jane replied.

'That's right. They aren't.' A rather smart insult from Melissa; she tossed her hair proudly. 'You never sent Julie a birthday card, Miss Fish'n'chips. People notice these things.'

'That's because I can't stand Julie.'

Melissa bridled. 'You'd better watch yourself. We can make life very hard for you in this school. If you want to be picked for any teams, or sit with anybody, or get a part in the play, or go to parties . . .'

'Yeah, well, I don't.' Jane Morgan snapped the book shut. 'That's what you don't get. So tell me again why I should give a damn what you think?'

'Watch yourself, weirdo,' Melissa repeated, and stalked off. Damn! That ugly Brit. She was so arrogant. Every year she managed to survive the worst they could throw at her. She should have been hounded out of Miss Milton's by now. Of course Melissa, Julie, and everybody else knew why it hadn't happened. One word.

Sally.

Sally. The country bumpkin. The dumb blonde from the West with a stupid Texas twang, Barbie's hair, and illegal curves. A few more years and she could be starring in *The Dukes of Hazzard* as Daisy. There was nothing hip about Sally, nothing cool. She didn't listen to the Beastie Boys or Mötley Crüe. She always had that boring ass country and western playing. She didn't wear the right clothes – no black leather jackets and metal studs, no Madonna fingerless black lace gloves, or spiderweb tights in exotic patterns.

But Sally had two things in her favour – at least, Melissa only admitted to two. First, she was rich. And not just film-biz, Beverly Hills common-or-garden rich like most of them, with their daddies working producers, driving Mercedes and flying business class. No, Sally's family was Money with a capital M. Her pa, Paulie Lassiter, was in the oil business, and had long ago stopped counting his wealth in millions. Estimates in school varied from one billion to four.

One thing was definite. Her daddy could buy all their daddies ten times over and still have plenty to spare.

Insults to Sally Lassiter were muted. Even the daughters of studio heads had to mind their manners.

And second – even worse – Sally was *gorgeous*. You could sneer – and they did. Dumb blonde. Texas rose. Bimbo. Cheerleader.

Yet, as their own reluctant eyes, and their brothers' admiring stares, confirmed, Sally Lassiter's looks were devastating. Her skin glowed, warm and tanned. Her long, rich-girl blond hair was glossy and smooth like a Timotei commercial. She had coltish legs, slender arms, large, bright blue eyes, and over the whole package, a white-toothed, milky, all-American wholesomeness. She was always smiling, always upbeat; narrow waisted, but with large breasts and a tight, curvy butt that suggested she was fit and healthy, and some day would make a good-looking mom of good-looking babies; when she laughed, she lit up the entire room.

Sally made sophistication and cynicism seem like a waste of time.

She was the best-looking girl in the school. Some thought she was the best-looking girl in the city.

So she wasn't a brainiac. So what? She was an only child, heir to a vast fortune. And it seemed so unfair, Melissa recollected, absently touching her own rather bulbous nose, that she wouldn't even have to waste any of it on plastic surgery.

It was hard to condescend to a girl like Sally. Richer and prettier than you, of course she had confidence. Buckets of it.

Yeah, she was a dumb hick; they all thought that, sometimes even dared to say so. But Sally just smiled. She knew she was untouchable, Melissa thought, knew she was better than all of them. It was so unfair! She didn't even work at being popular; she didn't have to navigate high school politics. Instead, she just went her own sweet way. And they had the uncomfortable feeling that all the time they were laughing at Sally Lassiter, the Texas honey was laughing right back.

And of course if she wasn't smart, she had a friend who was.

Jane Morgan.

They made such an unlikely duo. Best friends as long as anybody could remember, yet totally different. Jane was, in Miss Milton terms, a bum. Her folks had no cash; her fees were all paid by the British Embassy. She was doing this on the taxpayer's dime. She wasn't pretty, either, no style, no hipness to her whatsoever. Jane was a real little bookworm; unsuited to the sun, sea, sex of LA, the hot, dusty city of perfect bods and shiny cars. She lived an internal life, always in the library, studying; no crushes on actors, no gossip about boys – like they'd be interested in her. Melissa suspected strongly that was just a front. After all, Jane showed zero signs of being gay. So how come she was Miss Ice Maiden?

Jane Morgan would have made an easy target. She didn't have Sally's weapons. Status, sure; Daddy was practically royal, and the cars that picked her up sometimes had little fluttering flags on the front, which was cool. But this was LA, not Washington. It didn't count for a whole lot; not like having a movie with boffo opening numbers, owning a magazine, or being a top-notch sports agent, like Melissa's father.

Yet they could not touch her. Sally protected her. And as long as they stayed friends, those two girls, together, were so much more than the sum of their parts. Julie Manners used to say – damn, all the time – that Sally and Jane were like a jigsaw puzzle. They made no sense on their own, but together they were unstoppable. Jane had the brains. Sally had the looks. Jane had that smart mouth. Sally was loaded.

Melissa had to admit they made a hell of a team.

*

Jane watched, carefully, as Melissa's tense back receded into the distance, joining the throng of chicks hanging around Julie. It wasn't till Melissa was safely out of reach that she could breathe a sigh of relief.

Not that she would let it show. No way; never. Jane Morgan had no truck with weakness. But she *was* unhappy, even depressed.

Another bloody term. Stuck in this shithole. With no decent teachers, no good courses. Girls went to Miss Milton's for one thing – social cachet. How the hell would she get into Oxford or Cambridge after studying at this dump?

She buried her dark head in her hands.

Trouble with being clever, it was harder to deceive yourself. Of course, the lack of academic standards was a problem for an ambitious student. But that wasn't why she was unhappy . . .

Jane looked wistfully at the laughing, jostling crowd surrounding Julie Manners and wished she was the other girl. Just once. What would *that* be like? To be popular, to have people fighting for your attention. She had never had that, never, not as long as she'd lived.

She looked at the front gate, her knuckles tightening on her book. Yes, she was hoping to see a limo pull up. She had never wanted to see Sal as much as she did right now. The warmth of that smile, the native happiness, might pull her up a little. As long as she had Sally, it wasn't all black.

But Sally wasn't here yet. And as she sat by herself in the playground, pretending to be absorbed in her reading, young Jane Morgan felt a wave of loneliness crash over her. It was a wretched feeling, and she lifted her head; jutted her chin up, as though she were in physical danger of drowning.

Her dad. His Excellency, the Hon. Thomas Morgan. Jane thought of him, smiling that politician's smile at her. As she tried to persuade him to stay with her, to want her close . . .

to love her, just a little, the way she loved him, always had; a child's needy love, which was still unrequited.

'But Daddy . . . I really hate that school.'

She'd been hovering on the landing, at the top of the stairs, her suitcases all packed, in the limo already.

'We all hate school, darling.' He gave her an absent-minded kiss.

'I want to be with you.' Jane's words tumbled out, although she'd promised herself she wouldn't beg; eager, desperate. 'I want to stay here – in Washington.'

'No, you should mix in other surroundings. The political hothouse . . .' he waved his hands vaguely. 'Not good for teenagers. And I'm so busy, you'd never see me. Boarding school is best. We did it in my day.'

'I live in the guest house, with Consuela.'

'Same thing,' he lied. 'Now run along, darling, your driver's been waiting ten minutes already.'

'But . . . Dad.' Her voice, already pleading, whiny. 'If I were here, you could see me more. And you'd like that, wouldn't you?'

'Of course I would.' His voice softened, just a fraction, and he leaned over and kissed her on the forehead; a brief touch, but manna to Jane. She wanted desperately to hug him, but he pulled back, and his clear grey eyes regained their professional detachment. 'And I'll see you this summer, sweetheart.'

Sweetheart. Darling. If only that were true.

But Jane Morgan squared her slim shoulders and pasted on a smile, as brisk and impersonal as Daddy's always were.

'OK. See you then,' she said, and gave him a hug; he patted her stiffly on the back. 'Love you, Daddy.'

'Love you too, Jane.'

As she walked down the stairs, she heard him turn and go back to his office. He didn't even wait to wave goodbye to her.

The memory was bitter. And she had chewed on it, like a foul herb, all the way to the airport, and then all the way to the smart, lonely, rented house she lived in when she was at school. There was a mixture of longing and loathing when she thought about the school; bleak despair at yet another term of being the outsider, the outcast. Her life sometimes seemed like one long story of rejection. And yet, that bright spot, her best friend; Sally, who was the closest thing, Jane sometimes thought, that she had to real family; Sally, who was almost a sister.

There was a sound; a large limousine rolling over the speed bumps in the drive. Yes – that was Sally's car, straight out of Texas, a large, gleaming white monster; Jane would know it anywhere.

Her blues temporarily banished, she scrambled to her feet.

The car parked; the driver, neatly dressed in an immaculate uniform, got out and held the door open for his young passenger, like she was a princess. Jane hovered; behind her, she was aware of the rock music being lowered, the general drop in the hum of voices – everybody was looking this way, everybody was waiting for Sally. For that matter, they were looking at her, too.

Her friend was one of life's stars, brilliant and dazzling. And yes, those coltish legs, slim and tanned over the white bobby sox, tumbled out of the car's chocolate-brown leather seats; her skirt just that touch shorter, her long blond hair blowing around her shoulders in the breeze, designer sunglasses holding it back, her eyes thick with mascara in defiance of the no make-up policy – there she was, and the school collectively exhaled at the sight of her.

Jane gave a whoop of joy and ran out to Sally.

'I'm so glad to see you,' Sally cried, flinging her arms round Jane and enveloping her in a cloud of scent. 'It's been so boring while you were in DC.'

'Me too.' Jane felt awkward; she always did when Sally first appeared. Sometimes she was a little jealous; she was the moon, pale and serious, while Sally blazed like the sun; other times she felt all her vulnerabilities crash in on her, and agreed with the rest of them: why would Sally even be her friend?

But slowly she relaxed.

'What's going on? Bye, Jake. Y'all take care.' She waved to her chauffeur, who tipped his cap. 'Is that Melissa talking to Julie? Horrible haircut. She looks like a boy.'

'Tough is in this year,' Jane answered wrily. 'Have you seen Julie's black leather jacket? She's all over Whitesnake. And she had platinum highlights put into her perm, and it's gone all crispy.'

'No!' Sally squealed with delight. 'I gotta see. That girl has no style.'

'Knows a lot of movie stars, though,' Jane observed.

'Whoop-de-do,' Sally said. 'They're ten cents to the pound around here.'

Her pretty face reflected such total unconcern that Jane instantly felt lightened. And slightly ashamed. How could she have let Melissa Smith get to her? Sally and she were unbreakable. The in-crowd could do their worst.

'Can you help me with my vacation project?' Sally asked, lowering her voice. 'I think I got the Tudors muddled up. I could use an A, Daddy's kind of bothered about my SATs.'

'Sure.' Jane was on her own ground now. 'I'll write you something quickly at lunchtime, you copy it out, hand the project in tomorrow.'

'Thanks.' Sally blushed. 'I know I should have gotten it right by now.'

'Don't worry about it. I'm always here.'

Sal squeezed her arm, and they walked off into the playground, chattering away like starlings.

*

'. . . which concludes the assembly for this morning.' Miss Milton herself, her grey hair neatly wound in a steely bun, her doughy body encased in a couture Dior tweed suit, surveyed the room full of her well-heeled charges. 'Orientation for the new girls we welcome into the school this year will continue at first period.'

Jane glanced, without much curiosity, at the gaggle of new chicks that were standing off to one side like sheep waiting to be herded into a pen. Various different ages; every form had some turnover each year – a producer hit hard times and couldn't afford the fees, a rich plastic surgeon moved to the area and pulled strings for his daughter. She didn't see anybody interesting. Most of them, with an unerring sense of social accuracy, had tried to glom on to the crowd surrounding Julie.

There was one latecomer. Dark-haired, average height, slim without being skinny, her socks raised to maximum calf length, no make-up. Rather shy-looking. Understandable. Unlike Jane, she seemed to make an effort with her appearance; whitened teeth, plucked eyebrows, neatly brushed hair worn loose instead of scraped into a convenient pony-tail, no glasses. She looked uncomfortable, and twisted her fingers around as though wanting something to do.

Very tanned, though, and pretty enough not to be an obvious target for bullies; not like Jane, with her thick glasses and disregard for fashion.

'We will now stand for the Pledge of Allegiance. Foreign citizens are excused.'

There was a rustle of cotton as the room got to its feet; Sally stood, her blue eyes fixed patriotically on the Stars and Stripes displayed at the front of the room. She always meant it, when some of the other girls sneered and rolled their eyes; another reason to love her, Sally didn't have a cynical bone in her body.

'I pledge allegiance to the flag of the United States of America . . .'

Jane, from her chair, cast her eyes around the room, picking out the other diplomats' daughters.

'. . . and to the Republic for which it stands, one nation, under God . . .'

Cecile Perron wasn't here, then. Stuck in Paris, or had Papa been reassigned? That would be great; Jane couldn't stand Cecile.

'. . . indivisible . . .'

Wait. The new girl wasn't standing either. One lone chair had been provided for her, and she was sitting in it, sticking out. The other new girls were casting sidelong glances, sneering at her. Jane looked closer; that wasn't a tan, she was from the Middle East. Large dark eyes, an aristocratic nose. Israeli?

'. . . liberty and justice for all.'

The bell rang, and Miss Milton left the stage.

'I got art history first period. You?'

'Maths,' Jane responded, still looking at the new chick. She was being jostled. A wave of empathy broke over her; it was almost exactly the same as had happened to her when she first got here – before she'd found Sally. 'Hey, Sal. See that new girl over there? They're picking on her.'

'They always do.'

'Let's go and say hi,' Jane urged. 'Come on, it'll be your good deed for the day.'

Sally sighed; art history was the one lesson she enjoyed, and the teacher hated it if she was late. All those glorious dresses they wore back in history. Fashion meant something then, it was more than a Donna Karan bodysuit or grey Armani dress. Sally liked colour, and style; gold cloth and lace.

'Sure, why not?' she said.

Chapter Two

Sally walked towards the new girl.

Jane was her conscience; Sally knew there was a streak of iron in Jane, something she respected, even feared at times. Jane would have gone over to that chick whether she had come too or not.

She scrutinized the object of her friend's attentions. Modest, shy, a clever look about her, disturbingly pretty . . .

Sally felt a moment of misgiving. She never felt dwarfed by Jane's formidable intellect, because Jane, let's face it, *wasn't* attractive. Both of them had strengths, but not in the same areas. This new girl was looking threateningly gorgeous, and also had a sharp light in her eyes that Sally recognized from a long association with her English friend.

Would that work? What if the new girl wanted to be real friends? She might be clever enough to rival Jane and pretty enough to steal her own thunder, too. Not right now, but with a little work – some caramel highlights, a pair of heels, some berry lipgloss . . .

Then she blushed. Those were mean thoughts, worthy of Julie or Melissa, not her. The new girl needed help. And Sally Lassiter, even though she schemed and gossiped and loved her own reflection almost as much as everybody else did, was fundamentally kind.

'Hey!' she called out, waving brightly to the new girl, who was heading towards the door. 'Hold up, hon! We want to talk to you.'

The other girl hesitated and nodded.

Jane fell in behind her friend, slightly annoyed. Now Sally was marching over there, taking the lead, like she did in everything. Jane sighed and followed her, smiling softly at the new girl.

'So what's your name?'

Sally flicked her curtain of blond hair over her shoulder and treated her to that patented, dazzling smile. Behind her, Jane grinned. One thing you could say about Sally, she was no snob. She had no need to play cliques, or make the new chick earn her friendship.

'I'm Sally, Sally Lassiter,' she encouraged. The warm Texan tones matched her mahogany tanned skin. Sally was a hot little butterfly, and even the sedate uniform of Miss Milton's couldn't disguise that.

The new girl's dark eyes swept over the blonde, drinking her in.

Sally was a million miles away from her own long hem and high socks. Sally wore her grey pleated skirt hiked up an inch or two, with her socks down to her ankles. Her cream shirt had an extra button undone, revealing a tiny glimpse of bountiful, all-natural breasts. The boys all stared, and some of the men, too, when Sally walked by.

That was the way she liked it. Such brassy confidence!

'Helen,' the new girl muttered. 'Helen Yanna.'

'I'm Jane.' Jane moved forward, adjusting her glasses up the bridge of her nose. They were thick, and made her eyes disappear behind them. Helen pegged her as English at once. She had her hair neatly tied back in a ponytail. Not a likely companion for this Sally Lassiter.

And nor, Helen thought, am I.

Olive-skinned with an aristocratic, aquiline face, Helen had hazel eyes flecked with green, and lush, black hair, glossy and sleek. Where Sally's shirt was undone, Helen's was buttoned up; the extra button under the chin, tightly drawn. Her thick hair was loose, and her dark eyes peeked shyly out from under her fringe. But, like Sally, Helen's frame had dangerous curves that no amount of buttons could hide.

'How do you do?' Helen replied, formally. Warily. Were they about to start teasing her like the other girls had done? She already hated this school. When she got home tonight she'd beg her father to reconsider.

But Helen was a realist. Baba was a bit of a social climber. He was thrilled when his daughter was accepted here – they weren't ambassadors, or princes, after all, just mildly successful business people.

And whatever her differences with the other girls, they all had that one vital thing in common – cash.

It required *mucho dinero* to make it here.

Everybody tried to get their kid in. The school had an unofficial policy against the Biz – only the finest directors, Oscar-winning actors, and truly determined studio execs and producers managed to get past admissions. Miss Milton's Academy preserved its cachet by attracting a better class of girl. The daughters of congressmen and senators, the mayor and the governor. Senior lawyers, major player bankers, and real estate moguls. And huge numbers of girls from the diplomatic community. They liked exotic – French, European, Israeli, even Arab. Once there had been a couple of genuine Russians. Sending your girl to Miss Milton's Academy guaranteed her an instant shot of culture.

Of course, the Americans still ruled the roost. This was their home turf, and they knew all the unspoken rules from day one.

Helen had already suffered from that.

'You're new,' Sally observed. 'We figured maybe you'd want somebody to show you round? Help you fit in.'

The olive-skinned girl nodded shyly. 'That would be very kind.'

26

Jane noticed at once she spoke in full sentences, didn't use contractions, or slang.

'Where are you from, Helen? Israel?' she guessed.

The girl didn't take offence. 'Jordan. It is very close nearby.'

'You're an Arab!' Sally said, blue eyes widening.

Helen nodded, and Jane noticed her back stiffen. 'Does that upset you?'

'Of course not,' Jane said quickly. 'We have people in the school from all over. I'm English, my dad works in Washington.'

Helen made a face. 'How sad, to be separated from your father.'

'Not particularly.' Jane tried to harden her heart to match her words. 'My father's a diplomat. He mostly thinks of politics. I don't think he'll be winning father of the year any time soon.'

'Your mother, then.'

The English girl shook her head. 'She died, when I was three. Car crash.'

Helen looked horrified. 'I'm sorry.'

Jane shrugged. She sometimes wondered about that night. Her father had been driving, had emerged almost unscathed, apart from one long scar on his back. Who knew the truth? Maybe he had been drunk.

Her mother would have loved her. As it was, Jane had nothing but herself and her friend. She had learned to live a self-sufficent life, and books and studying were her salvation. You could rely on brains; tests never let Jane down, and it was good to struggle and win validation. Every time she got an A, it soothed her, deep inside. Intelligence was the one area where she was more than good enough. She was outstanding.

Jane had big ambitions. Oxford or Cambridge. A Fellowship of All Souls. After that, tenure somewhere in the

Ivy League. Permanent respect, a job for life, and worth that did not depend on something unreliable, like men, or ephemeral, like looks.

She knew her best friend felt sorry for her.

'I can handle it,' she said shortly. 'I'm a day girl here. And I have a nanny in our place by the beach.'

'I'm day too. Daddy has a house in Bel Air,' Sally said artlessly. 'Right next to Aaron Spelling, but twice as big. We're in oil.'

'My father is a businessman.'

'What business?' Sally zeroed in.

Helen spread her hands. 'Many.' It was true, her father had his fingers in many different pies. 'He arranges contracts, meetings, for Americans who want to work in the Middle East. They build roads, apartment buildings, water facilities . . .'

'That's swell,' Sally said, losing interest. 'He's not in oil?'

'Jordan has no oil.'

'So he's not a sheikh or a king?'

Helen smiled. 'I'm afraid not. Just a businessman.'

'Oh well, never mind.' Sally was too bubbly to be put out for more than a few seconds. 'Come with Jane and me and see the school. We'll introduce you *way* better than orientation.'

Helen looked behind her; a bossy-looking matron with white hair in a stiff bob was taking the rest of the new intake towards the labs. Rebellion was not her strong suit, but the enthusiasm of the American and the friendliness of the English girl intrigued her.

'Why not?' She tried out her practised English vocabulary. 'That sounds like . . . fun!'

The three of them went round the school grounds. Jane watched Helen as she drank it in. It was nice, she realized, to have somebody else there. Good to have more back-up.

On days that Sally was sick, or travelling, it was not particularly pleasant to be in this school.

And of course Helen Yanna was a foreigner, too. That made her even more of a target. It was something they'd have in common. Plus, Jane could tell at once that the girl was clever, brighter than Sally. It might be nice to have somebody around she could chat with about the stuff that didn't interest Sal. Like her exams.

Jane found herself nervously hoping that they'd hit it off.

'That's the fountain.' Sally beamed. 'Impressive, no?'

'No,' replied Helen, thinking the question was serious. 'We have much better in our garden in Amman.'

Jane bit back a smile.

'And the statue, it's old. *Real* old. Victorian, imported from San Francisco. Almost *two hundred years*.' Sally was determined to show off. 'A genuine antique.'

'I think she's seen older.' Jane smiled at their new friend. 'Have you ever been to Petra?' she asked, with a touch of envy.

'Yes, of course.' Helen returned the smile. 'One day you can come with me? On a visit.'

Jane glowed. 'Really? I'd love to.'

'And here's the pool.' Sally wasn't interested in archaeology or ancient sites. She waved her hand, her enthusiasm infectious. 'Olympic size, and it's got a current. The gym is fully equipped. Rock-climbing walls, TVs on stands while you work out, treadmills, free weights. Even kick-boxing.'

That did it. Helen's eyes roamed excitedly over the massive pool. Yes, this was fun. Kick-boxing! Why not? This was an all-girl's school. She'd *love* to do that.

'And come on in.' Sally strode commandingly through the steel door entrance to the architect-designed school building. It was modern, clean, everything brand new. Helen saw rooms full of new personal computers. A theatre, with a real lighting rig.

'Room 102 – drama – the aspiring movie stars love that. Right next door is crafts. They do pottery and all that stuff. Computers – you have to get with the programme, right, Jane?'

Jane snorted.

'Sometimes I have to physically drag her out of there. And here,' Sally went on, 'are the classrooms.' Her pretty mouth made a moue of dislike. 'Gotta say, I still hate class. It's such a waste. Learning about General Custer, and stuff. When are you gonna use that in real life?'

'History teaches us about the future, too,' Jane said.

'Deep. Teacher's pet.' Sally winked at her friend. Helen looked at her enviously. She wished she had that American confidence. And she secretly wished for beautiful golden hair. Would Baba let her dye it?

Probably not, that would be a Western step too far.

'And this is the chapel,' Sally continued, gesturing at a long room with benches, an altar and a crucifix. 'Non-denominational. I pray there . . .'

'When?' Jane demanded.

'Sometimes,' Sally lied. She turned to her new protégée. 'Want to go inside?'

Helen shook her head. 'No thanks. I'm a Muslim.'

Sally stopped walking. 'Huh?' she asked, really amazed.

'Of course she is,' Jane swooped in quickly, to cover the faux pas. 'She's from Jordan. What did you think she would be, Sal?'

'That's OK.' Helen was amused at the blonde girl's discomfiture. Didn't they understand not everybody was like them? 'Actually there are lots of Christians in Jordan. More than five per cent. But my family is Muslim.'

Sally made a good recovery. 'That's cool. There are lots of Jews here anyway. And here's where we eat lunch. Do you want to sit with us and eat lunch?'

Jane looked at her best friend, and felt a rush of warmth.

Really, Sal was a kind, good girl. Asking somebody to sit with you at lunch was a big deal. She was offering to support Helen Yanna, in public, in the full view of all the nasty, cliquey, bullying teenage girls that otherwise could make this shy young Arab's life a perfect misery.

And Sally was doing that to a girl from the Middle East with no connections, no cool factor, nothing that indicated she'd do the blonde girl any good.

Sometimes Sal aggravated her, despite their friendship. That blinding beauty and the huge wealth, the careless, confident dismissal of academic things. But at bottom Sally was a big-hearted Southern belle. And she'd just opened her arms to somebody who needed it.

Jane was proud to know her, and proud to be her friend.

'I'd like that too,' Jane said softly.

'I'd love to sit with you.' Helen felt nervous for the first time that day; she peered in to see the refectory full of loud, noisy, American girls, already bonded into their little groups. She wanted to cling to her two companions. 'But . . . I can't eat the food. It isn't halal. My father made an arrangement. They will bring me my food especially.' She hesitated. Was that too weird for them? If they left her, she would be the new, strange Muslim chick, and the brash American students would bully her. Helen felt the butterflies crawl in the pit of her stomach.

'I *dig* that!' Sally sensed the fear, and hastened to reassure her. 'See? You're special. Like waiter service, right in hall!'

'Thank you. *Shokram*.' The Arabic slipped out, from habit. 'Do you two have other friends?'

'Sure! Plenty. But we're *best* friends,' Sally said confidently, squeezing Jane's arm. 'We're our own group.'

'And can I be in your group?' Helen asked artlessly.

Jane smiled warmly at her. 'Absolutely! We'd be delighted.'

'Thank you,' Helen said again, with a grateful smile. She

loved it. This was a great school. And these two were nice girls. Helen thought she would be like the best of both of them, intelligent like Jane, gorgeous and sassy like Sally.

The ache that had been in her heart since their family had left Amman started to dull, just a little.

It was so great to have friends.

Chapter Three

'What you doing, freak?'

Helen touched the mat in front of her with her forehead and tried to concentrate on her prayer.

'I *said*, what you doing?'

There was a sharp kick in her ribs. Helen flooded with anger and fear. She knew that voice. That was Julie Manners. Queen of the cliques. And first-class bitch.

'I don't like Ay-rabs,' Julie announced.

Helen gritted her teeth and raised herself, kneeling back on her heels, praying for forgiveness. Especially for the fact that right now she wanted to smash Julie Manners' teeth in.

'You ignoring me? You better *not* be ignoring *me*. Towel-head!'

'*Allahu Akbar*,' Helen whispered. She knelt down again, putting her head to the ground, towards Mecca and the holy shrine.

'Look, girls. Little Miss Sand Nigger here thinks she can act all hoity-toity in the U S of A— *oof!*'

There was a gasp and Helen, her eyes closed, heard shouting. She continued to pray. There was the sound of a sharp slap and a howl of rage.

'Y'all better back off *our* buddy.' That was Sally, Helen thought, with a rush of gratitude. 'You're a fat ugly waste of skin, Julie. They ain't made the surgeon yet who can turn you into a babe. You'd best get to prayin' somebody puts a padlock on your refrigerator.'

'Leave me alone!'

'Let her *go*!' Julie's groupies, chiming in.

'I suggest you leave Helen be. Permanently. Otherwise I will go directly to Miss Milton and report what I saw. You'll be expelled.' Jane Morgan, speaking with that proper British accent. Daring them to continue.

'Screw you, you Limey bitch! And *you*, you redneck slut! The whole world knows that Jimmy Quiznos turned you down last Saturday!'

'Yeah, like I'd give Jimmy the time of day. He's so ugly even you could go out with him!' Sally retorted.

'Bitch!' Julie shrieked again, but Helen could hear it was from further away.

'*Allahu Akbar*,' she whispered again, a little more fervently, and stood up, finished. She opened her eyes and saw Julie and half her gang skulking off to the other end of the playground. Julie stuck up one manicured finger.

'Don't mind about her. She's ignorant,' Sally said, as Helen rolled the prayer mat up.

'Did she hurt you?' Jane touched her friend's ribs through the grey jumper.

Helen winced. 'No,' she lied.

It would make a pretty fair bruise, that was for sure. But the insults kept ringing through her head. *Sand nigger. Towelhead. Weirdo. Ay-rab*. 'Why do they talk like that?'

The irony was that as the months ticked by, Helen felt she was losing some of her identity. Baba always spoke English to her, and her Arabic was disappearing. She grew confused by some of the customs, and couldn't follow her parents when they rowed and slipped back into the mother tongue.

She was trying to keep rooted in her culture. But of course the bullies didn't see her becoming more Westernized. Helen was just an *Ay-rab* to them, always would be.

'Just showing off. They think you're strange because you never have any boyfriends.'

'Nor does Jane.'

'Ouch,' Jane objected mildly. 'You don't understand tact, do you, Helen?'

'What does it mean, "tact"?'

'Never mind.' Sally was full of beans. 'You want to be accepted, don't you?'

'She has us,' Jane retorted, still mildly stung.

'But the other girls . . .' Helen had an outsider's longing to fit in. 'The rest of them. You know.'

Jane nodded. She did. She glanced at Sally. 'I agree. They never let up. Especially Julie and Melissa and co. It can get wearing.'

'Then we should do something about that.' Sally stretched, her tanned schoolgirl body catlike in the sun. 'Serve them out for what they just tried to do to Helen.' Underneath her milk-and-honey Southern tones, Jane heard real anger, and she half shivered; Sally might not be academically bright, but she wasn't dumb. There was a streak of steel to her. And right now she was furious.

'Let's throw a party,' Sally said, after a pause.

'A party?' Helen asked.

Jane smiled. Subtle.

'Yes. A real party. Like, party of the year. Must-attend, social death if you don't show up. Crack the whip a little bit over these girls. Prove to them that y'all really *are* my friends.' There was a dangerous light in Sally's eyes. 'And there are consequences if they mess with you.'

Helen's dark gaze flickered over the loud, obnoxious gaggle of girls at the other corner of the playground; they were laughing, most likely at her.

'But they won't come to our party,' she said. 'I don't understand.'

Sally smiled at her friend. Sometimes, she felt a little lost when Helen and Jane were talking together; both the other girls were smart as a whip, and they could get their minds around things that either stumped her or bored her.

But when it came to pure, glorious style, Sally Lassiter was in her element.

'Oh, they'll come,' she said, coolly. 'Right, Jane? They'll come. We just make the party big enough and hot enough and they'll be begging me for invitations. You can handle it just fine, if you've got style.'

She reached out and patted Jane and Helen on the shoulder.

'You need to understand. Glamour is a weapon.'

And she winked.

Helen Yanna stood in the kitchen of her house and carefully watched her mother fixing tea; she made it fresh, the Moroccan way, with mint leaves and lots of sugar, served in small, decorated glasses on an ornate silver tray. An afternoon ritual with them, and one that always made her feel comforted. A slice of home.

'Do you want some?' her mother said, speaking carefully in English. Baba insisted they use it, even at home.

'Thank you,' Helen replied, politely. She accepted the glass and sipped carefully. Wondering how to broach the subject.

'I found some beautiful peaches at the Farmers' Market today,' her mother said, starting to chatter. Helen glanced around the kitchen; it was modern and stylish, but relatively small. Baba wanted to be in the best areas the family could afford. Where they lived now wasn't yet Bel Air or Beverly Hills, but it was central LA, Third Street, near the Writers' Guild building, and inside a prestigious gated complex. Helen knew her mother and sister Jasmine loved the security; the manicured lawns, the little houses in the development all the same size, the community leisure centre with its pool and gym. Everything was neat and clean here. Baba had bought them one of the smaller properties, and was spending the rest on school fees for Helen. That, and a really big Mercedes, a fancy TV, a home computer, and the right kinds of suits and watches.

With Baba, appearance was everything. Helen calculated; could she use that to advantage now?

It was a strange way to grow up, living between two worlds. With loving parents, but hypocritical ones. Yes, Baba and Mama desperately wanted to fit in. And Helen knew all about that longing. She felt it, every day, at school. But they were also Muslims, not very devout, hardly practising, but still, it was one rule for them, another for her. To this day, she had not dared to bring Sally or Jane home. *Especially* not Sally. They were too Western, too determined. If Baba ever caught sight of Sally's deliberately shortened skirts, he'd order Helen never to see her again.

Was it likely he'd let her go to a party?

Helen twisted her fingers around the glass. She didn't think so. And yet she wanted to go, oh, so, so badly. It wasn't like she'd do anything, she thought resentfully. She wouldn't drink alcohol or kiss some boy. She just wanted the chance to go, to be with her friends. To be at the heart of things. To get her own back on the bullies.

To see what it was like to be like Sally – just one time, one night.

'You know, Mama, there's a big party at my friend Sally's house in two weeks. It's for her birthday.' Helen strove to sound casual. 'She's very rich, her father owns an oil company.'

'Your friend is too young for that sort of thing.' Mama sniffed.

'Well . . . there won't be any alcohol,' Helen lied. 'And Sally's parents will be there . . . you know, as chaperones.'

Mama turned to her daughter, her mouth drawn in a thin line.

'Absolutely not, Helen. It sounds forbidden, with boys and mixing. That sort of decadence is not for a good girl like you. Your father will say no. Put it out of your mind.'

'But—'

'No,' her mother said, then lapsed into Arabic, for emphasis. '*La-a.*'

Helen shrugged as if she didn't care and finished her tea. The direct approach hadn't worked. A year ago, before Sally and Jane, she would have accepted that; quietly, resignedly, like she always had.

Tonight, she refused to give up.

The answer would come to her. Helen was determined.

Her father came home, kissed his wife, and started telling her about his day. Average, not too many orders. Possibly a deal importing cosmetics. Mama started gabbling, in Arabic, which Helen was starting to forget, as her memories of her old life in Jordan slipped through her fingers

She suddenly had a brainwave. She got up and went into the kitchen as though unconcerned, getting the cutlery out for dinner.

'Helen.' Baba's voice was stern. 'What is this your mother is telling me? About some party? You should know better than to ask.'

'Oh,' she said, lightly, taking water glasses out of the cupboard. 'It's nothing, Baba. Just a grand affair at Sally's estate in Beverly Hills. Mama didn't understand – I would never be invited anyway.'

'What?' He blinked.

Helen shrugged. 'Sally is nice to me in school, but of course she and Jane move in different social circles.'

'Explain that,' Baba said, darkly.

'Well, you know, Jane's father is an Ambassador. And an honourable. It's an English title, he is aristocratic. And Sally is one of the wealthiest heiresses in America. I mean, come on – *our* family can hardly hope to be seen in public in that company. Sally's party is very exclusive, strictly for the top girls in school. I don't mind.'

Her father's cheeks had gone a nice shade of puce.

'You mean she is supposed to be your friend, but she didn't invite you?'

'Yes, she invited me – after I told her you would never allow it. That way she gets to say she invited me but she knows I won't show up to mix with the important girls. All *their* fathers are major movie producers at the very least.' Helen flashed a smile. 'That's life, Baba, you know what this town is like.'

'No. No way.' Her father shook his head. 'We are as good as any of them.'

'The party will be chaperoned,' Mama broke in. 'Maybe the Ambassador will be there. It would be good for our daughter to know such people.'

'I have made my decision.' Baba's voice was stern. 'You will attend. Tell her I said you may go. I will pick you up at half past ten. Of course you will be modestly dressed. And you will stay with your friends from school. All the girls.'

'But Sally doesn't think—'

'She can hardly take back her invitation. No! *My* daughter is as good as any of them. As is our family.' He sniffed. 'You will go, Helen, do not argue with me.'

His daughter turned aside so he could not see her triumphant smile. Her parents confused her these days, but she still knew how to play Baba at his own game.

'Of course not, Baba,' Helen said meekly. 'I wouldn't dream of it.'

Sally was going to make her over, too. It would be modest, and she didn't see why she should not accept. The best way to handle that was simply not to tell her parents at all. Better to ask forgiveness than permission.

*

Jane turned the pages of her calculus textbook, trying to absorb the maths. But outside her sitting-room windows the path down to the cliff-tops beckoned. It was a glorious October day, and she couldn't concentrate. Maybe she would drop the numbers and pick up one of her biographies instead. That was a hobby of hers – delving into the lives of others. She especially liked ones where the subject had made it after a tough childhood. She could relate to that.

OK, so here she was in her luxurious little rented house in Malibu, with every modern convenience, a nanny/housekeeper and a driver. But nobody who really gave a damn. As she reminded herself, you couldn't pay people to love you.

She wondered, with a pang, what her father was doing right now. Last time he had called, Thomas Morgan had sounded even more stressed than usual. She shouldn't care, but she did. The hope that he would love her one day never really went away.

'Jane!' Her nanny, Consuela, was calling from the sitting room where she was watching *Arsenio Hall* with a big bag of Doritos. 'Your friends are here.'

Jane jumped up, pushing the book away. What? Sally never came out here. There was nothing in her cottage that Sal didn't have ten times better at home – they always hung out on the estate. But sure enough, her personal white limo was pulling in at the front gate, or trying to.

'Make sure you're home by nine, remember the curfew,' Consuela said, half-heartedly.

'Yeah, sure.' She treated that with the contempt it deserved. Consuela wouldn't care if she jumped off a bridge.

'Hey, get in.' Sally flung open the door. 'We're going to a beauty salon. And an opticians.'

'What for?' Jane asked suspiciously, pushing her glasses up the bridge of her nose.

'Don't argue with me, honey. We're going to fix you right up.'

Helen poked out her head, smiling. 'I'm going too.'

'You both are. I won't take no for an answer,' Sally said firmly. 'Get in. Now.'

'Try these.' The optician leaned forward and handed her another pair of lenses. 'Don't worry, you'll get it; everybody drops them at first.'

'Sorry . . .' Jane was embarrassed. She hated clumsiness. Any lack of control, in fact.

'On the tip of your finger . . . *there* you go.'

'Ah.' Jane gasped. But she could see! She blinked.

'Now the other one.'

She put it in, blinked again. Her vision swam, then settled.

'What do you think?' the optician said.

'She looks hot!' Sally approved.

'You're very beautiful,' Helen agreed. '*Very.*'

'Don't be silly,' Jane said gruffly. But she couldn't suppress a smile. Without glasses, her face was so . . . different.

Better. Prettier. Yes, almost beautiful, in its way.

'Thanks, doc. Messenger her lenses to our house, 'kay?'

'Sure thing, Sally.' Dr Madrid smiled benignly. The billionaire's daughter got whatever the hell she wanted. If they asked him to act like a grocery boy, that was A-OK by him. 'A pleasure . . .'

'Come on.' Sally was tugging Jane along by the hand. 'We haven't even started with you yet.'

'I don't know . . .'

Jane shifted uneasily in her seat; the hairdresser was holding a large lump of her hair. She was still getting used to the lenses; as she blinked, her face swam in the mirror.

41

The hairdresser had swooped on Sally as though she were his long-lost best friend. Then when she'd presented Helen and Jane, there had been a lot of clucking and sucking air through the teeth.

Now he was prancing around like a circus pony, grabbing great fistfuls of her hair in exaggerated movements. Not that Jane really cared about looks, but still, she didn't want to come across as a nun.

'Of *course* you don't know. If you did, would you look like *that*?' Maurice snapped his fingers. 'Nuh-uh! I'm the artist, baby, you're the canvas. Let's leave it to the experts. You got it?'

He drowned out her protests. 'See your girlfriends, sugar?'

Maurice spun the chair – there was Sally, getting her golden mane blow-dried, and Helen, having her nails manicured.

'Now they got it going . . . Sally the most. The dark one's shy, but she's at least at first base. *You* need help. Major help. You do *know* that, right?'

Jane swallowed her pride. 'Right.'

It wouldn't do much good to go to the party of the year as guest of honour – queen it over Melissa, for once – if she was also wallflower of the year.

No. No way. Like it or not, Jane Morgan was about to compete. In a new arena.

'Go for it,' she said shortly.

'Really?' He beamed.

'You got it. Give me the works.'

No pain, no gain. It took hours, long and, for Jane, boring hours. There was washing, combing, cutting, dyeing and blow-drying.

'Does it always take this long?' she complained, as Maurice wrapped the millionth piece of foil around her newly shorn head.

'You have to suffer for beauty,' he sighed.

Jane returned to her shopping magazine. It was as dull as all hell. Shopping! Who on earth would be interested in that? Green was in, was it? So what? There were only so many colours in the rainbow. Would anybody complain if she wore blue? Course not.

Were women really this moronic?

'Head back,' Maurice commanded. 'This is going to sting . . . a little.'

'What's that?'

'Hot wax. You're way too cute for that unibrow.'

'Aaaargh!'

'I'm giving you French.'

'Excuse me?'

'Mani-pedi. No colours, you're not ready to graduate.'

'If you don't use colours, what's the point?' Jane asked, staring at her hands. The other two had gone off for a coffee in the diner across the street. She was *still* stuck here, and that tyrant Maurice wouldn't let her see a mirror.

'You'll see,' he said mysteriously.

Finally, it was over. Ten minutes after Helen and Sally sauntered back in, cradling their non-fat frozen yoghurt-to-gos, Maurice flicked the switch off on his sleek steel dryer.

'Of course, I don't make her up yet,' he said modestly. 'And you understand she need clothes . . . colours. But still!'

He beckoned them forward, spun the chair around, and whisked away the black silk drape he'd placed over the mirror.

'Holy Toledo!' Sally shrieked.

Helen gasped.

'Oh my goodness.' Jane was reduced to childishness. She placed one hand over her mouth. 'Oh my goodness . . .'

Her hair, cut to just above the shoulders, was streaked with subtle lights of bronze. It was full of bounce and fullness, the lack of weight giving it a lift it had never had. Without that thick coil pulled into a ponytail, Jane felt as light as air. Her beetling eyebrows had vanished in favour of high arches that opened up her face. And the hand clasped across her mouth boasted neat, shiny nails with attractive white cuticles.

'Wait till we get some make-up on her.' Maurice preened. 'I am magician, no?'

'No – you had great stuff to work with,' Sally said, smiling. 'But you *are* good.' She pressed forward and gave the outraged stylist a kiss on the cheek – and put five hundred dollars into his hand.

Maurice smirked back. '*Merci, chérie*. It was *un plaisir*.'

'Now we get you a dress,' Sally announced, briskly.

'You'll look fantastic,' Helen said, delightedly, beaming at Jane. It was so good to see her blossom – she was so clever, but not always feminine. But they had brought the beauty out from the shadows. Now, who could bully Jane? What girl would even dare to try? Her friend was transformed, prettier than she was. But it wasn't in Helen's nature to be resentful, she was happy for Jane. She had some beauty herself, after all, a consolation, like their friendship, in what Helen instinctively understood was a tough life. Poor Jane. For all Baba annoyed her, at least she had family. Like Sally. What did Jane have? A useless father, not worthy of the name.

And Jane Morgan was so cold, so walled off all the time. Angry at the world. At life. Helen, who was soft and gentle, hoped her friend would marry one day, but she wasn't sure. Sometimes Jane gave every indication of wanting to be a bright, crabby professor somewhere – a distinguished old maid. And that would be a pity, because if Jane needed one thing, it was family. A real family, of her own. Maybe loving her own children would heal her, Helen thought.

'Not just her – *you*.' Sally's warm Southern tones interrupted her reverie.

'You can't get me a dress!' Helen was half flattered, half offended. Unlike Jane, her family had their own cash. 'I'll bring my own.'

'I want to style you,' Sally wheedled. 'Like Jane. Just imagine when we get the make-up girl on her!'

'Nuh-uh.' Helen shook her head. 'I don't do low-cut, Sally. I'm not like you.'

'What? Are you calling me trashy?' Sally's eyes flashed. If she had a weakness, it was being laughed at. She just hated that. So what if she wasn't book-smart? She was *street*-smart.

'Of course not,' Helen prevaricated. Her eyes slipped to Sally's tight white dress, which left very little doubt as to the impressive curves and golden tanned skin beneath. If Baba saw her wearing something like that he'd have a fit! 'I just don't think we have the same style.'

'Relax. I know that, I know what'll suit both of y'all.' Sally nodded. 'I'm throwing this party *for you*. Trust me.'

'For us,' Jane said, nudging her. Come on! Sally loved being the leader of the gang of three. The party was hers, it would only underline her untouchable star status, her truly limitless wealth.

Whatever Paulie had would be Sally's. So what if the other girls' fathers were famous directors or noted producers? When Sally Lassiter grew up, she'd be able to *buy a damn studio* and hire – or fire – any of them.

The party was Sally flexing her muscles.

'OK, then. For us. The three musketeers!'

'Excuse me?' asked Helen.

'Never mind,' Sally said. Impatiently, she tugged at the two girls. Making them over was like playing with grown-up Barbies. She adored her friends, and wanted them to look as hot as she knew they could. 'Neiman Marcus. Now. I got a personal shopper waiting!'

Helen looked at Jane and shrugged. Sally in this mood was a force of nature. Might as well go along!

'You ladies look wonderful.' The manager was gushing as hard as he could. Of course it meant sales for him, but Jane could see the light in his eyes; he really did seem enthused. 'Truly, you are something else. You're going to *wow* them!'

'What do you think, ladies?' Sally didn't trouble to keep the triumph out of her voice. Her two friends had emerged from the chrysalis, and they had her to thank for it. 'We make a pretty cute trio, don't you think?'

The reflection in the mirrored wall opposite confirmed that diagnosis.

Sally – blonde, tanned, stunning in a knockout dress of golden sequins, with a scalloped neckline, tiny fluted sleeves and a fishtail. She looked like a mermaid from a fairy story.

Jane – newly beautiful, now made up by the counter assistant from Chanel, her hair bouncing with life, her delicate features enhanced with a natural, glossy make-up that emphasized her youth – she was wearing a sheath of dark green velvet that picked out her emerald eyes and bronze-highlighted hair.

Helen – exotic and aristocratic. Playing to her heritage, Sally had chosen for her a long-sleeved gown with a dramatic sweeping train, a satin and lace confection of pewter and grey, with a matching cape of lambswool, soft as thistledown. A collar of seed pearls was knotted around her neck.

Her friends had protested they couldn't possibly accept anything so expensive.

'Screw that,' Sally said forthrightly. 'My daddy don't count his money, girls, he weighs it. And if he wants to spoil me, I want to spoil *you*. We're friends, so don't be stupid.'

Lots of people sucked up to her. But she knew these two really liked her; would do, in fact, if she had nothing. In

Sally's position, that meant a lot. In fact, it meant everything.

'If you say so. Thank you.' Helen kissed her on the cheek, thrilled. It was an exquisite gown, modest as well as stylish, and her parents would have no objection.

'Thanks, hon.' Jane gave Sally a bear hug. Anything more, and her voice would have started to crack.

She could hardly believe how Sally had transformed her. Lose the glasses, get some make-up, colour and cut her hair – she barely recognized herself. And the nasty bitches that tried to make her life a misery weren't going to either.

Jane was big on brains. Not so much on self-confidence. After this party, that was going to change.

Chapter Four

Paulie Lassiter glanced around his home, and tried to forget the troubles he was going through at the office.

The big mansion soothed him. It was the most obvious manifestation of his wealth. A man who lived in a house like this couldn't have any real problems at work, now could he?

His home. Green Gables. Named after the L. M. Montgomery novel. Mrs Mona Lassiter was a big fan.

Green Gables. The biggest and most fabulous estate in Bel Air.

Paulie Lassiter loved it. It was his home, his castle, and the definition of his status.

LA ran on star power, the electricity that truly supplied the city grid. And Paulie had none of it – nothing but the thick black ooze that poured out of his desert wells in the Lone Star State. He'd grown up poor, and he wanted only the best for his little girl. In America, Hollywood was the best, and Paulie Lassiter, despite his lack of connections, was determined to be a big fish.

That meant one thing. Conspicuous consumption. The buzz word of the eighties.

So what if his name was never mentioned in *Variety*? Mona, his wife, would be at all the right parties.

So what if he had nothing breaking out at the box office? He would have the biggest pad in LA.

Sally was doing fine at Miss Milton's. And Paulie kept a

fleet of six luxury cars. Ferrari Testarossa, Porsche, Rolls-Royce, Aston Martin . . .

Even the garage wing that housed them was specially made. Yeah, Green Gables was the greatest thing since sliced bread. A canny purchase of some sloping, dusty land in a good part of Bel Air, and unashamed bribery – make that *campaign contributions* – had got Paulie Lassiter, from Belmont, Texas, all the planning permission he needed.

And boy oh boy had he gone to town.

Spielberg – in your face!

Lucas – fuggedaboutit!

The main house had twenty-two bedrooms – some he'd never gone into. There was an enormous heated pool complex, two kitchens, ten en-suite bathrooms, eight dressing rooms, stables, an apple and pear orchard, and a goddamned maze. On top of that, the 'guest wing' of the estate had tennis and squash courts, three guest bungalows – modelled after the famous Beverly Hills Hotel – a formal Italian garden, planted with lavender, rosemary and olive trees, and dotted with fountains and statuary, and a vast enclosed private gym with full-time trainers on staff. And all that was before you counted the staff accommodation for his 'n' hers chauffeurs, the maids, the cooks, and the trained private barman . . .

Green Gables had its own private golf course, eighteen manicured holes.

Green Gables had a fully stocked poolside bar.

Green Gables had a helipad, a landing strip, and an aircraft hangar for Paulie's private jet.

No wonder he was happy about showing it off!

Paulie glanced out of the huge windows of his den, down his manicured lawns to the glassy surface of his private boating lake. Yes, Green Gables was his. What they were telling him about the pension fund just had to be wrong. You couldn't afford a place like this unless you had made it, really made it. He had come from the roughest part of Texas, and he was never going back.

'Daddy.' Sally put on her best little-girl voice. It was Saturday, and she was sitting in the enormous eat-in kitchen, eating buttermilk pancakes with syrup and watching their real fire blazing in the grate. Even in LA it occasionally got chilly in winter, and the Lassiters knew how to make the best of it. 'Can I have a party?'

'What kind of a party, honey?'

Her father moved to the refrigerator to grab a glass of fresh-squeezed juice. It made him feel healthy, even if Conchita was fixing him a pile of bacon and sausage for breakfast. Just chuck some fruit on top, get those antioxidants. Right?

'A biiiig party,' Sally wheedled. 'For my sixteenth birthday and my best friends, Helen and Jane.'

'I love Jane!' her mother said vaguely. An English diplomat's daughter was pure class, and wasn't that why they paid Miss Milton's the big bucks? 'Who's Helen?'

'A new girl.' Sally wasn't certain Daddy would love the whole Arab thing, so she kept it to herself. 'She's real nice. But some of the others been acting up, you know how uppity they get, the actors' daughters and all that. I thought it'd be cool to have a nice party . . . You know, all the works.'

'The works, huh,' Paulie grunted. 'Sounds expensive.'

'I bet all the papers would write it up,' Sally said winsomely. She knew marketing. 'Party of the year! At Green Gables!'

'That'd be nice,' Mona Lassiter mused. She'd missed making the society pages for the last four weeks in a row. It was hard for 'civilians' to be anywhere in this town. What Paulie had was cash – and cash was made to be spent!

'I don't see why we can't live a little.' Mona walked over to her husband and trailed her long nails through his thinning hair, scratching his skull and making him purr with pleasure. 'You can't take it with you, Paulie . . . It'd be nice to see all the young people enjoying themselves.'

'Ah . . . My two best girls,' Paulie said expansively. He shrugged in a hopeless gesture. 'Guess I'm outnumbered!'

The same impulse that made him look round his billionaire's pad prompted him to say yes. Whenever he felt stressed, Paulie would buy something. Or do something. A truly rich party for his little princess and her friends, a night he'd enjoy, show off his money, put aside the gnawing anxiety over the balance sheet. Why not?

'Yay!' Sally squealed. She did a cartwheel out of her cheerleading routine, her skinny legs tumbling forward gracefully in her jeans, blond hair flying. Paulie looked at her fondly. He'd have liked a son, but really, Sally was pitch-perfect, his little honey, and he adored her. Since Mona wasn't able to have a second, he'd ploughed everything into his baby.

'We'll definitely get the works.' He grinned. 'Mona, take care of it, will ya? A carousel . . .'

'A carousel!' Sally rolled her beautiful eyes. 'Dad, I'm not *eight*. We need one of those flight simulators! You know, from the fairground. You strap in and take a rocket to Mars . . . And we need fireworks, a *huge* display. And candles all round the pool.'

'Fairy lights, lanterns, a marquee, tented silk – we should get Chasen's to do the catering . . . or Zanzibar . . .'

'Not Moroccan,' Sally said hastily. Didn't want Helen to get upset. She was touchy sometimes. She ran over, kissed her mother and father exuberantly on the cheek. 'Thanks, you guys! You're the best!'

They hugged her back. Yes, her parents were the absolute best, Sally thought happily. And so was her life. She was queen bee, and she was taking her friends with her!

*

'I'm having second thoughts about this party,' Baba announced that evening.

They were preparing for dinner, and Helen was happy, humming to herself as she chopped the coriander. Their last outing, for coffee, had been cool: lots of chat with her girlfriends, laughing and giggling, sneaking glances at the movie stars. Well, a sitcom star and a hot director, better than nothing.

And plenty of people had stared at them, too. Not just at Sally, at all three of them. Helen was only human; like Jane, who sat there, blossoming under the attention like a parched plant getting water, she had enjoyed herself.

A warm-up to the big event.

As her father spoke, Helen's fist tightened in mid-air, her knuckles whitening on the knife. Baba couldn't stop her – not now!

Little Jasmine looked round at her big sister, then lost interest. *Fraggle Rock* on the TV held much more fascination for her than Helen's social life.

'But I would never do anything wrong.' Helen burned with resentment. Her father was such a hypocrite! He wore Western clothes, gave them anglicized names and drank like a fish. She hardly ever saw him attend prayers, or go to the mosque. Baba made his friends call him 'Al', which sounded less foreign than Ali. She strongly suspected their family had settled in LA, not New York, because with year-round tans on everyone their Levantine skin stood out that much less. 'There are going to be chaperones,' she reminded him.

'See? Chaperones. If it's so innocent what do they need them for?' asked her father. This was the great leap of logic. If Sally's parents weren't coming, he'd have moaned about no chaperones, she just knew it.

'Anyway, Helen, there's no need for you to go. And mix with these Western boys.'

'No need?'

She had a sinking feeling she wasn't going to like what came next.

'You tell her,' Baba said to her mama.

'We found a nice man for you.' Aisha stirred the sauce, not looking at her daughter. Deliberately, Helen suspected. 'He's family . . .'

'Distant family.'

'My cousin Lallah. Her nephew. Ahmed is his name. He's twenty-four . . .'

Ugh. An old man.

'He's a merchant, in Cairo. Has a very nice house – a large garden, like our old house in Amman. You'll like it. You'll like him.' Aisha's back stiffened. 'Baba and I are all agreed.'

'Well, isn't that nice.' Helen was surprised to hear the bitterness in her own voice; rebellion wasn't her thing. But she was saying it, all the same. The words tumbled out of her. 'But you forgot to ask me. I'm not agreed.'

'You've always been a good girl,' her father grunted. 'You knew this had to be.'

'Not now. Not any more.' Helen stood firm. '*I'm* going to decide who I marry, Baba.'

'But Ahmed is a nice boy!' Aisha was scandalized. 'It's a lot of money. An excellent match, a good family. Cairo is perfect for you! We've discussed it.'

'You will obey me on this, Helen, I am your father,' Baba reminded her stiffly. 'Our family has position, reputation to think of. Maybe I should pull you out of that school!'

Leave Sally and Jane? Like hell!

'I tell you what, Baba.' It suddenly occurred to Helen that her father was a businessman. They could do a little old-fashioned horse trading. 'It's going to be a major social event, you know. Paulie Lassiter is a billionaire, all from oil. There are going to be movie stars, diplomats, bankers. And of course Mrs Lassiter is overseeing the entire thing. You should let me go, it'll be a feather in your cap. You already said yes. Just stick to that.'

His eyes narrowed. 'And if I do? You'll marry Ahmed?'

'I'll *meet* him,' Helen countered. 'I'll consider it. Certainly, why not? Cairo is very cosmopolitan, and like you say, he has a good family . . .'

'You're in no position to bargain!' said her father, crossly. He marched to the dresser and took out his bottle of whisky.

Helen knew that look. She just waited.

'I suppose if there are chaperones, you can go. We want you to fit in. Ahmed will like it if you have friends here . . . he can expand his business . . .'

'What business is he in?'

'Carpets.'

Helen looked away so Baba would not see her roll her eyes. Carpets, great. What a cliché. Did he have any flying ones? she wanted to ask, but bit her lip.

'*Very expensive* carpets,' Aisha announced. She was sharper than her husband, and knew something about the set of her daughter's back. 'Priceless works of art, some of them. Only the real Hollywood types could afford them.'

'That's great!' Helen lied. She tried to give it some of Sally's cheerleader pep. 'I'll see if I can collect business cards, Baba. Anyway, a woman has to think of her social position. For the family, ours . . . and his.'

Yeah, lay it on thick. Was this a sin? Maybe. But she had no intention of marrying somebody she'd never met. And in her religion they couldn't make her.

It didn't hurt to give them a bit of flannel, though. Agree to meet this guy – anything, as long as she could go to the party. Live it up a little! She was working hard at school – why not? She deserved a reward.

Helen looked at her father. She could meet Ahmed, be nice to him, try to manage a few sentences in Arabic. Who cared, really? She would promise anything as long as she could go to the party . . .

'That's very true. You'll make an excellent wife . . . Very well, you can go. You're a good girl,' Ali pronounced, smugly.

He watched his daughter, dark head bowed, turn back to the coriander. That had gone surprisingly well. Of course he loved America, and the lifestyle here, but there were limits. He had not been blessed with sons, and he had no intention of either daughter shaming him.

Helen was disturbingly beautiful. Her body was ripening daily. He could see it under her uniform. When the family went out to restaurants, men looked boldly at her.

She was ready for marriage. If they waited, like Western girls did, it would be a disaster. Let her complain, Ali thought; she will enjoy her life, once she has a husband, some babies, and a fine house. He himself had grown up poor and had made it through the sweat of his back. Things would be altogether easier for Helen.

Yes; he had done well. And he knew what was best for her.

Jane sat in her favourite nook in the library. There was a comfy window seat, padded with soft green cushions, and it looked out over the lush lawn that sloped down towards the carp pond. There was a great view of the permanently flowering garden – Miss Milton's, like the rest of the town, was *big* into image. Best of all, it was a tucked-away spot, near the reference shelves.

Hell, the library in general was pretty tucked away. The school had cachet, sure, but not the academic kind. The glossy Angeleno teens who populated it didn't care too much for books. The ones who did use it were like her, pre-makeover. Natural loners, a bit shy, usually not so easy on the eyes. Fat Debbie Fulford was in here a lot. And Soon-Yi

Kiwasa, the Thai girl with the serious acne problem. All of them using books as a get-out clause from life.

'Well, well, well.'

Jane sighed. It was Julie. With her two sidekicks right behind her, Melissa and Kate.

'What do you want? I'm studying.'

'You're always studying,' Kate Menzies piped up. 'Lame brain. Don't think anything's changed, just because you look good now.'

'Normal.' Julie corrected her, sharply

'Get out of here, or I'll go get a teacher.' Jane brushed them aside. She was with Sally; untouchable.

'Ho ho.' Julie looked triumphantly at her hangers-on. 'Maybe *Miss* Jane Limey doesn't want to know our news.'

They all smirked.

'Maybe I don't.' Jane forced herself not to ask.

'Course it isn't set. Just a rumour. But I do have *great* sources.'

'Seems a certain fancy diplomat's getting himself into trouble.'

'Like *real* trouble.'

Jane shrugged. 'You should know by now, I don't care *what* my father does. Nice try though, girls. Better luck next time.'

'*Oooh,*' they chorused.

'I think you'll care about this one, babycakes. When it all goes down,' Melissa said nastily. 'No more mansions. No more limos . . . I'd be using this library while you can. And make sure to say all your goodbyes to Sally and the towel-head.'

'I told you to get out of here. Don't speak like that about Helen Yanna. I'll report you, in a heartbeat.'

'Course you would – sneak.'

Jane made a supreme effort and lightly shrugged her shoulders. 'Everybody knows how mad you are you can't get an invite to Sally's party, Melissa. So sad to be left out like that. Rob Lowe's coming – I hear you like him. But really, don't take it out on the rest of us. It just looks pathetic, don't you think?'

Melissa flushed a satisfactory shade of puce. 'Bitch! Let's see how long Sally Lassiter hangs out with a *goddamn bum*. You're going to be on the streets. Maybe you could come to our house – we need a new maid!'

'Or you could sell oranges on the roadside. Like a wetback.' Julie laughed loudly, and her companions snickered. 'See ya, welfare girl.'

Jane yawned and went back to her book.

Only when they'd left the library did she lift her head. She wouldn't have wanted those cows to see the anxious expression on her face.

Chapter Five

'So how did it go with Dad?'

'Fine! I can come,' Helen replied happily. She had no intention of telling Sally about Ahmed and the arranged marriage. That was so backwards – it was embarrassing her parents even *thought* they could get away with it.

'That's great. Julie was begging for an invite earlier.' Sally smirked as she contemplated her party-throwing skills. Some of their enemies had thought they could get away by blanking her, but Sally had played it carefully. Stacked the party with rides and treatments until it sounded like paradise – manicure tents, masseuses on hand, firework displays, flight simulators, camel rides – then added cool little gifts, like necklaces personally designed at Frederick's of Hollywood, and lastly, the killer ingredient – boys, and stars.

The seniors from the *most* exclusive LA boys' schools were all invited before *any* invites went to the girls of Miss Milton's. And Paulie Lassiter knew actors. Mona was able to get several of the younger, hotter Hollywood set. Molly Ringwald was an acceptance. There were producers there, aching for some of Paulie's cash for financing. Actors followed producers, and in a feeding frenzy, like lissom teen pirhanas, the girls of Miss Milton's followed the men.

Nobody tried to play it cool.

Sally was accosted.

'Hey, Sal. Where's my invite?'

'Sally. Can I come?'

'Hon, you haven't forgotten about me, have you?'

She enjoyed them all. Usually accompanied by a wheedling tone and a cajoling sort of smile. Anybody who thought they were too cool for Sally Lassiter had another think coming!

'We'll let her crawl a little while,' Sally decided. 'And then she's gonna be seated at the *worst* table – I'm talking Siberia!'

'Out by the tennis court?'

'Yeah, with my mother's tennis coach! And the guy who comes to teach Dad French.'

Helen laughed. Yes, Julie would *hate* that. Plus, it would be the talk of the school.

'And Melissa nowhere . . .'

'She ain't coming. Baby, I gotta have me some standards.'

'I can't wait,' Helen said truthfully. She would be at the centre of things for once, right at the epicentre. Top table and in the thick of it. The idea gave her a buzz. 'And we have to help Jane . . .'

'Of *course*.' Sally lifted one perfectly plucked eyebrow. 'That's what this whole deal is about! We'll bring her out of her shell. She'd be a *babe*, once she got introduced to the human race. And a pair of eyebrow tweezers. *You* know what I'm talking about. Grooming, 101.'

'Exactly,' Helen responded. Thrilled that her friend considered her hip enough to help.

Make Jane Morgan in Helen Yanna's image. Wasn't that a kick?

'Jane.'

'Pennnn-eeee.'

Sally swooped down on her as she walked along, staring into the middle distance. Helen snapped her fingers in Jane's face.

'Hello? Anybody home?'

'I'm sorry.' Jane snapped back to the world around her. 'I was miles away.'

She didn't mention her worries. Neither one would understand. But Melissa Smith's father was a lawyer – a very high-priced, Washington, *criminal* lawyer. He had got countless embezzling billionaires and rich, murdering husbands a 'Get Out of Jail Free' card. OK, not exactly free – Mr Smith's fees cost more than the President made in a year.

'Yeah, well, forget all that. What are you doing tonight?' Helen snaked a buff arm through hers.

'I have archaeology club . . .'

'No. You don't,' Sally announced. 'You're coming with us.'

'I've got obligations . . .'

'And *I've* booked a table at Morton's. The most exclusive restaurant in LA. Just for starters. You can consider yourself kidnapped. You're coming with us.'

Jane tried a small smile. 'Party stuff?'

Despite being a brainbox, she was still sixteen years old. And the idea of being guest of honour at the hot party Melissa couldn't get into was delicious.

'Sort of.' Sally grinned. 'Practice! I want you to hang out, let everybody see your new look. Give you girls a little confidence. When you come downstairs at that party we have to *wow* them. I don't want y'all to be timid.'

'OK. I'll come.'

Being stared at was a new idea. She could use a little practice.

Helen squeezed her arm. She loved the freedom she got hanging out with her friends. Milkshakes and very expensive pizza, a little star-spotting . . .

'We'll have fun. Put that book down.'

'OK.' Jane smiled back, excited despite herself.

She'd practically forgotten the acid tongue of Melissa Smith.

*

The house on Washington Avenue. He loved it. It had been the scene of so many of his triumphs. The intimate party for the Princess of Monaco. The state dinner for Vice President H. W. Bush. The negotiations – tremendously secret, but bugged by both sides – between the UK and Russia over the Ukraine . . .

And more. The scene of his personal rise – and he did mean rise.

The Hon. Thomas Morgan took a last, unsteady walk through his house. It was like taking a walk through a film – of his life, starring him. And hadn't that been how it really was? He, the star? Emerging from the shadow of his oh-so-lucky big brother, James, the one with the title and the fabulous Elizabethan manor house. Second sons were awkward. James was the heir and he was the spare. In bygone ages they'd have shoved him into the Church. Right. He laughed wildly. Some priest *he'd* have made!

Ah yes . . . the billiard room. He particularly loved it, because it had been the scene of so many great screws. Two of the sexy young nannies, right there on that table. A couple of desperate Washington housewives, longing to climb that social ladder. What a room! It was there that he lived and breathed, there that he had his power.

Nobody more charming. Nobody more brilliant . . .

The grip of the drugs subsided in his mind, and for a second melancholia swept in. What the hell . . . what the hell did it all mean?

The unwelcome thought arose that maybe he hadn't been *that* brilliant. Maybe he'd just been the best kiss-ass in town. A natural politician, one that could groom his lords and masters in London just as well as sucking up to the Yanks and assorted foreigners who comprised the social scene in America's capital.

Maybe that wasn't something to boast about. Fucking

desperate women, poor immigrants without the right papers, nannies longing to keep their job and their shot at freedom, obsessed wives of other men, dumb enough to see the world through the same shallow blinkers he did.

Maybe he should have paid more attention to his daughter.

Maybe he shouldn't have gambled.

Maybe he shouldn't have neglected his job . . .

Thomas Morgan let out a loud, wretched sob. He felt piteously sorry for himself. He didn't deserve this, any of this. He was a good person! They were all picking on him . . .

The maudlin wash of regret peaked on another chemical dip and turned into anger. Morgan strode back into the bedroom, sat at his antique William and Mary dressing table, and snorted the next of the thick, fat lines he'd chopped out earlier this evening.

Wow! Instant rush.

His dismissal, hand-delivered from his boss, lay ignored on the bed. Morgan was flying, riding a fresh wave of self-confidence and pride. He looked at himself in the mirror, a tall, handsome man in his mid-forties, a dusting of powder just under his nose – that, he brushed off. The white tie, Washington's most formal style of attire, looked *fabulous* on His Excellency. As ever.

Swap it for an economy ticket home and a cheap pension? Live in a semi-detached somewhere cheap? He thought not.

His Excellency the Hon. Thomas Morgan walked over to the Victorian sash windows of his boudoir, threw them open with one arm, and swung his legs over the edge. Fuck them, fuck them all! They'd never catch him. They were no match for him!

His daughter, Jane, briefly floated back into his mind. But he didn't want to think of her now. Wasn't the moment. She was *his* daughter. She'd be OK, and besides, her mother was waiting, expecting him . . .

He tossed himself over the edge, high as a kite. Falling, his arms spread out, as though he were flying, offering himself to the elements.

But he wasn't flying. He was dying. In that long second before the death, Thomas Morgan knew it. His mind threw up a vision of Jane, all grown up – she was happy, he thought.

He blew her a kiss as the ground swallowed him up.

'Baby, baby, baby,' Mona said. She sighed with satisfaction, walked across the kitchen and gave him a hug. 'You wouldn't *believe* the response I am getting for this party. Shelby Cusack's agent just called to ask me if we could squeeze her in!'

'That's great,' Paulie said absently. Normally, he'd have been thrilled to bits that hot new starlets were paying court to his wife. But right now, his attention was fixed on the screen in front of him.

'We've got Feliz, too. You know, the Amazing Feliz? He's the big lion tamer from Vegas! It's like the most incredible act. And Melissa Ugoretz wanted him for *her* wedding anniversary but she couldn't afford him . . .'

'How much is the party costing?' Paulie asked suddenly. The figures . . . They didn't add up. He suddenly had a dry mouth. His business brain was stuck, like a slow computer dragging; he just couldn't process this.

'Why?' Mona asked innocently. 'We haven't had one this year . . .'

'No. I know.' It hit him that he didn't want to know the answer.

'Well, Feliz was a hundred fifty . . .'

'Thousand?'

Mona laughed. 'I love it when you make a funny, baby, you crack me up.'

'I like to see you smile,' Paulie responded, mechanically. What would this party cost? With fireworks fit for a county park, fairground rides, a private zoo, party designers on an eight per cent budget and the best of everything, it would be plenty.

No way did he get out of this for less than a mil. Judging by past triumphs, one point five.

He didn't blame his wife. It was what she did – a world expert on spending cash.

Up until two weeks ago, Paulie Lassiter had loved it.

'You OK, Paulie? You're looking kinda pale.'

'I'm fine.'

'If your tummy's bothering you again I can get you some pepto-bismol.'

'Nah. I think I'm gonna go into the office,' he said.

There had to be some mistake. What he needed was an hour with his accountants, and his lawyers. Maybe fire some of these dumb-ass executives, if they were dumb asses. Starting to look like they might be crooks.

But he, Paulie Lassiter, was in the clear. He hadn't done anything wrong.

He tried to calm the churning in his stomach by reminding himself of that. And anyway, it was the party on Tuesday. His wife would expect him to be upbeat. This was only the second major party he'd given for Sally – her sweet sixteenth!

It would be a golden moment. Worth every damn penny of a mil five.

Paulie was a good dad. He wanted nothing he did to detract from this party. The reckoning could come later. A couple days would make no difference, not right now.

Sally's party. Sally's day. Whatever he did in life, it was for her.

'Do you think we're doing the right thing?' Aisha asked nervously.

'Of course.' Ali gave her a quick peck on the cheek. 'She's ripe, you know it.'

'But to force her . . . What if he's not the right boy? We brought her here, darling. Sent her to that school . . .'

Ali's face darkened. He wasn't sure if that had been the right move. Helen was growing too bold, too rebellious. Of course he wanted a spirited daughter, but not one who would defy him on the fundamentals.

'I never met *you*,' he reminded his wife. 'Aya Muna set us up. Do you recall?'

She smiled. 'I didn't want to marry you.'

He scooped her up and nuzzled her ear. 'I wanted you, though.'

'Because you came to my father's house and climbed up the olive tree by the garage.'

'It's true.' Ali was proud. 'Had to scope you out.'

She had been so beautiful, his young bride, her raven hair flowing loose over her beige cotton dress with the embroidered sleeves, hanging out the washing on the line her mother had strung up. He had wanted her instantly, felt his destiny calling. 'I won you over.'

Aisha blushed, remembering her wedding night.

'That's right. Sweetheart.'

'The old ways are the best ones. We're not doing this *to* Helen, we're doing it *for* her. Think of that – her happiness. Why should young ones make their own choices? Who says they have any idea how to do it? All these American marriages ending in divorce – how many ex-wives do you know, stuck with babies?'

Too many. Aisha nodded.

'In the end, it is the solemn bond, the friendship that wins through. We are doing what's best for our little Haya.'

Aisha smiled. He hadn't called Helen by her original name since they'd arrived in America.

'Ahmed lands tomorrow,' she said, reassured by her husband.

'Good. That is the day of her big party.'

'He can take her to it!' Aisha suggested, brightly.

'I don't think that's the best idea.' What if Helen had been wrong? What if there was decadence, after all? Ali had no intention of letting Ahmed see his daughter in any light other than as a modest and suitable bride. He loved the idea of Helen, wife of a Cairo businessman, contentedly walking through her garden lined with trees, prosperous and, *insh'Allah*, pregnant.

'But he can be here, waiting, the next morning. As soon as she wakes up. We will organize the meeting in the morning, and in the afternoon, the *nikkah*. What do you think?'

The engagement ceremony. Under Islamic law, they would be as good as married. It didn't matter then how long till the party, and the wedding reception. Helen would be a married woman. All the rest, just so much paperwork.

'She might refuse,' Aisha fretted. 'You know her, Ali!'

'She won't understand what she is getting into. Her Arabic is rusty. Once she realizes . . .' he shrugged. 'We'll have her in Cairo, and it will all be different. She will accept it – and be happy.'

'Jasmine will miss her,' Aisha sighed. She knew this was best, but the thought of sending her first-born away made her want to cry.

'We'll all miss her.' Ali hugged his wife. 'But if we want her happiness, we will have to make sacrifices. Once she's pregnant and has accepted him, in her heart, they can come here, and we will all be a family again.'

Aisha nodded, but wept a little into his chest.

Ali stroked her hair fondly. His own marriage had been the most solid thing in his life, and he loved his strong-willed child enough to do right by her. Of course, at first she would feel betrayed, but soon she would be accepting.

Chapter Six

The day of the party dawned bright and clear.

All over town, girls were getting ready for it. Half – the lucky half – of Miss Milton's Academy. Daughters of movie stars, studio heads and other powerbrokers. Some models and actresses, and wives of famous athletes.

Everybody who was anybody.

Melissa Smith was *not* on the invited list. And nor were half her friends.

They sat in the walk-in closet of Julie Manners, watching her try to pick between eight different outfits. Seething with envy. Why couldn't *they* go to the ball? Where was a fairy godmother when you needed one?

The Brat Pack were gonna be there! And maybe somebody from Guns n' Roses. For heaven's sake!

'You think the blue?' Julie held up an electric-blue mini dress, no longer than a T-shirt with pretensions. 'Or the white?' Body-hugging in the extreme, it was practically see-through.

'Either'll look great.' *Tramp*, Melissa thought. Just because they hung out together didn't mean she had to *like* Julie.

'Don't know why you're bothering to go,' Swan Cohen said petulantly. 'It's gonna be a real drag. None of *us* will be there.'

'Oh, I only want to see how *lame* it really is, so I can report back,' Julie lied, smiling sweetly at them.

Miss it! The party of the year! Hell, no. Sally Lassiter was a real bitch and so were her two stupid friends. But if you weren't at this party, you were *dead* in this town.

Everybody in the room knew it.

'Jane Morgan looks hot now,' Swan said morosely.

Julie scowled. 'She's just passable.'

'And Helen Yanna . . .'

'That towel-head just trails round after Sally. She ain't nothing to write home about. I don't think Rob Lowe's gonna be asking *her* for a dance.' Julie was scornful. 'If the point is to show off those two, Sally's gonna have wasted a whole lot of Daddy's dollars.'

'Don't be so snippy, we all know you crawled to get that invite,' Melissa snapped.

'Sweetie,' Julie retorted acidly, 'I don't *crawl*. I think it's gonna be fun to show the world that *we're* the stars of *Sally's* party. When all her hot dudes are asking for *our* phone numbers, Sally's gonna feel way dumb. You get it?'

'Oh yeah,' Melissa said sourly. 'We' and 'our' included Emma Lightfoot and Caroline Noakes from their gang, but not her, Swan or Patsy. For the last two weeks they'd been at each other's throats. 'I get it all right.'

She wasn't going to give Julie that cool new hands-free phone she'd been planning to get her for her birthday. Not any more!

'I'll have Emma take some pics to show you,' Julie said in a mollifying tone. She held up a green silk dress with an obscenely plunging neckline. 'What about *this* one? Should steal the show from Sally and crew, don't you think?'

'Whatever.'

'Maybe.'

The other girls chewed on their resentment, torn between wanting Sally's party to fail and wanting Julie to get shown up.

'You better *hope* so,' Julie warned, reading their minds.

'Because we're *friends*. Do you want that Ay-rab and the Limey laughing at you on Monday morning?'

They all shook their heads. Hell no. After all, Sally had the power. She was the one withholding the invites – all to prop up her little gang of three.

They didn't like Julie much, but they *hated* that lot.

'Go for the white,' Melissa said, speaking for all of them. 'It's *way* sexy.'

She hoped Helen and Jane didn't get so much as a second glance from all the boys! Let this party be a disaster. Then, at school, they'd show them who was boss!

Green Gables was on fire.

Helen ran excitedly to the window of Sally's enormous bedroom. It had a walk-in closet that was bigger than Helen's lounge, its own bathroom complete with jacuzzi and stand-alone power shower, a separate dressing room *and* a private kitchenette!

Wow. Helen wondered what it'd be like to have this much money. Her dad was comfortable, rich middle class, but compared to Sally they were nothing but paupers.

She wanted this kind of success.

'Look at that!' Another rocket arched into the sky and exploded, a fiery rain of stars and whistling comets descending on an awestruck crowd. The air was full of *ooohs* and *aaahs*. 'Come on, Sal! We *have* to go down!'

The party had been raging – and that was the word – for two hours already. Mona kept popping her head in to report this movie star or that supermodel had arrived.

'Yes, let's go.' Jane was surprised at her own eagerness. Dressed in the gown Sally had picked out for her, carefully made up by a pro, spritzed with a little rosewater, she looked astonishingly lovely, and she knew it.

'We want to make an *entrance*.' Sally smirked. 'This is our *moment*, ladies. We're not going to blow it.'

'Aww, please,' Helen said. She did not want to miss the fireworks!

'Five more minutes. Momma's getting them all ready.' Sally was in her element, supremely confident. 'You'll see.'

'Damn.' Julie Manners seethed. She was gyrating on the dance floor, but it was having no effect. Rob Lowe had been here but hadn't even looked her way.

'That preppy kid from Beverly Hills High was checking you out,' Emma suggested helpfully.

'Screw him!' Julie pushed her fringe out of her eyes. Who cared? He was probably some dentist's kid . . .

She was frustrated. All the girls from school were watching her and Emma like hawks. It was a battle for supremacy. The party was supremely, awesomely great, so now all that remained was to see who was the most beautiful. Those three girls had been the talk of the school since they arranged this party. How dared they hang out just with themselves? They were freaks. But Sally Lassiter had been the protector. Julie did *not* want to see Helen and Jane Morgan making it by themselves.

She was possessed by a sudden, deep loathing, a bully who suspects she's about to see her victims succeed.

The music suddenly stopped, leaving Julie in mid-grind. Emma sniggered. Julie scowled at her.

'Ladies and gentlemen,' the voice of the Lassiters' real English butler came over the tannoy. 'Please welcome the birthday girl, Sally Lassiter, and her best friends Miss Jane Morgan and Miss Helen Yanna!'

The glittering crowd, gathered around the dance floor, buzzed in anticipation. Everybody's eyes were fixed on the top of the stairs.

Julie Manners had a sinking feeling in the pit of her stomach.

And there they were. At the top of the stairs.

'Oh – my – *gosh*,' said Emma. 'Oh my gosh!'

There was a collective gasp.

Sally – in the middle. Long blond hair, va-va-voom body, illegal curves, in her glittering gold sheath, scalloped neckline, looking like a Greek goddess – Aphrodite, the queen of love.

Helen Yanna. Flowing robes, statuesque as a model, make-up emphasizing her natural beauty, a diamanté circlet in her hair, her Arabian features exquisitely calm and confident, was holding her left hand. Golden slippers glittered on her feet.

And holding her right hand, glasses vanished, hair light and gorgeous, high cheekbones glowing under radiant skin, dark-eyed Jane – perhaps the loveliest of all. The ugly duckling turned swan, with all the extra firepower of good old-fashioned shock.

The crowd froze for a moment. Sick with jealousy, Julie glanced around. She saw the men's eyes narrowing with interest and admiration; the girls from school staring as if star-struck.

Then the applause broke out – and the cheering.

The orchestra struck up 'Happy Birthday To You' and the three girls started to walk downstairs, holding hands. Three babes. Three best friends. Unbreakable. Perfect.

Flashbulbs popped as the official photographers captured the moment. Julie knew just how that picture would look – a glorious capture of youth and a level of beauty that neither she, nor any of her friends, would ever be able to match.

Just before the well-wishers – and boys – swarmed in on the glittering trio, Julie saw Sally Lassiter scope the crowd and find her.

The birthday girl gave her an insolent, triumphant wink.

I hate her, Julie thought. I've got to destroy her!

But what could she do?

Those three girls – they were untouchable!

She saw that hot new movie star, the one from the serial killer flick with all the Oscars, go up to Jane Morgan – and ask *her* to dance!

It was just horrible.

Julie turned to Emma. 'I'm leaving,' she said.

But Emma was gone. She was pushing through the crowd, shouting to get some attention. 'Helen! Hey, Helen!' Julie heard her calling. 'That's a great dress. Who's the designer?'

There were two new queen bees in town. Furious, Julie stalked off to the cloakroom.

'I want my bag!' she yelled. 'Like, pronto!'

Time to split. Seething, she stewed in her failure. Damn it all to hell. Would anything ever go wrong for these bitches? Well, when it did, she, Julie Manners, would be right there waiting.

She had no idea just how soon it was going to be.

'So, how did it go?'

Helen's father helped her into the car. He had to admit she looked marvellous – modestly gowned but at the same time splendidly beautiful. He was pleased – young Ahmed would be a most amenable bridegroom.

'It was so much fun.' Helen sighed with contentment. In all her young life, she had never had such an evening.

The spectacle of it – that was something else. The camel rides and free manicures, the fabulous food and sneaky drinks from the hidden beer keg – not that *she'd* indulged – the fortune tellers and fireworks! Too much fun.

And then, herself. The girls had all adored her outfit, and she'd felt simply beautiful – not different, just the centre of attention. The solid friendship of Sally and Jane had buoyed her up. And if young men had asked her to dance, asked for her number – well, she didn't have to say yes – that was nice, too.

'Excellent. I trusted you,' he reminded her.

'I know, Baba.' Helen gave him a reassuring hug. 'It was all fine.'

'Tomorrow morning Ahmed is coming.'

She sighed, but a bargain was a bargain. 'I'll be there. I'll be nice to him, I promise you that.'

'Good girl.' Her father kissed his tired daughter gently on the forehead, and reminded himself that what he was doing was for her own good.

The sun was streaming through the window of her bedroom when Jane woke up. It was a glorious winter's day in LA; sunny, but not too hot. The Malibu ocean was crashing against their private beach, and as Jane tossed in bed, she smelled the welcoming aroma of Consuela's bacon and tomatoes, sizzling in the pan. The rented house the Embassy provided for the Ambassador's daughter was small, but lovely, on a high cliff overlooking the sea, with large windows, modern designer furniture, and of course the latest live-in nanny.

Jane pushed a hand through her tousled hair and smiled.

For the first time in a long time – maybe forever – she woke up happy.

Last night had been truly wonderful. She'd been asked to dance by no less than three film stars, one soap actor, and a rock star – and asked for her number by countless hot-looking studs. And the girls had fluttered about her, offering compliments, gazing wonderingly at her hair – wow, it felt fantastic!

The tribute paid to beauty. Moth-like Jane had never known it. She was overwhelmed with gratitude to Sally. She'd never look down on that again. Call it superficial all you want – as bookworm supreme, Jane certainly had – but being pretty made *all* the difference. She felt confident, feminine, as if the missing puzzle piece had been added to her life. Maybe she'd never have Sally's brazen, starry glow, but Jane Morgan felt good about herself.

She swung her slim legs out of bed and padded over to the mirror. Jane slept in a pair of plain navy pajamas. But even without make-up, the beauty was still there; the great hair, ruffled by sleep; her pretty face, without the glasses; a little mascara on her lashes that hadn't come off with the cursory wipe she'd given her face last night.

Jane Morgan was seventeen, carefree, and single.

It was to be the last day of her life she would ever feel that way.

She wandered into the shower and was washing her hair, revelling in the sensation of the powerful jets, when Consuela hammered on the door.

'Mees Morgan – phone – for you.'

'Take a message,' Jane yelled. 'I'll call them back.'

'They say ees important. Ees Washington.'

'I'll get dressed, call them right back,' Jane snapped. Damn! Couldn't she at least put her clothes on?

Still, it wasn't like Daddy to call her and insist on talking. Reluctantly, she hurried through her routine, pummelled out the conditioner and stepped out of the shower. Jane dried off fast and selected black jeans and a matching T-shirt, then went to find Consuela.

Her nanny put a plate of food in front of her. 'Here.'

'Gracias.' Jane minded her manners. 'That number?'

Consuela passed her a scrap of paper and Jane dialled back.

'British Embassy.'

'This is Jane Morgan,' she said, confidently. 'I believe my father called me?'

There was a long pause at the end of the line.

'Hold please, Miss Morgan.'

A couple of beeps, and Jane found herself talking to Cyril – Sir Cyril Clark, her father's senior attaché.

'Jane?' he said.

She knew instantly, from his tone. Something was wrong

– very wrong. Automatically, Jane pushed the plate of bacon and tomatoes away, untouched.

'Cyril, it's me.' She could hear the anxiety in her voice. 'What is it? Let me speak to my father, please.'

Another leaden pause.

'Now listen, Jane,' he said heavily, and her stomach curled into a knot. 'You're going to have to be very brave.'

'And this is my daughter, Helen.'

Baba was speaking in Arabic; Helen's was rusty, she was ashamed of that. After the party, she'd been too excited to sleep much. This morning she was groggy with exhaustion, but she'd got up anyway, to keep her end of the bargain. Helen even wore a long, traditional dress, the *al thoub*, to please her parents, instead of her normal jeans and a button-down shirt from Gap.

'*Wa-es salaam*,' she said politely.

He nodded back and said something too fast for Helen to understand. Ahmed was a young man of reasonable height, and a pleasant enough, unremarkable face. He looked about as enthusiastic over the whole exercise as she did herself. Helen smiled at him – he, too, probably had parents to placate. They'd get through this together.

'Ahmed's father is also visiting town. He'll be here this afternoon for the ceremony.'

'What ceremony is that?' Helen asked, confused.

'The friendship ceremony.' Ali spoke in English, and Ahmed looked on uncomprehendingly. 'Traditional in Egypt. You will go through with it, Helen?'

'Course I will.' She nodded. Fair's fair – they'd let her go to the party, the greatest night of her life. At the very least, she could show willing. 'It will be good to meet your father,' she added to Ahmed, haltingly.

'Thank you.' He added, 'I am very happy.'

He didn't look it.

'And I have a surprise for you,' Ali added. 'Tonight we are all going on a family trip – to Cairo. Your mother is visiting her cousins. Afterwards we'll go back to Amman.'

'Really?' Helen asked, thrilled. Back to Jordan? It would be so good to see her childhood home again. She thought of all her friends, Fatima, Lallah, little Rahma, wondered how they'd grown up. 'You mean it?'

Baba reached up to the mantelpiece and patted the envelope that sat there. 'Got the tickets and the passport,' he said. 'You know, Helen, one thing that matters in this life is staying close to your roots.'

'I totally agree,' she said. Did that mean he was going to give up the whisky?

But she didn't say that. It was a nice moment – no need to spoil it.

It was all a bit hazy, a bit confusing, and she was very tired. But Helen loved the idea of going back to Jordan, and if it meant being nice and polite to this older, distant cousin for a little while, she would go along with that. Besides, who wouldn't want to see Cairo? She'd had the great LA party with Sally and Jane; a short holiday to reconnect with her family would be a perfect idea right now.

'Will you excuse me?' she asked Ahmed. 'I want to go and see my friend Sally. Thank her for that amazing party. I'll be back this afternoon, for the ceremony.'

'No later than noon – your mother has a special dress for you to wear,' Ali told her.

Helen kissed him on the cheek. 'I promise.'

Chapter Seven

The cab dropped Helen out front. Green Gables was already immaculately clean – she could hardly believe it. An army of servants had descended on the place in the night; after only a few hours, you'd never know there had been a party there at all, apart from a few hoof prints on the grass where they'd had the camel rides. And Helen suspected they would soon be gone, too.

Wow. It was astounding what money could do.

She rang the bell, eager to see Sally. Maybe they could take a ride in Sally's Porsche over to Malibu, see Jane. She had a teenager's eagerness to relive her night of triumph. And just wait till Miss Milton's opened on Monday morning! The gang of three would become a gang of *twenty*-three – at least.

Helen finally felt like she fitted in.

A moment later and the door swung open. Richard, the second butler, greeted her.

'Good morning, Miss Yanna.' All the staff here knew Helen by name. 'Please come in. Miss Lassiter is in her bedroom.'

'Thanks, Richard.' Helen half ran up the stairs, feeling as light as thistledown. She knew the way, third on the left at the top of the sweeping marble stairs. She hammered on the door. 'Sally! You sleeping? It's Helen. Let me in!'

'Just a moment.'

Helen blinked; she could hear that Sally was crying.

Why? Last night had been perfect. Some drama with a boy after she had left?

'What's up?'

Sally opened the door, red-eyed, tear tracks streaked down her face. 'It's Jane. There's been . . . an accident.'

Helen's stomach turned over. 'What kind of an accident? Is she *dead*?'

'Not her. Her father. He fell out of a top-floor window in his house in Washington . . .'

'Oh, my God.'

'The British Secret Service came . . . took her away. Took her to Washington. She called me before she left.'

Sally would never forget the bleakness, the desolation in Jane's voice.

'Does she have family there?' Helen, always practical, tried to process the information. 'Maybe an aunt? A grandmother?'

'Nobody. Her father never got on with them.'

'Then who's going to look after Jane?'

Both girls flopped down on Sally's huge California King bed with its silken Pratesi sheets.

'I guess I am,' Sally said, finally. 'She's my best friend. I told her she can come live here, like in one of the guest cottages. We can afford it . . .'

'Her family will take care of the money, I'm sure. Won't she inherit—'

'No, that's the thing.' Sally Lassiter wasn't book-smart, but she had some of her father's savviness. 'It was all government stuff – dependent on her dad's job. Now that's gone, so's everything else. She has no house . . . nothing.'

'But her maid. Her driver . . .'

'Helen, her dad didn't really fall. It was suicide.' Sally dabbed at her red eyes. 'He got caught . . . drinking on the job, taking drugs. They fired him, dismissed him for cause. He was going to be shipped back home to the UK. And he had a gambling problem, apparently. There was no money there at all.'

'Oh God!' Helen cried out. 'Poor Jane.'

'Everything he *did* own will be forfeit to the bailiffs, it was all bought on credit.'

'But the British have to look after her. She's still a child legally,' Helen pointed out.

'I guess.' Sally mulled that over. 'She didn't sound like she wanted anything to do with them.'

Helen bit her lip. 'We'll have to stay with her at school – all day. What about the nasty girls? They'll be hounding her. Calling the press, maybe.'

Even with the party and Jane's newfound beauty, Julie and the other bullies would see their chance now. No way could Helen let them snigger over her father's death.

'That won't be a problem, Jane told me the Brits are going to cover it up. They're just calling it a suicide.' Sally sighed. 'But she's not coming back to Miss Milton's.' Sally rubbed her eyes; the thought of losing Jane, whom she felt she'd known forever, the closest thing to a sister, was dreadful. 'She says she never wants to see that school again. And you know what, I think she means it.'

'Well, whatever she decides, we'll be here.' Helen knew it sounded lame. 'Maybe I could get a transfer to her new school – wherever the Brits decide to send her.'

'Maybe.' Sally was anxious. She didn't think Jane Morgan would want to go to *any* new school. 'They might try to send her home . . .'

'This is her home,' Helen said stoutly. 'LA.' She looked at Sally. 'My family's taking a short trip too, but I'll be back very soon. Look after Jane for me.'

On the way back to Third Street, Helen thought of nothing but her friend. She was worried – extremely. What if Jane went off the rails? There was a strange streak to that girl.

What if she wanted revenge, on the Embassy? Was that so crazy? Surely she wouldn't think of killing herself. No. That was not Jane's way. But Helen could not blame her for not wanting to deal with the shame. School would be appalling. Who needed it at such a time?

Selfishly, she was also afraid on her own behalf.

As the cab sped under the palm trees, waving gently in a perfect LA sky, baby blue with a couple of fluffy clouds, Helen was ashamed for worrying about herself, too.

Jane had been the glue between herself and Sally. The older friend, but clever, able to bridge the gap between them. She could discuss politics with Jane, or history, or anything. With Sally it was all movie star gossip and the latest trends. And rock bands . . .

Helen loved all those things, of course. But Sally and she were just so *different*. She was frightened now. Maybe with just the two of them it wouldn't work out.

Sally and Jane had history. Not Sally and her.

'Eighteen fifty.'

'Thanks.' Helen gave the cabbie twenty-five, absent-mindedly.

'Thanks, hon. Have a great day,' he said, speeding off down La Cienega with a screech of tyres.

There were ribbons tied to her gate, and balloons. Oh, man. Baba was having a party for Ahmed! Helen was not in the mood, but still. Baba had let her go in the end, and the party had been blissful; she was grateful to her father. And Jane's father was dead – the last thing she needed was more drama right now. No need to make a scene, she'd go along with it.

Exhaustion and worry had seeped through into Helen's bones. Well, she wouldn't make a fuss. She could sleep on the plane to Cairo.

Aisha hurried out of the kitchen door.

'Come with me upstairs. I have your betrothal dress.'

Helen allowed herself to be pushed upstairs. 'What do you mean, betrothal?'

'The ceremony, the friendship ceremony,' her mother said hurriedly. 'Now here, put these robes on! Where have you been? They are all waiting. With the contract . . .'

Helen quickly got changed; her mother had got her a beautiful Jordanian robe, traditional and, she thought, antique. She admired her reflection as Aisha fastened a flowing headscarf of cream silk around her hair.

'Can I keep this? It's beautiful.'

'Of course you can. Now run downstairs, Baba is waiting for you. Jasmine and I will come down in a minute.'

'Mama, you know I'm not actually going to marry Ahmed.'

'Just do this for your father,' Aisha said vaguely. 'Hurry! His father is there waiting for you.'

Helen sighed and walked downstairs. Her father was waiting with an ornate-looking document. Ahmed was there, looking as embarrassed as she was, in traditional Islamic trousers and hat; he didn't meet her eyes as both their fathers embraced.

Baba put Helen's hand into his. Feeling every sympathy for Ahmed, she gave him a surreptitious wink. He looked at her properly for the first time; his eyes widened, and he gave her a very small smile.

The things we do for our parents! Helen thought.

Baba was speaking in Arabic now. She didn't follow what he was saying. He told her he would lead her, she should repeat after him.

Helen willingly agreed. She wanted to please her father; to ease the tension for poor Ahmed; and to forget today's troubles.

Get to the airport, get on the plane. Do some thinking.

When she returned from Egypt, Jane would have worked out what she wanted to do. *Insh' Allah*, she would be back at school, with Helen and Sally protecting her. Like always. They were best friends and they would stick together. An unbreakable trio. A few days' absence would not hurt that.

Her father was placing a golden pen in her hand.

'Sign here,' he said. 'Darling. My little daughter.'

He kissed her on the forehead and Helen pressed her head against his. She adored her parents. Their little ceremony was over now, and they seemed happy with her. Tired, confused, she signed the papers.

'Do you like it? We'll sit here.'

Ahmed smiled at her – his English was as rusty as her Arabic.

'Yes, brilliant.' Helen laughed, she loved flying business class. She wasn't Sally Lassiter – it took a chunk of her parents' money to send her to Miss Milton's. For her this was an adventure, a kick. The air hostesses were hovering, so she hurried to take her seat. They were seriously late.

Helen was tired, but running to make the plane had given her a surge of adrenaline. It had been very chaotic at the airport, with her parents running and shouting and waving boarding passes. Helen was handed hers separately and asked to sit with Ahmed by Baba. She agreed. Why not be pleasant? She'd sleep most of the flight anyway.

They had barely made it on to the plane, Baba stopping to sort out their cases and waving Helen and Ahmed ahead. She hadn't seen her parents and sister in the departure area, they were probably already seated.

'Ladies and gentlemen, we are about to depart. Please ensure your seat belts are securely fastened around your waist, and that your seat-backs and tray tables are in the upright position. Cabin crew to cross-check, please, cabin crew to cross-check.'

Helen spun round in her seat. She couldn't see her parents. Where were the others? And Ahmed's father, her mother's cousin? This was a family trip – were the rest of them sitting in coach?

She shifted uneasily on her seat. Politeness to Ahmed was one thing, but she did not want her mother in economy while she flew up here.

'Ahmed,' Helen said urgently, summoning her Arabic as best she could.

The plane groaned, shuddered and started to accelerate as the pilot eased it on to the runway.

'Where are Mama and Baba? Where is your father? Are they all sitting by themselves back there?'

'I do not understand,' he said heavily, dark eyes fixed on her. 'What are you asking me?'

Helen tried again. 'Where are our parents?'

He blinked. 'In America. The airport, they said goodbye. Why are you asking me this?'

The plane heaved again and then pushed up into the sky, the retraction of the wheels shaking the undercarriage.

She felt sick. 'Ahmed . . . *I* don't understand. Are my parents on this plane? Where is your father? Isn't this a family trip to Cairo?'

'Of course,' he said, and for a second her stomach unknotted. 'It is a family trip – a honeymoon trip. Yours and mine.'

Helen repeated dully, 'Honeymoon?'

Ahmed showed the first signs of impatience. 'We are married, are we not? You and I. Married. *Mash 'Allah*,' he added but, Helen felt, with a sense of duty. Thanks be to God.

'Married?' she repeated, almost hysterical. 'Who told you that? Who said we were married?'

Ahmed stared at her anxiously. Helen could almost see him wondering about her mental health. Reflexively, she gripped the armrests of the seat in front of her.

'Helen,' he said slowly and, she noticed, gently, as one

addressing a frightened child. 'What of yesterday? You and I signed the *nikkah*, did we not? We are married now, in the sight of the Most Compassionate.' He offered her a tentative smile. 'We have done our duty, you and I, to our parents – as is pleasing to Him – and we will make the best of it. You also believe that, do you not?'

Stunned, she was silent.

'I promise you, I am a gentle man.' He reached across her seat and took her hand, and stroked it. 'I did not want this either. But if we surrender our selfish desires, we will find true peace, *insh'Allah*. You also believe this, I think?'

The puzzle pieces fell into place with slow, terrible clarity for Helen.

That 'friendship ceremony' had been no such thing. It was her *nikkah*. The binding engagement ceremony between Muslims – in the eyes of God, she was already married.

Helen's head spun. Yes, Mama had said it – engagement ceremony. Helen just had not pushed it. Was she being wilfully deaf? When Baba read from the sacred Qu'ran, God forgive her, she had not been paying attention. But she had happily gone through with it. Ahmed had no idea she was not consenting to be his wife.

'Our parents thought it would be best,' he said, artlessly. 'In truth, I had already lost my one true love. I could have lived forever by myself. But they decided otherwise. And you and I can be friends, I think? Is it not so?'

Helen understood, in a second. She had underestimated her father, her mother too. And even now, she did not blame them. There was no anger there. Her father and mother had schemed a little, and arranged a marriage for her after the old ways. And she, a believing Muslim, had to admit she had gone through the *nikkah* of her own free will, after being advised what it was . . .

An imam would likely tell her it was invalid. But Helen

looked at Ahmed, older than her, his own face drawn from duty to his parents and indeed to God. He was, she knew instinctively, a good man. None of this was his doing. And Helen was mature enough to believe that what her parents had done had been from sheer love of her. She knew their own had been an arranged marriage, and she knew, too, they had been extremely happy.

Ahmed had his hand in hers.

Helen had no wish to disgrace or humiliate him. After all, her American passport was in her pocket. Whatever her parents' well-intentioned schemes, she was a free woman.

But she would not hurt this man. Or her parents. There could be a divorce – after a decent interval, of course.

'Yes. We can be very good friends,' she agreed, with a generous smile.

'That is well.' He beamed at her.

'And friends should be honest,' Helen ploughed on. 'So tell me, why didn't you want to go through with the *nikkah*?'

Ahmed blew out his cheeks and sighed.

'I don't want to offend you.'

'You won't.'

'Her name was Firyal,' he said, eventually. 'I thought . . . well. I thought we were destined for each other. She was not from a good family, but I saw her, in the mosque, each day. I found her outside, one time, and started to talk to her. She was an exceptional woman. She had a job working for the Department of Antiquities. Firyal was beautiful, modest, and brilliant,' he said with fervour.

Helen was strangely moved. There had been nobody in *her* life – nobody she had loved like that.

'But your parents disapproved?'

'I would not have cared for that,' Ahmed said firmly. 'I loved her.' He looked across at Helen. 'She died,' he added, simply. 'A car accident. Cairo traffic. So mundane.'

'And you did not want to marry again?'

'I was never betrothed to her.' He fell silent, and stared out of the tiny window at the cloudless sky below them.

And you're not really betrothed to me. Helen picked up her headphones and plugged them into the seat. She would stay in Ahmed's house for a week or so, then, once the divorce was concluded, come home. Her father meant well, but this was not for her. She would arrange her own marriage – to a man who actually *wanted* to be her husband.

'Sally. It's Jane.'

Sally gripped the receiver. 'How are you? Where are you?'

'At LAX,' Jane said. Her voice sounded tense and miserable, and Sally's heart sank to hear it. 'Can you come and pick me up?'

'On my way. Hang tight.'

Sally bounded down the stairs. Jonathan, their butler, was polishing a statue in the hallway.

'Any of the cars ready?'

'The Aston Martin is around, Miss Lassiter. It's Richard's day off, but Mike could drive you—'

'That's just fine, thank you. I'll do it myself.'

She snatched the keys from the rail, checked she had the right set – Daddy had so many cars – and made to rush out the door. Paulie waddled out of his study and almost crashed into her.

'Hey, hey, princess. Where's my princess going?'

'I got to pick Jane up at the airport.'

'She came back from Washington, good. Poor little girl.'

Sally stopped for a second; her dad was all red-faced.

'You should go easy on that bacon at breakfast, Dad,' she said.

'You're as bad as your mom. I drink OJ, I'll live for a

thousand years.' Paulie patted his rotund stomach. 'You'll never get rid of me.'

Sally flung her arms round him and gave him a hug; poor, poor Jane.

'I might not be back till late. I'm gonna drive to pick up Jane, we might spend some time together.'

'That's fine.' Her dad looked distracted, a little anxious. 'Something came up at the office. I'll be late too.'

'Mom'll be stuck with *Jeopardy* and a TV dinner,' Sally joked. She knew she ought to have asked Daddy what the matter was, but she was more worried about Jane right now. Didn't want to keep her waiting. 'See you later, Pop.' She kissed him lightly on the cheek and ran out the door.

'See you later,' Paulie said to her departing back.

But he would never see her again.

Chapter Eight

Jane was standing with her suitcases, right on the kerb, and Sally felt a thrill of anxiety when she saw her. Her friend was still beautiful; her good looks hadn't disappeared, she hadn't turned back into a pumpkin, but all that new self-confidence was gone. Evaporated. She cut a bedraggled, forlorn little figure on the sidewalk, shoulders slumped, the picture of misery.

Sally screeched to a halt and jumped out, hauling her case into the back seat.

'You ride up front.' She crushed Jane in a big bear hug. 'Tell me everything.'

'Nothing to tell.' Jane laid her head back against the headrest as Sally pulled smoothly out into traffic. 'A diplomatic funeral, but under the circumstances very quiet. Just me, his secretary and the pastor. Then the lawyers; they read the will and told me what my options were.'

'So . . . it wasn't good?'

Jane shook her head. ' 'Fraid not.'

Sally glanced across at her. 'He left you nothing, hon?'

'Some personal effects. I can't bear to keep them, so I asked they be donated to charity.' Jane's voice had a clear, cold determination to it that tore at Sally's heart; she had seen her friend throw up walls like this before, a crab scuttling back under her shell. 'He had debts up to the eyeballs, but the Embassy got a lawyer and they won't attach to me, as I'm a minor.'

'Which means they have to look after you . . . You should

really consider coming back to school. Helen and me will look after you.'

'They refuse to pay for Miss Milton's.'

There it was. Sally's worst nightmare. Split from Jane forever. Their threesome broken up.

'That's bull,' she exclaimed. 'If they won't pay for you, we will. Daddy will, I promise you that.'

Jane reached over and squeezed her hand.

'Sally, I love you for that.' Tears started to prickle in both their eyes. 'But I can't go back there, don't you see? It's less than a year till I'm eighteen now. Then what? College? There's no money coming in. Without Daddy's salary, how am I going to pay for the Ivy League? I can't go to Oxford or Cambridge either – I'd need money to support myself. And once I hit eighteen, they wash their hands of me.'

'Oh, Jane.'

'They offered me a small place in Washington in a not great area, and the last year at a local private school. I said no way. Murder capital of America.'

'So what are you going to do?'

'Stay right where I am. Consuela will be with me till her wages run out. And then I guess I'll go get a job. And an apartment.'

'But you're not a legal adult. And without a degree what kind of job can you get?'

'I'll work something out.'

Jane sounded definite about that. But Sally could hear the tears lurking just under the bravado.

'Y'all can come and live with us,' Sally suggested. 'The maid and you. We'll pay her wages . . . you can have a guest bungalow. It's what they're there for. Daddy won't mind.'

'Thanks, honey.' Jane smiled at her, gratefully. 'But I want to see if I can figure something out for myself. I want to rely on myself. Does that make sense?'

'You always were ornery,' Sally said, but she did

understand. Jane had always had that fierce pride, as long as she'd known her. Her father's final abandonment meant she would need to try to stand up for herself. 'We'll go see Helen, go get a long lunch somewhere. I think her phone's down, she hasn't been answering.'

'Sounds good,' Jane said.

They pulled up outside the Yannas' compact little house. Sally looked at it with interest, never having been there before. Jane smiled, reassured; Helen Yanna's parents must be reaching to send her to Miss Milton's – one more thing she had in common with Helen. Who knew? Maybe Helen's dad could do with a bookkeeper.

'You stay here,' Jane suggested tactfully. 'I'll ring the bell.'

Sally was wearing one of her typical short skirts, just off the knee, with a sexy pleated kick to it, and an outrageous tight white T-shirt that played up her glorious breasts and golden skin. Somehow Jane assumed that her own plain black trouser suit would be more reassuring to their friend's parents.

She climbed out and pressed the buzzer; there was the sound of footsteps, and a young girl wrenched the door open. She was pretty and slight, not more than ten, Jane guessed.

'Are you Jasmine?'

The little girl nodded, eyes wide.

Jane offered a hand. 'I'm Jane Morgan, Helen's friend from school. Is she in?'

'Helen's never coming back,' Jasmine said, and her eyes brimmed with tears.

'Excuse me?' Jane asked, bewildered, but an adult figure filled the door, a stocky, bearded man, and he was gazing at her very coolly.

'Mr Yanna, I was just telling Jasmine that I'm Jane, Helen's schoolfriend. Is she about?'

'No.'

Jane tried again. Maybe his English wasn't too hot.

'It's just that we wanted to—'

'My daughter is not here any more. She has got married.'

He obviously wasn't joking.

'I – I don't quite understand. We went to a party last week together, and—'

'She got married to her second cousin Ahmed and they have gone back to Cairo to set up house,' Helen's father replied flatly. 'She may not be back here for many years.'

'But she didn't say anything to us.'

'A wedding is a private family matter,' Ali Yanna said. 'If she wishes to call you, she can.'

Jane digested this.

'If she speaks to you, will you tell her Sally and I would like to talk to her?' Jane asked.

He shrugged. 'Goodbye then.'

The door closed.

Sally wound down the car window and poked her head out. 'What happened?'

Jane got back in the car, her face troubled, and motioned for Sally to drive off.

'He said she left the country. Got married to some distant relation and left for Cairo.'

'You're messin' with me.'

'Apparently not. I don't think her father approves of us, Sal. He didn't seem to want to talk.'

Sally's face was a picture of dismay. 'That can't be true. She never said a damned thing to us.'

'Mr Yanna told me it was a private family matter.' Jane chewed on her lip. 'I know Helen . . . still waters run deep, but I don't think she would do that.'

'She's been hanging out with us long enough to get her some street smarts,' Sally said. 'She knows our numbers. Guess we'll just have to wait for her to call.'

'I guess so.'

'Oh, man,' Sally breathed. 'It just hit me. I'll be all alone at school now. No you and no Helen. I don't want to go back.'

They both contemplated Julie Manners and Melissa Smith.

'Don't,' Jane said, boldly. 'Sal, just don't. Get your dad to pay for a private tutor, or go to a different school. You don't have to take that. I wouldn't.'

'Maybe you're right,' Sally said, wearily. 'I should think about it. But that's about all the change I can handle for one day.' She grinned at Jane. 'We still got each other. Let's go get some coffee.'

'So.' Paulie Lassiter shook his head. He was getting worked up. He was in the Century City offices of his extremely high-priced corporate lawyers, surrounded by suits, and not one of them was coming up with any damn solutions!

'What do we do? We gotta fix this.' His stare said, *you* gotta fix this.

'I don't know, Paulie. These accounts . . . they're fiction.'

'Fiction!' He snorted. 'Three accounting firms signed 'em.'

'Yeah, but your CFO was cooking the books.'

'I told you, I fired the sonofabitch.'

'That won't do it.' Lionel Javits, head of the lawyers, pushed horn-rimmed spectacles up his nose. 'You have to notify the Feds, the Dow, the regulatory authorities. The stock is going to go through the floor. Jack Lessing is going to jail.'

'Damn right he is,' Paulie snapped. The lawyers exchanged looks. 'My concern now is to save the stock. Nobody's selling, not while this is going on.'

Ugh. He hated delegating. A month away to look at a new field, some possible strikes in northern Canada, and what happens? His asshole executives cook the books. Paulie Lassiter was an *oilman*, not a damned accountant. Billion-dollar company and he was having to do every little thing himself. He mopped his brow, struggling with his breath. Anger was not his usual emotion.

'Paulie, they already did. Most of your board, even the non-execs. They've been quietly dumping stock for the last eighteen months. It's your workers who are going to be ruined.' Javits paused; it was clear to him that Lassiter had no grasp of what was happening. 'And if you haven't been selling, then it doesn't look good for you either.'

'But at least it proves you're honest,' a junior suit piped up brightly. '*You* won't be going to jail!'

Javits glared at him.

Paulie glanced outside at the bright, blue sky. It seemed such a normal day in LA. How could everything look normal when his world was coming apart!

'That *can't* be right,' he said patiently. 'We're not some paper company. We got *assets*. Oilfields. Six in Texas, one in Ghada, maybe a new one in Canada . . .'

'Doesn't cover the expansion into natural gas, the pipeline in Kazakhstan that was smashed by terrorists. Your corporate policy was breached.'

'Not enough security.'

'And four of the Texas fields dried up.'

'Lassiter Corp's been trading pretty much on its reputation. And some fancy footwork.'

'Your executives have been living pretty high on the hog, Paulie.'

Well, he knew *that*.

'But the money was there,' he said, weakly. His heart started thumping. A picture of his wife, doing the breakfast cooking herself, chattering about Sally's party, floated into his vision. How the hell would he explain this to her? He'd never disappointed Mona.

'No, it wasn't, Paulie,' Lionel Javits said gently. His client was such a big, lumbering bear of a man. A *good* man, and there weren't too many of those left in Los Angeles. Paulie was an oilman, not into business. And, unfortunately, far too trusting.

'It's corruption.' The junior suit was piping up again. Eager to explain. 'Oil company . . . theft . . . That's what the lawyers call it.'

'Corruption?' Paulie ignored Javits' death stare at his employee. That was something he *did* understand. 'You mean my workers . . . the pension fund . . .'

'It's bankrupt, Paulie. In fact it's looking to me like the entire company is going belly up. We'll need to show you are an innocent party. I don't want you speaking to anyone. I'll contact the authorities myself. You say, on the advice of counsel I assert my Fifth Amendment rights not to incriminate myself . . .'

Paulie Lassiter felt needles in his left arm, then a huge stabbing pain in his chest. He couldn't breathe.

'Ugggh,' he groaned, and struggled to his feet. A glass-topped coffee table crashed to the ground.

'Paulie!' Lionel Javits shrieked. 'My God! He's having a heart attack!'

'Call 911!'

'Aspirin – it's in the cupboard – *get* it,' the lawyer screamed.

But it was too late. Paulie, clutching ineffectually at his chest, gasped and tumbled forward, the blocked blood rushing to his face. Two lawyers dived on him and attempted to roll him over, start CPR.

'Leave it,' Javits said. He found he had tears in his eyes. This was a massive coronary – you didn't need to be a doc to see it.

Paulie Lassiter was very dead.

And Lionel Javits knew what was coming – for Lassiter Corp, and for Paulie's family. Ruin – lawsuits – total humiliation – ostracism.

He liked Paulie. Paulie was dead now. And Javits thought he was better off that way.

Chapter Nine

'Who is it?'

Jane had the door on the chain.

'Repo!'

The man's voice was gruff. She put her head to the fisheye lens in the door. Yeah – they were repossession guys, uniforms, van, everything.

Jane swallowed hard and opened the door.

'Hi there!' She gave them a bright smile. 'Come on in. You guys want coffee?'

The guy entered with three other men.

'No thanks.' He couldn't meet her eye. 'Which way is the living room?'

'Right in there. I unplugged everything. It was mostly too big to move by myself, though, I'm sorry.'

'That's fine.' Now he looked at her. 'You work here? You the maid?'

Well, you could hardly call it living here. 'Sort of,' Jane agreed.

'Let's start with the TV.'

The men moved into her living room and got to work. They moved fast – probably used to doing it whilst under attack. Her favourite big screen TV, the stereo system, the furniture, the statues and antiques – just like house movers, they took everything. Efficient as ants at a picnic.

Jane withdrew into the kitchen and put the kettle on;

they had already removed the cappuccino machine.

'Sure you won't take that coffee?'

'No thanks. We got to get to West Hollywood.' The leader sighed and wiped away some sweat. 'At least they didn't have the family here, that's the worst. Crying and begging, you know? Like, have a little dignity. Not *my* fault you fucked your life up.'

'Right,' Jane agreed. 'That's so pathetic.'

'The bed . . .' He looked back into her room. 'That's not on my sheet – the inflatable bed.'

'Yeah, I think that belongs to the daughter. She picked it up after the dad bought the farm.' Jane smiled. 'Maybe she knew you guys were coming!'

'Cool. We can leave that, I guess. And you can keep that kettle!' He grinned generously at her. 'They won't notice a sixteen-buck kettle in my office.'

'Thanks. You guys have a great day.'

Jane saw them to the door. She shut it, leaned her head against the wood, and listened as the truck doors slammed and it drove away.

Finally, she was sure she was alone. She glanced around her empty house – not hers, any more; the Embassy had made it clear that the lease was up, end of the month. It was bare, stripped of everything down to the last framed print. There was nothing but the cheap single bed and the white goods in the kitchen.

Oh, and her coffee mug.

She went over to the bed and flopped down on it. And finally, she allowed the tears to come.

When she was done, she went and took a shower – at least the hot water was still on, and she had a towel and clothes in a suitcase. Sure, the Embassy wanted to 'look after' her – on *their* terms.

Jane was not into that. Stuck in some hideous

Washington two-bit school, where everybody would know who she was? Laugh at her? Humiliate her?

Hell no. School was a brutal exercise in social Darwinism. Jane Morgan had no room in her heart for further bruising. And what would she get out of it, with her grades disrupted and her exams disturbed?

She finished with the shower, carefully brushed her teeth, and got dressed. Then she let herself out the back door with the key Consuela had left for her when she was fired.

'You'll be OK,' her former nanny told her. 'I never saw anybody like you.'

Jane had bit her lip, to stop it trembling; a rare moment of weakness. They'd never been close, but at least Consuela was familiar. And now she was leaving too.

'You'll be fine.' Aggravated, the older woman pretended not to see the teenage girl's eyes reddening. 'I gots to go,' she added, and hustled off down the driveway to the street where her Ford Fiesta was parked. What the hell – did she have to care? She had troubles of her own. Like no job! That English chick was a piece of work, she'd land on her feet . . .

Jane glanced at the driveway; empty now, like the house. She was ashamed of herself. But after all, she was only seventeen, and everything in her world had fallen apart.

Her father – useless; unloving; selfish. But *hers*. Deep down, she had hoped that one day they could forge a relationship. When he was retired, and she was grown-up.

That chance had gone. Forever.

And her lifestyle. At least that had been great – independent, stylish, and rich. Her driver; her maid; her nanny; the beach house, the security guards . . .

Miss Milton's, for heaven's sake. Who'd have ever thought she'd appreciate her lousy, unacademic school?

The money – she felt she could have managed without that. In other circumstances. Because at least there had been the girls.

Her best friends – no, her *family*.

But, like her father, like Consuela, like the money, her friends had gone. Just like that. One week, and they'd evaporated.

Helen. Vanished from school, the day after the party. And now, gone back to Egypt to get married. To a distant cousin.

To get *married*! She'd never spoken of the guy to them. Not a word. Nor of the fact she was thinking of leaving the country. The three girls were inseparable, how could Helen not tell them? She hadn't left an address, a phone number – nothing. Just vanished.

Helen Yanna had left Jane's life the same way she'd arrived – quietly; definitely.

And Sally, her older friend? Far different, and far worse. Jane ached to see Helen, to cry on her shoulder, but at least she knew Helen was happy – was doing OK, getting married. For Sally, life had exploded, in almost the same way it had done for her.

Paulie Lassiter's heart attack had been Monday morning's big news. But the afternoon's big news was the collapse of the company. Jane had watched, horrified, on her TV, as the squad cars proceeded to Green Gables; as a black-clad, half-fainting Mona was taken into police custody, accompanied by her lawyer; as Sally, a blanket thrown over her head to protect her from the paparazzi, joined her.

She'd called – of course. But the phone had been disconnected. Sally eventually called Jane, too distraught to speak much; her bubbly vivacity, her lightness, her optimism – everything Jane loved about her – was extinguished, just gone.

Jane almost envied her her agony. Sally was mourning a beloved, kind, attentive father; her grief, welling up from the depths of her soul, reflected real love. Real family. And at least Sally still had a mother.

But there was no doubt her best friend was facing trouble. Very serious trouble.

'The Feds are taking everything,' Sally confessed to her, once she'd stopped sobbing.

'What do you mean, everything?'

'We're bankrupt. They froze Dad's accounts . . . it all belongs to the creditors.'

'But what are they leaving you to live on?'

'The auditors gave us a payment of twelve thousand dollars for the year.'

Jane gasped. 'A thousand a month?'

Damn, that wouldn't even cover rent on a one-bed in their old neighbourhood.

'And they took the cars, the artwork – everything. Mom's still under investigation, but they think she'll likely get off with innocent spouse defence.'

'You sound angry.'

'Innocent spouse? Makes my dad seem guilty. And he wasn't no crook.' Sally sobbed. 'Do you know what Julie Manners said to me today?'

A tear rolled down Jane's own cheek, and she fiercely brushed it away. 'Don't . . . just don't. You can't go back there . . .'

'Without you and Helen, no way.'

And without the cash that had always protected her.

'I decided to move to Washington after all,' Jane said. It wasn't true, but she didn't want Sally to worry about her. And she had to figure out her future. Sally wouldn't be able to help; Jane had to deal with this, on her own.

'Yeah.' Sally sounded so dull, so depressed. 'We're going away, too. Mom's friends – her so-called friends – they've all vanished. Ever notice that in this town they treat failure like a disease? One that might be catching?'

A grim smile. 'Yes, I did.'

'I told her she needs to get out of Dodge. We have family in Texas she can go to.'

'You'll like Texas, right? That's home.'

'Was once.' Sally sighed. 'I think it's better, away from the press. They live in a small town.'

There was a long, wretched pause.

'Take care of yourself, hon.'

'And you, Sally.' Jane was unused to the emotion that washed through her now. First Helen, then Sally. Their friendship was breaking up. 'Be kind to yourself,' she said. Her voice cracked a little, and she hurriedly replaced the receiver.

Now Jane sat in her still-neat garden, on the iron bench they hadn't bothered to remove, and looked at the sea. The ocean was clear, blue, and immense. It crashed, and crashed, eternally, on the beach below her; mindless, soothing noise.

She had come out here to think.

The disasters, one on top of the other. No friends, now. No money. No contacts. At the end of this month, no house.

She was entirely on her own.

A sleazeball lawyer was the right start. Emancipation – Jane had read about that in the library. A teen petitioning to be designated a legal adult, usually due to marriage. She'd stay well away from that. If you got too close to anybody, you exposed yourself. They left – and your heart shattered.

Once she had the important pieces of paper, she'd be two things. An adult; and an American. She could go anywhere she liked in the country, do whatever she wanted.

Her first change – no more bookworm.

Jane had learned a hard lesson, and learned it fast. Money counted in this world. When she'd had privileged access to it, she had despised money. She'd only sought prestige, position as a tenured professor somewhere.

Now, she wanted revenge. And that meant cash. The kind that Paulie Lassiter used to have – but legitimate, all hers. The kind that protected schoolgirls from taunts, that enabled people to fulfil their every whim. The kind that could help get her own back on Julie, and all those snobby bitches at school. That could help Sally deal with the rich friends who'd seen fit to dump a devastated and grieving widow.

Money was protection. Money was control.

Money was something *women* didn't have.

Yes . . .

Jane watched the ocean and let that thought sink in. Plenty of rich girls in her orbit . . . except they weren't, were they? It was always somebody else's money. Those removal men had swarmed like locusts on her house, stripping it bare, because it wasn't her stuff, just on loan from the Embassy. And Sally had nothing of her own, it was all in Daddy's accounts. When they were cut off, so was she.

Helen Yanna, daughter of a wealthy, middle-class man, now married, apparently, to another wealthy, middle-class man. Passing from one comfortable lifestyle to the next, but not under her own steam. Jane worried about her. What happened if she fell out with her husband? What happened if her father cut her off? Helen, at school, had been bright, quiet, God-fearing, and shy. Yes, there was a core of determination – but still. She was exactly the type of personality to depend on men.

And the world didn't prepare people like Helen – or Sally – for the moment the Jericho walls crashed into rubble.

What would Sally do now? Regroup, heal – then marry somebody? She still had those blond Barbie looks, and right now it seemed she'd be reduced to trading on them.

Jane didn't want that for herself. No way. She didn't want to depend on some university board, either. She was here, by the ocean, in LA. And she still had assets. Brains – thank God, for everything stemmed from that. Beauty – not like Sally's, but she would never go back to her dowdy self.

Sally had once told her glamour was a weapon. It got you

through the front door. After that, your brains had to take over.

It was time to grow up.

Jane saw things much more clearly now. She went inside, picked up the phone book now lying on the dusty floor of the living room, and called the DMV.

'Hi. I'd like to make an appointment for a driving test.'

'Then there's the matter of my fee.'

The lawyer looked at Jane down his nose, expectantly.

She sighed. The office was filthy; there was a fat bluebottle buzzing lazily and hopelessly against the glass; the windows were dusty, and he had papers all across his desk.

'Two hundred,' she said, hopefully.

'Two hundred!' He snorted. '*Fifteen* hundred, *and* that's a discount because you're a minor.' He leaned across his desk and leered at Jane. 'In *one* sense. In another, of course, you're legal . . .'

She knew exactly what he meant.

'Maybe we could work something out.' His gaze travelled slowly up her legs.

'Look, Mr Richards.' Jane stood up, wanting to get away from the stare, but he just transferred it to her breasts, so she took a walk to the window. 'Can I speak frankly to you?'

'You can be as frank as you want to, honey.' Josh Richards regularly screwed desperate women who couldn't pay him any other way. Mexicans mostly. And seeing as how he had bad breath, wonky teeth and a widow's peak at only thirty-one, it was the only way he got any play.

None of those *mamacitas* were as hot as this Limey, though. Damn! She was fine, with her delicately styled hair and peaches and cream skin. He dug the accent, too, all cold and haughty. She'd look great bent over his desk with that—

'You're a loser,' Jane said.

That brought him up short. He blinked, not sure he'd heard her right.

'Excuse me?' He was outraged.

'You're a loser,' Jane repeated flatly. 'Going nowhere fast. It's why I picked you to handle my case. I can't afford a decent lawyer, and you desperately need some work.'

'Two hundred ain't work.'

'I mean real work. Cases. You need your name in the papers. Nobody's going to hire you for so much as a quickie divorce if you slob around like this.' Disdainfully, she lifted one of last week's papers, the sports section, lying on the edge of his desk. 'You got to get yourself a secretary – not somebody who's going to sue you for sexual harassment, either. A neat office, a decent suit, and some real clients.'

Richards wanted to tell the schoolgirl to take a hike. What a ball-buster! That twitch between his legs had vanished like she was pouring cold water on it.

But it was true, he did need work. He was already behind on the rent here.

Graduate from a mediocre school with a mediocre record, and it was tough to make it. The big boys didn't want to know, and clients – forget it.

'All that takes cash. And I got clients like you who don't want to pay it.'

'I bring more than cash. I bring you a *chance*. Represent me, and you'll get publicity. You'll have a major client. I can guarantee you press coverage. In fact, forget the two hundred. You'll do it pro bono – much better PR that way. And once it's taken care of, I'll give you a fabulous quote.'

'A quote?'

'Yes. Let me see.' Jane composed herself and looked at him; her eyes were suddenly brimming.

'After my father died the Brits abandoned me,' she said, her voice breaking. 'Nobody cared, nobody would help me. Except Josh Richards . . . I know what they say about lawyers but he's one who *really cares*. You can trust Josh Richards. I owe this all to him.'

She brushed away the tears and snapped back into business mode.

'Wow,' he said, impressed. 'You should be an actress.'

After Sally's makeover, Jane heard that ten times a day.

'No thanks. Five thousand chicks chasing twelve low-paying jobs.' She had no intention of getting into that; a totally ephemeral business, where success often depended on pure chance. 'How about it?' She snapped her fingers. 'Focus, Josh, focus!'

He blinked. He had the uncomfortable feeling he was being railroaded. By a *schoolgirl*.

On the other hand, she did sound like she knew exactly what she was doing.

'I take you on – for free. And you organize some publicity?'

'Hey, you read the papers. Even if you start at the back.'

He defended himself against Jane's contempt. 'I like baseball—'

'My father was a high-ranking British diplomat who gambled away his money and took lots of drugs. They had the goods on him. He was going to be fired.'

As she recounted this tale, Jane Morgan seemed almost totally devoid of emotion. Josh flinched – the chick was a robot.

'Anyway, he cheated them – flung himself out of a top-floor window. In full evening dress.'

'So where's your mom?'

'Dead.' Jane shrugged. 'I never knew her. And before you ask, there are no aunts or other sundry relatives. I'm orphaned and on my own.'

'I'm sorry,' he said, awkwardly.

'It's been that way for a while. Point is, I don't inherit a dime. And I need to get to work. The *minor* thing is getting in the way. The Embassy doesn't want any more bad publicity, they're trying to force me into a lousy Washington school and a cramped little apartment.'

'What's wrong with that? At least it's a place to stay, right?'

Jane didn't bother to answer. Maybe he was the sort of person that accepted *at least*. She wasn't.

'I want to be a legal adult. And I want US citizenship. I've been here almost all my childhood. I'm naturalized. You take care of the emancipation and get me a pass from the INS. I'll get you great PR for your pro-bono work for the Ambassador's orphaned daughter. Deal?'

She strode back to the desk and offered him her manicured hand.

'Deal.' He couldn't suppress his curiosity. 'Where are you staying right now? Do you need someplace? I have a couch.'

Sure, and watch his towel 'accidentally' slip as he emerged from the shower?

'I'm getting somewhere to rent. I'm fine.'

'Whatever you say.'

'I'm serious about this,' Jane told him as she turned to leave. 'I want emancipation. Legal adult status. I need that to work. No time-wasting – you file those papers this morning. Or else I'll walk down the street and find myself another hungry lawyer.'

'Don't do that,' Richards said hastily. 'I'm on it, I'll file this afternoon.'

'Good.' She walked out, closing the door behind her.

Damn! He pushed a hand through his thinning hair. Why was he worried about getting fired from a job he was doing for free?

But Richards knew that was a stupid question. The girl was right – one hundred per cent. It could be a publicity bonanza for him. A lifeline.

When she'd come in through the door, he'd seen only two things: a fee or a screw.

But Jane Morgan had her eyes on the bigger picture. And he suddenly knew that this was his one shot. Working for a seventeen-year-old schoolgirl who wanted to grow up fast.

He didn't want to blow it. He turned his computer on, and got to work.

Chapter Ten

'So what do you think?'

Think? Jane thought the place was a dump.

Studio apartment, above a dive of a record store on Sunset Strip. Winos and crackheads outside the door. Tiny, filthy bathroom, with cracked shower tiles, mildew and a stain in the loo.

'It has a separate kitchen.' The fat landlady puffed her cheeks out. 'Y' can see if ya like.'

Kitchen! What a joke. A tiny alcove, one cupboard and an electric socket.

'Fridge is broke,' the landlady said succinctly. 'Y' can buy a microwave to cook with. They go for cheap outside the Farmers' Market, got a wetback store selling second-hand electrics.'

Jane watched as a fat black cockroach scuttled up the kitchen wall. She shuddered.

'Five hundred a month and the same as deposit, minimum one-year lease.'

'Forget it. Two hundred and no deposit.'

'You forget it.' She was outraged. 'Get out, you're wasting my time.'

Jane stood firm. 'Think about it, lady. You won't get anyone in here but section 8. And they'll just trash the property. Now what *I* am is an English lady down on her luck. You rent to me, and I'll clean up this shithole. No more roaches – it'll smell good and it'll look good. I'll make it

Bohemian and funky, and when I'm gone you can rent to a student at a thousand. Or, you could sell it – having a human being live here will add fifty grand to the price at least. I don't do drugs and I'm not a hooker. Plus, I pay cash – no contracts – meaning no taxes for *you*. And you get to kick me out whenever you feel like it.'

'I dunno.' The fat woman hummed and hawed. 'Two hundred ain't enough.'

'It's all I got, so it'll have to do.' Jane reached into her purse and pulled out two hundred-dollar bills. She waved the portraits of Benjamin Franklin temptingly in front of the owner. 'By rights, you ought to be paying *me*. What I'm going to do for this place is like a month of Molly Maid *and* a free contractor. Come on, you haven't been able to move this apartment, it's been on the market eighteen months – even the welfare types don't want it. Two hundred, I'll only be here three months, and there'll be something rentable when I've gone.'

'What's gonna happen after three months?'

Jane tossed her head. 'By then, I'll have a real job.'

'*Suuure* you will.' But she snatched up the money. 'Three months, girlie, then the price goes up to five hundred. Call me if you want to do porno, I got a cousin who's always looking.'

'Thanks,' Jane said wrily. 'I'll bear that in mind.'

'You get free electric – no heat. Here's the keys.' She fished out a couple of grimy copper Yales and threw them at Jane, who caught them single-handedly.

'Enjoy,' the woman said, bustling out.

Jane exhaled. She stood by the window, watching until the landlady drove away. Then she turned round and went through her handbag.

Let's see, a grand total of . . . three hundred and twenty-two dollars.

All she had in the world.

Carefully Jane hid the money under a squeaking floorboard, after she had extracted thirty bucks. There was a Shop Smart within walking distance – great, since she didn't have a car. They sold the cheapest of everything. And Jane needed to invest in some sponges, some serious disinfectant, and the cheapest new bedding she could find.

She stripped the bed, emptied the stinking fridge and the garbage pail, nearly gagging, and hauled the black bin liner downstairs. Then she came back up, threw the window open and locked the door.

For a second, despair overcame her, but only for a second. No, this wasn't bottoming out. This was independence, she told herself. The start of a brand-new life. And she, Jane, was going to make a go of it.

That night, she worked her tail off. Mopping, scrubbing, even painting her window sill. Jane pulled the dusty net curtains from their slide and washed them in the sink, with a capful of Dettol. While the drunks and hookers fought and screamed below her, and her floor shook with the dull thud-thud of the booming base from rap tracks on the stereo, Jane cleaned. She wore out three scrubbers and got her hands raw from rubbing alcohol. The stinking refrigerator she emptied of bugs and droppings, closed tight and then switched off. There'd be no way to get rid of roaches other than keeping zero food in the house.

When the place was done, she unpacked her other purchases. Amazing what you could get for a dollar or two in the bargain bins. A mattress protector for the single bed – who the hell knew who'd last slept on it. A shade for the bare lightbulb that hung from her ceiling; it transformed the bleak glare into a pretty, peach-coloured light. Fresh sheets on the bed – not exactly matching, but all basically white or cream; a pillow and a comforter. Gave it a tone-on-tone look that was perfectly acceptable. A snap-up wardrobe made of fabric and plastic, with a zipper, and hangers for her clothes. A cheap Mexican rug, for a splash of colour. A shower curtain, discontinued, clear plastic and decorated with little white suns and moons.

Finally, Jane had blown a whole $2.50 on a cheerful yellow plastic vase and a bunch of carnations.

She hung up her curtains, closed the window, and put water into the vase. The flowers sat on top of a white cloth on her chest of drawers. No TV, but she didn't want to see the news anyway. She had about as much reality as she could handle.

Carefully she undressed, folded away her clothes, and showered again, this time using a tiny amount of cheap coconut bubble bath. It felt so good to be clean.

On her kitchen table lay an application form. Shop Smart, always looking for helpers – 'greeters', they called them. Paid minimum wage. That was fine by Jane. All she was asking for was someplace to start. She had a driving licence – tomorrow she would be legal. Jane knew quite a bit about Shop Smart, a large company with lots of potential. She had no qualms about getting in on the ground floor.

Jane didn't plan to stay there long.

'Jane! Jane!'

'Babe! Over here!'

She emerged from the courthouse to find a small knot of reporters, and two local TV cameras. Dressed in her best suit and carefully made up – cosmetics, clothes, and shoes were about all the bailiffs had left her – Jane walked out on to the courthouse steps, her head high, one arm threaded through her lawyer's.

Josh Richards was wearing a suit, too. He beamed – he looked almost presentable.

'Can we get a comment?'

'Do you blame the Brits?'

'Jane!'

She held up a hand. 'Thank you, ladies and gentlemen. No, I don't blame anybody. I have a very good lawyer, who worked on this case for free. And I'm grateful to be recognized as both an adult, and an American.'

'How does it feel to lose all that cash?'

'I never expected to have anything handed to me.' She smiled dead at the camera. 'Tomorrow I'll be going for a job at Shop Smart. I want to work my way up, and that's an all-American company.'

They snapped and took pictures, and eventually drifted away. Richards was ecstatic.

'Hey, thanks, babe. I think one of those guys was from the *Times*.'

'I don't doubt it.'

'You want to get lunch?' he asked hopefully. Hell, she *was* an adult now, totally legal in every way. 'I'm buying . . .'

'No thank you. I have work to do.'

'Thought you didn't have a job,' he sulked.

'That's the work – finding one.'

He had a brainwave. 'Hey, I'll give you a job. Come be my assistant. I bet you could clean the office up real nice – you'd look great in reception. Clients would love you.'

'No thanks. I don't need all the staring. And I don't want to be anybody's assistant.'

'In Shop Smart you get minimum wage – *if* they take you on. I heard the Sunset Store is full. It's menial work. And no lunch break.'

'Yes, but they have a management programme,' Jane said. 'Goodbye, Mr Richards. Maybe we'll meet again.'

She strode away from him, towards the bus stop. Living in LA, no car, no cash – still as confident as all hell.

'Maybe,' he muttered. But somehow, he doubted it.

That girl was made for bigger things than him.

*

Mrs Doherty saw Jane coming, and smiled, despite herself.

'Good morning. I was wondering if any vacancies had opened up?'

The English girl was well dressed, and groomed. Good accent, too – the customers would love those classy Limey tones.

'Saw you on TV. You said nice things about Shop Smart. My boss said if you came back to give you a job.'

'Great.' Jane felt a wash of relief surge through her. 'If you've got a uniform, I can get changed right away?'

'You need to fill in a form first.'

Jane opened her purse, took out the neatly completed form and handed it to the recruiter. Disbelievingly, the woman scanned it.

'Damn, girl. You in a hurry?'

Jane didn't reply.

'There are uniforms in back. Put one on and clock in. You're going to be a greeter. Seven-day trial, be here at seven a.m. tomorrow. If you're late, you're fired. Got it?'

'Yes, ma'am,' Jane said. She hurried away into the back, before her new boss could change her mind.

'Good morning! Welcome to Shop Smart. I hope you have a lovely day.'

Janice Esposito, junior manager, sourly watched the new girl at the front door. She was standing behind a video cassette rack – Jane Morgan couldn't see her. Ticking off performance stats. Looking for a fault.

Janice couldn't believe the new girl really *wanted* a shitty job like this. She'd read the papers – an Ambassador's daughter? Celebrity orphan? Right, like she was really poor. Why the hell would she want a minimum-wage job that was strictly for the unqualified? The hours were easier at McDonald's.

Janice instantly disliked Jane Morgan. But she had a job to do as well. And it involved ticking off little boxes. Plus, sometimes they checked up on their own Human Resource people, so you couldn't fake it – not to mention there were cameras at the entrances.

Jane Morgan had learned something. Sell the sizzle, not the steak.

Bosses already loved her. She'd brought them free PR. They wanted her to succeed – the new citizen, the American dream.

Friendliness – check.

Neatness – check. Not a hair out of place, looked like she'd been wearing that uniform for years.

Smile – check. Crocodiles had smaller smiles than this chick.

Enthusiasm – check.

Janice's pen hovered as she watched Jane Morgan quickly glance at her watch. Finally, a no-no – she was *supposed* to be looking out for new customers, one hundred per cent of the time.

'Good *afternoon*.' Jane Morgan beamed. 'Welcome to Shop Smart!'

'Well, would ya look at that, Dick,' the portly matron said to her husband as they waddled in past Janice and her clipboard. 'Bang on twelve noon and she switches to "afternoon". Ain't that a kick!'

'Yeah, real impressive,' her husband said. He glanced behind him at the check-in girl's *impressive* figure. What a piece of ass!

Janice sighed. Unfortunately, in a job where there was no such thing as taking the initiative, this girl had just found a way to do it.

There was a box at the base of her form. 'Consider for promotion?'

Reluctantly, she ticked it.

*

Jane didn't do a lot of crying. Mostly, she was too tired. The cheque at the end of the week was unbelievably tiny; man, she resented those taxes and social security payments, yet she still had to save from it. Needed a deposit on a car. Never mind how much of a wreck, she had to have *something*.

The minutiae of grown-up life was unbelievable. So much to do – forms to fill in, stuff to organize. Now her citizenship had come through, she had to queue to get herself a social security number, a driver's licence, a bank account. Credit was the worst. America trapped you: if you didn't have any, it was hard to get any.

She managed it somehow; a starter card at an exorbitant rate. Yet your score only rose if you used it. Daylight robbery, but Jane started an account, and set it up with her bank so that payments were made automatically, on time.

All through Jane Morgan's childhood, she'd been living large. Now, she was living lean. It was amazing what you could get, for free, if you were persistent. Most every day, Jane ate in the staff cafeteria, where food was plentiful and cheap. It was hard to keep healthy, with the disgusting, calorie-laden stodge they served the workers, but she managed it, always opting for the fresh fruit and salad, taking just a little of the protein-based dish and leaving the glutinous baked desserts. There was no private gym in her life, but she still had her clothes, and they included a pair of Nikes and a comfortable jog suit. Jane ran daily, every morning at 6 a.m; a golden hour, when the junkies had finally crawled home to bed, and the regular Joes hadn't yet surfaced. She ran up and down the Sunset Strip, ignoring the detritus of needles and beer bottles, keeping her eyes fixed on the sun rising over the horizon.

And when she got back to the apartment, Jane forced herself to do forty push-ups before her stretch routine.

Punishing. But energetic. When she got into work, there

were free bagels and orange juice – a daily shot of C – and she had the energy she needed to push her through the day. Because on minimum wage, you needed all the hours they'd give you.

When she finished greeting, smile never wavering, there was lunch – ten minutes flat, and a bathroom break. Next, Jane swapped uniforms and went to the checkout till, where she worked two sessions. She got home nights at 9 p.m., showered, and tumbled into bed.

It was a disciplined routine. After a while, it became automatic. And with the free stuff she got from the store – spoiled items, unwanted bottles of shampoo, frayed T-shirts you could sleep in – Jane spent next to nothing. Rent and utilities – that was it. She worked seven days, and actually watched her savings start to mount.

One day blended into another. It was mindless. And that suited her fine.

Jane Morgan didn't want to do too much thinking.

'Let's go see her.' Julie Manners stretched out on her lilo in the pool.

'What do you mean? She's gone.' Emma Lightfoot laughed meanly. 'Ain't that a bitch?'

The girls extended their legs and applied a little oil. Got to love those private beaches! There were some fine-looking preppy boys across the way checking them out.

'Did I tell you guys? Momma got me a birthday present,' said Melissa Smith, tossing her silky black hair.

'We know. A yellow Maserati. You told us already,' Emma complained.

'Not that one, another one. Season tickets to the Dodgers. A *box*.'

'Oooh,' Julie said, instantly seeing the possibilities. 'Great for invites, let's have a party there.'

What dude could resist tickets to the Dodgers?

'There are some UCLA guys coming. I heard the Governor's son was going to be there.'

'Boooring.'

'And Pete Easterman, you know, from the new Arnold flick?'

'That's more like it!' Julie patted her acolyte's arm. 'Definitely a little party. I could like baseball.'

'Get the guys to teach it to you,' Emma said, seeing herself playing dumb – men *loved* the pouty, little-girl-lost look.

'Right. And we'll drive some of them in your Maserati. And my Jeep. It'll be way cool.'

Not exactly Sally Lassiter-style cool, but what the hell? Sally was gone. All three witches were gone.

Julie returned to her theme.

'It'll be even cooler if we go to Shop Smart to pick up the party gear – invitations and stuff.'

'Shop Smart?' Emma looked at Julie like she was mad. 'My mom knows this great woman on La Cienega who will do invites, like, with calligraphy and pressed flowers and shit like that.'

'Yes, but *Jane Morgan* doesn't work for her.' Julie gave her friends a silky smile. 'You girls heard the news, right? Hoity-toity Miss Jane is a *greeter* on minimum wage! Right on Sunset!' Julie snickered at the delicious thought. 'We should go see her,' she repeated, cruelly. 'It'll be fun. Let's have her wrap our purchases, call us "ma'am" . . . bow and scrape like a little shopgirl. Which she is. And if she acts up, we can report her to her bosses. The customer is always right, you know.' Julie cackled.

'Oooh.' Melissa's eyes widened. 'You are *evil*.'

'Come on, you know she deserves it. Don't you remember how *mean* she was to all of us? She stopped you getting invited to that damn party.'

'Yeah, it's true,' Melissa said, angrily. That still burned. 'Let's go there and show her who's boss!'

The girls laughed.

'I got the new car parked outside,' Melissa said, eager to curry favour.

Julie rewarded her with a smile. 'I like it – let's have her walk our groceries to your Maserati, and if she does a *real* good job, maybe she'll get a tip.'

'Yeah, like two dollars!' Emma said, and laughed.

Chapter Eleven

Jane was exhausted. The night before, Will Fox, the student, had cancelled his checkout shift and her boss had asked her to stay – till eleven. She made it a practice never to say no, but she couldn't cope with only six hours' sleep. Not on her schedule.

But she'd done her running, just like always, and here she was, trying to smile, trying to be effusive.

One thing about Shop Smart, they *always* watched you.

It was why she'd chosen them.

But Jane couldn't afford an off day.

Rhodri Evans, Shop Smart's Senior Vice President of Marketing, West Coast, looked over the store carefully. Hollywood – an important location. They were expanding from the Midwest, moving into the cities. He wanted to keep the prices rock-bottom but soften the image, away from vast concrete warehouses in the middle of nowhere.

This store had been open for two years, and he wanted it to succeed.

Good – so far it seemed busy.

He walked through the front doors.

'Good morning, welcome to Shop Smart.' A young African-American college kid shook his hand with a perfunctory smile.

Evans was not impressed, but it was a perennial problem. They didn't pay enough to attract the best staff.

'Good morning! Welcome to Shop Smart. Great to see you!'

He turned his head, distracted. A young woman with a foreign accent, beautiful enough to be a model, was standing at the opposite door. She was smiling like she'd just won the lottery, and her uniform looked like it had come from the dry-cleaners.

'Who *is* that?' he asked the greeter.

'Jane. Y'all can't have her number, though,' the kid said, wearily.

'Do lots of people ask?'

'Lots of *men*,' he said with contempt. 'She's all about work, though. Wants to get noticed. What the hell she's doing here I don't know. She could have got work lots of places. Like been a teacher. Or a rich man's nanny, she's good with the kids.'

'OK. Thanks.'

Evans walked into the store and pretended to browse. He never began an evaluation without actually doing some shopping. You could read all the management consultant reports in the world, and it wouldn't help you.

Jane . . . Jane who?

He stood in front of a rack of video recorders, looking confused, rubbing his chin. Nobody came to help him. One black mark.

The beautiful girl was still there, smiling and shaking hands as if the customers were long-lost relatives.

Rhodri was fascinated. He edged back to the front of the store and pretended to be interested in a pile of discount khaki pants, made in Taiwan from one hundred per cent polyester.

'Good morning! Welcome.'

'It's great to have you at Shop Smart today!'

'Welcome, what a beautiful day for shopping!'

Wow! She was always beaming, always performing. He was impressed.

'Well, well, well, look who it is.'

There was a pause. He looked up from the polyester pants to see a small knot of beautifully dressed teenagers – girls that were far too rich to be shopping in *this* store. A slim girl wearing Prada, another in a Chanel jacket twinned with designer jeans . . .

'Good morning, Jane,' said the lead girl cattily. The others sniggered. 'Hey, great place. Nice to see you've landed on your feet.'

Abandoning his pretence, Rhodri Evans stepped back from the table and folded his arms, watching.

'Good morning, Julie,' Jane said stiffly. 'Do you need help with something?'

'Actually yes,' said Melissa Smith, smirking. 'We're having a little party. My mom bought me box seats at the Dodgers. Some of the boys from Fulbrook High are coming along.'

'We want napkins and party items.'

'They're in aisle three.' Jane gritted her teeth, but her face was flushing from the humiliation. 'I'll get somebody to help you.'

'Noooo,' Julie purred. '*You* help us. Then you can carry it all out to Melissa's brand new Maserati. What are you driving these days, Janey? Or do you take the bus?'

'The name's Jane, and I'm afraid I can't leave my post.'

As Evans watched, a pudgy woman, a store manager, bustled over to see what the fuss was about. What was her name? Oh yeah – Eileen something. Doherty. And a Personnel woman. Janice Esposito. She had an unpleasant look on her face.

'Hello, ladies,' cried Mrs Doherty heartily. 'Are you getting good service here today?'

'I'm afraid this young woman was saying she was too busy to help us,' Julie pouted. 'Which is a shame because we were going to spend a *lot* of money in this store. Oh well, guess you don't want our business.'

'Jane, is that true?' snapped Janice.

Evans didn't like the way this was going. He moved towards the knot of women. Other customers had started to stare.

'You know,' the girl called Melissa said nastily to Jane, 'if you had been willing to help, we'd have given you a tip. On *your* wages I'm sure you could have used it.'

'Of *course* she could have, ma'am. I'm so sorry you've had this trouble today,' Janice said triumphantly. Finally! An end to all those positive evaluations. She couldn't stand the hoity-toity Englishwoman, little Miss Perfect making everybody else look bad.

'That wasn't the case,' Jane said calmly. She struggled to keep her voice under control. 'I told these young ladies where their goods were located and I was going to fetch an assistant to help them, since I'm a greeter this morning . . .'

'We don't *argue* with the customers!' Janice snapped. 'Get back into the staffroom immediately, Ms Morgan!'

'That's right,' Julie triumphed with a little snicker. Her eyes danced over Jane with total contempt. 'Get back inside immediately, *Jane*, so I can be sure you're fired from your crappy little job. Go on, get!'

Jane stood there, and he watched her tense shoulders slump, and painful tears of humiliation fill her eyes. He understood at once.

This was a black, bleak moment in this young girl's life.

How could the other rich girls be so foul? And why weren't his staff standing up for their young colleague? He'd heard staff morale was at rock bottom in LA. Perhaps this was why.

'Didn't you hear me? You move,' spat Janice Esposito, her own face suffusing with pleasurable outrage. 'What do you think you're doing?'

That was it. He strode towards them and addressed his personnel manager.

'What do you think *you're* doing?' Rhodri Evans stood in front of the group, angry. He glanced at his young greeter – tears were spilling from her eyes now, but she was standing her ground, even as they all glared at her. The ugly looks of satisfaction on the faces of the rich girls annoyed him intensely.

'You did not observe the situation,' he said coldly to Janice Esposito, 'and you are making a scene in front of the customers.'

'Who the hell are you? Security!' said Janice, flushing scarlet and snapping her fingers.

Two security guards, who'd been watching the altercation idly, wandered over.

'This guy's *leaving*,' snapped Janice.

'No.' Rhodri withdrew his wallet and handed the guard his business card. 'My name is Rhodri Evans, I'm Senior Vice President, Marketing, West-Coast. You're fired,' he said to Janice. 'Human Resources will be in touch to return your personal effects.'

'You can't do that,' she hissed. 'I *am* Human Resources.'

'Not any more.' He nodded, and the guard took her elbow.

Janice went bright red. 'I'll sue you!'

'Try it.' Evans shrugged. 'Don't you know the whole thing's on camera?' He turned to the security guards. 'And these young *women*' – the term was deliberately insulting – 'are also leaving. They attempted to harass a member of our staff. They aren't welcome here.'

'Fuck you!' Julie Manners went bright pink in the face. 'My father will—'

'Save it. There's a video. The contents of which I very much doubt any of your fathers would wish released to the press. You know, bullying is very unattractive.'

'You don't know who I am,' Melissa Smith hissed.

'Sure I do – you're somebody who's just been banned.'

He turned to Mrs Doherty as security hustled the shame-faced girls away.

'Who is this young lady?' he asked, gently.

'Her name's Jane Morgan, Mr Evans,' she said eagerly. 'I hired her myself, and she's always been one of our best workers. I fully supported you just then, Jane, I was just about to step in . . .'

Sure you were.

Evans turned to Jane. 'You handled that well.'

'Thank you,' she said. He realized her voice had thickened; she was struggling not to cry.

'Mrs Doherty, find another greeter.' To Jane he said, 'You come with me. I want a word – privately.'

Jane fought her tears all the way to the office. It was hard – so hard. Somehow it was easier to be strong when she was being attacked. No damn way she'd let those girls see her crumble. But when this man, this stranger, defended her – the emotional walls she'd erected tumbled down. The hard work, the exhaustion, the low pay – and then, pure humiliation. Jane felt naive; why hadn't she assumed they'd come looking for her?

Maybe she was being dumb. Maybe she should apply for something in the comfort zone – librarian, or public school teacher. It would pay higher out of the gate, enough for a real apartment, a second-hand car. But it would be a dead end after that – no career prospects, no advancement.

She had come here with a purpose.

For the first time in her life, Jane Morgan was gambling. Was she about to win – or lose?

This manager – he'd stood up for her, yeah. But he *was* a guy. She had become adept at brushing aside advances. From customers, from staffers, from other worker bees at the base of the food chain. Funny, what being beautiful did for you. Until Sally made her over, it wasn't a problem Jane Morgan had had to deal with.

Did Rhodri Evans have a motive? If so, this could be the end. Because she *wasn't* going to sleep with anybody. This guy was major league. He could end her career.

'Right in here.' He opened the door. 'Take a seat.'

'Thanks,' she muttered.

Jane drew her legs together and tried to tug down the hem of her Shop Smart uniform's skirt.

'Don't worry.' Evans was looking at her sympathetically. 'I'm not going to hit on you. I'm gay.'

'Oh.' She smiled, weakly. 'That's great! I mean . . .'

'I know what you mean.' He studied a file on his desk. 'You're seventeen?'

'A legal adult,' she said quickly.

'There's a note in your file of how you came to us.'

Jane didn't say anything; she waited for him to speak. Evans smiled; that was clever.

'You must have known Shop Smart would take advantage of the free publicity and hire you.'

'Yes, I did.' She started to feel more confident. 'Publicity has value; you can trade it for many things. I traded it for free legal advice, and then this job.'

Evans decided he was enjoying himself hugely. When did moments like this ever happen in his tightly wrapped corporate life? She was a most unusual girl, indeed. Seventeen years old, and, simply from the way she spoke, obviously keenly intelligent. Far more so than himself, he suspected.

'All right.' Rhodri pushed his chair back and adopted a light frown. 'Why were you looking at Shop Smart? We pay low wages . . .'

'Minimum wage.'

'And require low skills – we are always oversubscribed for jobs. With your qualifications . . .'

'Firstly, I have no qualifications. I never got around to taking my SATs.'

'You could have been a nanny. There are many rich

families in this city who would pay highly for a girl with an English accent, from a good school.'

'Nannies aren't Senior Vice Presidents, West-Coast.'

'Ah.' He grinned. 'So that's what it is? You wanted to get into the management programme?'

'I wanted to get into *management*,' she corrected him. 'Get noticed – and promoted.'

'You always knew this day would come?' Evans teased her.

But her reply was deadly serious.

'Yes. Because if you do something brilliantly, you'll get noticed. And promoted. If it hadn't been you, it would have been someone else. Eventually.'

'And you think you were brilliant, at the door?'

'I know I was,' she said confidently.

'So I should make you a manager, huh? Give you a department. Just like that.'

'I've worked in this building seven days a week for three months. There's nothing I don't know about this store – and nothing your management programme can teach me.'

'What do you know about business?'

'Try me. I read the *Economist*.'

He arched an eyebrow.

'I do,' Jane insisted. 'I take a bus to the library every Saturday morning – it's my break from exercise. And I read. Magazines, and the *Wall Street Journal*.'

'Amazing,' he breathed. He believed her. And he realized he was staring.

'OK, rookie,' Evans said. 'You're up. Tell me. I put you in charge of women's merchandising. What happens next?'

'I say I want a bigger job.'

'What?'

'It's part of the problem. Managers for every section of the store, all fighting for their patch. It's one store. It needs integration, not turf wars.'

'Example.'

'Electronics are in aisle six. But telephones are in aisle two. You need to store similar goods together. Food needs dedicated checkout lines. The layout needs to be thought through – they shouldn't be able to walk right out. You need tempting quick purchase items by the tills, not the same old medley of magazines . . .'

Jane went on, sketching a vision for the store. He listened attentively. The girl made a lot of sense.

'You realize this would mean slashing jobs.'

'Slashing a wasted layer of management jobs. For a company so concerned about wages, you waste a ton of money on pencil pushers that don't do anything.'

'And how do you know that?'

'I've *watched* them,' she said simply. 'With the savings, you announce an incentive scheme. Bonuses to staff who get special commendations. And an invitation to study for the management programme once they reach a level of excellence. You really need to improve morale. Get some family picnics going, events. Better food – the canteen can do a lot better on the same budget.'

'How would you improve morale?'

'Shop Smart needs to be an excellent store – that means running it smoothly. When I'm manager, I will actually watch staff. All the staff, including the backroom operators, the caterers, the security guards. Rewards and employee excellence certificates for those that do best. Nobody will put the extra effort into it if they think they'll get nothing back.'

He nodded. 'I'm not going to make you a manager.'

Jane sighed, disappointed.

'It's too much of a risk. I take a seventeen-year-old girl, pluck her from the greeters, and put her in charge of a multimillion dollar store? If you fail, I become a laughing stock. And get fired.'

'I see.' She did.

'So what I'm going to do is test you. I'm promoting you to junior manager in charge of staff.'

'Reporting to Mrs Doherty?' Jane's tone showed her disdain.

'Only technically. She will be instructed to let you have your head, but on paper you will report to her. It covers my back.'

She grinned back at him.

'Your brief is to get this lacklustre bunch of employees into a team that could be Disney World cast members. You talk a good game – I expect you to deliver. I better see something outstanding. You have six months.'

Jane flushed with pleasure. 'Yes, sir.'

'And that's not all. I want you to continue your observations of the store. Logistics, and cost-cutting. Write daily reports, collate them into a monthly assessment, and send it to me at central office. When you have six months of cost-based analysis, maybe I can see about a promotion. What is your current weekly salary?'

'I do about seventy-five hours a week, sometimes more, on minimum wage. So that's two hundred and fifty a week.'

'From now on your salary is forty thousand dollars a year basic. There will be incentives – I'll send you a contract. The signing bonus is five thousand dollars – you can pick that cheque up today – and you'll get use of a company car. Junior management gets a Ford. Any colour as long as it's black.'

Jane sat quietly. 'Thank you, Mr Evans,' she said eventually. 'Thank you very much.'

'You didn't tell me you can't believe it,' he observed.

'But I can believe it,' she said coolly. 'I believed it from the start. It's why I came here.'

He stood up, indicating the meeting was over, and offered her his hand.

'Then your plan is working out.'

She allowed herself a brief smile. 'Yes – it is.'

*

'I don't see why you gots to go.' The landlady was sulking. 'You wanted the place pretty bad first time I talked to you.'

'And I kept my word.' Jane looked at her calmly. 'You ran a filthy squat, now it's a student apartment. If you're smart, you'll sell it. Otherwise it'll just get wrecked again, and that's money out of your pocket.'

'You got a big mouth, lady.' The woman glanced round her apartment. It was bright, clean, repainted a gleaming white, with pretty curtains and furniture. It smelled good and she could see no bugs. She wanted to have a pop at the arrogant young missy, but the niceness of her place defeated her. Shheee-it! A contractor would have charged her plenty to get it looking this nice. She had to admit, that two hundred in rent had come with some sweet added value. 'Pick yourself up a fancy new boyfriend?' she sneered.

'No. I got a real job, and a car. Just like I told you.'

The landlady admitted defeat. Besides, something told her it wouldn't be the best idea to make an enemy of this young woman.

'Well, you did good. The place looks nice. Thanks,' she said, grudgingly.

Jane inclined her head.

'You gonna rent someplace fancy now? One a those swish apartments over at Park La Brea?'

'Rent?' Jane was dismissive. 'I'll never rent again. I'm going to buy my own house.'

Chapter Twelve

'So here we are,' Ahmed said. *'Mash' Allah.'*

They were in a crowded Cairo street, and Helen was tired, and hot. It had been a long flight, and the city seemed strange to her; even after LA, overpowering – the flood of traffic, the constantly honking horns, workers on bicycles, a choking sense of dust.

She felt out of her depth. Lost – and she was slightly ashamed. Helen had been foreign in LA – too dusky, too Arab, only protected by her girlfriends. And now she felt foreign here. Her native tongue had atrophied; she thought in English, she groped about for Egyptian words. The garish billboards with their smiling photos embarrassed her; she could not read the Arabic inscriptions.

Helen felt herself between two cultures – and not fitting in with either one.

'Mash' Allah,' she repeated, bowing her head.

Whatever happened, she was determined to use this time. How long would it take to arrange a divorce? Let them bathe, and eat, get some sleep, and she would discuss it openly with Ahmed in the morning. But since she was stuck here, Helen vowed to use the time – a week, maybe longer – to familiarize herself with her own language, her own people. And once she got home, she would ask Baba for an Arabic tutor – either that, or they should stop using English in the home.

The doorway was hidden, almost secret, a grey-painted

nothing of a door, set anonymously into a wall of the city street. While Helen waited with their suitcases, Ahmed reached into his wallet and pulled out a small brass key, old, she thought, with intricate casing. He inserted it into the lock; she heard the clicks and tumbles, like a puzzle solving, and the little door, heavy, swung open on its hinges. She had to stoop to enter, and then they were inside. He stopped to pray when they entered the courtyard.

She looked around. The place was magical. When the small door closed, the sounds of the street disappeared. She was standing in a high, ancient courtyard, where the walls were many feet thick, strong enough to drown out the traffic. The height offered a pool of natural shade. The garden was green; shady palms, as many as seven, were placed strategically around gravel paths. Tiny bricks, painted blue, fenced off flower beds, dotted with azaleas, blossoming cacti, and thick beds of lilies. In the four corners of the garden, low-level fountains bubbled with water; it spilled, burbling, into square pools, giving the air a moist feel, a sense of a true oasis. There were birds in the trees, singing; she saw Ahmed had discreetly placed feeders and boxes for them. Butterflies darted around the flowers.

The garden was set in a Roman peristyle. There was a covered walkway around the outside, with flagstones like a European church underfoot, and the pillared arches were covered in mosaics, in the Moroccan style; tiny squares of glass, blue, and green. Islamic art and architecture, and she felt her soul thrill with unexpected pleasure.

'This is our house.' For the first time, Ahmed smiled warmly at her. 'I worked on it – many years. The garden, especially. I hope you like it – since that is your name.'

She nodded. Helen Yanna – al-Yanna, the garden. She'd always liked that part of her name.

She glanced around, drinking it in.

'Do you approve?' He was hopeful. It touched her that Ahmed desired her approval.

'I do.' Helen nodded. 'This is beautiful.'

'It isn't rich, not a big house,' he said, apologetically. 'My business is not as good as it should be, not yet. But you will like it, I hope so.'

'We can try in Arabic,' Helen said, switching, awkwardly.

'You've forgotten?' Ahmed spoke softly, and looked into her eyes, with a new confidence. As though he were assessing her. 'I will remind you,' he said. 'I will teach you.'

To Helen's amazement, her stomach started to churn. She blushed and lowered her eyes. A tendril of something—desire, she realized – was trawling over her belly.

To cover her confusion, she said, 'I would like to bathe . . .'

'Of course. How tired are you? Can you manage dinner?'

She was rocky with exhaustion, but she nodded, still blushing.

'And then . . . bed.'

Helen's head snapped up. He was still looking at her in that way. As she opened her mouth, wondering what to say, Ahmed lifted his hand and traced a fingertip across her mouth, softly and possessively.

'You are afraid – like a mare, before saddling. No, not tonight. I do not want you tired. I want you fully awake.'

'The bathroom . . .' she said dry-mouthed. 'Please?'

He grinned, and extended his arm, opening the house to her. And as Helen walked inside, she was aware of Ahmed watching her. Wanting her.

She didn't know what she was feeling.

The house was not as spectacular as the little garden; it had some tile work, old wood; she thought it was beautiful, modest and comfortable. Three large bedrooms, a master suite with a bathroom and two dressing rooms; a kitchen, servants' quarters, occupied; a living room, and a dining room, and a small ornate room set aside for prayer, with the mats and a window facing Mecca.

But the decoration! Every room carpeted with a priceless antique – Persian silks, rough kelims, each gorgeous, lining the house with beauty. There were mosaics, brass lamps that cast intricate shadows, scrollwork on the walls, glass vases, sculpture. Small pieces, but carefully collected. The house was like a museum, she thought, but lived-in, warm; the servants who bustled through it, wearing baggy linen trousers and shirts, or traditional robes, greeted her kindly and seemed genuinely happy that Ahmed was home. He introduced Helen, and she was polite.

Now that the moment had passed, she was getting a grip; getting her control back.

'I will bathe, also.' Ahmed stood back from the master bedroom. 'When you are ready, come downstairs; they have made us a little supper.'

'OK. Thank you.' She turned aside, towards the large copper tub with the modern, rain-like shower attachment . . .

. . . and then his hand was on her shoulder, firmly turning her towards him, and a strong arm lowered her down into the crook of his shoulder, and his lips pressed on to her mouth, teasingly, lightly brushing over hers, his tongue flickering against hers, probing, owning her.

Helen shuddered, taken utterly by surprise, and feeling his strength; she had never been kissed, and he knew what he was doing. She was light, nothing in his arms; she could feel the strength, the hardness of his muscles under his shirt . . .

And then, as she was in turmoil, he let her go. Stunned, Helen, seventeen, stood there, her thumb on her mouth, her lips half open, staring at him.

'Later,' he said. His dark eyes swept across her again. And then he suddenly turned, and went down the stairs.

Helen went into the bathroom and shut the door; mechanically, she turned on the taps. She didn't know whether that word 'later' was a promise or a threat.

She chose, deliberately, a Western dress for dinner: a long-skirted, fitted, navy blue dress from Armani that Sally Lassiter had treated her to. It was modest, with long sleeves and a square neckline, but chic and simple. Helen teamed it with the tiny diamond studs Baba had given her for her sixteenth birthday.

Very important to keep that connection to home. She vowed not to be angry about the fast one her parents had pulled. They only had her best interests at heart; but Helen was determined that she would be the judge of that.

The kitchen was full; servants, cooks, had materialized out of nowhere. Helen greeted them, shyly, and went through to the dining room.

Red silks, gloriously embroidered, hung from the walls. Antique glass and brass lamps were lit, casting detailed shadows across the walls. Perfumed candles, scented with attar of roses, were dotted about, floating in water in the powder-blue ceramic bowls Ahmed had laid out, their flames adding a cheerful light to the ambience.

In one corner of the room, a musician, his head studiously lowered, played a tune on the sitar.

Ahmed had changed, too. He was now in traditional dress. Long black trousers and an open-necked shirt revealed to her that he was slim, but strong. It was his own house, and he was sprawled comfortably against the Moroccan cushions piled on the divan. Master of his own domain.

'Good evening,' he said.

'Hello.' Helen blushed. After that kiss, she did not know how to look him in the eyes.

'Will you start with a drink?'

'Thank you,' she said.

'They have spent a month deciding on the menu,' he told her. He lowered his voice. 'So I hope you eat something.'

There was coconut-scented rice, and small roasted birds; Moroccan *tabbouleh* salad and some delicious local pastries served in a dish of sweetmeats. Helen, not really hungry, picked a little at everything; it was all good, delicious, she was sure, if she had her appetite back. For dessert, Ahmed's servants laid out chilled fruits: lychees, dates and pomegranate seeds, carefully scooped out and laid in a crushed bed of freezing ice crystals.

For drinks, they offered freshly squeezed orange juice, pure, icy water, or hot mint tea, heavily sugared and served in frosted glasses.

Slowly, she began to relax. After all, he had said he wouldn't come to her tonight. So why worry?

'This is wonderful. Thank you.'

'You don't need to thank me,' Ahmed said, dark eyes on her. 'You are not a guest here. This is your house.'

Helen bit her lip. Should she tell him?

But no, they were both zoning out, exhausted from the flight. This was not the time.

She made polite conversation instead.

'How long have you lived here?'

'Four years. Since I found the market in America, and my business has done well. It is also four years since Firyal died,' he added, unembarrassed. 'Had she lived, we would have married and settled in her father's house. He owned land in Qatar – she was in Egypt to pursue her studies.'

'And you loved her?' Helen was curious.

'Infinitely.'

The answer overcame her reserve; she was conscious of an unwanted, new feeling, a stab of jealousy.

'Then why agree to this? We never met, before that

day at my parents'. Why would you want to marry me?'

'Because,' he said. 'Because your mother and mine are related, and I knew you were a Muslim girl, of good family. Because I heard tell that you were a believer. Because I loved Firyal so much that I thought never to be in love again, as long as I lived, with anyone.'

Helen noted how he put that in the past tense.

'Because I want to have the joy of a family, and of children, *insh'Allah*. And what better for that than a young girl, intelligent, a believer, of good family? I saw it as my duty. What was the point of looking for love?'

'And now?' she demanded. Her pride, stung. It was *she*, Helen, who was doing her duty here. Ahmed should be *desperate* to marry her. Inflamed for her. Who was this Firyal? And she thrilled to the unpleasant idea of competing with a ghost.

'And now I find you interest me,' he said. 'You seem . . . on the brink. Like a ripe plum, not yet fallen. You stir me . . . you are different. I want to train you.'

His eyes bored into hers.

'I am not an animal,' Helen managed.

'You are. We both are. Human animals.' Ahmed smiled, confident and suddenly attractive. 'Tomorrow . . . in our marriage bed . . . I will show you, little American.'

'I'm going to want to talk to you.'

'Talk all you want.' He grinned, not allowing her to drop her eyes. 'You are a virgin, untouched, and terrified. After tomorrow, you will be mine.'

'You're very sure of yourself,' Helen said.

He smiled. 'That's right. I am.'

She had no idea how she made it to bed. Ahmed, soon afterwards, clicked his finger for the aya, and the woman came, and helped Helen away from the table, and through the house to the master bedroom. 'Here,' she said, opening the bathroom cupboard. There were new toothbrushes, in their packaging, cosmetics, and flannels.

'Thank you. *Shokram*.' Helen bowed, and eventually the woman went away.

Drained, she brushed her teeth and passed the flannel over her face. It made her feel clean, good; combine it with the bath, and she no longer sensed dust and grime clinging to her every pore. Air travel . . . such a nasty, unhealthy way to go.

She did not have any energy left to hunt around for a nightdress. As soon as her ablutions were done, Helen flopped on to the bed, and she was asleep almost before she had closed her eyes.

'What time is it?'

Helen rolled over, on to her side, to find Ahmed lying next to her, dressed in white, his eyes closed. Groggily, she rubbed her eyes.

'Ah.' He sat up. 'I thought you would never surface. I was about to call the doctors.'

'It can't be that late . . .'

'Try three p.m. You've been asleep for almost eighteen hours.'

Helen groaned. 'It'll take me days to get over the jet lag.'

'I would not worry. You have years.' Ahmed smiled down at her. 'I have taken a nap myself, after lunch; very civilized, the Spanish siesta. So I will be full of energy tonight, also.'

Helen sat up. She was thirsty.

As though reading her thoughts, Ahmed clapped his hands, and a woman materialized, bearing a pitcher of freshly squeezed orange juice and two enormous glasses.

'Better than water,' he said. 'It will also replenish your body salts.'

She didn't need telling twice. Helen thirstily gulped down two enormous glasses of the golden nectar, and it tasted beyond delicious; the oranges themselves even richer and sweeter than those harvested a touch too early in the California sun.

'Excuse me,' Helen said, after she was finished. Ahmed nodded to his servant, who melted away as quietly as she had come, and Helen, self-conscious, fled to the bathroom to do her teeth and take a bath.

Once she was finished, wrapped securely in her big towelling dressing gown, glad to have escaped him, she went back into the bedroom.

But Ahmed was there. Sitting on her bed. Their bed.

'Talk,' he said, in English.

'Excuse me?'

'Talk. I have now sent the staff home. We will not be disturbed. Whatever you have to say, whatever request you want to make, now is the time.' He grinned. 'And then I am going to begin training you, Haya.'

She was outraged. 'What did you call me?'

'Haya,' Ahmed said. 'It is your name. What you were given at birth. It means modesty, and it suits you. I asked your father. He put "Helen" on you when you went to the United States, so that you would fit in with all the other girls. But you are not Greek; you are Arab. And your name is special, as you are. Ordained and written in the book of life. You are my Haya. I will never call you by that fake name again.'

His speech stopped her anger dead. But she felt obliged to add, 'You can't train me, Ahmed. I told you that last night.'

'Let us see if you are telling me the same thing three hours from now.'

'I won't be telling you anything,' she said, feeling out the name 'Haya' in her mind. It was, in truth, very beautiful, much better than boring Helen. Maybe now she understood why she had never liked her name. 'I'm not yours, Ahmed. I'm mine.'

'What is the contradiction?' he asked, dark eyes on her. Not backing down.

'I . . . didn't understand what I was doing. When I signed the *nikkah*,' she said.

For the first time, he registered shock. Amazement, then scandal.

'What?' he said. 'Do you not understand the purpose of the *nikkah*?'

'I do,' she said. 'Of course . . . but I did not realize I was signing a *nikkah*. They spoke so fast . . . My Arabic is poor.' She blushed. 'As you know. And my father told me it was a friendship ceremony.'

He considered this for a second. She had expected him to curse, to stand, perhaps to be abjectly apologetic. But he was none of these things. Instead, he looked at her calmly; and with that same assessing stare that had disturbed her yesterday.

'Then tell me, Haya,' Ahmed said. 'Were they wrong when they informed me you were intelligent, and a believer?'

She flushed. 'No. Of course not.'

'Then you know the faith. What "friendship ceremony" did you think this was . . . exactly?'

She had no answer.

'And was marriage never mentioned to you?'

'It was,' she admitted. 'But I said that I would choose my own husband.'

'Yet you met me, and of your own free will went through this ceremony. Is it not so?'

She blushed. 'Yes.'

'So on some level you knew what was going on. You are not stupid, Haya.'

It was true. She knew it in the depth of her soul.

'I have the right to choose my own husband!' she said.

'That is so. I will not force you.' He leaned across the bed, and his face was inches from hers; a young man, but older than her, confident, and on his home turf. 'In fact, my Haya, I would make you go through a second ceremony, now, before I permitted you to touch me. And even after that, I would make you come to me, and beg for it.'

Her eyes widened. 'You are so arrogant!'

Ahmed inclined his head. 'And you want me. Do you not think I know my own?'

'How could you tell I am your own?'

'I tasted your lips,' he said to her. 'And you will yield to me.'

Ahmed stood up, gave her a little bow, and withdrew.

Chapter Thirteen

She woke up in the middle of the night, sweating, unsure where she was. The hum of traffic and the splashing of the fountains seemed wrong, strange and wrong; as she came to, Helen longed for the reassuring quiet of their house off Third Street, her compact, American bedroom . . . her parents.

She shoved the covers off her and walked to the window, shivering as the night air hit her. The moon was half hidden behind the clouds; it looked different here, in the southern hemisphere. Her nightdress was thin around her legs. Helen cringed; she felt so alone, so vulnerable, unprotected, no family, no friends . . .

Briefly her mind flashed back to the two girls. What would Sally say? Some crude joke about Ahmed and their wedding night? She wasn't sure if Sally was a virgin; that was an indelicate question, not one she'd wanted to ask. Jane was, she was sure of that. Jane had only been made beautiful recently, and had never been seen with a boy.

Ahmed, in America, had been very different. Lost, confused. Polite. Here, in Egypt, he was on his home turf. Transformed. Predatory.

Helen twisted her dark hands, confusion springing up in her. He terrified her. Ahmed had all the power in this situation, all the money, all the knowledge. He spoke the language . . . she was his, in his house.

And it scared her even more that she was starting to feel

for him. A dark, violent attraction in the pit of her stomach. A longing, in the belly of her, when he was close; wanting him to go away, but wanting, at the same time, for him to reach out, to touch her cheek, her neck, to kiss her, even . . .

She was disturbed. She hated her own powerlessness. Helen's fingers tightened on the window sill, and she bit down in anger on her soft lips. She had herself to blame for this, for her modest obedience to her parents, for always wanting an easy life, always wishing to avoid confrontation. Yes, she still loved them. But how, how, had she given the impression that this would be acceptable? That they could ship her off to Egypt, and choose the man to whom she would belong?

The traditional ways? While her father drank alcohol whenever he felt like it, and her mother neglected prayers often enough and sometimes snuck food during Ramadan, Helen had seen her do it. Why was it one rule for them and another for her?

No, she thought. No. She would not bow to this. She would not submit to Ahmed's rule of her body. She wanted to go the hell home, right now.

A night breeze came in through the arched window, fluttering the thin cotton of her nightdress. Helen shuddered and ran to her suitcase. Frantically she tugged on her underwear, her socks, a pair of jeans, and a shirt. She had no sweaters or coat – who knew it could get so cold here at night? It was a desert country; too late she remembered that. Well, it would have to do. Frightened, she worked quietly, grabbing whatever she could. A few American dollars – not many, she had about thirty bucks, she'd assumed Baba would bring the cash for the holiday. No airline ticket, but she had a credit card. She tried to remember exactly what was left in that account, from her allowance. Four hundred, maybe less. Not enough for a last-minute ticket to the States. Then she would go to Europe, she thought, go to England. Get somewhere safe. And her passport, *mash'Allah*, she thought with a fervent rush of gratitude and relief. Her passport was still here . . .

She put on her sneakers and quietly opened her bedroom door. It was oiled, and didn't squeak. Helen's heart thumped wildly in her chest, crashing against her ribcage. What if he heard her? Would he be angry, feel betrayed? Hit her . . . beat her? Worse, drag her back to her room and rape her? She did not know this man at all. What if he regarded her as his possession, as a disobedient chattel out to humiliate him?

Carefully, delicately, she tiptoed down the stone stairs, their ancient surfaces pocked and pitted. Helen cast her eyes around, in the gloom, watching for any door to open – he had enough servants, a cook, a nightwatchman . . .

But nobody came. They were all asleep. She looked at the clock in the hallway; it said half midnight. She reached the door to the kitchen, then the door to the garden. Outside, it was very chilly, and she shivered again. The water looked eerie, bubbling in the dark. Helen ran across the courtyard, quietly in her sneakers, unlatched the gate, and made it out into the street. She didn't know Cairo; she had no idea where she was. She picked up her heels and ran, blindly, fast, towards the sound of traffic.

It was dark. Helen, terrified, thudded through the streets, her sneakers pounding the pavement. There were few lights; she thought she must be off the centre, somewhere. The storefronts were all shuttered. A man rode by on a donkey, pulling a cart full of trash; he scowled at her. She turned left into a major street, her breath ragged, and slowed to a walk.

OK, OK. Don't panic. The street signs were in Arabic, she had forgotten how to read it. No English subtitles. She looked around, hoping for a taxi, a bus – did they run at night? Anything. A way to get to the centre.

A group of men walked past her and laughed raucously.

She heard them say something, it didn't sound pleasant. She thought they called her a whore. Helen hesitated, desperate to ask for directions, but one of the group, a thin man with a scarred face, whistled at her and started to move in her direction. Hurriedly, she crossed the street, starting to feel that this was a mistake. She looked like a tourist, and judging from the broken windows, the tin cans in the gutter, this was a rough part of town . . .

Helen felt the fear rise in her throat. The gaggle of men were conferring, looking over in her direction. Would they follow her? Rape her? She didn't wait to find out; she raced off down a narrow alleyway, and heard them cursing. Oh God! She prayed desperately, her mind racing. What could she do? She was totally lost, it was pitch black, cold, no place for an American girl in a thin blouse . . .

She needed a landmark. Clutching her wallet in her jeans pocket, Helen forced herself to breathe more slowly. She was panting from exertion and fright. Look for a crescent, she told herself, look for a crescent rising above the modern apartment blocks and ancient tumbledown houses. She would find a mosque . . . it would have directions near it, and she would be safer. Who would hurt a girl in the shadow of the minaret? Helen steadied herself against a wall and peered into the gloom. There – towards the north-west. It looked far away, but there it was, the crescent glinting against a street lamp. She walked towards the north, down another alley, and then into an open street. More men, staring at her. Not a single woman to be seen anywhere. Helen picked up pace. She'd keep moving . . .

There was a squeal of tyres and a beat-up red Ford Fiesta screeched to a halt beside her. The window wound down; the driver stared at her, calmly.

'How much?'

That, she understood. And realized with a shock of nausea he thought she was a prostitute.

'Leave me alone,' she said, in English. He flashed her a sick grin, displaying yellowing teeth.

'Taxi,' he said. 'Pretty lady want taxi to airport?'

'Go away,' Helen hissed. She started to pick up speed, but he pressed his foot on the gas.

'What you doing out here at night? Ladies don't come here. Give me money, I take you hotel. Airport.' He cackled. 'Pyramids!'

Helen squealed; he thrust his arm out of the window and took a swipe at her handbag, cursing at her as she flinched. But his arm was strong, and as she screamed for help, he wrenched the bag away, ripping at her shoulder. Helen grabbed, but it was too late, and now his scrawny hand had closed around her wrist.

'You get in car,' he said. 'Now!'

In her blind terror, Helen remembered a self-defence move from kick-boxing class. She bent her hand backwards, naturally breaking his grip. He shouted in rage and slammed on the accelerator. Helen pivoted and ran the other way, leaving him to execute a sharp turn in the street.

And then she blinked, thrust her hand in front of her eyes, as headlights, full on, dazzled her and lit up the whole street. Another car had turned into the road, at speed, a shiny Mercedes, its horn blaring. It rammed the Fiesta, hard, then pulled back and rammed it again.

She stood, frozen to the spot, her fists crammed in her mouth. The red car lurched and skidded from the impact, but the thief slammed his foot down and it lurched off, fast, down an alley.

The silver car was now sideways across the street, blocking her exit, blocking off the entrance to the alley from which Helen had come. She breathed in, shuddering, scared, looking around her wildly for any escape. Oh God! It was one of the other men, one of the drunks from before, he had tailed her. She had no passport now – and she was going to be raped . . .

The door was opening. A man was getting out. Helen struggled against the scream that rose, choking, in her throat.

'Wait!' he said, in English. 'Don't be afraid, Helen. I won't hurt you.'

She stared. It was Ahmed.

He rushed across to her, his eyes searching her body, her lips bluish with cold, her blouse torn where her attacker had ripped off the buttons.

'I heard you leave . . . when I got up you had gone.' His words tumbled out. 'I followed, I asked men on the street where you were headed. In the end, I found you. Did he hurt you?'

Numbly, she shook her head. 'He tried.' Her teeth were chattering, she could barely speak.

Ahmed looked her over. 'You didn't have to run. You were always free to go. It's your decision.'

'If it was my decision, I wouldn't be here,' she said, wildly. 'Stuck in this hellhole.'

And then she burst into tears.

He got her into the car. That was an easy choice; it was obviously safer. As she buckled up, Helen thanked God for the small things – the soft leather, the clean seats, the warmth coming from the heater.

'I went too fast with you. You are too young for marriage.' Ahmed shrugged. 'I would never force any woman. Do not worry, I will drive you to a hotel.'

Helen's eyes swam. 'I only have thirty dollars.'

'I'll pay,' he said, easily. 'All you will need is your passport. And I'll arrange for a one-way ticket back to Los Angeles. You can call your parents to come and collect you.' A cold smile. 'Chalk it up to experience.'

She shook her head, plunged back into misery even as her body started to thaw.

'He stole my passport,' she wailed. 'It was in my bag.'

He was silent, turning the wheel of the car, easily negotiating the narrow streets of the old quarter, on his way back to the house.

'Hotels here will not register a foreign guest without one.' He sighed. 'It would appear you are stuck in my house, at least for a day or so. I promise you, I will not bother you. I will not come to your room, or even your part of the house. A woman servant, my cook, will take you to the Embassy tomorrow so you can start on the paperwork.' He glanced across at her, hunched and shaking in the passenger seat. 'At least do me the justice of understanding that *I* never forced you. My family and yours are related – distantly, perhaps, but the bond is still there. I would not attack any woman. Still less one who is mostly a girl.'

She nodded, feeling a little embarrassed.

'It was scary, to be alone in your house.'

'A lot worse out here. Which is why I followed you.'

Helen stared at her lap; she noticed the ripped-off buttons and the gape in her shirt and miserably pulled it tighter.

'I . . . thank you,' she whispered. 'I owe you.'

He shrugged. 'I think of you as a guest in my house, one under my protection. We will get you safely back to your family, and you can forget all about Egypt.'

'I'm sorry,' Helen muttered. 'I just didn't ask to be here.'

Ahmed drove her back in silence to the house. They were not too far away; he parked, and allowed her to get out of the car herself, averting his eyes as he walked into the kitchen. Helen heard him shouting, and the cook, rubbing her eyes, emerged in a night coat with a cloak that she flung around Helen's shoulders, warm, black wool, covering her modestly. The older woman clucked and fussed as she led Helen up the stairs, back into her bedroom. The fountains were still splashing, gently, in the courtyard, but she was no longer menaced by the sound; Helen felt stupid, but safe.

She undressed, put her nightgown back on – it had remained, crumpled, on the terracotta tiles – and crawled into bed.

Within seconds, she found herself drifting off. Emotionally exhausted, jet-lagged, and fatigued, she could not keep her lids from closing. And as she slipped into sleep, she thought of Ahmed, his dark eyes ranging over her body.

When Helen came down to breakfast, he had already gone. There was a short note on the table, and a pile of Egyptian dinars. Ahmed wrote that the cook had only a few words of English, but she would drive Helen to the American Embassy, wait with her and bring her back. He included a list of telephone numbers just in case she got lost. There was a small tourist guide to Cairo next to the note; Ahmed had placed a bookmark next to a city centre map.

It was very thoughtful but very brisk. An efficient little package from a benign stranger. Helen read the note, and felt a pang of loss. Of course, it was insane to suppose they could marry. She was miles too young. But . . . under other circumstances . . .

She figured it would have been good to get to know him better, the handsome merchant with the probing eyes. They might have dated . . .

But her world was an ocean away. There was no point in pining over him now. Last night she'd been afraid he might rape her. No wonder he was keeping his distance.

The cook bustled in, pointed at the note, smiled, and talked to her in rapid-fire Arabic.

Helen shook her head; the woman repeated herself, slower.

Still no dice. She felt ashamed she had lost her own language.

'Eat,' the cook said then, pointing at the breakfast. 'You will like it.'

'Thank you.' Well, at least she still had the simple words. And the food did look delicious: a chilled pitcher of freshly squeezed orange juice, a plate of dates, some hard-boiled eggs in a warm sauce of tomatoes and onions, a bowl of *ful mudammas*, bean dip with pita bread, and a samovar of mint tea.

Helen found she was starving. She ate, and the cook, who said her name was Fahdah, watched approvingly.

'Master Ahmed ordered it,' she said. 'He says you must eat.'

At the Embassy, it was hot and crowded, and it took Helen forty minutes to get through the gatehouse without ID. She queued for over two hours, and finally explained her plight to a bored young man with a Boston accent who hardly looked at her.

'We gotta backlog.' He barely looked up from his paperwork. 'We'll take your prints and details, but likely you won't get a passport for two weeks.'

'But it's an emergency,' Helen spluttered. 'I'm a citizen. Can't you help me?'

He looked up. 'Are you in physical danger, miss?'

She shook her head.

'Do you have a place you can safely stay in the country while your papers are processed?'

'Yes, but—'

'Leave a number. We'll call when your passport becomes available. You are a semi-priority after cases with no funds and no accommodation.'

'Look—'

'Miss, there's a long queue. We'll be in touch. Next,' he called, beckoning a fat woman in a *niqab* up to the counter.

Helen rode home dejected, trying to pick out a word here and there as Fahdah gave her a running commentary. How humiliating. She would have to explain, and then presume on Ahmed's hospitality. For two whole weeks. Her clothes would need to be laundered here, she would eat his food, walk in the safety of his garden . . .

That is, if he let her stay. But, somehow, that was one thing she did not doubt.

The cook left her alone in her room. Helen waited for Ahmed to come home, but lunchtime bled into afternoon, and he still did not come. She sat in her room, and walked outside to sit by the fountains, not daring to venture beyond the walled garden, bored out of her mind. She had nothing to read but a copy of *Vogue* she'd bought on the airplane. And that had been worn to shreds ages ago.

Helen washed her hair, carefully blow-dried it, and plucked her eyebrows. And then, for want of anything better to do, she made herself up, beautifully and carefully, just neutral, natural shades, the way Sally had taught her, and picked out her prettiest shalwar kameez, something she had packed for the sun, a delicate white and yellow chiffon layered thing, shot through with gold. She tried on her various sandals, picking a white pair with a curved heel and blue lacy detailing, and regarded herself in the mirror, as though she were dressing a doll.

She was playing with an armful of thin bronze bangles when the knock on her door finally came.

'The master is here,' Fahdah said, smiling. 'He's waiting in the kitchen.'

Helen jumped up. 'Thank you.'

'Very nice,' the older woman commented, nodding at Helen's outfit. And then she slipped into broken English. 'You pretty – make good wife.'

Helen blushed.

Chapter Fourteen

'She explained what happened. I'm sorry you have been put out.'

Ahmed was standing in the kitchen, reading some papers. He looked at her, just once, and Helen saw his eyes flash with interest. But then he turned away, back to his paperwork, and did not make further eye contact.

'You are welcome to stay here. Under the same rules as before. I can also make some calls, see if I have any contacts amongst the workers hired by the Americans. Perhaps we can speed matters up.'

Helen flushed. 'You're very kind.' She wanted him to look at her, wanted him to compliment her; maybe that was wrong, but he was handsome.

'Or, of course, you can call your parents, and they can arrange for a hotel.'

Helen thought about that. She really, really didn't want to speak to them right now. Her anger with Baba had grown white-hot. When she got home, she would confront them.

'I'd rather not do that. I have some issues with my parents.'

'Some issues? How very American of you. Then your friends, perhaps. Did you not tell me you had rich friends?'

'Well – one.' Jane didn't have two cents of her own, Helen knew she was better off than the English girl. 'To be honest with you, Ahmed, I – I don't want her to know.' She blushed at the thought of Sally's incredulous stare when she found out what Mama and Baba had done. 'I feel so foolish. I just want to get home, and get a job and my own apartment. I know it's a lot to ask and it's presuming on your good graces . . .'

'I don't understand that. What are good graces?'

'Kindness.'

He nodded drily, still refusing to look at her. 'You are Arab, you should learn Arabic properly.'

She blushed again, this time with shame.

'If I can stay with you for this time, I will send you some money when I get home and get a job.'

Ahmed's head snapped up, and the dark eyes bored into hers. Angry. She shrank back; his strong body was coiled, like a predator's.

'You insult me,' he said. 'Did I not tell you you are a guest in my house? Did I not come to find you, and protect you, when you ran from me? Did I not say we are distant cousins? You have been made welcome here and offered every comfort. And now you think to offer me money, as though I were running some kind of boarding house? Even now, you do not think me an honourable man.'

'No! I – it's just – it's such an imposition . . .' Her voice trailed off, and under his unflinching stare she quailed, and dropped her gaze. He was right, of course he was right. She was offering him a dire insult, and he had been nothing but good to her.

'Forgive me,' Helen said, speaking in Arabic the best she could. 'You have been a good friend and cousin. I would like to stay under . . . under your generous roof. If you will permit it.'

He was silent, and when she looked up, he was still glowering.

'Please . . . I'm sorry. I meant no offence . . . Ahmed . . . I want to stay with you, if you will have me.'

'And you will regard me as your host, trust me not to

force myself upon you, nor speak again of money?'

'No. As my host.' Helen bit her lip. 'My kind host,' she said.

She half wanted to stay, half to run. Feeling him so near was disturbing. And she was so much at his mercy. His anger at her dishonouring him made him all the more attractive to her.

'Very well then. It is settled. I'll call the Embassy tomorrow. Will you eat supper?'

'Yes please. And you can tell me all about your work.'

Ahmed's eyebrow lifted. 'I was going to arrange for your meal to be sent to your room.'

Helen started. 'Oh no, please don't. I want to talk to you, to spend time with you. It's been so dull without anything to read, and I don't dare go outside and get lost . . .'

Now he looked at her with a flicker of amusement, and the dark eyes ran assessingly across her pretty outfit.

'But we are not staying married. Do you think it is proper?'

Helen had the strong feeling he was teasing her, toying with her. She felt a rush of desire across her skin, her knees weakening.

'I am your guest. And we are relatives,' she reminded him. 'So I think . . . it's OK.'

'Very well then, we'll eat.'

He clapped his hands, and one of the serving man ran in.

'Bring us some supper,' he said. 'My cousin and I will eat.'

Helen lifted her face and smiled radiantly at Ahmed. She was so grateful. And she was longing for his company.

He chatted lightly and pleasantly enough, as the servant bustled about them, bringing *fattah*, *kaltah*, spiced kebabs with tomato paste and cumin, a dish of tomatoes and herbs, vine leaves wrapped around goat's cheese, figs and honey, and wine. Everything was hand-cooked, and there was a pitcher of iced mineral water and another of pomegranate juice. The flavours of the Middle East blended against her tongue, everything natural, nothing processed. Ahmed ate lying sideways, lounging against his silk divan, and Helen, nervously at first, imitated him, picking at a date or a grape and then the meat and rice dishes.

It was so good to have conversation; she'd had no idea how isolating it was not to speak the language. Her *own* language.

She could hardly look straight at him. Helen felt so grateful, and so indebted. Without Ahmed, she would be confronting her parents right now. Or exposing their behaviour to Sally.

And Ahmed was so confident; so tough, upright, uncompromising. The thought of how he had driven through the night, sought her, saved her, danced in Helen's head. His proud distance from her, afterwards. His eyes, just now and again, sweeping across her, and finding her beautiful.

And she found she desperately wanted him to find her beautiful.

When he was angry, she wanted to please him. To placate him. His dominance lit up something fundamental in her, and the female animal in her responded, setting her blood throbbing, making her long for his arms, his deep, owning kiss.

Of course, Helen didn't have Sally's dazzling style or blond halo of hair. And she didn't have Jane's strength and grace, or her newly discovered pale English good looks.

But there was something about Ahmed that assured her he would not glance twice in either girl's direction. He liked her; she was not 'foreign' to him, except in so far as she had lost her culture. He would – you could argue, did – marry her.

As he talked, politely and inconsequentially, about his business, about the Embassy, the Cairo traffic, Helen stared at him.

And she realized she wanted him.

The evening stretched on, and Helen ate, slowly, trying to

draw it out. When he finally washed his fingertips in the small bowls of rosewater, she did the same, then scrambled lightly to her feet, and walked round the table to be closer to him.

'We could have some coffee in the garden,' she suggested. 'Talk some more.'

Ahmed grinned. 'Dinner is over . . . *cousin*. And I am sure you know you are far too delectable for me to linger over with coffee and sweetmeats. Already you tempt me. You should go to bed. We can dine together tomorrow.'

She sighed. 'I will miss you.' Helen blushed. 'I like to be with you.'

His eyes darkened. 'Don't play with me, little beauty. I am not the sort of man to be teased. You have signed the *nikkah*, but you say you want to leave. And yet now you want to be with me. Which is it?'

She stepped back; the longing to kiss him raged in her. Or rather, to be kissed; to have Ahmed reach out and pull her to him.

But he wouldn't make it that easy. He would force her to be explicit. To make the choice for him. Ahmed stood.

'You know you are free to leave any time you desire,' he said. 'Go back to the West, go and find some gum-chewing surfer who will call you Helen, or some boring lawyer who will want you to dye your hair blond. You can call your parents any time you choose. The international code for the United States is double zero one.'

She watched in dismay as he walked towards his own bedroom; but then he halted at the door.

'I will be sleeping on the second floor,' Ahmed said, once again answering her unspoken question. 'If you want me, come to me. But come as Haya. And come prepared to be my wife. In all things.'

Her heart pounded, and her palms broke out in a sweat. Pure adrenaline.

'Ahmed . . .' she began. But he had turned, and left her.

In turmoil she rose and went to the window. He was arrogant – son of a bitch, he was arrogant! But a good man, all the same. There was nobody here to police him. Yet there had been no hint of force, no question he would make her do anything against her will. She could see Ahmed was a believer, that he knew her rights, knew his faith, would not attempt to deprive her of her natural liberty.

And yet, if she chose, freely, to go to him, it would be on his terms.

The heat of the afternoon was just starting to fade away. Helen turned from the window, and ran down the stairs, towards the courtyard.

Come as Haya, he had said.

The fountains were dancing, the birds sang. It was quiet, and cool. Helen – no, Haya. She tried out the name again in her mind, and it felt right. Her birth name, her Islamic name. Haya. That Ahmed had given it back to her, that she was here, in Egypt, learning her native tongue, with him, felt now as if she were crossing into another, ancient, more fitting world.

Haya sat on the edge of one of the flower beds, and tried to think.

The studious, shy young man she had met in her parents' dining room was no more. Here, Ahmed was in charge, successful, a man who had arranged his house, and his life, in his own way.

And a man who loved another woman.

A dead woman. A ghost.

Haya probed herself. She wanted Ahmed. Her body was in turmoil now. Was it because he was the first, the only one to have kissed her, to have made her squirm? She didn't think so. The boys she'd seen in America, at Sally's party, on the street – none of them had ever made her feel this way.

The bland, handsome movie stars and rock singers had left her cold.

Ahmed was different. His dominant, masculine side – you could call it arrogance – Haya knew it aroused her. And Ahmed was good, there was that to admire; none of her father's heavy-handedness, combined with hypocrisy. Ahmed didn't drink, nor did he attempt to trick her.

If she went home, what then? The rage of her parents. School politics at Miss Milton's. Wanting to be as pretty as Sally, or as clever as Jane . . .

Of course she would see her friends again. But what was to stop her doing that as a married woman?

A few days here, in her own land, and Haya already felt her childhood slipping off her like a snake skin. She was grown; she had passed into womanhood. And the thought of Miss Milton's and schoolyard politics was ridiculous. She had left that behind her when she landed in Egypt.

Haya al-Yanna was a woman now. And she knew that she would one day marry. If not Ahmed, then whom?

True, Haya hadn't chosen him – yet. But Ahmed was demanding she do so, before he touched her.

What was there for her back in LA? Somebody more 'suitable'? More Anglo? Richer?

Haya put her fingers to her lip, tracing where his mouth had crushed hers. She felt weak with desire. Ahmed made her stomach churn, excited her in a way she'd never known before.

Right now, at this moment, Haya realized she had no desire to go home. If LA was still home. She knew that if she did go, she would never see Ahmed again.

Then what was her choice? To confirm the *nikkah*. To do it all over again . . . to go into him, and let Ahmed touch her . . .

Her lip trembled. She was afraid.

For ten minutes she sat there, paralysed, staring at the water that cascaded into the pond.

Then finally Haya rose, and went back into the house. She turned left under the peristyle, and climbed the stairs to the guest bedroom suite.

Ahmed was sitting in a carved wooden chair, piled with cushions, facing a western window, watching the sun set over the roofs of Cairo. A book lay open, face down on the mantelpiece.

'You have come to me, Haya?' he asked, without looking round.

'I don't know,' she said, and her voice wobbled.

Ahmed stood up, came over to her, and enfolded her in his arms, gently this time. Haya started to cry. She didn't know why, not exactly. But she was here, in Egypt, and it was strange, and her parents had sent her here. And she wasn't sure if she had fallen in love.

'Come on,' Ahmed said, when she had finished. He kissed her lightly on the top of the head. 'Do you want to be a tourist?'

'What?' she said, dabbing at her eyes.

'Let's go out to the pyramids,' he said. 'See the son et lumière. It's . . . what do you Americans say?'

'Cheesy?'

'Exactly. But it's fun.' He stood up and reached for a lambswool cloak, very fine, a soft pure grey, reminiscent of the one she had worn to Sally's party. 'The desert gets cold at night.'

'Thank you,' she said. 'And . . . I like it that you call me Haya.'

He was right; the desert was freezing. She was amazed at how bitter it was. Ahmed got them chairs at the back, and they sat together, the cloak thrown over them, watching the eerie green light over the pyramids, the booming voice of the announcer.

The head of the Sphinx reared, massive, in the spotlight. Haya gasped.

'Do you like it?'

'Like – that's not the word. I mean, I've seen pictures. But they are so inadequate.'

'This is your heritage,' he said. 'Not a sports car, or a hamburger.'

'Amazing,' she said.

'Tomorrow we will go and see it, in the day. And maybe next week we can take a boat. You must see the Valley of the Kings. But I won't overwhelm you. The tourists try to see all Egypt in seven days, and as a result see nothing. It blurs into one.'

'We'll take our time,' Haya said. She looked up at him; his profile was strong, his jaw set against the red and green lights on the sand. He was handsome; he cared for her. And she did not want to go home.

Already, home seemed distant, and a little tawdry.

'*We* will?' Ahmed turned his face to her, his dark eyes above hers. And Haya wanted, longed for him to bend down and kiss her. Her lips moistened, parted . . .

'No,' he said, softly. 'You did not sign the *nikkah*.'

'I did,' she said. 'I did . . .'

He lowered his mouth, close to her, not touching her. Teasing her, cruelly.

'Then who are you?'

'Haya,' she said, and now her voice was thick with desire. 'Haya . . . your wife . . .'

Still, he did not kiss her. And desire curled like smoke across her breasts and belly.

'Please, Ahmed,' she whispered.

He laughed, softly, and pressed his lips on hers; his arm around her back, supporting her, he kissed her, hard, this time, no teasing, his mouth almost crushing hers, his teeth on her lips, the hard muscles of his chest against her breasts.

Haya gasped; she felt lust flood through her.

Silently he rose and offered her his hand. Haya stumbled to her feet, blushing; it felt as if everybody could see her wanting him. Ahmed flung the cloak around her shoulders, and led her to the car, while the ghostly lights of the show danced over the ancient monuments behind them.

His home – their home, now, she supposed – was still, silent apart from the sounds of the birds and the fountains. Without the servants, it seemed very empty; and Haya felt Ahmed, his body, his strength, his nearness, now, exciting her and scaring her.

He turned to her in the garden. She opened her mouth to speak, but he put one finger across her lips, then scooped her up into his arms, as though she were light as silk, and carried her into the house, and up the stairs, and laid her down on the divan bed in their room, where the intricate shadows from the Moroccan lamp played across the walls.

'Ahmed.' Haya attempted a smile. 'Carrying me across the threshold?'

He did not smile back. The look he was giving her bored into her eyes. He reached down, and started to unbutton her dress, with one practised hand.

'Be gentle,' she said, gasping as his fingers stroked the soft flesh at the top of her breasts.

Ahmed lowered his mouth and kissed her again, hard.

'At first,' he replied. 'Only at first.'

Chapter Fifteen

'*Tisbah ala-kheir*,' Ahmed said quietly to her, when the moon was starting its descent over the palm trees in the garden, and Haya lay, drained, and sore, and deeply in love, in his arms. They were both sweaty, but she loved the scent of him, and did not want to let him go. 'Good night.'

'Good night,' she said, copying his Arabic. 'My darling.'

The next day, when she awoke after a deep sleep, Ahmed had ordered that breakfast be brought up to their room. He handed her an iced glass of juice, and watched her as she drank it, blushing, remembering what he'd done to her.

'Look at me,' he said.

Haya could hardly hold his eyes.

'Will you come home early?' she murmured, staring at the floor.

He put a calloused finger under her soft chin and tilted up her head, forcing her to stare into his eyes.

'I said look at me.'

Haya flushed; her breathing seemed to be coming raggedly. Ahmed put a hand to his wife, and she gasped.

'So eager,' he said, with a grin. 'I'm not going to work today. It's our honeymoon. And I want to show you what pleasure means.'

He led her into the shower later, and bathed with her, washing her, until she was so stimulated she had to reach for him again. Haya found her husband was exactingly patient, deliberate as a lover; he insisted on knowing every inch of her, and discovering what brought her to the boil.

Haya realized her world had been black and white. She could hardly cope with the feelings Ahmed induced. At times he was rough, and dominant; at other times gentle, erotic, slow with her. The day ticked by wonderfully slowly, and she lost herself to her body, and his body, and the ferocity of her newly awakened love.

Their first month together passed in a daze. Haya was beside herself; her emotions ran at fever pitch. Love of Ahmed, and desire for him, consumed her. And yet there was anger, which started slowly and simmered into rage, against her father. On the plane, what Baba and Mama had done hadn't seemed that important. But happy though she was now, Haya had grown furious that this major change had been done to her, that she had never had the chance to decide for herself to come here.

Baba had tricked her, and now she was in Egypt.

Every time she could not make herself understood in the marketplace, or one of the servants turned away from her, pretending her accent was too strange, Haya felt out of her depth. As though only Ahmed could protect her. And that, she hated.

Her period came and went, and came again. It seemed so wrong that she did not conceive, right away. She could hardly stay away from her husband. Ahmed was a dominant lover, not gentle, not soft, and he excited her, made her ready and hot in a way the dull American boys never had. Her passion excited him; her naked desire, visible to him even when she was fully robed, made Ahmed want her more; he was on her, all the time, taking her by surprise in the shower, locking the doors of their study, coming home from work at lunchtime, burning for his wife, and wanting to have her again.

Haya was unused to the sensations which rocked through her at his touch. She had never thought of herself as particularly sexual; never mooned over posters of the latest hot actors, like the other girls at school; never really considered men. And now she was addicted. The more he came to her, the more she wanted him.

Desire made her sick, almost. Haya was so feverish for Ahmed that she could not concentrate, could not get herself together. Her days and nights centred around wanting him. The depths of her responsiveness scared her.

And still there was no child. And as Haya stayed in the house, barely improving her Arabic, she became restless.

'I need to do something,' she said, after they had finished a sticky session of love-making one afternoon. 'Ahmed, I'm going stir crazy here. I was not made to sit still in a house, even a beautiful one, and I have no friends, nobody but you.' She missed her girlfriends, dreadfully. 'Maybe we should go back, the two of us, to America. Visit my parents. Have it out with Baba,' she added grimly.

'I can't.' He leaned over and kissed her on her naked stomach; she drove him crazy, lean and young and hungry for him. 'I can't take time off work. I already spent a week in LA before we came here. And you can't go.'

'I can do whatever I want.'

'No way. I'm not letting you out of my sight. I want you far too much for that.'

She softened, smiled.

'But you are going crazy. Even the birds in the garden fly elsewhere over the city.' He thought about it. 'Why don't you come with me? Into work.'

'Your work?'

'Yes, why not? Come and see what I do. Do you object to wearing the hijab?'

'Not at all.'

'The women in our workshops are very traditional. It

162

would save some questions . . .' He grinned. 'And anyway, your hair is so beautiful, I want it all to myself.'

'Fine by me.' Haya groaned, and pushed his hand away. 'Don't . . . Ahmed.'

'And why not?'

'We just did . . .'

'I remember.' But he was ready, again. The woman made him feel like a teenager. 'Come here.'

She rolled to him, eagerly.

Maybe it was better he take Haya to work, Ahmed thought. When he was away from her, he spent every moment looking for excuses to get out of the office. And he loved her, and did not want her to get bored, or restless. Until the children came along, *insh'Allah*, could it hurt? Why not? She was still a teenager, after all, even if she carried herself like a young woman.

Business would be a fascinating diversion. And it wouldn't last too long. Once his wife got pregnant, that was it.

'And this is the workshop.' Ahmed bowed, greeted the women that were sitting there, weaving; they smiled and nodded at Haya. 'They make some carpets here. Mostly, I deal with importers, or find goods myself. It is all in the eye. Come upstairs.'

She smiled at his workers and followed him up the wooden stairs. Every inch of the place was hung with beautiful carpets, and the storeroom smelled a little fusty.

'Mothballs,' he said, in answer to her question. 'Nothing works better. No technology, even today. Mothballs to keep the carpets from being eaten alive. And here we are, this is the showroom.'

'Amazing.'

It was. A long room, full of windows, but they had muslin drapes across them all. She understood; daylight would bleach out the precious fibres. Instead, even in the day, the room was gently lit with candles. Piles of gorgeous silk and woollen rugs lay on the floor, they hung from the walls, they were suspended from the ceiling. To counter the mothballs, he had placed scented oil burners in strategic places; there was a strong smell of frankincense.

'Do you want some tea, pastries?'

Haya was hungry; she nodded, shyly.

Pleased to be showing off his work, her husband nodded at an employee; the man disappeared into a side room, and returned with a silver tray holding a teapot, glasses, and a delicate selection of tiny cakes, placed on a lace napkin.

'We keep a kettle boiling for customers,' Ahmed explained. 'I serve them mint tea. It is a way of forcing them to stay, to take time, and then the beauty of the goods . . .' he shrugged. 'They sell themselves.'

As though to underline his point, there was a commotion downstairs. Haya recognized the guttural accents of German, stabbing at English.

'Would you like to watch?'

She nodded.

Ahmed bent down and kissed her on the cheek. It was a modest gesture, but he allowed the tip of his tongue to graze her cheek; he licked her, just a little, where the others couldn't see.

Desire rushed through her, electric, insistent. Haya struggled not to gasp; she forced a smile, and withdrew to the side of the room. She wanted to watch her husband in action; and she couldn't let anybody else know she was turned on . . .

There was a cushioned bench towards the back. Haya took away her tray, and busied herself pouring out the mint tea.

'Welcome. Come in.' Ahmed was smiling at his customers, but it was a smile without warmth. 'Would you care for some tea?'

'Thank you,' said the wife. She was rather fat and kept

her sunglasses on, even in the darkened room. Haya instantly disliked her.

Ahmed signalled to another employee; more cakes and tea were brought.

'Are you looking for anything in particular?'

'We're not going to pay over the odds,' the husband said, rudely.

'Of course not.' He glanced at Haya, and winked at her, quickly. 'You will find we offer excellent value. What size of carpet or rug are you looking for?'

'Something medium. That one.' The husband jabbed at a large red Persian silk carpet. 'Or something like that,' he added, pointing to a completely different Afghan kelim in bright blues and yellows.

'Ah yes,' Ahmed said, with a sigh. 'Two of the finest pieces in my collection. But you knew that, of course. Are you a dealer? We do special prices to the trade.'

'*Nein* . . . no . . .' The little man puffed out his cheeks, and his wife smirked. 'But I know quality when I see it.'

'Those rugs are very expensive. Can I show you something a little more moderate?' Ahmed nodded, and two workers swiftly ran forward and unfolded a large, extraordinarily fine Persian rug in creams and blues. Haya's eyes widened; she was no expert, but she saw it was antique, and worth many thousands, maybe ten thousand. Or possibly more. She'd seen one in Saks just like it.

'No thank you.' The clipped tones were full of disdain. 'Don't try to fob me off with that cheap stuff. It's clearly inferior. How much for the yellow one?'

Ahmed shook his head, sadly. 'That one is over four thousand euros.'

'A thousand,' he barked. 'Not a cent more.'

Haya grinned, and ate a pastry. Fat fool! Her husband was going to fleece this idiot. He'd been so rude and aggressive, he deserved it.

She hated that sense of moral superiority they'd come in here with. As though they were instantly going to be cheated. Well, their insults had created the fact. And she was glad. If she had watched Ahmed bow and scrape, and allow himself to be talked down to, it would have changed them, her and him, forever. How could she feel as owned, as possessed by him as she did, surrender herself to him, if he were weak with other people?

Instead, he was expertly slicing these obnoxious tourists up. Not boorishly, with violence. But deftly, with words. And it was not theft, they were paying only what they wanted to.

She listened carefully. He did not lie, or tell them the kelim was a work of art. Instead he praised its general qualities. And why not? It was a perfectly workmanlike rug. Haya would not have expected a man like her husband to give house room to anything else. But it was worth nothing like what they were paying for it.

What fools, she thought. Demeaning another people, a great people, just because they saw them as poorer. It was an instructive lesson in manners.

As they went through the motions, paying with a credit card, filling out customs forms, Haya drank her tea, and drank in her surroundings. Beautiful carpets, impressive. Ahmed had a good business, she could see. Large offices, a staff, a comfortable house, prosperity, and servants.

She thought about herself. Now she was his wife, they were a team; they could be more.

She was here, and married, very happily. Against the odds. She had never thought it could happen. Her parents' choice . . . Far more importantly, her own.

But she had tasted fun and independence in America, as well as romance in Egypt. Why give that up? Why put all those dollars spent on her education to waste?

Haya didn't see why Ahmed should stay here,

comfortable, prosperous, a man trading well within his limits. She admired him. But couldn't he be more? And even if Haya was Ahmed's, in his arms, outside them, she was her own woman. His wife.

Couldn't *they* be more?

The fat Germans left, talking loudly in their own language. Haya didn't know the words, but she recognized the tone, the same sneering contempt they had walked in with. Probably laughing at how they had ripped off the poor little carpet merchant . . .

She was surprised to find a sudden surge of anger, almost violent loathing, ripping through her. She wanted to kill them. No . . . she wanted to *show* them.

'So what did you think?'

Ahmed, slipping back into Arabic, came over to his wife, grinning. 'Happy customers, no? And so generous. Eighteen hundred, in the end, for that hundred and fifty euro kilim.'

'You are a wonderful businessman.' She leaned across, put her lips up to him, and kissed him. 'And your carpets are magnificent.'

'Thank you, darling.'

Haya ran her hand possessively over his sleeve.

'Do you think I could be involved?'

'Involved?'

'Help you. With the business. I have better English . . . I know America. My father could get some contacts. Maybe you could export.'

Ahmed, surprised, smiled back at her.

'That would be good. I'd like you to take an interest.' He slid his hands up and down her waist, resting his fingertips on the underside of her breasts, stroking lightly.

Haya shuddered with pleasure, but pulled away, glancing downstairs in case one of the workers came up.

'That way you could be with me all day.' He released her breasts, but laid a hand casually against the flat of her stomach, letting her know he could feel the warm blood pooling there, hot under the skin, her belly tense with desire. Ahmed bent down, placed his mouth against her ear, and Haya pressed herself against his hand, her knees buckling.

'Please,' she murmured. 'Take me home . . .'

'I should make you wait,' he whispered.

'Please, Ahmed . . .'

He straightened, and called to his staff that they were going home for lunch.

'Working together. An excellent plan.' He grinned.

He left her at three, bemoaning his lack of self-control. But Ahmed was so slow, so patient, a master at heating her and re-heating her. He could awaken desire when Haya thought she was drained. The Lord only knew when, exactly, they would do *business* . . .

Haya was excited at the prospect. The last of her doubts had lifted with it. Now she would go to America, too, see her family and her old friends. A wave of guilt ran through her at her immolation here, lost in Ahmed to the exclusion of all else. But since he was the first, the only man in her life, the other girls would understand, wouldn't they? It had only been a few months. Extended honeymoon, if you like.

Haya dialled Jane's number, squaring her shoulders, preparing to get a blast for being out of touch for so long. She knew she deserved it!

'The number you have called is not in service,' said a tinny American voice. 'Please check the number and dial again.'

She did. Same message. Damn it, Haya thought. Jane had changed her phone number. Had it transferred back to the Embassy in Washington?

Never mind, Sally would know. She rang Green Gables. This time the phone did ring.

'Wasserman residence. May I help you?'

'I'm sorry; I must have the wrong number. I was looking for the Lassiter residence.'

There was a pause.

'They don't live here any longer, ma'am.'

Haya blinked. 'OK – sorry—'

But the caller had hung up.

She felt bad. Just a few months and both her friends had changed numbers? It was Haya's own fault for not staying in touch. OK, first she'd been embarrassed, but once she'd fallen in love with Ahmed, decided to stay married . . .

Haya thought for a moment, then dialled the British Embassy in Washington.

'I'm looking for Jane Morgan, daughter of Ambassador Thomas Morgan. I'm a friend of hers.'

'We have no information on her whereabouts.'

Haya tried again. This was fruitless.

'Look, I went to school with her at Miss Milton's in Los Angeles. I've been out of touch . . . I got married. I'm in Egypt. She's not at her house they rent in Malibu. I called our friend Sally Lassiter—'

'Just a second please.'

Haya waited. There was a click, and another voice came on the line; cool, modulated English tones.

'This is Emmeline Berkley. I was Ambassador Morgan's private secretary. Can I help you?'

Haya explained.

'Yes, I remember Miss Morgan mentioning you. And you left the country . . .'

'Three months ago.'

There was a sigh.

'I regret to have to tell you,' she said, not unkindly, 'that we've lost track of Jane Morgan. Miss Morgan had herself legally emancipated as an adult, and after that we had no responsibility for her. I believe she is somewhere in Los

Angeles still, but I have no contact information. I'm sorry.'

'Oh. I see. Poor Jane,' Haya gasped. Now she really did feel low. 'I have to find her. I'll contact Sally . . .'

'Sally Lassiter? That was Miss Morgan's other close friend?'

'Yes,' Haya said anxiously, not liking her tone.

'Then you might not have heard . . . Mr Lassiter's oil company collapsed, and I'm afraid he had a heart attack. The government confiscated the assets, it was rather a big scandal.'

Haya's knuckles tightened around the phone. Sally had been close to her father, very close.

'And where are Mrs Lassiter and Sally?'

'The press reports said they went to Texas.' There was a touch of real sympathy in the firm tones now. 'I'm sorry, that's all I know.'

'Thanks for your help,' Haya said, and hung up.

Well, there was nothing she could do now. Nothing she could do from Egypt, anyway. Haya was wracked with guilt. Both her friends had lost parents – not that Jane's had been much use. And Sally, glorious confident Sally, how on earth would she cope? Life without money . . . Haya couldn't imagine it. Sally had even had her own personal limo and chauffeur.

She gave herself a little shake. No point in beating herself up, she had to get on with it now, travel back to the States and find them. She could set up some contacts for Ahmed while she was about it. Haya was convinced of her husband's eye, his drive and talent. He needed to swim in a bigger pond. And she needed to find her friends.

Chapter Sixteen

Haya took it slowly, at first. A week or two meeting the staff, getting to know Ahmed's stock, his prices, how he found his carpets. Brushing up on her written Arabic, learning how he kept his books; the old-fashioned way, in leather-bound volumes. Her husband was a visionary, and in love with the beauty of the things he sold. Haya's first move was to buy a computer, enter all his data onto spreadsheets, and start filing on his customer base. Ahmed didn't like it much, but she ignored him, and kept plugging away. And within a few days he was staring, amazed, at the simple, easy system she had set up, and then trying to use it himself.

Haya called her father. They had a long, stilted conversation. She decided to avoid talking about the marriage. What was the use? He would only act defensive. Instead, Haya demanded her father's assistance.

That was the price of forgiveness. She didn't say it openly, but they both understood it, just the same.

Baba, chastened by her tone, promised he would help. He could set up some meetings, talk to some people who knew people, that sort of thing. There were exhibitions, trade fairs. Retailers, although many of them already had suppliers . . .

'We will undercut their suppliers,' Haya said, ruthlessly. 'Tell them that.'

Ahmed, overhearing, grinned. 'And once they're hooked, the price goes up.'

He kissed his wife on the forehead. She was intelligent,

and now she was a true help to him. No more long nights grappling with his books in the fading light. No more riffling through his papers to find the right number. She had even helped him with his taxes.

He liked it. Last week, Ahmed had gone on an acquisition trip to Fez, and without rushing things the way he was used to, had picked up better stock at lower prices.

And it turned him on to see his intelligent, dark-haired wife, the scarf draped modestly over her hair, concentrating on the figures, her fingers flashing over the keyboard. She was not one to stay at home, or spend her days gossiping with friends. She engaged with the world, and her spirit was fiery, the same fire that clawed at him and writhed under him in their marriage bed . . .

It was his business, of course; he was in charge. But Haya argued her case, and Ahmed listened to her.

'I have some ideas,' Haya said, one evening, after a fine sale. Ahmed had won an order from an Egyptian hotel chain in Sharm El Sheik, a large order for their lobbies and conference rooms; he had supplied pieces worth forty thousand dollars. They were flush with cash. He had been half expecting her to pounce on it.

'What do you mean?'

'Business ideas. I think you should change.'

'Change?' Ahmed blinked. 'Change what? This works, my love. I've been doing it since I was younger than you.'

'Not the goods . . . well, maybe. Maybe we could diversify.' Ahmed frowned at that, so she hurried on. 'But I think you should find a new way to sell. Don't deal with these little people. They are not worth your time, my sweetheart.' She kissed his arm through the fabric of his shirt. 'You need to do it differently, to sell these beautiful carpets the way they are meant to be sold. Each individually. Displayed like a jewel. We need to find more customers like the hotels, and fewer like Begum Sistanti.' The rich, fat widow of the Interior Minister, who always came back to them when she bought a new villa or Parisian apartment, probably with ill-gotten gains from the taxpayer.

Ahmed was listening, she saw. Emboldened, she ploughed on. 'They should be given space in windows, each one selling for many, many thousands. Why should you not be like the owner of a gallery?' Her Arabic was rough, but she continued. 'They give stories to their artwork. Provenance . . . catalogues. You can sell your carpets that way. They are all unique. Why should arrogant tourists from Europe, with no appreciation of them, buy them and place them in their homes?'

He smiled, but his eyes were intrigued.

'And how would you propose to do this?'

'We must export,' she said, confidently. 'To America. To the quality stores. Perhaps first to a gallery. Somewhere very expensive.' Haya switched to English. 'You know that American expression? "Sell the sizzle, not the steak." My friend Sally taught me that.'

He chuckled. 'I like that.'

'I can help,' she insisted. 'I speak perfect English. I also know them, the richest Americans; what they want, what sells to them. Let me be your export director. Let me work for you.'

Ahmed's arm stole around her waist. 'You *do* work for me.'

'That's not work.'

'And I told you, I don't want you leaving me for the States. Even for a week.'

'Then come with me,' she said, persuasively. 'Come with me. I can teach you better English. The same way you teach me Arabic. And I know people. I've spoken to my father . . .'

He thought about it. 'You really think I could sell these better?'

'No question,' she said confidently.

Ahmed leaned down and kissed her, hard, on the lips. 'Then let us try it,' he said.

He believed in his wife. She was young, but she was brilliant. There was that core in her that a man could rely on. They could be partners in business, as well as in life. Let her give him that start, and he would take over. Soon, anyway, she would be preoccupied in the nursery.

'Can I call home again?' Haya said, beaming.

He was mildly offended. 'I've never stopped you.'

'Then you have no objection? I can tell Baba we're coming?'

Ahmed leaned in to her. 'Since almost the first night, I believed in you, Haya. Let's try it.'

Chapter Seventeen

It was amazing how fast Sally's world collapsed.

Her father's death leaked by somebody in that scum-sucking nest of lawyers. It was on the radio and hit the TV before anybody placed a call to Green Gables. Mona had been in the beauty parlour. Her chauffeur had hustled her out and driven her home, sobbing, chased by the paparazzi.

Sally herself had refused to believe it. She'd rushed out of school – nobody daring to tease her, not even Julie, not that day, at least – demanding loudly to talk to the police, then calling them liars as they tried to pass on the news.

As long as she lived, Sally would never forget that day. The howling rage of her loss, the sick feeling in the pit of her stomach. The photographers, like locusts, camped outside the gates of her house; news helicopters chopping loudly overhead, their intrusive spotlights beaming down into their lawns. Rushing in to hug her wailing, disintegrating mother, turning off the TV that showed her father's ample body being loaded onto a gurney, wrapped up in a blue tarpaulin.

'They shouted at me,' Mona choked out. 'They called me the merry widow.'

Even in her grief, Sally had felt the rage rising, blocking the air from her throat so she could hardly breathe. Bastards! Some wiseass had yelled her way, when her white car was entering the gates, 'Hey, baby! Are you the richest heiress in America?'

What the hell did he know? she thought, tears brimming

and helplessly tumbling down her cheeks. Didn't he understand she didn't give a damn about money? That she'd trade every red cent for one more minute with her daddy's arms around her?

For the first time in her golden, charmed life, Sally Lassiter experienced grief and loss. The devastation almost overwhelmed her. Every moment, thinking how that was it, she'd never speak to her father again. Not in this world. Not for all the days of her life. He'd never walk her down the aisle, never hold her children . . .

It was bad. The pain was a hurricane, battering at the hatches of her heart and dignity.

And it was all going to get much, much worse.

The next months were a haze of pain and fear. First the funeral – long-lost relatives, people Sally never saw from one end of the year to another, crawling out of the woodwork; charities, colleges, lobbyists, all calling with their palms out, grubbing for cash. Sally, throwing dirt and a rose on to Daddy's coffin. Walking away from that graveside. Trying to support her mother, who was falling apart.

And after that grim event, worse to come. The lawyers – first her own, then the government's. And the companies. The executors, and the insurers.

Her father, she discovered, was accused. Fraud and embezzlement on a massive scale. Thousands of workers had lost their pensions, ordinary families bankrupt. Her mother – who could hardly sleep and at times barely dress herself, who had stopped washing, or brushing her teeth, or combing her hair – Sally took care of her as though she were a child. Her mother offered nothing but a blank, Valium-induced stare.

And so the police and the investigators talked to Sally. And roamed through her house. Rifled everywhere, like burglars, looking for documents. Took away every computer. Impounded her parents' cars.

She dropped out of school, and hired her own lawyer. Not for long, though; the federal government froze their bank accounts. And the worst thing was that as she forced herself to watch the news, long after Mona had crawled into bed, Sally couldn't blame them.

Sick with dismay, she was forced to confront the idea that her father might have been a crook, that the luxury they lived in might have been built on the suffering of others. Her father's lawyer, Lionel Javits, promised her privately it was not that way, and Sally clung to that.

'He died right in front of me. You could say of shock.'

'Shock,' Sally repeated.

The lawyer spoke compassionately, but slowly, as though she were stupid; he does think I'm dumb, Sally's brain told her. Dumb blonde. The old classic.

'There were thieves in that company, Sally, but your dad wasn't one of 'em.'

'And this house?'

He flinched away from her cool gaze and stared at his hands.

'Please tell me the truth, Mr Javits,' Sally said, her soft Texan tones demanding his respect. 'My mother's having a hard time with this. The police and FBI come around here every day. The staff already quit because I can't pay their wages. Tell me what's going on, and I can make a plan to deal with it.'

That impressed him – his own children, his teenage boys with their Metallica jackets and studs in the ears, they would never be able to cope, never be as strong as this golden butterfly with the weight of the world dropped on her slender shoulders.

'It's not something you can make a plan for. Your father didn't realize, but the oil profits that paid for this estate were built on paper. What my office is hearing is that the government is about to repossess.'

'Can we fight that?'

'Not in my judgement. They've seized all the liquid assets of the estate. This is next. No lawyer can make a case that this,' he waved a hand inadequately around the vastness of their kitchen, 'that this is necessary as a dwelling.'

Sally drew herself up. 'I see.' She paused, mulling it over, the dreadful news in all its bitterness. 'And what will they leave us with?'

'Nigel Farrar is the prosecutor. He's oily, looks slick on TV, wants to run for Congress . . .'

'Wants to look tough on criminals?'

Javits nodded. 'I'm very sorry, but he gets good press if you and your mother are left with nothing.' He sighed. 'Like all the other Lassiter Oil families.'

'Nothing? No settlement?'

'He has an excellent case. The longer you drag it out, the better he likes it. Your mother can try innocent spouse relief, but they'll never let you keep above a token amount.'

Sally stood up. 'When are they going to do this to us?'

'Maybe next week. Is there somewhere else you can go?'

'You mean that Daddy didn't own? Not really.'

'Believe me, Sally, Nigel Farrar wants a circus. I think you should do your best to get out of here. Go stay with friends.'

Ouch. That cut. Friends. Where were they?

Helen had run off to get married, and Jane – Jane was dealing with her own troubles. Sally felt the abandonment almost physically.

'I tell you what,' she said slowly. 'Can you negotiate with them for me? My mom's got some jewellery . . .'

'Anything Mr Lassiter gave her is forfeit.'

'No. Her own. She was a society belle back home. Brought some into the marriage.' Sally almost choked on it. 'I have a diamond brooch I can give you for a fee. You go to the prosecutor and get us free and clear on my mother's personal savings account – that was frozen too. It was a dowry, she never touched it. There's fifty thousand dollars in there.'

Fifty thousand – that used to be the wage of their live-in chef. All of a sudden, it looked like it was all she had left in the world.

'I can do that.' Javits thought about offering to represent her pro bono, but he was not a strong man, and it wouldn't have looked good. He didn't want to damage his reputation.

'Thank you,' the glorious blonde creature said, with a calm smile that made him feel four feet tall.

'Where will you go?' he asked, wretchedly.

'My mom has a niece in Texas. We'll go live near her. It's a small town, very quiet.' Cheap too, Sally didn't say. 'I'll go get that diamond pin for you, Mr Javits, and you get that account unlocked.'

Javits worked fast. And so did Sally. Once her mind was made up, there was nothing more to do. She called Jane, asked her to come round and help her pack.

'I'm so sorry.' Jane stood by, feeling useless, as Sally packed up her suitcases with a brisk efficiency that Jane had never known.

'Wasn't your fault.' Red-eyed, her friend bent down and zipped up the last of the cases. 'And I'm so sorry for what happened to your father, too.'

'Yeah, well,' Jane said, her throat dry. 'I never had much of a dad to start with.'

'My daddy was perfect.' Sally bit down hard, on her lip, and Jane turned away so she could compose herself. After a moment's struggle, Sally straightened herself, and surveyed her room: all mind-blowing luxury, a Barbie palace, with designer dresses, pink silk walls, a four-poster bed, enough sweetness to give you a toothache. The ultimate girlie paradise.

'You're strong,' Sally said. 'Give me a hand to load up these cases, hon?'

Jane hesitated. 'But we're not done packing.'

'Yes we are.'

'We need another case – your toys, your bear . . .' She held up the much-loved fluffy brown teddy with the lopsided eye. 'You can't leave Mr Snuffles, Sal. Come on!'

Her friend shook her head and lifted the largest suitcase.

'Yes I can.' She nodded for Jane to do the same. 'I don't need him any more. My childhood is over. It's time to grow up.'

The girls lugged the heavy cases down the long stairs, one by one, and loaded them into the back of the rented van.

'Long drive,' Jane observed. 'Sure you won't fly?'

'I don't want to face them at the airport.' They both knew she was talking about reporters. 'By the time we get to Texas, this story will be done. Something else will have happened. I don't need to expose Momma to a plane full of angry people.'

In truth, Sally didn't want to expose her mother to people. Period. Mona was losing it, and Sally couldn't bear for her to be seen in public.

'So what about you?' Anything to change the subject. She dragged her thoughts away from her disintegrating mother, and fixed her pretty blue eyes on Jane. 'Going to DC?'

'Yes,' Jane lied. Why burden Sally with the knowledge that she was staying in LA entirely alone?

'Right.' Sally hopped from foot to foot. She wanted to get the hell in the car, get in and drive; go and wake her mother from the drunken stupor she was doubtless sunk into.

But that would be so final. DC. Texas. They might as well be in outer space.

'Hey.' Jane read her thoughts. 'We're best friends. We'll find each other.'

'I'll write you with our new address, OK?'

'OK,' Jane agreed.

'I'll send it care of the Embassy.'

'Sure. That works.'

'And Helen?'

'When she finishes her honeymoon she'll be in touch. You bet.'

'Friends forever,' Sally said. She tried for brave, but her voice quivered.

'Forever,' Jane repeated. She enveloped Sally in a big bear hug and, so unlike her, gave her a little kiss on the cheek.

'I'll go get my mom. I better scoot. I hate goodbyes.'

'This isn't goodbye,' Jane insisted. 'It's "see you later".'

Sally nodded, not trusting herself to say anything else, and ran back into Green Gables to find her mother.

When she was out of sight, Jane quietly crept in behind her. She walked up to Sally's room, retrieved the teddy bear, and came back to the van, slipping it into the largest case. This was her sweeter side, her vulnerable side. But Sally's unhappiness brought the tenderness out.

She wanted Sal to have a friend, because right now Jane thought she'd never see her again.

Chapter Eighteen

'Well, now.' Emily Harris glanced from Sally to Mona, and Sally squirmed inwardly.

They were sitting uncomfortably on her cousin Emily's velvet antebellum sofa, in a small, richly decorated, and soulless guest parlour, and Sally felt as out of place as a beggar in a ballroom. Her cousin was stiffly, properly dressed in a white poplin blouse and long cotton skirt, but Mona was a wreck. Sally had done her best to clean Mom up this morning, before they checked out of the final hotel; forcing her to brush her teeth and swig with mouthwash, although she suspected Mona was swallowing the minty stuff just to get the alcohol; eight per cent, as good as beer. Washing her hair was no-go – Sally wasn't strong enough to physically wrestle her mother, so she had to make do with scarfing a brush through it, tying it into a ponytail and dousing it with hairspray. At least that should take care of some of the dirty, sweaty smell. Mona had agreed to get in the shower; a small mercy, though Sally looked and saw she wasn't washing, just standing there, slumped against a wall, as the water sluiced over her.

In truth, Sally was frightened. Depression had turned Mona into another person. A helpless, sick person, listless and lifeless. If her mom had her way, she'd never even get out of bed.

The speed and shock of loss was too much for her mother to deal with. The loss of the only man she'd ever loved had devastated Mona, but then came everything else on top, and it finished her. The scandal, the shame, TV headlines – and all her fair-weather friends melting away like New York slush in April.

As the money vanished, so did Mona's support network. Half of them dropped her before the funeral, afraid to be pictured on the news at the graveside of a world-class crook. The other half vanished one by one as the lawyers and federal government closed down their accounts. Susan Ermine, her mother's supposed best friend and wife of a senator, suddenly discovered she had to be in Washington. Milly Fawcett and her husband disappeared on a 'round the world' cruise. Lola Montez actually called Mona, said the family had deceived them, and they were no longer friends. Her mother had cried then, shocked for a second out of her apathy. But Sally was fiercely grateful to Lola. At least that one had some guts. At least she'd told them the truth.

The Lassiters, once the billionaire kings of Beverly Hills, were pariahs. And Sally could see the same, wary, disgusted look in the eyes of her cousin Emily. Dad's niece had married exceptionally well, into an old Carolina family, and disapproved of her aunt, the brash, working-class barmaid that Paulie Lassiter had plucked out of the gutter twenty years ago.

'Well,' she repeated, and her smile was bright and cold. 'It certainly is a surprise to see y'all here. What can I do for you?'

'We've left LA for good,' Sally said, taking the lead. 'We're going to settle back home. In Texas. Near family.'

Family, right. What a joke. The only family Sally had was sitting next to her, staring into space.

'I don't know if that's such a good idea,' Cousin Emily said, smiling all the brighter. 'Surely you have friends back in LA. You're hardly Texans any more.'

'I was born here,' Sally countered. 'Spent my childhood

here. I'm as Texan as you are. And of course you're one of our nearest relations.'

There it was. She waited to see what her cousin would say. Emily was a mighty rich woman, not oil rich, but plantation rich; her dead husband had left her plenty of land and some big condo developments. She was in a position to turn their lives around, if she chose to. A grace and favour apartment. A nice car. An office job, something undemanding, to occupy Mona's time.

'I think we better get some things straight,' the older woman responded. 'When Uncle Paulie left for California, well, some of us thought that was best. There was distance, you understand. We were never very close. Y'all never visited me here, and I never came to you. We're not really family in that sense. And I have to tell you, Mona,' she turned and addressed her remarks, coldly, to the glassy-eyed woman propped against a corner of her couch, 'that I'm really highly disappointed in you and my uncle. You stole from hard-working families—'

Sally jumped up. 'Daddy did no such thing!'

A long sigh. 'That's not what the federal government says. And now y'all turn up here, poor as church mice, disgraced . . . I declare, Mona, if I don't smell liquor on your breath at ten o'clock in the morning. Well, I think it's just too bad.'

'I see. Thank you for your hospitality.' Sally tossed her golden hair, defiantly. 'Come on, Momma. We're leaving.'

'I'm sorry, but I think it's better to get these things straight. I have a position in society . . .'

'Yes.' Sally gave a mighty heave and hauled her mother to her feet. 'It's better to know where we stand. You're certainly not family. And yes, you are sorry. A sorry excuse for a Christian woman.'

The tears were threatening now. She was tired, exhausted. Her back hurt from days of driving, she had

184

nowhere to go, and her last hope was looking at her with total contempt.

'Please leave,' said Emily Harris, flushing with anger.

'Don't worry. We won't bother you again.' Sally thrust up her chin, her slim shoulders set firm. 'And I won't forget this, either.'

'That's as may be,' said her cousin, following closely behind as Sally dragged Mona, stumbling, to the door. 'But I'm certainly going to forget you. Your family has embarrassed us all.'

Sally pushed her mother out of the sweeping, gracious porch that had looked so welcoming when they first arrived, all whitewashed wood, cane sofas and heaped cushions; an old-fashioned Southern veranda.

'Don't come back here,' Emily shouted, as Sally opened up the van and helped her mother inside. 'We have security.'

And she slammed the door.

'Now what?' Mona asked, as Sally, brushing away the tears, angrily spun the van around. 'Where do we go? My head hurts.'

'Don't worry, Momma.' Sally refused to give in; mingling with her embarrassment and fear was a sense of white-hot anger, and she used that anger to keep her strong. 'We'll be OK. We have some money, enough to rent a place. Look.' She turned left, into Hartford, the nearest signposted town, and slowed as they reached main street. 'This place has everything.' Sally gestured as they rode by. 'Look, a drugstore . . . banks . . . a post office . . . rail station.' It was small, and the houses were not all that big – a place for the working middle-classes, Sally assessed instantly. Which was just what they were, as of now.

Sweetwater. An anonymous American town. It even had a high school. Perfect.

'Let's pull over, get a local paper,' Sally decided. 'I'll have a house legally rented by the end of the day. This is home.' She glanced at her mother, who was watching the dashboard, betraying no interest.

'We'll be happy here,' Sally insisted, bravely. But even she didn't believe it.

She worked hard. First, finding a place. That afternoon, Sally trooped round apartments – mostly rundown, with the paint peeling off the walls – and houses, some with leaking roofs or mould. In the end, forced to raise her price, she found a two-bedroom tract home, on the edge of Hartford's main road, near a drugstore and a garage. Poor location, but all the basics; neat, clean, with no more than a square patio to look after in the back. Sally put down three months' rent to avoid a credit check, and breathed a sigh of relief. The utilities were connected. There were no roaches. It was poor, yes, but respectable. And she could afford to rent there for a couple of years, at least.

Mona was making noises about going to the local bar, so although Sally hated herself, she went out and bought liquor, cheap gut-rot vodka, in the forlorn hope it would turn her mother's stomach. And not at the liquor store, either; she could just imagine what gossip would do in a one-horse joint like this. They'd go crazy over the new arrivals, a mom and daughter whose first stop was to pick up alcohol in a brown paper bag! Instead, Sally went to the grocery store, passed the time of day with the clerk, and shopped, for almost the first time in her life; awkwardly putting groceries into the trolley, trying to learn the prices of different brands. She picked up milk, eggs, cheeses, and fruit; meat was expensive, so she bought spaghetti and mince for bolognaise. Simple; she'd liked to cook, at times, as a hobby, and that would be cheaper than prepared sauces.

She also bought bread, and a few little luxuries. The exhaustion had not dissipated, but Sally was discovering the fire she had in her belly. Damn it all, she was going to survive. One step at a time. Get a little money, rent a normal house, fill the refrigerator. And they were not going to live like slobs. For only a couple dollars, she picked up pretty scented soaps and some potpourri. Candles could come later – Sally didn't trust Mom not to knock them over and set the place on fire.

In the discount racks, Sally found other things. A couple of framed samplers. Cheesy, perhaps, but this way they would have art on the walls, not just bare white space.

She came home to find Momma passed out on the couch. That was a relief. Sally quietly unpacked, and took a long, hot, relaxing shower. Then she stashed away the suitcases and left a note on the table. She drove out of town to a Shop Smart they'd passed on the way in. That place was paradise for shoppers down on their luck. For an hour or so Sally forgot her troubles; she scoured the aisles, looking for bargains, looking for bright, stylish touches – a five-dollar rug, some artificial silk roses, a white wicker wastebasket, fluffy towels for the bathroom, over-sized and under-priced.

When she got back, Mona was still snoring. Her limbs drained, Sally nonetheless managed to unpack, hammer, and hang; to make the beds, fluff the cushions, lay out the towels, put the toothbrushes in the holder.

By the time she was done, it was late. Sally walked around the house, with the blinds down, a grim little smile on her face. On less than seventy dollars, she'd made the place look normal; it was cheerful and clean, a respectable, basic house.

Quite an achievement. She thought of her mother, staggering around motel rooms, knocking over full ashtrays the maids hadn't bothered to clean. When she woke, hungover, it would be in a proper house for a family to live in. Not what they were used to, but miles away from Skid Row.

She undressed, carefully slipped on her pyjamas, and tumbled into bed, enjoying the feel of the brand-new sheets. Tomorrow there was lots to do. Return the hire vehicle, buy a new one, register for school, contact the lawyer . . .

Sally knew her father was proud of her. Misery probed at her, but she was too tired to dwell on the past. Tomorrow was the start of a new, tough life, but she knew she could handle it. She slipped into a deep sleep.

'Mom . . .' She hated the way her voice sounded, all whining and pleading. 'You don't need that.'

'Hey.' Mona gripped the vodka bottle, all the way to the sink. She swayed in her slippers. 'Don't lecture me, missy. I can't stand it when you get all uppity.'

'You've already had too much.'

A fat tear of self-pity rolled down her mother's cheek.

'Why can' you leave me alone?' she slurred. 'Can' I have a lil bit of pleasure left in this world . . . He's gone . . . he's gone.'

'I know.' Sally fought back her own tears. 'He's gone, Mom. And he'd hate to see you like this.'

Mona reached out to grab the sink to steady herself, missed, and fell over; the vodka bottle slipped from her grasp and smashed on the floor. She burst into loud, drunken tears.

'We gotta go out,' she whined. 'Gotta go out and get some more. I don't have no more here.'

Thank God, thought Sally.

She went over to her mother, carefully picking her way through the broken glass.

'Never mind, Momma. I'll clear that up. You come with me. Just take a little lie-down . .'

'Yeah . . . lie down.'

'This way.' Sally was a slightly built girl, but she was strong, and getting stronger. Hauling Mona's dead weight around was something she did a lot of lately.

'I don' feel so good . . .'

Mona was turning a nasty shade of green. Hastily, Sally shoved her into the loo. Thank God it was downstairs.

'Go ahead, you'll feel better . . .'

Mona had already slipped to her knees and was puking violently.

Sally leaned back against the wall and tried to count her blessings. This was gross, but at least her momma was getting it out now. She was frightened that one day Mona would fall asleep and choke on her own vomit, like a seventies rock star but without the glamour. Or just die of alcohol poisoning.

She'd drawn down the blinds. Their house was now permanently shuttered, and they lived in a darkened, gloomy atmosphere, like a Spielberg movie just before the aliens come. But Sally had learned to cope with just the cracks of sunlight that beamed through the dusty windows. No way did she want any of the neighbours to see her mom looking like this. Worse still, the press . . .

They had come crawling around here, those damn vultures. Sally had learned to manage them. When they door-stepped her on her way to her new public school, Sally would just smile and say that she was settling in, and her mother was still in mourning. That it was a beautiful neighbourhood. That her daddy always taught her to take the lemons of life and make herself some lemonade.

And then she would politely remind the snapper that she was still a minor, on her way to school. Could they please back off?

That always worked. Whether it was from fear of legal action or shame, they left her alone.

The tabloid articles were out there. With their pictures.

'Brave Sally, starting over.' 'Sally Lassiter, staying strong for Mom.' It was human interest, and at least it was better than the alternative – nasty realms of print, castigating her and her mother for living off the backs of the poor.

There was some of that too, of course; the shrieking phone calls, late at night, the hate mail, notes from people swearing her mother was a greedy bitch, that they had money stashed away in Switzerland or the Caymans. Sally tried to remember that these folk had lost everything. Lassiter Oil Inc. had collapsed, the pensions of the workers had evaporated, and her dad's old buddies at the top were mostly in jail.

Good – she'd rather have seen them dead. They were murderers – they'd killed her darling father.

And events were killing her mother.

Sally dealt with grief. She had to. There was only room for one invalid in the family, and Momma had taken that slot. While Sally tried to piece things together, just the most basic stuff – talking to law enforcement, swearing out depositions, arguing with the bankruptcy courts – Mona had dived into the clear, numbing depths of her vodka bottle, and she wasn't coming out any time soon.

But Sally had discovered within herself a core of stone. A parting gift from her dad, perhaps.

Sally knew she was not brilliant, like Jane, or even smart, like Helen; Helen, so graceful and diplomatic, aristocratically feminine; Jane, the librarian Limey, both girls far more sophisticated than the pretty Texas rose who'd had life handed to her on a plate.

But Sally had something. Something more than long blond hair, flawless limbs and a tan. Sally had street smarts. She knew how to sell herself, and how to sell situations.

Despite it all, she had managed – still was managing – to change the story from 'embezzler's widow' to 'brave survivors'. She had negotiated a settlement with the IRS that left them without any more creditors, at least. And she learned how to shop on a budget. Sally took care of school enrolment, and signing Mom up for benefits and Medicaid.

Sally wasn't embarrassed to go on welfare; she couldn't afford to be.

The most important thing was to look after Momma. Sally didn't mind the press stalking her; but she couldn't bear them to see the wreck of her mom, a slovenly drunk, hell bent on killing herself and oblivious to shame.

No. Although no reporters had been round for months now, Sally drew the blinds. Just in case.

As Mona retched and heaved, Sally glanced around their home. This was getting to be a routine. Put Momma to bed, force her to drink a glass of water and choke down two aspirins, then clean the place while her mother snored in a drunken stupor.

She was getting to like cleaning. It gave her a very small sense of control. At least their home would not be a disgrace.

Mona gave one more dry heave and collapsed.

Sally quietly went to the sink, moistened a flannel, and washed her mother's face. She flushed the loo, and heaved her mom back into the living room. Mona had already passed out – no way to get her up the stairs.

Carefully Sally laid her mother on her side, in case she was sick again, and put a blanket over her. No water – she was unconscious.

Then she went upstairs, to her own room. To think.

Sally's room was a little haven. A tiny box, sure; her dressing room at home had been twice as big. But she had decorated it as best she could with cheap touches from Wal-Mart, little pink cushions and swatches of gauze; it had fresh flowers on the window sill, her clothes hung neatly in the wardrobe, and she had candles to give the place a soft glow at night. It smelled good and looked fresh, and Sally hung a framed photo of Laguna Beach, California, right over her desk.

There was a calendar underneath that picture, and she noticed the next day was ringed. Oh. Right. Her birthday.

Yeah, she thought, morosely. Happy birthday. To me.

A year out here. A year of suffering. Of being ogled by the boys and teased by the girls at a little hick school, where pupils were content to make low grades and scrape by. A school with no Helen or Jane. And knowing she was friendless, the boys hit on her. One even offered her money . . .

Sally opened her window, to let in a cool winter draught. It was chillier than usual, to match her mood.

She needed a change. Desperately.

But what could she do?

And then it dawned on her. Seventeen – tomorrow she was seventeen. She could *leave* school. Why not? It didn't offer her anything. Mediocre SATs, and no money for a paying university. Community College – that was worthless.

Sally had no doubts. She wasn't clever enough, or qualified enough, to go work for somebody else, in some office. That way lay grunt wages and a dull life. The most she could hope for was an eventual slot in middle management, perhaps a tract home in Dallas.

Hell no. If anything was going to happen, she had to make it happen.

She felt like pacing her room, only there was no space. Sally smiled at the irony and checked herself out in the mirror. So what *did* she have? What had she got that other people couldn't offer?

Well, beauty, of course. But Texas had lots of pretty girls. Still, there was something else. She was dressed in a sharp jacket, tucked in at the waist, seamed stockings, and a pleated, swinging little skirt – about the only nice clothes at the discount store, but they fitted her perfectly. Even after she'd had to sell all her designer outfits, Sally realized with a thrill of pleasure, she still managed to look good. For all the 'Barbie' taunts, girls in the playground copied her style.

Style. That's what Sally Lassiter had. That's what kept those photographers at bay. That's what kept their heads above water, even now, when the bottom had fallen out of their world.

And if there was one thing Hartford needed, it was style.

Chapter Nineteen

Style had kept her sane, kept her strong against the press and, later, the nasty kids at school. Style had helped her fight her mother's descent into the pit. She could only slow it, but at least Sally had done that. She made sure that, like it or not, Mona was washed and dressed every day. Once a week, even as her mother gazed blankly at the TV, Sally insisted on giving her a manicure.

She was fiercely determined they would be decent. And Sally Lassiter never left the house without her eyebrows styled, mascara, and a slick of lipstick – at the very least.

The kids were starting to accept her. One of her male tormentors had even asked her out the other week, this time for real. And when she'd laughingly turned him down, he hadn't been able to shield the look of disappointment in his eyes.

What did style mean to her? Bravery and beauty. Glamour, as a weapon . . .

That thought made her wince. Just a little. A reminder of past history. When she, and Jane, and Helen, had come walking down those stairs . . .

Sally wondered if her friends ever tried to find her. Of course, she had intentionally disappeared. Put that down to style too, if you like – the shame, the deep shame, that lurked around the edges of the brave face Sally put on things. She just could not bear for Jane to know how small her life was, or for Helen – kind, gentle Helen, who once had been the least of them, less bright than Jane, less rich than Sally – to pity her. She hadn't reached out for them. Survival, for herself and Mom, was her first priority. Of course Sally had told herself that one day in the future they'd be back. All of them rich. All of them on top, like it used to be, only better.

Why did I give that up? she wondered. Why did I stop thinking about it?

The fact was that small-town Texas life, with an alcoholic mom and a dwindling stack of cash, was hard. And Sal hadn't had time for her own dreams. Or her memories. In fact, she had blocked out thoughts of Jane and Helen very deliberately.

Her friends were part of a happier time. And thinking about that hurt.

Damn. I can do better than this, Sally thought, swallowing hard to push back the tears that were threatening. I can make sure there's a chance to get that back. Daddy would be proud of me for keeping it together, but survival ain't enough. I've got to have more.

And style was Sally's way out.

She had it. Hartford needed it.

Sally came to a decision. It was time to go get a job.

When she came downstairs the next morning, Mona was already lying in front of the TV, with the soaps on.

'Momma? Did you wash your face?' Sally called brightly, fixing herself an orange juice.

'Yes. And I did my teeth,' Mona said, like a little girl.

'Shower?'

'I'll do that later.'

'OK.' Normally Sally would have argued, but today she didn't have time. At least her mother had worked out that basic hygiene was the path of least resistance. Mona didn't want to look after herself, but even less did she want Sally to poke around her in the bathroom. So these days Mona was brushing her own teeth and taking care of the basics.

Sally checked; her mother was in her favourite large pair of elasticated jeans and big floppy shirt, with her house clogs on. That was fine; not the height of fashion, but at least she was dressed.

Sally ate a slice of dry toast – always watching her weight – and scurried back upstairs. This was going to take some time. First, she washed and blow-dried her hair – no cheating today, no ponytails – then she selected her outfit.

It had to look sexy, but demure. She knew just the thing. A dark-blue pair of boot-cut jeans, spray-on tight, to show the curves rising above her slender legs. Next, a crisp white shirt, three-quarter-length sleeves, to emphasize her hand-span waist and rich, golden tan. A cute silver cuff, to show off her delicate hands and carefully manicured French nails. Next, towering high-heeled cowboy boots. PVC, because she couldn't afford real leather.

Mmm. She smiled at her reflection. That looked fine.

Next, make-up. That was easy; she was going for healthy and young. Mascara, good and thick, on curled lashes that opened up her eyes. A sexy smudged black liner, to give her that bed-head style. A good rust-coloured blush, half blusher, half bronzer – real 'rose of Texas' stuff. Gold eyeshadow. Natural lipgloss, sheer with just a touch of pink, no liner. A spritz of perfume, and she was done.

Sally didn't normally go to this much trouble but today she had pulled out all the stops. She pirouetted in the mirror, loving what she saw. Yeah. She looked like a model, or a cheerleader for the Dallas Cowboys; every boy would want to be with her, and every girl would want to be her.

Sally glanced at her school uniform, hanging neatly in the closet. She had no use for it any more. She took it on its hanger and folded it neatly over one arm.

'Bye, Mom,' she called, running down the stairs. 'See you later.'

'Be good in school,' Mona called back.

Sally grinned. Well, yes. She would.

The gates of Hartford High were open – she was normally in here half an hour earlier, but that was as a pupil, on the bus. Today she had walked.

Lucy Drew, the hall monitor, was lounging about on the door. Her eyes widened.

'I have to give you a demerit for being late. Two – it's half an hour. And what happened to your uniform?'

Lucy was a nice enough girl – average face, brown hair, average body. She'd been kind to Sally when she first appeared, sometimes eating lunch with her if one of her own friends was sick.

'I'm quitting.' There, that was a juicy piece of gossip. 'You can feel free to tell the girls.'

'Quitting school? Why, can't y'all afford the meals?'

Sally flinched; Lucy thought Mom and she were dirt poor. Well, the sorry truth was, with only eight thousand left in the bank, they were getting there.

'We're doing fine,' she lied. 'I'm just fed up with this place. Say, you know where Leo Fisk is next period?'

Lucy blushed; like every other girl in school, she was sweet on Leo. He played football, his daddy owned a chain of garages, and he drove a Porsche already. Plus, he had classic Texas good looks: cleanshaven, strong-jawed, slim and fit.

'Not sure,' Lucy lied back, 'but I think it might be math,' she admitted.

'Cool. Thanks.'

Sally sauntered past her on her way to the principal's office, and Lucy watched her sashay by with a deep sigh from her soul. Damn. She'd almost be glad to live in a tiny box house with Mona Lassiter if she could look like that. Just once, for one day . . .

'But I don't understand.' Mr Rogers, the principal, looked dismayed. 'You were doing very well in your studies, Sally.'

This was truly shocking news. Rogers liked and admired the young blonde girl, his teachers thought of her as a ray of sunshine, determined and fierce. He personally knew folks who had lost their life savings in the Lassiter Oil collapse, and he had been almost determined to loathe the billionaire princess who had turned up out of nowhere once he realized who she was.

But it had soon become clear that there were no billions left. Whatever else the Lassiters were doing, they weren't living high off the hog. The government had done a pretty good job wringing every last cent out of Paul Lassiter's estate. And in Hartford, gossip soon discovered the mom had serious problems.

Sally had tussled with the press when they first found her, and then with the sneers and jibes in school. He never saw her flirt or sleep around, although clearly she wasn't prudish – she was just too busy keeping her world together.

Prudish – definitely not. He was almost glad to be shocked by her news, because it was hard not to stare at the sensational young woman busting out of that shirt and jeans. Hell, she would tempt a statue. John Rogers kept his eyes determinedly above her collarbone.

'I was doing OK,' Sally corrected him. 'So-so SATs.'

'You could make college.'

'I want more than a basic college education and a job as a bank clerk,' Sally replied, with a frankness that took him aback. 'I have other talents. I want to go get a job, and then maybe start my own business. Doing what I'm good at.'

'And what's that?'

The gorgeous butterfly gave him a dazzling smile that made it somewhat hard to breathe.

'Glamour,' she said. 'Style.'

He had no comeback. Undeniably, Sally Lassiter was a born expert there.

'And where are you going to get a job?'

'At Fisk's Beauty Parlor.'

Her principal blinked. Well, it made sense, if you considered that Elaine Fisk's little store was the only beauty place in town. But he thought that Sally Lassiter got on badly with young Leo Fisk; she'd refused his advances, and he amused himself making sexual cracks about her, loudly, and laughing with his buddies, whenever she came within earshot.

'I wish you the best of luck, young lady.' Sally had made up her mind, and he got the sense there was no point in arguing. 'And if it doesn't work out, come back to me. There are plenty of jobs around the school . . .'

But not, he thought, in his office. He'd been married for fifteen years, and he'd like to stay that way!

'Thanks. Same to you, Mr Rogers.' She shook his hand, and was gone, leaving nothing behind but the faint scent of jasmine.

John Rogers sat on his comfortable swivel chair and wished he were eighteen again.

'We-e-ell,' Leo said, giving a long, low whistle. His eyes flickered hungrily up and down Sally Lassiter's knockout body. 'Damn, baby. You look about as pretty as a peach like that. What's up?'

Leo wasn't too smart. A meat and potatoes guy, he'd hated being humiliated by the leggy blonde from California – she was supposed to be as grateful for his attentions as all the other chicks. And he'd made sure to punish her when she didn't play ball. Rich girl on hard times? She should have been dying to lose her cherry to him.

But at least she'd come to him now. And out of uniform. Man. Sally could make just a pair of jeans look like it should come with a triple X certificate.

His buddies stood behind him, book bags over their shoulders, murmuring and ogling. Leo was pleased. The hottest chick in school had never looked hotter. There would be an especial pleasure in laying her now they'd all seen what a grade A piece of ass she was.

'Leo,' Sally said, straightening her back. 'I'm fixin' to leave school and get a job. And I'm hoping you'll be a gentleman and won't stand in my way.'

'Stand in your way? Why would I want to do that?'

'Wanna earn some money, baby, I can think of an easy way to go,' one of his jackass friends piped up. Leo turned and scowled at him.

'Shut it, Duane.'

'We haven't always seen eye to eye. You know that.'

Her voice was soft as melted butter, and there was something strong and beautiful about how she carried herself. He started to think he had been dumb, that maybe she'd make a good date, as well as a good lay.

'I'd love to let bygones be bygones,' he said, his gaze travelling the entire length of her tall, delicious body. Imagine what that would be like in a see-through teddy from Victoria's Secret . . .

He felt himself stirring, not good in a school corridor.

'That's mighty good of you, Leo. Because I'd like to go work in Mrs Fisk's beauty parlor.'

He couldn't stop a broad grin from spreading across his face. Perfect! The sassy little minx would be in Mom's little shop every day, and she'd be real beholden to him. He could have her fired any time he liked.

'You go right ahead,' he said. 'I'll put in a good word for you, too. How's that?'

'That'd be real nice of you.'

'And maybe you'd consider stepping out with me Friday night. That new *Die Hard* movie's out . . .'

'Why, that's a very sweet offer,' Sally said, smiling at him. 'But I never mix business with pleasure.'

He flushed with anger and opened his mouth for a sharp retort, but then thought better of it. As a matter of fact, he just couldn't do it. The girl was too blindingly hot. Better to just put his time in. So she wanted to make him crawl – it'd be all the sweeter when she tumbled into his bed.

'I understand that,' he said slowly. 'So I'll call Mom for you. Maybe see you around.'

'Sure thing. And thank you again,' Sally said, and this time gave him a real smile, one that reached all the way to those clear blue eyes.

She knew the store well, passed it every day. Fisk, the only beauty place in town. Really, it was drab and underused. Mostly, Elaine Fisk just used it as a talking shop. All her prosperous friends came in for manicures; Elaine employed two bored twenty-somethings to do manicures and blow-drys, with the occasional hair trim. It seemed to be well stocked but with old cosmetics, since nobody actually used the store. The ladies of Hartford preferred to drive over to Catfield, closer to Dallas and with a bunch of Korean-run manicure places.

But Sally never liked to leave Mona that long. So once a month she had gone into Fisk's and had her eyebrows plucked. Five bucks, but worth it. She liked that sense she was treating herself. But she'd never go there for anything else. Not worth it; Mrs Elaine Fisk, a fat woman into velour pantsuits and diamonds at all times, knew as much about style as she did about advanced calculus.

Which was why this was such an attractive prospect. Far better than a Korean place, where the canny owners knew their business, or a fancy store with up-to-date magazines and tinted-glass windows. Fisk was perfect, Sally had decided. A central spot, and a blank canvas.

'My son speaks highly of you,' Elaine Fisk said. 'Says you are a very proper young lady.' Her stern eye danced over Sally's breathtaking outfit. Elaine doubted it but hey. She couldn't quite work out quite what was so sexy. The jeans weren't too low-waisted, nor the shirt unbuttoned . . . But just looking at Sally made Mrs Fisk uncomfortable; she wished she hadn't eaten that second muffin for breakfast.

'Leo's been so kind to me,' Sally said sweetly. 'He's a credit to you and Mr Fisk, ma'am. Y'all have raised a real gentleman. Everybody says so.'

That did it; Elaine liked nothing better than to hear Sally Lassiter talk that way about her Pookie, her little baby. And maybe Sally could shake things up, she thought, vaguely. Not that Elaine cared about making money, nothing so vulgar! But her friend Sheila Gunn had recently abandoned her place, not even coming for coffee any more – she said Betsy-Lou had messed up her trim and taken off two extra inches!

'Well, I could certainly use somebody to sweep the floor, maybe get me a couple of cushions, wash hair in the basins,' Elaine conceded.

'Actually, I want to be your beauty therapist.' Sally stood firm. If she didn't get it right now she'd never get another chance. 'What I'd like to do is work with you on a new vision for Fisk's. Your beauty parlour will be *the* place in town, Mrs Fisk. You'll have the ladies fighting each other to book a slot. You may have to change your phone number, because all your friends will be *begging* for appointments . . .'

Elaine looked sceptical. 'And how are we going to do that? What do I use to attract all this attention?'

'Me,' Sally said, proudly.

'Honey, you don't have two cents to rub together. What could you know about fancy cosmetics?'

Sally didn't flinch. 'You remember all the stories? A couple of years ago I used to know everything about them. And you know, Mrs Fisk, I was in LA, and we mixed with the top Hollywood celebrities. I can tell you all the style secrets.'

'Hollywood Dazzle!' Elaine cried. 'That's the new name for the store!'

Sally bit back a smile. Hell, at least the woman was getting enthusiastic.

'We should stick to what we're known for. Nobody'll buy that down here. At least, not yet,' she added, diplomatically. 'This is your place so it should reflect *you*, Mrs Fisk. How about this – Rodeo Girl.'

'Rodeo Girl!'

'It's down-home, it's sassy, it's pretty, it's us.'

'I like it,' Elaine said, excitedly. 'And so I'll start doing the treatments. More treatments! We can offer makeovers . . .'

'We'll need a little money. Just a little. Some paint, some new lights, letters for the storefront . . .'

'My husband will give me that.' Elaine waved her fingers dismissively, lost in the dream. Her store, her place, the hottest thing in town. But then her eyes narrowed, and she looked at Sally. 'But just because *you've* got style, how can I tell if you'll be good in the store? You would look good in a potato sack. We don't make a lot of money here, I don't think I can give you more than minimum wage. We're taking losses . . .'

'I want a thousand dollars a month.'

Elaine Fisk's eyes widened, and she laughed.

'Young lady, you are plumb crazy talking like that. We don't even take a thousand dollars in a month. Not even half.'

'But we will. Much more than. Look, Mrs Fisk. You're a beautiful lady yourself,' Sally lied. 'But when was the last time you had a real romantic date with Mr Fisk? Tell you what. Why don't you let me style you? I'll show you just how good I am. You'll look ten years younger. He'll think he's romancing your little sister!'

'He better not,' Elaine Fisk said darkly. But it was a tempting pitch. 'OK . . . I'll try it.'

Well. This would be a challenge. But Sally gritted her teeth. She could certainly make Elaine look, if not good, at least better.

'We'll start with hair and make-up,' she said. 'No cutting – just styling. And then we'll go shopping for a new outfit. I'll do your nails and brows. The whole bit. Why don't you come on over here, and we'll start with washing your hair.'

Elaine hesitated.

'And I give a fabulous head and shoulder massage,' Sally tempted.

'All right. I'll try it.' Elaine waddled over to the washbasin and sat down. 'Although I've no idea why I'm agreeing to this. You certainly are a sweet-talker . . .'

Sally hastily ran the warm water into the basin and wet down her new boss's hair.

She didn't want to give Elaine a chance to change her mind.

'My stars,' Elaine Fisk murmured. 'Oh, my goodness.'

She put one hand to her mouth, then lowered it again. She gaped at her reflection.

'I can't believe it. It doesn't even look like me.'

Although she was twenty years younger, Sally stood back, beaming like a proud parent. Of course Elaine wasn't about to win any prizes in the Miss Texas pageant, but still . . .

Her heavily sprayed, stiffly backcombed hair was softly washed, blow-dried, and styled into a long bob around her face. The layers of thick mascara that only a young woman could get away with had gone; Sally allowed her one coat of brown mascara to pick out the blue in her eyes. Similarly, the ugly rouge on Elaine's cheeks, and the face powder that caked in every wrinkle, were replaced with a sheer anti-ageing formula that tightened up her skin a little, and a neutral blush which Sally cleverly used to design cheek-bones that really weren't there.

The vile pantsuit had been replaced by an expensive, well-cut dress in a heavy fabric, which made Elaine look stately rather than fat. The flashy diamonds Sally had swapped for some luminous, cheap freshwater pearls, and she'd picked out a lace shawl to complete the effect; and finally, the masterstroke, a pair of sturdy, stacked heels, which forced Elaine to stand differently and stretch as she carried herself.

She looked younger, thinner – *better*.

Elaine couldn't contain her delight.

'Mark is going to go wild,' she said. 'Oh, Sally, you're a genius.'

'Just wait until you send your friends out looking like that,' Sally prompted. 'I want to offer makeovers, hairdressing, and a styling service if they pay enough – for the elite customers, two hundred dollars a session. I'll go shopping with them and show them what to get.'

'Oh yes – yes certainly,' Elaine said, dreamily staring at her reflection.

'Ask Mr Fisk for a budget to renovate the store? And I want to throw an open day on Saturday. Free makeovers. Believe me, that'll get them talking.' Sally was almost dizzy with her success, high on her plans and dreams. She *could* make it happen. 'If they want me to make them up they have to give us their mailing address and sign a consent form to receive special offers . . .'

Her new boss wasn't listening; she was turning around in front of the mirror, absorbed in herself.

'You know, this dress looks like what Oprah wore on the

Grammys. Except for I'm a white lady . . . but it's so *sexy*,' Elaine hissed, lowering her voice. She blushed. 'Do you think you could come shopping with me for lingerie?' she whispered.

'Sure. You'd look great in . . . a teddy. Or baby-doll nightdress,' Sally managed. 'But first, you should hire me. I wrote up a contract. A thousand dollars a month plus basic healthcare benefits . . .' Sally produced a neatly folded, typed document from her handbag. Elaine signed it without even a murmur, went to her desk, took out her chequebook and scribbled in it.

'Delighted, dear,' she said. 'Say, could you look after the store for me this afternoon? I want to go and surprise Mark.'

'Of course. Just give me five minutes while I call Mom,' Sally said.

She ran out of the front door, an annoying little bell tinkling, and went straight across the street to the bank. Not that she didn't trust Elaine, but a thousand dollars seemed like a small fortune. She wanted to bank it right away. Back in the store, she ushered Elaine out.

'You go on home, Mrs Fisk. I'll look after things here.'

Elaine drifted out, dousing herself in perfume as she went; Sally put her into Chanel No. 19, a lighter fragrance, since she knew Elaine was addicted to the nozzle.

She looked around the store. Dingy, drab, and under-used. Well, she could change all that. Sally moved to the back to grab a broom. In the morning the two hairdressers would come in, and she'd start to teach them how to do a real blow-dry.

I'm in charge now, Sally thought, and it was the first bit of real optimism she'd felt in ages.

Chapter Twenty

And things changed. Not overnight; Mark Fisk, stunned though he was at his wife's appearance, moaned over the fifty thousand dollars – Elaine's place had never been more than a drag on his finances. The two current employees were jealous of Sally, and tried to rebel, until Elaine laid down the law. The builders and decorators were lazy, and it was a constant struggle.

But Sally persevered. She had to. She had a job now, and a purpose. If everybody else was lazy, she worked like a demon, painting, decorating, sourcing cool artwork, fancy mirrors, bronze letters three feet high, designing and re-designing the ad for the local paper. And if the renovations took three months, well, that was plenty of time for Hartford to get good and curious.

When the grand opening happened, all Elaine's friends were there, as well as several curious teens from the high school. Sally had trained the other two girls in beauty basics, properly, and left them doing pedicures and neck massages while she flitted from chair to chair, flash-styling the small-town girls in ten minutes each; plucking eyebrows that hadn't been touched for decades, wiping away bright, ugly make-up and replacing it with neutrals, blow-drying out previously gelled-up hair, showing housewives addicted to plaits and buns what natural styling looked like.

The oohs and aahs from the mirrors didn't put any cash

in the coffers, but Sally had faith. There was no business as sound as beauty. If you could show women you made a difference . . .

And the store, after all that hard work, was amazing. Rodeo Girl looked like it belonged on Rodeo Drive. Gone were all the yellowing magazines and peeling paint, and the old-style radio blaring out traffic and weather updates. Sally had installed tinted windows, sleek new graphics, a sexy logo of a rodeo chick in heeled boots and a tie-under shirt. Banks of televisions were tuned to CMT, the country and western version of MTV, with buff unshaven cowboys and modern Western divas slickly belting out their hits.

It celebrated Texas – and it celebrated style. Hartford had never seen anything like it. The older ladies booked the place up almost immediately, and their daughters scrambled for appointments. Sally was busy, nine to five, every day, and sometimes on weekends as well. It was exhausting, but it was a rush. And her salary enabled them to afford little luxuries.

After a month or so, she began to get sizable tips. Instead of wasting the cash, Sally banked it. She didn't know exactly where she was going yet, but she was sure of one thing. She was not going to stay here.

Elaine Fisk basked in all the glory and took all the credit. Sally didn't mind, as long as she kept getting paid. And Elaine allowed her to keep all the tip money, which almost doubled her basic salary. As long as Sally's first priority was to keep Elaine looking good, the owner didn't complain. Her husband was actually getting money back after the third month, so he was happy. And, watching Sally work her magic on the small-town women of Hartford, Elaine discovered a vestige of pride in herself. She confided in Sal that she wanted to lose weight, and Sally put her on a walking regimen, something she could do quietly, without her catty friends noticing. Sally told her where to pick up good, ready-made salads. After a while, Elaine dropped a dress size, then two . . .

For the first six months Sally's life moved into a routine; working, banking her salary, learning on her feet. She spent her spare time at home, looking after Mona as best she could. Sally felt guilty, at times, that she couldn't turn her mom around the way she was shaping up Elaine Fisk. But fighting Mona's depression and alcoholism would need Sally to be there full time, and she had to make choices. Right now, Rodeo Girl was letting her save some cash and giving her a better education than a third-rate college could ever provide.

Sally tried not to think too much. She let her days fill up, her savings account slowly increase. It was easier to cope that way.

'Look at her,' Leo Fisk said.

His Porsche was parked across the street, with three of his buddies sitting inside. The top was down, and they stared at Sally as she sauntered out of the front door, kissing Lucy Drew on the cheek.

'Dude, which one? Lucy's hot now,' his friend Barry replied.

'Come on.' Leo was scornful. Certainly he wouldn't say no to Lucy Drew, with that cute new haircut and the figure-hugging clothes and dramatic, pouty lips Sally had given her. But Sally Lassiter was still way out of Lucy's league.

Or anybody's. He'd been watching her coming in and going out of his mom's store for months now. The original plan was to drop by, hang around, watch her doing menial tasks like sweeping the floor – he vaguely thought that would be sexy – and have Sally flirt with him, begging him to notice her. After all, without his say-so, Mom wouldn't have hired her.

Only it hadn't worked out that way. Since day one, Sally

was surrounded, first by workmen, then by customers. And obviously she was key to Rodeo Girl, whatever his mother told people. Leo had no power over her any more.

Today she was wearing a short skirt, kitten heels, and a cream silk blouse. Her smooth, tanned legs seemed to run on forever. Her flaxen hair was caught back in a smooth ponytail, worn low at the neck, and her mouth showed wide teeth when she laughed.

All the eager, desperate schoolgirls he'd fumbled with or taken to bed paled into nothingness compared with Sally. And the further away he got from her, the more he wanted her.

'Yeah, she's fine,' Barry agreed.

'Pity you didn't bang her when you had the chance,' Simon Bernardillo said.

'He never *had* the chance. Remember? Chick turned him down flat,' piped up Keith Brand, from the back.

'That's right,' Barry said, and laughed.

Simon started to hum 'Dream Dream Dream' by the Everly Brothers, and his annoying friends fell about laughing.

'Can it,' Leo said, shortly. 'She's just another piece of tail, fellas. Let's go play ball.'

Aggravated, he put the Porsche into gear and slammed his foot down. The car screeched off; in the side mirror he saw Sally Lassiter glance in his direction idly then, unconcerned, go back into the shop.

It burned him. She'd tricked him, that minx. She'd come up to him, sweet as pie, and teased him, knowing she was never going out with him. He resented it. Sally should have been grateful, and pliant. Submissively asking him to be pleased with her. Now, their roles were neatly reversed. She had a job, she was effectively an adult, and he still went to high school! OK, he was a senior, but it was still totally humiliating. The working woman and the schoolboy . . .

Leo was a peacock. He hated it when his friends laughed

at him. Unacceptable. He was going to have to teach that girl some manners. She damn well *would* go out with him, and in public. Or else.

He left after practice, so as not to be obvious about it, and went over to his dad's garage on Fifth Street, where they had a liquor concession and nobody asked questions. Leo took a little supply, some crates of beer and a pint of vodka. He liked that best because it didn't leave a smell on your breath. And it was hard liquor. A man's drink, something to get riled up on before he confronted Sally. She had a snappy, cool way about her when she put you down, and Leo wasn't taking any chances. He wanted to stand up to her. He packed the beer into the trunk, then unscrewed the vodka and took a good, fiery swig before stashing it in the glove compartment. His throat burned, and he felt himself gearing up. Carefully, not wanting to attract the cops, he turned the car south, heading back to main street and the way Sally walked home. It was a long walk to the tract on the outside of town, and she never got the bus; she liked the exercise. Perfect for him. He raised his headlights, and started to scour the side of the road.

Sally was tired, but glowing. Saturday night, and a particularly great week for tips. Mrs Ellis, the wife of the local realtor, had been so thrilled with her personal shopping session – Sally guided her to a whole new wardrobe in one afternoon – that she'd pressed five hundred-dollar bills into her hands. And there had been over four hundred from the rest of the clientele, which meant she'd got almost a month's worth in just a single week. There was some real money now in their bank account. They lived on a thousand a month, and with what was left over from LA, and all her work this year, Sally now had thirty-two thousand saved, with the promise of more to come.

It would be almost a year soon, and then she'd ask for a rise. A big rise. Rodeo Girl was a huge success. Three thousand a month, just for starters, and Sally thought she might walk Elaine through share structure and get her to give her a slice. Once they'd done that, she could hire staff, maybe start a new store, maybe even one in Dallas. She didn't have to work here for twenty, twenty-five thou a year.

Maybe, Sally suddenly thought, maybe she could even go home . . .

But no; not yet. Not till she'd accumulated at least, what, eighty? That way she and Momma could get a little apartment. And she'd need working capital to set up a beauty parlour in LA.

How much did rehab cost? Maybe more than she had. And Momma needed it. No, not ready yet, not ready to go back. Perhaps in a few years, when she was twenty-one.

I should set my sights in the middle, Sally told herself, managing the emotional comedown. Aim to get my ass over to Dallas, work the big city first . . .

A car honked; she jumped out of her skin, spun around, her hand flung up against the dazzling light.

'What the . . . Oh, hey. Leo.' She dropped her hand and drew aside as his big Porsche slowed down. 'You startled me.'

'Hey, what's up?' Leo Fisk was smiling at her, with that familiar, lascivious look in his eyes. 'You're far too cute to be tramping home in the mud, Sally. Let me give you a lift.'

'It ain't muddy,' she replied. 'I like the exercise.'

'I know, but take a load off. You should relax once in a while. Go home early.'

Well, it was unseasonably chilly. And she didn't want to be rude to Leo, he was Elaine's son, after all.

'OK, why not.' She opened the door and climbed in. 'Thanks.'

'So,' he said, pulling out into the road again. 'Sally, you never did give me that date. I reckon that call I put in for you with Mom came out pretty good, huh? You owe me a dinner, at least.'

Sally sighed. Not that she hadn't been expecting this moment to come. She was only surprised it had taken him this long to get around to it.

'Leo, look. You're a real good-looking boy' – hell, he hated that, he wasn't a goddamn boy – 'and I know all the girls are wild to go out with you, but I'm just not ready for a romantic relationship right now.'

'What are you talking about? You're eighteen, baby. Legal in every state. I can't believe you've never had a boyfriend.'

Well, she sort of had – dates, back when she was fourteen, fifteen. Boys she met from church or sports, or sons of Daddy's business partners. The odd movie, a kiss in a parking lot. Fumbles. But nothing more.

'I've dated,' she said evasively. 'But really I'm just focusing on work right now. I want to save up and get a place of my own.'

'All work and no play makes Sally a dull girl,' Leo said. He slurred the ss, and she realized with a shock that he was more than a little drunk.

'Make a left right here, Leo,' she said. But he missed the turning and shot past the intersection.

'Oh, you missed our street. Never mind.' She didn't particularly want him to turn back, in the traffic. 'Just pull over and I'll walk.'

He didn't look at her; his eyes were fixed straight ahead, and he pressed his foot down on the gas.

'Just pull over,' Sally repeated, uneasily. 'And thanks for the lift.'

Leo drove on.

'I don't think you're being fair, Sally,' he said, and there was a silky tone to his voice she didn't like. 'I think you tricked me. Day you came to see me in school. All dressed up in them tight jeans. Made me think you'd go out with me. If you weren't coming on to me, what was all that make-up for?'

They were going fast now, very fast. Too fast. The dial was on ninety, and the car was wobbling. The lights of Hartford disappeared in the distance.

'Please stop,' she begged.

'Answer the question,' he said.

'I wanted to impress your mother with how stylish I could be.'

'Yeah, well. You impressed me, honey. Made a *real* impression.'

The car pulled to a halt.

'What the hell are you doing?' Sally cried.

'You wanted me to pull over.'

She glanced wildly around. They were in the middle of nowhere, a corn field to the left. Quiet road, no traffic.

'Leo, you're drunk. I'm walking back and we're gonna forget this ever happened,' Sally said. She tried for confident, but her voice cracked with fear.

He reached for her, one hand brushing against her breasts.

'Come on, baby, you'll like it. All the girls do.'

'Get away from me!' Sally shouted.

'No, I've had it. Enough teasing. You're gonna get just what you asked for.'

She tried desperately to twist away, but he was strong. Slight, for a man, skinny, not the type of body she liked. But a man is far stronger than a woman, even a weak man. Sally knew that, instinctively. She was frightened.

'Leo, you're better than this . . . What would your mom think? Don't, don't touch me!'

Angrily, he backhanded her across the face. Sally gasped

in pain and shock. That would leave a welt. She kicked back and tried to clamber out of the door.

'You're trying to ruin it,' he hissed, grunting. 'Bringing my mom into it. That ain't sexy. You're just an uppity bitch.'

'You're a bully and a coward,' Sally sobbed. 'I'll scream . . .'

The light in his eyes was manic. She couldn't believe it. She knew this boy, had seen him at school every day.

'You do, and I'll kill you,' he snarled. 'And dump you right in that damn corn field and you can rot away in the fall.'

She didn't know if he meant it or not. Sheer terror froze her to her seat.

'Now,' he said, fumbling at her shirt. 'Let's get this off of you. Yeah . . . yeah, you sure are well built, baby, and I'm gonna be your first, just like I told them boys . . .'

His hand was on her. She was tight, dry as a bone. He didn't care. Sally sobbed and leaned her head back. She didn't want to die, so she said nothing.

And Leo Fisk raped her.

He dropped her home afterwards. She said nothing. Leo was full of good cheer. Told her she was sexy, she was hot.

'Don't worry, I'll see you again,' he said. 'Take you out to the movies tomorrow. How's that? It'll be better next time. You'll get the hang of it, baby, you're too hot-looking, you got it in you.'

She climbed out of the car, and he was gone, tyres spinning down the road.

Sally had seen true crime shows about rape victims. How they would get in the shower and scrub themselves till they bled. Or went to the police, and pressed charges.

Sally did neither of those things.

Instead, she ignored the prone figure of her mother, snoring upstairs on the bed, and went to grab her suitcases. Sally furiously started to pack.

The police would not believe her. There were no witnesses. The Fisks were popular. She knew that, sick as it was, deep down in her bones. And she didn't want the publicity – vultures crawling over her, all that prurient interest in the rape of a teenage blonde. They'd find Mona, too, drunk and depressed, still eking out the days in her personal hell.

Forget this shithole of a town. Sally was gone. Earlier than she'd expected, or wanted. But she had thirty thousand in the bank. They could rent, back in LA. And she could start her own store. Buy a lease – get it done. Screw working for Elaine. She was angry, angry in the very depths of her soul. She was going to go the hell home, make some money, show all of them. The bastards who'd dropped them when her dad died. The snooty friends who never called. All the bullies, all those snooping vultures in the press.

Sally needed money. If she had money again, she'd have had some protection. If she wasn't poor, Leo could never have got away with raping her, treating her just like a chattel.

Never again. She knew how to make it. She was a real Steel Magnolia. First, she was going to change their lives, again. Next, she was going to cure her momma and get rich. And last, she was going to take revenge.

Not just on Leo Fisk. On the whole damn world.

Chapter Twenty-One

'You can't fire me.'

He was young, but still older than Jane. Thirty at least, in his fancy Armani suit, with a Princeton degree and an arrogant air she disliked. Plus, he was looking her over, checking her out, with a degree of impertinence Jane objected to. Violently.

'I can and I am. You know our policy, Michael. Up or out. The San Diego store is failing to attract customers and growth.'

'A rise of nine per cent. Read the report,' he replied with contempt.

'That is insufficient. The Sunset Boulevard store is making between twelve and fifteen per cent growth per year.'

'That's a special case,' he said.

'Of course it is.' She smiled thinly. 'I run it. And now staff have been trained to follow my principles. Which is why I'm sitting here in head office, and you're being sacked.'

He stared. 'My God, you're every bit as much a bitch as they say you are.'

'And I hear that you've sexually harassed every new immigrant worker San Diego took on.'

'Bullshit. Prove it.'

'I don't have to.' Jane shrugged. 'I have your lack of performance. There's a severance package on the table, but it won't be there for long.'

'What the hell do you know?' He jumped to his feet, puce with rage. 'You're just a kid – no college degree, no MBA. A couple of *fluke* years in LA and all of a sudden you think you're Jack Welch.'

'Grow up,' Jane said dismissively. 'And get out. I'm busy, I don't have time for this.'

'I'm leaving.' He turned at the door, and stared at her, eyes angry. 'Everybody knows why you're here, *Miz* Morgan. You're the best little whore in the company. Fucking half the board of directors, no doubt. And I bet you're *real* good at it.'

'Security can be up here in thirty seconds. And they really are good at it,' Jane replied coolly. 'So if you value your ribcage, I suggest you leave. And by the way, the severance package just evaporated.'

He snarled at her, cheeks mottled with rage, but he left.

She stood up and walked to the window. The office was her favourite part of this job; below her, the office building sloped down and to the right, a curved arc of polished marble. The Manhattan skyscrapers jabbed into the hazy blue of the sky, smudged today with autumn clouds; the traffic crawled, in miniature, on the junctions at ground level, little yellow cabs crawling along like beetles, the sunlight flashing off the windscreens in diamond bursts of brilliance.

Her office. Vice President in charge of Personnel. And she deserved it, damn it.

She tried to brush off what Michael Tiersky had said as the rantings of a failure. But it bothered her; it certainly did. She heard it far too often, in this job. From any man, and half the women, she canned.

Sex toy. Hooker. Bimbo.

Sometimes they threw out names. Who, exactly, was she sleeping with? Rhodri Evans? Carmine Gallo? Richie Benson?

That she might deserve her position, be here on her merits – impossible. She was too young. Twenty years old.

And, Jane was starting to understand, too beautiful.

It aggravated her. Rhodri, her first and still best mentor, was *gay* – not that she would tell them that, or dignify the sleaze with a response. She'd proven herself out there in LA. In six months, she had transformed that workforce, and with it the whole store's productivity.

At first Mrs Doherty had resented it, but as the cash flowed, so did her bonuses. Before long, she was recommending Jane wholeheartedly for promotion. Amazing what a little influx of cash could do.

And Jane was not the monster they made her out to be. Under her regime, merit was rewarded. Yeah, she cut out the dead wood, but more at management level than amongst the grunts. People soon came to understand that with Jane Morgan watching – and she was always watching – slacking was impossible.

But if you were a worker, Jane made life good. Even for the lowest levels. She ordered the canteen redecorated, new coffee machines installed, and the food improved. Sexual harassment was no longer tolerated. For the college kids, she offered daily internships in the management offices, so that the stint packing groceries would look better on their résumés. For the working moms, Jane brought in a crèche. For the families, she negotiated discounts at Universal Studios and the museums. There were reward schemes, employee of the month awards, bonuses, and a better staff area and menu.

People were motivated. Jane revolutionized the store.

They promoted her three times, and then the call. Come to New York. A vice presidency of Shop Smart. Translate your methods across the country.

Jane had thought about it, but not for very long. She put her neat little house in Encino on the market, donated her stuff to charity, and moved into a smart two-bedroom flat on the upper east side. Her Ford had long ago become a Lincoln Town car; in Manhattan, they offered her a driver.

Jane demurred. She'd take the subway. It was cheaper and quicker into mid-town.

Her bosses loved it, and they loved her. Before she knew where she was, Jane was getting her photograph taken in studios and appearing on the Shop Smart corporate website. Along with a note on her tragic story.

She wanted to object, but didn't. It was all an irrelevance. And if the company looked good for having a woman at a senior level, then fine.

But now – now she was getting sick of it.

Not for the obvious reasons.

Not because her brand of human resources focused more on the resource than the human. She did not tolerate dead wood. A manager's salary was fifty grand a year, and if the university grads did not perform, she had a waiting list of hungry training programme workers, direct from the shop floor, ready to take their place.

She had zero time for lazy placeholders. No tears for Michael. Let him get another job. He wasn't her problem.

No, Jane's trouble was that she did this *too well*. Her success on Sunset Boulevard had blinded them. Shop Smart just wanted more of the same. And since her original aim had simply been money and position, she didn't want to turn this down – the complete package was worth almost two hundred grand a year.

But she wasn't a Personnel drone. What interested her in Shop Smart was *selling*. It was the store, itself. So she could run a team of workers – big wow.

Jane could do other, more important things. More crucial things. She wanted the chance to try.

But the board had other ideas. They told her they liked her where she was. Why mess with success?

Jane stared down at Manhattan, not seeing it. She sensed danger. This was a trap – a very comfortable trap, a middle-class trap, but a trap, all the same. Personnel had its limits. It was female-dominated, and like all female-dominated industries, underpaid. A safe place to stick your so-called high fliers. Get a nominal woman 'senior' executive, but not one in any danger of actually doing anything important.

Jane wanted to run supply lines, oversee buyers, construct new stores, award ad contracts. She had trained herself to be a *businesswoman*, not an overpaid nanny.

Five months in New York, and she was done.

She made up her mind. Go to Rhodri – he deserved the courtesy – and ask him for a transfer. Marketing would be a start. Buying, even better. She wanted to try her hand at stock and supply. And if they refused, she would quit.

Shop Smart had a formula. A very successful formula, but not one that allowed much creativity.

Jane Morgan was nowhere near where she wanted to be in life. Yes, she was out of the gutter. Yes, she was comfortable. Probably more so than her dad had ever been.

But she wanted so much more. And she was not sure Shop Smart was going to give it to her.

'I'll take it to them.' Rhodri Evans sighed, and polished his glasses. 'Really, Jane, you're twenty years old.'

'My age is irrelevant.'

'No, it's not.'

'Well, it damn well should be.'

'And you're gorgeous – so my straight friends instruct me.'

'Again, irrelevant.' Jane flashed on Michael Tiersky and his insults. Fancy girl. Slut.

'A gorgeous young girl in the boardroom would ruffle a lot of feathers.'

'You should know something,' she said. 'In terms of boyfriends,' she blushed, 'I haven't had any.'

'None at all?'

'No.'

What chance had she had? Working twelve-, eighteen-hour days, doing whatever it took to stay on top of the job. Jane sometimes believed a cloistered nun stood a better chance of getting married than she did

'I understand,' Evans said. He had faced plenty of prejudice himself, and he sympathized with her; she was a brain, no doubt about that at all. And a young girl, in a hurry to be going places.

He liked Jane Morgan dearly. She was an amazing woman, and Evans admired her.

That said, he remained a Shop Smart employee; and she was most valuable where they'd placed her.

'In Personnel nobody will question you,' he suggested.

'Rhodri.' Jane spread her hands, and he was again half amused, half impressed. An interesting young woman, to be certain. 'I am better than that. I came into this company wanting to learn the business, not wanting to be some glorified suit in charge of the parking rota who makes weight on Shop Smart picnics. I know all about Shop Smart picnics. I invented them.'

'You are *so* young, Jane,' her friend tried again. 'And you have no MBA. Not even a degree. Can't you see people are jealous of you?'

'Of course I can, and I don't see why I should give a damn.' Jane jumped to her feet, passionate. 'Who produces, who doesn't produce. That's all that counts. The eighties are over. Haven't we learned anything?'

'You're only twenty and already a vice president.'

Jane leaned across his desk. 'You know what I tell my juniors, Rhodri? Up or out. If they're not promotion material within a certain time, they are gone. Now tell me, why should the rules be different for me? You put me in as veep in charge of staff. OK, I've delivered. The dead wood is gone. The motivation programmes are there . . .'

'So you should see it through.'

'Like hell.' She stood and ran a hand through her long hair, and he admired her, dispassionately. 'I'm not into that. I want a real job, in business. Supply, management, marketing – there are lots of possibilities.'

Evans stood firm. 'So you're the no-bullshit girl?'

'Damn straight.'

'Then take some plain talking from me, Jane. You are a kid. And already you've been promoted five times higher than any kid would ever be. Whatever the numbers say, shareholders and, more importantly, analysts are going to bitch at seeing you promoted to board level.'

'Then explain why.'

'We did OK for many years before you got here,' he said calmly. 'And we would do OK after you left.'

'But this is so dumb. You gave me a brief, and I delivered—'

'And that's what you're trusted on.'

'But I could be so much more. Shop Smart—'

'Time for an object lesson,' Evans said. 'This store is at a peak of performance and sales. No director is going to give a crap if you come or go. You have to settle in to your at-bat, girl. And I can't help if you won't do that. At twenty years old, you can expect at least – at *minimum* – five years in this slot. And after that it's a distant maybe as to whether they would transfer you. You're good, and relatively cheap—'

'Don't I know it,' Jane said, angrily.

'So why change? Especially since any further movement would threaten their jobs.'

'And if I quit?'

Evans rolled his eyes. 'At twenty you're on two hundred k. If you quit, you're a moron. In *this* company you have a track record. Anyplace else, you're just another college dropout – because they won't be giving you a glowing reference.'

Jane snarled. 'Damn it!'

'You're an analyst.' He treated her with the same dispassion she treated everyone else. 'You figure it out. The fact you're so beautiful makes a difference.'

'You have a boyfriend. I don't,' she lashed out.

'Sweetie, if you want, I can fix that in five minutes.'

Jane grudgingly offered him a smile. 'Thank you, no.'

He was a smart cookie, Rhodri Evans, and a good friend. Maybe what he was saying made sense. She just didn't want to hear it.

'Seriously.' He stood up, and walked over to her. 'I think I know just what you need, Jane. You're frustrated, but maybe that's not because of work. You need a relationship.'

'Yeah, sure,' she said.

Rhodri didn't know why she dismissed the idea. Eighteen-hour days. Constant phone calls. Staring at the computer until you went blind. What was that? No kind of life for a young woman.

'You could date somebody who works on your schedule.' Evans thought about it, and ran through his single friends. The strong ones, at least; anyone else this chick would eat alive. 'There's John Rastone, an investment banker. Murray Krasnich, he's a politician, but dedicated. And Leroy Lassiter, he's a manager at senior level over at Wal-Mart – ahead of you, though.'

Jane shook her head. 'When it happens, it happens.'

'OK. Your call. I'm always there.'

For once she availed herself of the chauffeur service. Jane felt adrift, afraid about what to do next. She wanted a new job – and a man; somebody to silence the critics calling her a whore. She wanted the backing of her allies, but understood she was asking something outrageous. And yet the pure flame of capitalism told her she should already have the job.

On the slow drive up Fifth Avenue, stuck in traffic and wanting to get home, Jane thought about her life, about her past, and her friends. Where was Sally? What was she doing now? And Helen? Did she have children, was she enjoying herself in some Egyptian suburb? Did she ever even think of her and Sally?

But these were crazy reminiscences, Jane told herself. Friendships couldn't last forever – why had she ever thought otherwise? Well, maybe it was nostalgia but she was determined to find out.

The desire to avenge herself, to prove more than the pampered daughter of a worthless diplomat had been slaked. She was exhausted, and one way or another, she was on the way up.

For the last two years she had been a hermit, so deep in her work she might have been a nun. All the more funny that they called her a whore – but Jane wasn't laughing.

If she had friends again – that would be something.

It wasn't like she hadn't tried to find them. But the Yannas had remained tight-lipped, and there was no sign of Sally Lassiter anywhere in Texas. Jane came close, one time; she discovered Sally had been working at a beauty parlour in a small town in the Lone Star State. But then she'd upped sticks and left, and nobody had the first idea where she'd gone. Vanished in the night, her bank account closed, her landlord without a forwarding address.

I have to try again, Jane thought. Although she had no idea where she would start.

She tipped the driver, smiled briskly at her doorman, and rode the elevator to the twelfth floor. It had to be high – she'd stipulated that to her realtor. Manhattan, and her job, were full of stress. From way above ground, the city looked peaceful; in her office and at home, Jane Morgan wanted to be in the clouds.

Her apartment was laid out along the same lines. Cool shades of white, tone on tone, punctuated with the occasional soft cushion in soft beige or grey, like driftwood and bones on a beach; oyster, pearl and cream. Jane had opted for calming neutrals. Getting away from her father's leather-bound books and statues, she was sinking into Manhattan style, sparse, zen; a buffer between her and the world.

It was immaculate, too. No longer did she have to scrub out her tub with bleach or starve out the roaches. Her maid Janet came three times a week; the building's concierge delivered daily groceries and fresh flowers: lilies, white tulips, and snowy roses, the petals bright against dark green leaves.

By her low-slung designer bed Jane kept a couple of books; one on architecture; and a business biography or two.

She smiled as she picked up a tome on David Geffen, the legendary record businessman. Yeah, she was addicted. Her life, her home, even her leisure activities. All about the bottom line.

This was nice, but it wasn't nearly enough.

Next month was her review. If Shop Smart didn't transfer her, she was gone. She glanced around her flat, mentally saying goodbye to it, without regrets. In this life Jane Morgan had learned to travel light.

There was better waiting for her, elsewhere. And her friends – she *would* find them. It would be good to see Sally. No doubt Sal would need some help, too. Jane had a rush of guilt; she'd been so focused, she hadn't tried hard enough to find Sally, and offer her a place to stay, or a good job. Well, she'd put that right; a private investigator, if need be. Sal could be her assistant. And she'd be the one person in the world who wouldn't have to come up to her exacting standards. Sal would get a nice car, a great salary and a fat pension just for showing up. And if Helen wanted to come back to the States, the same applied to her.

Jane grinned. She'd earned the right to one freebie. In any other circumstance, Jane Morgan would have shuddered at the idea of hiring a makeweight. But Sally and Helen were special. They could have whatever the hell they wanted. Jane would see to that. Either in Shop Smart, or someplace else.

Jane needed her friends. But despite what Rhodri Evans said, she didn't need anything else.

She had absolutely no interest in finding a man!

Chapter Twenty-Two

There was a knock on her office door.

'I'm busy,' Jane said, not looking up from her screen. It was Friday, and her reports from the southwest were due in.

The door swung open and Rhodri Evans put his head around it.

'You're always busy. Make some time.'

She smiled, and clicked the spreadsheet shut.

'For you, sure.' Jane glanced at her diary. 'I have a free lunch, would you like to go and get something?'

'I've always believed in miracles,' the Welshman said. 'Come on then, I want to have a chat with you.'

She took him to Le Cirque; if they were going to eat on the company's dime, Jane figured it should be a good meal. They weren't paying her well enough as it was. She ordered caviar, smoked oysters, and a rare steak to follow; Evans, not used to quite such luxurious surroundings, stuck with a salad and roast duck. Jane insisted he take a glass of champagne. It was a new decade, 1991, and sackcloth and ashes were all the fashion. The stores did a roaring trade in lumberjack shirts, as everybody wanted to be Kurt Cobain; the designers were into black and grey aesthetics, monk-like chic.

But Jane rebelled. Even though she was twenty, she thought of herself as a true child of the eighties. Luxury, aspiration, pulling yourself up by your bootstraps; all that was in her blood, and it would never die.

'And you?' Rhodri wanted to see her relaxing, too.

'I'm not twenty-one yet.'

He raised a brow. 'You're not telling me you've never had champagne?'

'Of course not. Just that I don't want to be asked for ID in a restaurant I take business contacts to.' Jane smiled, coolly. 'I have some Krug chilling in my refrigerator. But I never fight a battle I can't win.'

'We'll toast you in here on your birthday.'

'That's a deal.'

She sipped at her freshly squeezed pomegranate juice while her friend enjoyed his champagne.

'So how did it work out with Peter Ralston?' The M&A specialist from Chase; newly divorced, older than her, considered handsome. Smooth, certainly.

'We had a couple of dates,' Jane said. 'Went to Nobu's for sushi . . . I just don't think we clicked.'

'Why?' Evans was upset. 'You never seem to get on with anybody. Are you really making an effort?'

'I'm an orphan. Shouldn't I at least get a pass on nagging about my love life? What, are you going to complain you'll never have grandchildren?' Jane chuckled, and Rhodri smiled back. It was good to see the girl laugh. He worried about her; sometimes he wondered if he had done the right thing, giving her that first promotion. She was so unnaturally absorbed in business.

'But he was perfect for you.'

'Evidently not,' Jane said, wrily. In fact, Ralston had said first that he thought they should knock it on the head, and she'd been relieved. He was coming on too strong, obviously expected her to jump right into bed. And she hadn't wanted to. He just didn't excite her. She didn't know what she wanted, exactly, just that Peter Ralston wasn't it.

'Then I have somebody else you should meet.' Rhodri nodded, determinedly. 'Somebody different to anyone you've seen before.'

'I'm not interested. Really, I'm so busy. And I'm young . . .'

'But this guy—'

'Another damn banker or congressman or highly paid lawyer. I don't think I can deal with that. Face it, Rhodri, I'm just not ready to date.'

'He's none of those things. A little slice of home, I'm thinking. Maybe that's what you need. He's English.'

That brought Jane up short. 'English?'

'Yes. From Sussex. His parents own a farm near the sea. Some place called Rye.'

'I know Rye,' Jane said. She took a large swig of pomegranate juice to cover her confusion. Instantly, she desperately wanted to meet this man. Maybe it was fate. But her lack of interest had evaporated.

'He went to Eton. No title but lots of cash. He's in town buying a place in the Hamptons. Going to build his own house on a plot of land. Just broke up with a girl, the daughter of some earl or something. I met him at a party last night. And he wants to meet you.'

Her response surprised him.

'Yes, that'd be great,' Jane said. 'Give him my direct line. Do you know if he's free tonight?'

'I don't—'

'Because I am. And if not, tomorrow.' She beamed at her friend. 'Thank you, Rhodri, he sounds interesting.'

Cheered, Rhodri tossed down the rest of his champagne. Finally, then, he had solved it, cracked the puzzle. What she needed was a guy from her own culture. He'd been born in the States, Welsh parents, but never felt the need to go back to the motherland. Jane, on the other hand, had spent her childhood in the UK. And that's what she was hankering after.

She seemed to come alive at lunch, animated, chatting, telling jokes. What a transformation, he thought. He could not believe it. As soon as she had paid and jumped into a taxi, Rhodri Evans telephoned his new protégé to give him the good news.

It put him in a good mood for the rest of the day. The young woman had fascinated him since the day he had met her, so brave and so tearful. He would love to see her find success in love, as well as a balance sheet. Because without that, what good was anything?

Jane floated through the day.

Jude was going to pick her up tonight at eight, and take her to a concert. How romantic! Carnegie Hall, a candle-lit dinner; his voice on the phone had sounded gentlemanly and urbane. It charged her; she was intrigued, impatient.

Unusually, she had rushed home at the end of the day, leaving her assistant open-mouthed. They usually worked till at least half six. But today Jane had better things to do.

She dressed with exquisite care: her favourite Azzedine Alaia dress, black and tight, bands of brilliantly-cut black silk tapering around her body, ending just over the knee; high Manolo Blahnik heels, with crystal-cut buckles; Wolford tights; Hermès 24 Rue Faubourg as her scent. Jane went to the hairdressser's first, and had her glossy brown mane blown out, smooth and beautiful, around her shoulders; she chose to make up with a daring plum lipstick and charcoal liner, emerald-green shadow on her lids. Vamping it up. A bold look, but the mirror told her, without a doubt, she had pulled it off. Amongst all the drab little minimalists, Jane would look like a flashing butterfly, a glorious Purple Emperor.

She finished the look with a dress watch, a slim gold Cartier set with diamonds; a present to herself from her last bonus.

Jane paced up and down her apartment, trying to contain her excitement. Come on, she told herself. He might be ugly, he might be short, he might be far too skinny, or fat as a house.

But it didn't work. Jude had sounded so different, with his modulated voice and easy-going, unpressured tones. So cultured . . . Miles removed from all the investment bankers who always gave the impression of wanting to check their phone messages.

Whole parts of herself that had been submerged for years now were starting to wake up, Jane thought, and she liked it. At least she wanted to see him. And that made a change.

The doorbell rang and she raced to answer it.

He stood on the doorstep with a large, expensive-looking bunch of roses, dark red, set with berries and twigs and glossy foliage. He was a tall man, light brown hair, hazel eyes, a handsome enough face, and wearing a good suit that looked a bit rumpled.

Jane felt her heart flip over in her stomach as Jude casually gave her the once-over; she suddenly, ardently, wanted to be found pleasing.

'My goodness,' he said. 'You might just be the prettiest girl I've ever seen.'

'. . . is the right answer,' Jane said, and they laughed.

He was absolutely smooth. He ticked every box. He held open car doors for her, walked on the outside of the pavement, offered her his arm as they climbed the stairs in Carnegie Hall to the box he had hired. Jane sat, fascinated, at dinner, almost unable to eat because of the butterflies in her stomach, while he told her all about himself – his parents' interests in land and property, his own desire to do 'something in art history'. Jude was finding himself, and didn't want to work. He told her he had no desire to join the rat race, and Jane envied him, and thought it amazing he could be so detached.

'But you're buying a place in the Hamptons?'

They cost a fortune; several million bucks for a decent house. She certainly couldn't afford one.

'I have a trust fund.' He shrugged. 'You know, the idea we all absolutely have to spend our lives working our fingers down to the knuckle is very recent. Did you ever read any Jane Austen?'

'Of course; all of it.'

'Well, Darcy never went and toiled in an office, did he? And nor did Elizabeth. So why should I, when I don't have to?'

'I think that's wonderful,' Jane said, a little starry eyed.

Gosh. Wasn't he handsome – and urbane. So charismatic, so confident! He reminded her, she supposed, of her father – something of Thomas Morgan's self-possession. But of course this was a date. And Jude actually seemed interested in her.

'Tomorrow's Saturday,' he reminded her. 'Maybe you could come out to the Hamptons with me. I'm going round a few places. You could help me choose.'

She beamed back at him, and wondered if this was what love felt like; her whole soul was bathed in sunlight, Jude Ferrers dazzled her. Briefly she thought of Sally, who had disappeared, and never called her again. That's what Jude made her feel – golden, just like Sally Lassiter.

'What do you think?' Jane said. She did a twirl for him.

Jude inventoried her dress. Very nice – really, *very* nice. Her dark hair fell in expertly coiffed glossy curls to her shoulders. She looked more like a model than a business-woman. Jude's groin twitched pleasantly, and he imagined every man in the restaurant looking at him with envy.

He had to fuck her. She was nothing like he'd been warned, cold and fiery, independent. Jane Morgan was eager to please him, bubbly, almost kittenish.

He'd been around girls like that before, of course, but they were usually in school. Sixth-formers. With crushes.

Whatever. Infatuation worked.

Jude was spoilt. He knew it, and he didn't much care. Life could be such a bore, when you had everything you want. It was a full-time job, trying to make life fun every day. Chasing the new girl with the mid-Atlantic twang, the one she didn't know she had, was definitely fun. A real change from the social register chicks and super-expensive hookers. A true New York career woman.

He dimly sensed that Jane Morgan's professional life was fantastically impressive. Younger than him, making well into six figures and a legend in her industry. Bully for her, he thought, with a stab of sharp resentment. He, of course, had inherited his money. Jude had an aversion to work that had started at Eton, and Jane Morgan, achiever and rising star, was a walking rebuke to him.

He thought of her with a mixture of lust, envy and patronising affection. The sexy little ball-buster. Well, she can bust *my* balls, he thought, and grinned at his own joke.

Jude liked it that this wannabe Gordon Gecko in the designer skirts and heels had melted into a puddle when he'd called her. It flattered his foppish vanity. She was suitably eager to please, and he was damn well going to give her the chance. A little flattery, some old-fashioned courtly English manners, and she was eating out of his hand.

Surely Jane couldn't be nursing any idea that he would actually *marry* her? His bride would be somebody English, properly so; somebody with no taint of scandal and no silly work obsessions. A girl who would reflect him, smooth and polished, like a mirror.

Deep down inside, he couldn't work out why a girl like Jane would want him. Jude Ferrers knew, on some level, that he was a vacuous, monied loser; that was one reason he struggled not to think too deeply. He desired Jane, and he resented her. And she was so easy to play.

'You look fabulous,' he said, laconically. 'Really, you

could dazzle any room you walked into.'

Despite the curl in his lip, it was absolutely true.

His body stirred at the sight of her, and he resolved to have her. Soon.

The next day she went for smart-casual, as English as she could: tailored corduroy trousers, green Wellington boots, and a tight, cute cashmere T-shirt; loose hair, neutral make-up for day, and a necklace of seashells.

'You look delicious,' he said, kissing her boldly on the cheek. And then, when she responded, lightly on the lips.

Jane blushed and smiled; she wanted him to desire her. And she'd hardly been able to sleep, waiting for him to turn up. A completely new experience for the ice maiden.

They took a helicopter ride to the Hamptons, and Jude showed her around: a modern, glossy house on the seashore; a cute four-bedroom white clapboard cottage, old by American standards; a red-brick Victorian in the centre of town. Jane loved each one. They were two million bucks apiece. She envied him such an effortless progress through life, and wanted that for herself. Jude bought her lunch at a clam shack in the Vineyard, where they drank a delicious, rough Italian white and ate deep-fried soft shell crabs, whole, and redcurrants with lemon sorbet for pudding, then a shot of espresso with a sour cherry dipped in bittersweet chocolate to finish it off.

Jane could not remember the last time she had enjoyed a meal so much. She sat, absorbed, as Jude told her all about Rye – a glorious medieval town, she remembered now, full of buildings from history, Queen Anne, Tudor, earlier, and the flat fields and rolling downs of Sussex. And she started to fantasize about what might happen. If he liked her . . . what if she gave up work, what if she just got married, maybe started a family?

Jane was careful not to eat too much. He told her about his exes, the models he'd dated. Code for 'I like skinny girls'. About the social register parties he attended, the London Season, the big events in Paris and New York.

He said he wasn't interested in buying anything on the spot. Jane waxed lyrical about the white clapboard cottage, but Jude's eyes glazed over. After a few minutes he interrupted her.

'There's the Old Shipping Inn in the centre of town. They have a suite open – I checked. It's Sunday tomorrow, you don't have to go to work, do you?'

Jane shook her head.

'I thought maybe we could stay over. Steal a night. Like honeymooners.'

She nodded her head, briskly, her throat dry, and he whisked her away to the hotel – in fact, despite the name, very modern and sleek – and up to the promised suite, which was nearly as big as Jane's apartment.

'Ever since I saw you in that tight little dress, I wanted to unwrap you, all shiny and new, like a Christmas present.'

Ever since? It had only been last night. But Jane didn't care. She nodded, half eager, half terrified.

'Mmm, baby, you've got fabulous legs,' he said. 'Long legs, like a colt's. Let's see what you've got up there.'

And he deftly undid her trousers while somehow popping over his own shirt, and tugged her, half naked, onto the bed.

Chapter Twenty-Three

'A virgin.'

He smiled afterwards, as though he'd won a prize. Propped up on one elbow, gazing down at her proprietorially.

'I can't believe you were actually a virgin.'

'Everybody has to start somewhere,' Jane joked, although she was afraid it sounded lame.

'But you're twenty years old. I thought virgins that survived their teens were myths. Like unicorns.' He ran a hand across her thigh, touching the drying blood that lay there. 'You can be my pet unicorn.'

'I'll take a shower,' Jane said, feeling gauche, embarrassed.

'How was it?' He yawned. 'What you expected?'

'Fantastic,' she lied. In fact, she'd been dry and tense, he had started too soon. But she blamed herself. She hadn't told him she was a virgin . . .

'Well, I'll soon have you trained up to be an expert.' He rolled over on the bed. 'Sex always makes me sleepy . . . I'll take a nap, we can do it again later.' As an afterthought, he added, 'You better get on the pill, darling, we don't want any complications. I just hate those, don't you?'

'Oh – of course,' Jane said.

She went into the shower; he had already closed his eyes.

She washed herself for a long time, covering her body in fragrant gel, scrubbing the embarrassing blood from her legs.

It felt as though the world should seem different now, as if the sky should have a different colour. But it didn't; everything was normal.

Except, she told herself hopefully, for Jude. The first man she'd ever felt something for. He had taken her virginity, and she was glad. As she dried herself and dressed, Jane snuck a look at him, lying there on the bed. So handsome . . . so charming. Rhodri had said all the women were flinging themselves at him. No wonder, she thought, and I've got him!

It was a brilliant feeling.

When Jude woke, he suggested they check out anyway.

'Nobody wants to wear the same clothes two days in a row. I'll pick you up tomorrow for brunch.'

'OK,' Jane said, happily enough. She had been looking forward to spending the night with him, but tomorrow would do.

He dropped her off at her door with a little pat on her ass, and Jane spun round to kiss him, deeply, romantically. But Jude laughed, and said, 'You're a lot of fun.'

She didn't like that. Something profound had just happened – OK, they hadn't been going out more than two days, but still, surely he must feel the chemistry, must feel the instant rightness of it all?

She went to sleep in her own bed, alone, and not wholly happy. But she tried to suppress her doubts. After all, she knew very well how beautiful she was. Men were always trying, and failing, to impress her. Jude would understand his luck . . . surely?

He did call. Bright and early, and picked her up at eleven. The brunch spot was crowded and hip, and Jane nervously picked at waffles with strawberries, while Jude polished off bacon and eggs and a mug of cinnamon coffee.

'So after this we'll go back to my hotel,' he suggested,

throwing down a hundred-dollar bill, carelessly. 'Work off the meal. If you want to. And then tonight . . . we could go to that book launch at the Metropolitan, and back afterwards for more?'

'Perfect,' Jane said, happy, reassured.

He still liked her. He was still interested. It wasn't wam, bam, thank you, ma'am. Yes, there was some reserve there, but she found it all the sexier, all the more exciting. For once, she was the pursuer. And every time he looked at her, every time that English voice complimented her, Jane thrilled with happiness.

The sex still wasn't great, but she didn't care. She went along, easily enough. It was the price of being with someone so charming. And that was what a relationship was . . .

Over the next week, at work, she floated through her days, her mind only half on her work. Thinking about Jude, waiting for him to call. They met at odd hours; in the middle of the night, at lunchtime, often, and then she would duck out of meetings at three or four. Nobody complained. Jane was invaluable. They gossiped a little about how starry-eyed she was, and she knew they could see she was in love. So what? Some day, she knew, she'd be announcing an engagement . . .

And then he rang, and her world crashed in.

'Baby.' That soft, familiar tone at the end of the work day. How she loved to hear it. 'You have to come over to the hotel.'

Jane glanced at the clock: 4:45. Good enough.

'On my way,' she said, grabbing her bag. And hung up. All Jude had to do was call, and she came running.

'So.' He rolled off her, stretched out for a minute, then jumped up from the bed. Jane grabbed the sheet and held it around her shoulders; when Jude walked away from her – he didn't like to cuddle much – she always felt more naked than naked. 'I'm going to miss you,' he said, grabbing his dressing gown and pulling it on, casually.

Jude wasn't looking at her. Jane was highly intelligent; she felt the tiny hairs prickle on her arms, and jumped out of bed herself, reaching for her clothes.

'Miss me? Are you going somewhere?'

'Well, the summer's over,' he said, lightly. 'Time to push on home.'

'I thought you were staying,' Jane said, worriedly. 'You're going back to England? I have a major project, re-staffing in Arizona. I can't get leave for a while.'

Jude sighed and reached towards the table where a packet of Marlboro Lites was half open; his eyes slid away from her, and he looked out of the window.

'Leave? To come and see me? I don't think that's such a great idea, darling.'

She shivered. 'What do you mean?'

'Oh, come on, don't make this difficult.' He started to pace around the room, then said, quickly, as though wanting to get the words out, 'I'm going home – you're staying here. This was a holiday romance, great while it lasted, but I don't think we've got a future. Not long-term. You've got your career . . .'

Jane was seized with blind panic. He was leaving her, abandoning her . . .

'Is there someone else?' she whispered.

'Yes,' Jude said, brutally. 'Actually, more than one. I just don't want to be tied down. You're beautiful, sweetheart, but you're just too . . . clingy.'

Numbly, Jane pulled on her panties and bra, and reached for her skirt.

'And we don't have an awful lot in common. In fact,' he said, sauntering towards the bathroom, 'there's history, isn't there? Your father . . . well, it wouldn't be right. Not in England, anyway. Not after what he did. I'm sure you can

see that, Jane. You'll be better off here, with a Yank –
somebody who won't ask too many awkward questions . . .'

Her hands trembled as she did up the buttons of her shirt.
Jane fought it, but the shock and loss . . . the embarrassment
. . . it was rejection, it was utter humiliation . . .

Deliberately not looking at her, he walked into the
bathroom, and she heard him switch on the shower.

Jane dressed as quickly as she could, her heart thumping
and her mind racing. Nothing in common . . . clingy . . .
better off here . . . *your father* . . .

Abandoned. Again. Was that going to be her destiny,
then? First her father, and then Sally and Helen, the only
two real friends she'd ever had? Rhodri was great, and Jane
got on with some of the other girls in Human Resources, but
there was nothing for her like it had been with her two best
friends. And they had run to ground, in Texas, in Egypt, and
she would never see them again. Everything she was trying
was coming up empty.

In fact, as she stood there, humiliated, in Jude's soulless
hotel bedroom, the pain of the loss of those two girls was
worse for Jane than what had just happened. Perhaps
because, unlike her father, Sally and Helen actually *cared*
about her. She flashed back on dark-haired Helen leaning
out of the window of Sally's car, calling her to come and get
a makeover . . .

Those girls were the only *real* family Jane had ever had.
And everybody needs a family.

Even as the tears were rolling down her cheeks, Jane
suddenly, in a flash of light, understood everything. Why
she'd felt so attracted, why she'd jumped on him, why she'd
wanted him, desperately, even when the sex was lousy and
the conversation strained . . .

Her father. Jude was English. In some weird way he'd
reminded her of Thomas, and he had wanted her. Praised
her. Spent time with her. Lavished attention on her . . .

She had been trying to claw back the love she hadn't received – romantic attention from a boyfriend instead of the fatherly love Thomas Morgan never gave her.

And the others? The Americans, with whom she was supposed to click? None of them had stood a chance. None of them could be a father substitute, none of them could pay back her pain . . .

She steadied herself, one hand pressed against her heart, looking out over Central Park, the leaves just starting to redden and brown. It was so clear, so revelatory.

Jude was nothing. She had lost her virginity to nothing.

Calm now, Jane reached for her coat. No more; no longer. That was all over. She would go on, and succeed, and win, despite what Thomas Morgan had done to her. If love came, it would come. But Jane Morgan was not about to go looking for it. And she would not use romance to heal a childhood wound.

Jude's clothes and his packed suitcase lay on the bed. Jane glanced out of the window; below them was a terrace. Casually, Jane tossed everything Jude owned out of the window – the suitcase was heavy, but she made it – and walked out of his suite, leaving the door wide open.

On the way home, she probed herself, her feelings. Yes, she felt a little stupid. But also lightened. As though now she saw clearly, saw the problem. Jane almost felt grateful to Jude. A stuck-up trust fund brat with no purpose in life except sex and snobbery; and he wasn't even good at the sex. But his careless betrayal had finally ripped the scales off Jane's eyes.

All in all, she told herself, cheaper than therapy.

She pressed the button and allowed the crisp, cool air to drift into the cab. It was refreshing, invigorating. The snap of autumn in New York.

Holiday's over. Time to get to work.

*

In her apartment, Jane found the answer machine was blinking. She pressed it.

'You bloody *bitch*!' She laughed. 'I've got to call damn housekeeping now, they might blab. This could make the gossip columns . . . I'll be a laughing stock . . .'

She pressed delete, went to her refrigerator, ignored the yellowing celery and Chinese leftovers in their cartons and went straight for the chilled bottle of champagne. Jane poured herself a glass, slowly, and sipped it, thinking hard.

She needed a change. Out of this relationship – that was done. Out of her job, too. It was no longer any fun in Human Resources. She could be comfortable there, but no more.

Jane wanted ownership. She wanted it to be *her* helicopter, *her* house in the Hamptons. She'd seen a slogan in a dime store once – 'It's a strong man who can prevail in the face of comfort.'

Too right. She was getting lazy. Middle management was not in her game plan. Let them promote her to the main board, give her a division to run. And stock. And she'd get on a plane, go back to Los Angeles. She was overwhelmed with a desire to recapture some of what she had lost. Find Sally Lassiter, even if Sally had disappeared – find Helen, even if Helen was babied up in a Cairo suburb. They had private investigators these days that were as good as the FBI. This was America; money opened every door.

Yes. As the alcohol cheered and relaxed her, Jane smiled. Time to put her cards on the table. Shop Smart and she would play a game of chicken, and Jane was not going to be the one who blinked.

Chapter Twenty-Four

Their first trip to America was a big success.

Baba and Mama met them at the airport; they hugged and cried, and were obviously so sincerely overjoyed to see Haya that she could forgive the smug look in her father's eyes. He was triumphant because she was wearing traditional dress and speaking Arabic, and so obviously in love with Ahmed.

'I was right,' he kept saying, on the drive back from the airport. 'You see, darling? I was right. We *did* know best.'

Haya wanted to explode, but Ahmed, in the back seat with her, kept pressing her hand, his eyes lit up with amusement. And then he switched to tracing an A with his fingers, slowly, in the small of her back. A for Ahmed. Telling Haya she was his. It turned her on, and her rage evaporated.

Ahmed, this time not wary of an impending arranged marriage, looked at LA with open eyes. With Haya's eyes. Yes, it was brash, and Western, and vulgar in lots of ways, but it was also exciting, big, and rich. His wife's enthusiasm was infectious. He loved that about her – that she made life an adventure.

And his father-in-law had kept his word. There was a meeting at Nieman Marcus, at Saks and at the Beverly Hills Hotel. And all three places agreed to buy a carpet or two; Ahmed had brought some of his finest examples. Before the month was out, he had a small, interested client base.

'We could do more,' Haya suggested. 'Sell in department stores, regularly. Of course, such things take time . . .' She looked up at Ahmed under her lashes. 'And also presence.'

And I could try harder to find Jane and Sally, Helen thought to herself, too. She adored Ahmed, but she missed her girlfriends. Dreadfully.

'You mean move here?' he said slowly.

'Talal could run the Egyptian store. We could buy a place, import some of the stock, just for a year or so. See how we like it.' Haya grinned. 'I'm a US citizen, remember? No problems there.'

'I don't know. It's a big step.' Ahmed looked down at her, sternly. He had already decided he wanted to do just that, but he enjoyed playing games with his willing, eager little wife.

'We should do it,' she said, her stomach flipping over in that sexy, slow way it did when he held her eyes. 'Please . . .'

He ran a finger down her cheek. 'Persuade me.'

In the end it was seamless. Haya trained Talal, his manager, on the computer; they organized insurance, and wages for his staff; a cousin from Aswan came with his wife to stay in the Cairo house, paying a peppercorn rent. And Haya took her dowry, which Baba paid to Ahmed, and some of the profits from their last year's trading, and purchased a property; Ahmed approved of the third place she showed him, a comfortable, modern villa in mock Spanish style at the foot of the Hollywood Hills, on a quiet street away from the tourist hotspots. The garden was small, but verdant, and they were in the thick of everything; and Ahmed enjoyed the large television, the power showers with multiple jets, the soft mattresses and air conditioning.

They moved in, storing a pile of their best carpets in a guest room. Haya helped set up the new American company, and Ahmed made the sales, and closed the deals. As easy as the move had been, business was not quite so simple. The famous stores had their suppliers already, and while he moved a carpet a month, the larger orders were slow in coming.

But America was an adventure for Ahmed. He enjoyed going to the beach every day, swimming in the ocean, trying the different foods, and taking trips: San Francisco, with the tall, prehistoric cedars of Muir Woods; the fortress of Alcatraz; and the disturbing cable cars. Haya blossomed even more, at home, where she was confident. They nestled in the modern house and made love daily, flew back to Egypt three times a year, and he pushed and pushed to establish himself.

Slow going, but the orders were there, and they kept their heads above water.

Yet he was disturbed by one thing: the months came and went, and still the wife of his heart was not pregnant.

Haya leaned on the balcony of the kitchen window; it was low-slung and looked out into their little garden, one of her favourite slots. The sun beamed down on the terrace; she might sunbathe later, under an umbrella, sipping a chilled grapefruit juice mixed with selzer, her latest favourite drink. But despite trying to relax, Haya was anxious.

There were things missing from her life.

Haya couldn't find her friends. When she first got back to the States she plunged into the search, calling Miss Milton's, checking newspaper reports in the public library, but it had all led to a dead end. Haya only had a grainy picture of Jane with some young lawyer, outside a courtroom, and one of Sally Lassiter, her head up, her hand in front of a camera, refusing to talk.

They were gone. And when she'd tried to look in the phone book, she found there were 407 Jane Morgans in Los Angeles County alone.

She gave up for the time being. Ahmed was happy, and so was she, but they had not spread their wings the way

Haya had hoped.

She wanted more.

Haya lowered her fizzing grapefruit juice and passed a hand across her forehead. A wave of nausea hit her, and she got unsteadily to her feet. She rushed back into the house and barely made it into their bathroom, throwing up wretchedly as she gripped the side of the loo.

Not good. She flushed and splashed water on her face. For the last week or so, as the pressure mounted, Haya had been feeling ill. She'd lost a little weight, as she could barely get anything down half the time, but today was the first time she'd actually thrown up.

It must be stress. Sitting around worrying was no good. Failure was enervating. Haya had been moping around the house feeling desperately tired, even after a good night's sleep. She cleaned her teeth frantically and resolved to talk to her husband. Haya wanted to get a grip. Maybe she needed to be more involved. Powerlessness was no fun.

When Ahmed came back that night – he had made five thousand on the placement of a beautiful Afghan in the beach-house of a famous actor – Haya asked him if she could come along the next day.

'Your meeting tomorrow. With Richard Drayson.' The sales director of Broderick Stores.

Ahmed was going to try, yet again, to get a department store to place a major ongoing order. It would be the sixth pitch meeting he'd had this year. Something was going wrong – they were failing, somehow. Just treading water. And Haya wanted to see why.

'If you'd like to,' Ahmed agreed. He too was unhappy. There was no progress, they were stuck in middle-class comfort. 'Sure. Why not?'

'We think you have good pieces, Mr al-Amin.' The buyer's eyes were flat. 'And we'll happily take two rugs.'

'We were hoping for a proper order,' Ahmed said. 'The small sales do not cover overheads. We are a reliable supplier and cannot be beaten on price.'

Drayson shook his head. 'Your goods are certainly superior, but I can't take the risk.'

'What do you mean by that?' Haya protested.

'Our traders deal with thousands of rugs per year. They have shipping systems and a constant supply of product. They get exclusive, or near it, presence in the stores because we rely on them. I can't offend them in order to take a chance with somebody who frankly is small potatoes. You have good carpets, Mr al-Amin, but you're strictly nickel and dime.'

Ahmed's eyes darkened, and he opened his mouth to speak, but Haya laid a gentle hand on his shoulder.

'Thank you very much, Mr Drayson,' she said. The buyer was only being honest. No point getting mad.

Drayson looked satisfied. 'So you'll sell us the two carpets,' he said briskly. 'Good.'

'No,' Ahmed said, suddenly, looking at Haya. 'I'm afraid not. We're going to go into business for ourselves, and from now on the line will be exclusive.'

She beamed back. Her thought exactly. She was so proud of Ahmed – they were hand in glove. *Mash'Allah*, Haya prayed silently, thank God for my husband.

That very afternoon, they got to work. They found a site – ironically, an old carpet warehouse – at a dusty road intersection; applied for planning permission, sought out an architect. Baba knew builders.

Haya suggested the name. Sekhmet. The ancient Egyptian goddess of vengeance and war, lioness-headed, beautiful and fierce – like they were going to be with the competition. She designed the statue that stood on the outside; striking, playing up their Egyptian heritage, and of course colossal, like everything in LA. Ahmed worked with the architect – huge windows, lots of light, UV protection built in.

No more fussy, dusty rooms.

It was their vision, and they worked to make it happen. A gallery. The carpets stretched out, displayed like paintings. Each as individual as a jewel. To keep costs low, they went for good light, clean walls, and little else. Baba contacted his network; Ahmed his sales prospects. On opening weekend they sold ten carpets.

Not brilliant, but respectable. Solid.

Haya brought in flowers and Moroccan mint tea. Ahmed placed a small advertisement in the *LA Times*. The second week, they sold another twelve carpets.

The gallery was profitable. They were on their way. It was hard work, but Haya enjoyed it; staying up late with Ahmed, making love in the bathroom, at home, on the back-seat of their car, like teenagers, in a secluded spot. They increased the trips back home, and she got used to dealing with suppliers, visiting the tribal weavers, talking to customs men. Haya's Arabic became perfect, and she was happy; she loved her husband, loved her job, loved her life. They were crafting a future; they became comfortable, and she still wanted more. And Ahmed, so dominant in the bedroom, outside of it was her partner and ally. Haya had everything, except her friends. And, *insh'Allah*, a child.

'It's so good to meet you.' Marcus Hardie, the sales director, looked at Haya and gave her a perfunctory smile that didn't reach his eyes. 'So often in our business we never get to see the family. Your husband has quite the business model; you must be very proud.'

Ahmed's eyes danced as Haya's flashed with annoyance.

'Actually, my wife had a good deal to do with this.'

'Of course. We all need the support at home. Couldn't get

it done without that.'

Support! The gallery had been *her* idea. Haya stiffened with anger. Now everybody – well, not Ahmed, but everybody else – was trying to take the credit away from her.

Baba insisted success came because of *his* contacts. The press ran stories about Ahmed, the backstreet carpet seller turned gallery owner. Now the Hollywood Mall marketing man was ignoring her too. Even when Ahmed specifically introduced Haya as wife and *partner*.

It made her angry.

Jane Morgan wouldn't let herself be ignored. And these days, all grown up, Haya al-Yanna wouldn't stand for it, either.

Haya suddenly remembered Jane and Sally fighting off those bullies in the playground, when she was at her prayers. The pang of loss came to her, sharp as a knife, The friends she'd made here – some of her sister Jasmine's girlfriends, the odd wife of Ahmed's customers – they were OK, but there had never again been anything like that true bond. A great friendship was like love, you knew when you had the real thing. But the private investigators were coming up empty.

Haya dragged herself from her memories, and focused on Hardie.

'Mr Hardie. The first consignment will be no more than fifty carpets,' Haya said, firmly.

'Per store? We'll want more than that.'

'Not per store. For the United States.' His chain of luxury goods stores was important, but not vital. 'You should have no more than one or two per store; in Manhattan and Beverly Hills we could go for five, at any one time.'

'That's not going to happen, little lady,' Marcus said, patronizingly. He switched his attention back to Ahmed. 'What numbers did *you* have in mind?'

'You heard my wife.'

'Our customers want product.'

'And they'll get it,' Haya said, 'eventually. After the carpets become impossible to obtain. When there's a waiting list – like a Kelly bag from Hermès.'

'A what?'

'We like to create excitement. These items are works of art. It is an approach that has worked here in the Sekhmet Gallery,' Ahmed pointed out.

'Always leave them wanting more. When you have orders in hand for fifty, we ship another ten. It will create a feeding frenzy,' Haya said.

Marcus parried. 'You can't run a business on hype.'

'Actually, you can. But in this case it isn't hype. Our goods are exquisite. We merely add to the joy of the purchase.' Haya warmed to her theme. 'Shopping is like a love affair, Mr Hardie, if it's done correctly. Prolonging the courtship is no bad thing.'

He barely refrained from rolling his eyes.

'I'll think about it.' He got to his feet. 'Tell you what, Ahmed, come and see me in the office, OK? And you, little lady, nice to meet you. See you again sometime.'

Haya exploded once he was out the door.

'Did you hear that? He wants to do business with *you*.'

'You can't let it get to you.' Ahmed stood up and walked across to her, standing behind her, his hands on her shoulders, tracing a line down them to her ribcage, possessively. She shuddered with pleasure.

'Not here,' Haya whispered.

'Why not?' He nuzzled her neck, biting it lightly, and ran his hands across her breasts and belly. 'Nobody will come in. Not without knocking. You're tense.' His thumb traced a line at the base of her spine, and Haya gasped.

'We'll go home,' she said. 'Let's go home, darling.'

'You go,' he said. 'Wait for me. I have to finish up here with Anita; some tax stuff.'

'Don't be long.' She was trying to get control of her breathing.

'Did you see the doctor?'

That broke the spell; reluctantly Haya calmed down.

'Results this afternoon.'

That was it; the one cloud in their happiness. A great business, houses in Egypt and the Hollywood hills, a foot in both worlds. But no children.

She had not wanted to make the appointment. What she and Ahmed had was so precious, so intense. To lay her womb open to medicine seemed clinical, intrusive. Like slapping nature in the face for the gift they had received – burning love, and a passion as hot now as it was the first night he had taken her. Surely such a love could not be barren? Wouldn't children come in time?

But Ahmed, on this one thing, had insisted. And she had obeyed him. Children mattered so much to him. It was why he'd agreed to marry her, before he fell in love with her.

Haya had submitted herself to Dr Felicia Nevins, one of Bel Air's leading ob-gyns. The woman had prodded and poked her briskly, drawn blood and taken tests. Haya felt like a laboratory animal.

At least there wasn't long to wait now. The results were due at 5 p.m. And she was nervous about them. What if there *was* something wrong? If, God forbid, she was infertile? Ahmed was hers forever, of that Haya had no doubt. But that would mean the end of this long period of perfect happiness. Their lives would never again be free of sorrow.

'Then hurry home and I'll help you pass the time,' Ahmed said. She ran to his arms, and he kissed her, pressing his palms against the soft swell of her breasts.

'*You* hurry,' Haya said.

She paced in their bedroom. Damn it. Where the hell was

he? Outside, their little garden was fragrant with bougainvillea and roses. She'd thought about scattering petals across the black silk sheets Ahmed preferred, but then decided against it – too much of a cliché. Haya was still aroused, her body holding the memory of his touch, not wanting to let it go.

This was not like him. Ahmed didn't blow her off for the sake of work meetings. If he said he was coming home, he came.

Haya picked up the phone and called their assistant.

'Claire? Haya.'

'Hi. What time are you guys getting back in? I have a ton of messages. Marcus Hardie—'

'Getting back in? Did Ahmed leave already?' Stuff Marcus Hardie.

'Of course – an hour ago.' Claire was confused. 'I thought he was going back home for lunch with you, sorry.'

'He was.' Haya wondered what the hell had happened. 'Maybe he stopped off for something. I'll call when he gets here.'

An hour later, she called the police. Supremely uninterested, they told her she couldn't report a missing person for twenty-four hours.

An hour after that, she started ringing around the hospitals . . .

Chapter Twenty-Five

'It can't have happened. No.'

'I'm terribly sorry.'

'He was with me three hours ago.' She felt stupid, just kept repeating it. 'He was fine. Can't you put him in a neck brace?'

Ahmed lay there – she could hardly believe it really was him. Bandaged and trussed, with drips and feeders running from his arm. Around her, there was chaos – an over-whelmed A&E, a really bad hospital in Venice Beach.

'Move him,' Haya said sharply. 'Get him into a private room.'

The machines behind her husband's bed beeped. It was a comforting sound. He was still with her, still alive.

'Mrs al-Yanna.' The doctor, a young woman, Korean-American, was trying to be kind. 'We don't have those facilities here, ma'am . . .'

'Then transfer him! A private clinic. I'll pay whatever it takes,' Haya said, tears welling. 'I have the money.'

'It's not that. There's no point, Mrs al-Yanna. It was a very bad accident – the other driver died at the scene . . .'

What did Haya care? They were just words.

'My husband is still alive,' she snapped. '*Mash'Allah*. And I want him to get the best care . . . and I'm staying with him, so I'll be needing a bed, or a cot, or something.'

'He is not still alive,' the doctor said, flatly. 'Ma'am, I'm extremely sorry, but you don't understand. Your husband is dead. He experienced total brain death. The stem of his brain is dead.'

'People come out of comas,' Haya whispered. Tears were rolling down her cheeks.

'He is not in a coma. He is dead.'

The woman was a devil! 'Then why . . .' Haya's voice broke on a sob. 'Why is that machine sounding? I can hear his heartbeats. I can see them!'

'Artificial respiration.' The doctor could see that the wife was semi hysterical. She had other patients. She had to move on. 'We kept him alive in the hope you'd be willing to donate his organs. All that means is his heart is pumping. It's up to you, ma'am.' For the millionth time that day, Dr Kim tried for patience. 'But I have a very sick father of two who needs a liver and an indigent lady waiting for a heart, with no other options.' Haya looked stricken. 'She needs it now. I'm sorry there's no time for you to decide. If the answer is no, we unplug him immediately and the Medical Examiner will take over. I need the bed.' She gestured at the wailing, sobbing crowd outside. 'You can see how it is.'

At these hurried, harassed words, a strange feeling of immense calm enveloped Haya. He was gone, gone to Paradise, and she was here alone. And Allah is the Most Compassionate, she said to herself.

Ahmed was gone. His tender heart would have reached out to the sick. In saving other lives there was a crumb, just a crumb, of comfort.

'Yes. I'll sign the form. Take what you need,' she said. 'And then return him to me, this day. He must be buried at once. He is a Muslim, a believer. We cannot delay the burial.'

Dr Kim couldn't believe it. She tried not to smile, but the relief and surprise was too great.

'Thank you – thank you. I'll get you a consent form and

a rush on the autopsy, I promise you. Tell me where you want . . .' Her voice trailed off. '. . . him sent.'

Haya went into automatic mode. She called Egypt, and his parents. Listened to the ululation of his mother. Called their mosque. Called Baba and Mama, forbidding them to come over. Not yet. Ahmed was lying in the funeral home, and she was here, in Hollywood, alone again, a widow at twenty. Who would marry her now?

It did not matter; she wanted nobody. Ahmed was her life, her love, the sun and moon to her. Without him, life seemed utterly pointless.

The funeral was attended by what few mourners she could muster, her friends, and the Muslims who worked for them at Sekhmet; not many people to stand around his grave, to mourn his shrouded body.

She tried to pray, but felt nothing. Nothing but darkness engulfed her. Without feeling, she stared into space.

The telephone rang. Haya answered, automatically.

'Hello? Ms al-Yanna?'

'Yes?'

'This is Dr Nevins.'

'Hi.'

'I have the results of your tests. And in fact I have some very good news!'

The American woman spoke with a professional chirpiness that made Haya want to slam the phone down on her.

No, you don't, she thought, there is no good news any more.

'You're not barren. These things just happen sometimes. It takes a little longer than planned. All *your* indicators are normal.' The doctor blabbed on. 'Maybe your husband had a low sperm count, you should get him in to be looked at . . .'

256

Rage surged in Haya. 'I have to go,' she said.

'But it's all academic,' the woman went on brightly. 'Because, you see, you're in fact pregnant. Congratulations!'

Haya shuddered. 'What?'

'You're pregnant. Only about three weeks from conception, but you're definitely pregnant. There's a heartbeat already, which *greatly* increases the chances of a successful first trimester. So lay off the booze,' Dr Nevins wisecracked.

'That is *haram*. I don't drink.' Haya was swaying on her feet. 'I have to go,' she repeated, and hung up.

Oh God! Pregnant!

So that was why she had been so exhausted. That was why she had—

Haya ran into her bathroom and was sick.

For the first two months, Haya did not tell anybody. She could not deal with that, not on top of everything else. The fussing and clucking – she would die.

It was enough to have to fly back to Egypt, and be plunged into a world she could hardly cope with: instructing lawyers, selling the house, enduring the anger of his parents, who blamed her for Ahmed's death. After all, she had dragged him to America, that godless, decadent land, and there, he had died.

Then there was everything else. The dismissal of all the staff, with compensation – generous; Haya arranged six months' wages for each of them, paid from the sale of the Cairo house.

Yet she could not bear to rid herself of the carpets, of the lamps, the silken cushions, everything he had acquired; the evidence of that eye for beauty that had assessed Haya herself, and found her pleasing. She had the stock shipped to LA. Everybody told her she should sell it off, in bulk; there were offers, now their brand had been established, for the carpets, the gallery space, for everything.

And in truth, Haya found she could not keep it going. Even if she'd had the emotional strength. She had been the inspiration, the spirit, of Sekhmet, but she had no idea about the details. Line management, staffing, wages, distribution; all that, Ahmed had confidently handled. She was out of her depth.

She wound up the company, offering three months to the American workers – their wages were far more costly – and sold the gallery. But the stock she put into storage.

Haya wasn't rich, but there was some money there, now. Enough for a year or so, for breathing space. Enough to see her through the birth of her child. His son or daughter. A small piece of her love that would come back to her.

Right now, that was all she cared about.

On the other hand, it wouldn't last. And Haya had no desire to go back to her father's house. She loved her parents, but she was independent of them. Which meant, one way or another, eventually she was going to have to make a living – more than a living. She had to give his child all he would have dreamed of. Anything less would be a betrayal.

Chapter Twenty-Six

'We're here. Momma.' Sally reached across the passenger seat and shook her mother, who was snoozing, her mouth open and her neck lolling against the headrest. 'Wake up. We're here.'

Back in LA. The very thought of it thrilled her. This was her true home, not Texas, this was the place where she had shone. With Jane and Helen, they were the three musketeers. Sally had tried to forget about her friends, back when her life was falling apart. Now she wanted more than anything else to find them again.

She remembered her last, greatest, day here, her party at Green Gables. The three of them, on top of the world . . .

Whatever it took, whatever it took to get that back, Sally thought, fiercely.

Mona opened her eyes. 'We are? Great.' She rubbed the lids. 'I want a drink,' she said groggily. 'A little champagne, huh? To celebrate. We're back.'

'Let's see what's in the apartment,' Sally suggested. She knew better than to refuse outright. Whatever would get Mona up the stairs. Sally was perfectly prepared to drug her mother, once she'd had a shower and eaten. A few sleeping pills, and she would tumble into bed.

Sally tried every trick in the book to keep alcohol away from Mona, to give her liver a few breaks. As soon as she'd saved enough money, Sally made the decision to try rehab. Betty Ford was permanently out of their budget, but there were other places. She couldn't afford those either, yet, but soon she'd be able to. That was her goal. That was why she needed a good job. One she would slave at.

It was worth it. And she didn't think Mona would fight that hard. Her mother had surrendered her place in the family, become the child, leaving Sally in charge. And if Sally issued an order, Mona obeyed it.

In her heart, her momma didn't want to be this way. Plus, they were back in LA. That gave Sally a chance for some prime emotional blackmail.

'You know, people might report us to the papers, Mom. You don't want Lucille and Kimberley,' Mona's ex-friends, 'to read about you in the society columns, do you?'

Mona shuddered. 'Read what?'

'That you were drunk in a cheap apartment? Just think – they'd be laughing at you.'

Her mom's eyes flashed with a spark of her old spirit.

'Hell, no,' she said. 'I'll just take a bubble bath.'

'There you go,' Sally said, relieved. She shepherded her mother inside and up the stairs. The apartment building was painted bubblegum pink, and the paint was tired; the rails on the stairwells were made of steel, and the flooring was cheap linoleum. But at least the place was clean; there was a strong smell of industrial disinfectant.

Mona clutched at her daughter as Sally fumbled with the keys.

'D'you think they will? D'you think they'll find out we're living here?'

Sally shrugged. It was good that her mother had some sense of shame, now she was back on her home turf. Perhaps Sally could build on that.

For now, she tried to reassure her.

'Listen, Momma, it's a decent place. Better than Hartford. It's got security and underground parking.' Sally pushed her mother inside the apartment. 'See? Not so bad.'

It was plainly furnished with the basic essentials. Couch, bed, a table and four chairs, and small seventeen-inch TV set. Functional beige carpets, and all the charm of a roadside motel.

She wondered what Jane and Helen would say if they could see her reduced to this. But Sally knew, and it glowed within her, that they would not be cruel. Unlike Mona's monied acquaintances, their friendship had been real.

'You take a bath.' There was a small tub, the kind where you had to raise your knees. 'And I'll go get the groceries.' Some hot chocolate with two sleeping pills would do the trick. Sally comfortingly patted her mother's arm. 'We won't be here too long, Momma. You'll see.'

Brave words. She wondered how she could make them come true.

Sally got a job the first week. It wasn't hard in LA, the world capital of glitz and glamour; every other block there was a beauty parlour. Beehive was a cute little place on Sunset with a customer base of hip West Hollywood teens; anonymous and boring. Sally agreed to work on commission in exchange for being off the books. She didn't want to be found in her own city.

Not yet. Not till they were truly on the up.

Of course, what applied to the press didn't apply to Helen or Jane Morgan. Sally rang around, made a few calls, even went to the public library to comb through old newspapers on the microfiche.

But she found nothing. They were gone. And although she kept trying, Sally knew she had to get to work.

She did makeovers, styled hair, and kept the place clean. Nothing exciting, but Sally was very good, and very popular. She got to set her own rates and kept fifty per cent plus tips. It paid the rent and fattened her bank account. They could afford to live, but Sally was still trying to get the rehab money together. Even the most modest residential place did not come cheap.

After a month she splashed out on a car, a respectable Ford Fiesta. But that was her only indulgence. Sally worked seven days a week, till late, and kept herself booked up to the eyeballs. She wanted to do something better, but the first step was to get established in LA. To fatten up their bank account until she had three or four months' reserve.

Sally Lassiter was tired of being an employee. She wanted to start her own business. And that required cash.

At night, when she got home, often to find Mona drunk again, Sally would go to her room and practise sketching.

She had ripped out pages from the glossies – *Elle*, *Vogue*, *Cosmo*. Sally wanted to design clothes – easy, wearable, hip. Style was more than make-up. Sally had it planned – her own designs, hand-sewn at first. Sold into stores. A boutique line, then more, rolled out across the city. Maybe the country. The sky would be the limit. She knew she had talent, and she certainly had glamour. Sally Lassiter had no intention of staying anybody's employee.

But for the first year, she paid the bills, worked her job, and saved the cash. And every day, Sally practised those designs.

She sewed up some clothes, put them on to work. Compliments flowed from the customers. Girls asked where they could buy the skirts and skinny jeans, and her favourite one-shoulder T-shirts.

'I love them,' Sue Joliffe, her friend from the salon, said, clapping her hands, red-painted mouth in an admiring O. 'They're so stylish, you sure do have a gift!'

'Thanks, sugar,' Sally replied.

Sue was a nice girl. They'd been for coffee a few times, and chatted about bands and where to get cheap clothes that hung right. But there just wasn't that magnetism she'd felt with the other two. Sometimes a lesser friendship downright depressed her, since the lack of progress in finding either Helen or Jane left her with such a void.

But Sue's opinion was better than nothing, that was for sure.

Sally grinned. She had enough money now, and the reaction told her she was ready.

One sunny Monday morning, Sally shook hands with the beauty parlour owner and told her she was quitting.

'But you can't.' Fiona Bryce's face was a picture of dismay. 'You're my best girl, Sally, people come here just because of you.'

'That's mighty sweet of you, Fi, but I want to do my own thing.'

Fiona tried to stop her.

'I'll put you on salary,' she said, desperately. 'With health benefits! And you can up the commission to sixty-forty. How about that?'

But Sally shook her head, and the long golden hair tumbled about her face.

'I want to make some real money. You only do that by owning your own joint. I've saved up enough now. Sorry.'

The older woman pouted; the determined glint in those beautiful eyes told her she wasn't going to get very far with this.

'It's tough, making it on your own.'

'I'm used to tough.'

'Well, good luck to you, honey. And if it doesn't work out, you always got a job here.'

'Thank you. That's real sweet.'

But Sally knew, as she walked out of the door, that she would never return. It was time for her comeback. She'd waited years, and finally, Sally Lassiter, tempered by tragedy, and poverty, and abuse, was ready for the big time.

*

The next step was the easiest. Sally booked Mona into a downtown rehab place. She brooked no argument; she bundled Momma into the car and drove off down La Cienega.

'I don't want to go without you.' Mona's latest excuse.

Sally didn't look at her. 'Mom, you'll be just fine.'

'It's too expensive. I don't need this, Sally. I can cut down. It's just the stress.'

'Momma, it's been more than three years since Poppa died. I'm nineteen years old. And I don't want you to be dead by the time I'm twenty.' Sally kept her eyes on the road. 'I can't face coming home every day, not knowing if you've choked on your own vomit. Your face is all red, you look like you're sixty years old. That ain't us, Momma. Daddy would hate it. We're back in LA . . .'

'We'll never be back,' Mona wailed, her voice full of the booze she'd chugged before Sally manhandled her into the Ford. 'We lived in Beverly Hills.'

'And we will do again.' Sally's knuckles whitened on the wheel. 'I'm going to be a designer. I'll sell my clothes. You'll see.'

'I should be at home, looking after you.' Mona's teary, drunken tones turned aggressive. 'Stop the car! You can't make me do rehab! I won't check in . . . I'll look after you, Sal.'

Sally pulled over to the side of the road and looked at her mother, all swollen-faced and drowning in self-pity.

'These past years, I've been looking after you. Paying all the bills. Running the house. Watching you kill yourself. The best I could do was to have you clean your teeth, Momma.'

'I've been fine looking out for you, Sally . . .'

Mona was delusional. Sally would not allow that to continue; not one more minute.

'Do you know why we left Texas, Momma? Because I

was raped. By Leo Fisk. One night when I was walking back at night after slaving all day to support us.' Her mother's mouth opened in a round O of shock. 'And when I came inside, you were passed out drunk. Again. That's when I packed up. And I came back here, to make something of this family again.'

Her mother started to sob now, in earnest.

'That's how I lost my virginity,' Sally said, coldly. 'To a rapist. And I couldn't even tell you. You were incapable. That all ends now, Momma. Today. You're going to rehab, and you're not going to lose your life inside a vodka bottle.'

'I'll go,' Mona whispered. 'Sally . . .'

She put the car in gear.

'Don't you worry. I won't let some no-account piece of trash ruin my life.' Sally raised her chin, proudly. 'Like I said, we're starting over. And today is day one.'

Chapter Twenty-Seven

'Momma.' Sally knocked on her mother's door. Two weeks back from rehab, and Mona hadn't touched a drink. On the other hand, she was spending all day in bed.

'Momma, what do you think?'

'What? I'm tired.'

Yeah, she was always tired.

'I want to show you these new sketches.' Sally was determined to have Momma awake, and aware of the wider world. 'What do you think?'

She was sure these were the best yet. A short sheath dress in buttercup yellow, with a careful ruched neckline and cinched at the waist. A business suit with sass – tailored jacket and kicky pleated skirt. A little navy dress with cap sleeves, full skirted, fitted at the waist and bodice – something for the girl who could no longer go strapless.

And, in addition, Sally had come up with jewellery. Forget minimalist, she was maximalist. Her designs glittered and sparkled with rhinestones and cheap semi-precious jewels.

'Very nice.' Mona wasn't even looking.

'Would you like to go for a walk, Momma?'

'Nobody walks in LA.'

'Well, when I get back, I'll drive you to the beach,' Sally said firmly. She was determined to get her out of the house.

'Where are you going?' Her mother was using that whiny, tearful voice again.

'I told you yesterday, I have an appointment. At DeMarco's.'

'OK, well. Good luck. I hope they have some positions, you could be a girl on the make-up counter,' Mona said, tiredly, and closed the door.

Sal shook her head and went back into the living room. She gathered up her sketches and the two pieces she'd actually run up herself. The first was her favourite skirt, a wild little thing in blue satin with a scalloped hem, bias-cut and full of motion. The second, a necklace, one she'd crafted very carefully: little round pebbles of semi-precious jewels, with a letter carved into each one; they spelled out 'Lucky'. She'd strung them on a silver chain, since she hadn't been able to afford a gold one.

They were good, she knew that. Stylish, and hot. Something a little different. She would wear them – any young girl would.

So far, it had been tough – buyers refusing even to see her stuff. But after weeks of badgering, Ollie Foster at DeMarco's had agreed to give her five minutes.

This was gonna be it. Her lucky break!

'So you can see the movement.' Sally smiled and turned the skirt around, letting the hem flute out in the breeze. 'And these stones – they're designed to be sold individually, with a chain. You can make your own message. It's like jewellery-as-pizza, you pay for each topping. They're like candy, no girl will resist.'

'Interesting.' Foster steepled his fingers automatically and moistened his lips. Sally noticed his eyes roaming across her ample breasts and steeled herself not to stiffen. 'You got anything else to show me, baby? It's hard to break into sales in this town – real *hard*.'

'I have these sketches . . .'

'I'm not talking 'bout sketches. Why don't you slip into

the changing rooms with me and model that skirt? You know, show me something. Got a cute little ass on you, girl. If you want a deal here, you know what you got to do. . . .'

Sally snatched her necklace back and turned on her heel. Sleazeball! She thought of Leo Fisk, and her eyes filled with tears.

'Where the hell do you think you're going?' he shouted. 'I got *connections*, girl. All the other big stores in this town. You gotta learn to play nice if you want to be in the game . . .'

But she was gone.

Sally didn't go home. She couldn't bear to. Go home and deal with her soporific momma. She was back here on her own turf, she had to make something happen.

Screw it, she thought, with uncharacteristic passion. Screw them all. The lechers and the sexists and the ones who just didn't care enough to even give her a chance.

So nobody was going to help her? Fine. She'd do it herself. It was just cutting out the middleman.

I have ten thousand dollars to rent a store, Sally thought, fiercely. Life was a gamble. Why the hell not?

Wiping the tears away, Sally walked from DeMarco's down Melrose. It was a long walk, hot, but she didn't care. Here was the epicentre of LA hip. All little biker bars, leather clothing stores, gothic fashion, witchcraft and palm-tellers.

The first four stores Sally tried turned her down flat. Their businesses were doing OK. Or they just didn't care. Moving was too much hassle. It took her three days and endless arguments before Sally found a candidate.

FINE FASHIONS. An optimistic name. Rundown and seedy, it was flogging racks of discount T-shirts from Taiwan at five bucks a throw, plastic earrings and elasticated bracelets.

There was nobody in the store, but it was a decent

location, halfway up Melrose with an empty parking lot across the street.

For the first time since she'd got back to LA, Sally felt a thrill of excitement.

She marched inside. Behind the counter was a little Korean woman, looking bored and reading a magazine.

'Hi,' said Sally. 'This your place?'

The woman was instantly defensive. 'We paid that fine, if you from City Hall.'

'I'm not. I need a shop. How long is your lease?'

'Six months.'

'I'll buy it out. Fifteen hundred a month.'

Her eyes narrowed. 'You serious, lady?'

'Totally serious. Another three grand for the fixtures and the stock.'

'I want five.'

'Don't push it,' Sally said. 'Your place ain't up to much, ma'am, I'm surely saving y'all from foreclosure. This way you keep a good credit rating, you can start over someplace else.'

'When you bring money?'

'You call your lawyer. I'll be back here tomorrow with a cashier's cheque and a contract.' Sally had another idea. 'You know any seamstresses? I need to hire some ladies who know how to cut and sew patterns.'

'Of course. Plenty.'

'I'll be hiring. I need four women. You could bring them with you, tomorrow.'

The woman stared. 'You serious, right?'

'Right,' Sally agreed. 'Deadly serious.'

'Well . . . OK.' The woman shrugged. 'This a rough spot, lady, lots of clothes shops, not enough customers.' She waved at Sally's neat little dress and chic platform shoes. 'But you rich, you can afford it. Learn the hard way.'

Sally smiled, her first real smile in a long time.

'See you in the morning,' she said, and left to find some walk-in lawyer.

'So this is what we're going to do.' Sally smiled at the women, as of now her employees. 'Cut one shoulder off every shirt. Neckline diagonal. And slash the hem like so.' She showed them her flame design. 'Then sew it back up. You see the pattern? I pay minimum wage plus a dollar. Once this stock is sold out, we'll get health coverage.'

An older lady with bags under her eyes spoke up; Sally could see she was used to life in a sweatshop.

'Health?' she asked. 'For real?'

'For real. And there's an hour for lunch; I'll get us sandwiches and coffee. We're in this together, ladies.' Sally's warm Texan drawl encouraged them. 'Do you think you can handle it?'

'Yes,' the woman said, smiling weakly.

'Yes, miss,' another of them said, looking hopeful. 'Here –' and she took a large, square, raspberry T-shirt, applied Sally's pattern, and started to cut.

'*L.A. Citizen*. Editorial.'

'Can I speak to Mike Reardon?' Sally gripped the phone. This was it – she was going all out. But she had no choice. Hiring the staff, buying the lease – the money she'd saved had almost gone. Sally had the stock. Now it was all about sales.

She was about to expose herself. And maybe Momma. But it was do-or-die time.

'Editor's office. Janice speaking. Who's calling?'

'This is Sally Lassiter.'

'From what company?' asked the bored assistant.

'I'm the daughter of Paulie Lassiter – you remember, the oilman whose company went bust and he died of a heart attack? Big story. Front page stuff.'

'OK . . .'

'Mom and I fled to Texas in disgrace.' That stung, but she forced herself to say it. The paper would see her as a human interest story or not at all. 'Now I'm back in LA and I want to give an exclusive interview. Tell our side of the story.' She gave her their number. 'Have him call me back on this number if he's interested in doing a feature. Goodbye.'

Sally hung up, her heart thumping with adrenaline, and headed to the kitchen to make coffee. She was opening the jar when the phone rang.

'Is this really Sally Lassiter?'

A man's voice. Sceptical.

'It sure is.' She tried to sound confident. 'I'm prepared to offer you a deal, Mr Reardon.'

'We don't pay for interviews, Sally, company policy.'

'Not what I'm looking for. I've started a little store – my designs. It's called Wave. I need the publicity. You come and do a feature on me, you include mention of the store and shots of my T-shirts. I'll pose in some of my clothes.' He started to say something, but Sally cut him off. 'I'll give you what you're looking for – plenty of emotional stuff about Dad and being poor, public school and taking the bus. All I want in exchange is the PR. Well?'

Reardon chuckled. 'You've got guts, young lady. I'll take that deal. But beware, we don't puff. I leave that to *Vanity Fair*. If your clothes suck, my journalist is gonna say so.'

'Fine with me.' Sally was elated. 'Let's do it.'

'When?'

'Now.' She gave him the address. 'I'll be at the store in twenty minutes.'

Sally made them take the photos first. She knew after she'd been speaking to the journalist her eyes would be red. Better get the shots out of the way while she could. She posed, sexy but demure, in her little blue skirt and a white cut-off

T-shirt that showed her tan; long blond hair flowing loose around her waist, nails with a simple French polish, her blue eyes laughing.

The photographer, a woman, sighed with pleasure. 'You look amazing, girlfriend.'

The interviewer was bespectacled and serious – the skinny black jeans and white buttoned shirt of a fashion maven. Sally poured her heart out; she sobbed, she railed at Miss Milton's lack of support, she castigated her mother's friends. Explosive stuff. She needed it to be; this had to make the paper.

'I'm filing it this afternoon.' The journalist clicked the off button on her tape recorder, clearly impressed. 'And Sally, I think your T-shirts are hot. *So* sexy. Plus, I adore those beads.'

'Here.' Sally jumped to her feet, collected a handful, and strung her a necklace. 'It says Annalise.' Her name. 'That's yours. If you like it, maybe you'll wear it, tell your friends.'

'Maybe.' The journalist smiled. 'This piece runs on Sunday. If I were you I'd stay open that day.'

The next morning was Thursday. Sally came to work to find her store already full; Koko, her Algerian counter girl, had opened early.

'There was a crowd outside.'

The photographer from the day before was back. And she'd brought her friends.

As the chic young women – Sally pegged them as grad students, lawyers, bankers' wives, non industry, civilian Angelenas – shopped, running through her stock like locusts, Sally reflected, you could be big in this town if you were hip and you were first. The rich girls wanted a jump on the hoi polloi who'd come here Sunday, when the *Citizen* ran the piece.

At the end of the day Sally was already showing a tidy

profit. She gave the girls a small bonus: fifty bucks apiece, all she could afford.

'There'll be more later,' she promised.

They laughed and hugged her, eyes bright with tears. Sally got the feeling her workers didn't often see fifty dollars all at once.

It gave her a thrill. Finally, her own money. Her own style. Her own success.

On Sunday, the piece came out. Sally didn't read it; she had no desire to relive that harrowing shit all over again. She just looked at the pictures; herself, golden, laughing, and supremely beautiful, with her kicky little skirt and innate confidence.

Annalise, the journo, had pegged it. Sally's shop was swarming with visitors. They sold almost every T-shirt, and the jewellery was gone in three hours.

After that, she started taking orders. Payment up front, delivery in two weeks; wait list only.

Sally Lassiter was still small-time. She didn't kid herself. But she was also a success.

Chapter Twenty-Eight

'You can't play chicken with me, Ms Morgan.'

Turnbull Scott, the doughy chief executive of Shop Smart, narrowed his piggish eyes at his young vice president.

'Your story is a good one – it reads well in the reports. But you're far too young for this sort of promotion.'

'When I evaluate executives, I go by results.' Jane felt strangely detached. A pigeon swooped past, outside the huge window behind Mr Scott; it made her smile, which infuriated him.

'You've used PR to advance your career. Think what it'll look like if we take a risk on a kid who can't even legally drink the wine we sell.'

'My track record proves I'm risk-free.'

'Look, get this straight.' Nobody ever talked to Scott like that. He loved what the chick had done to his personnel overheads, otherwise she'd be gone. 'We are *not* going to put you into a front-line division. You got an offer on the table.' The board had instructed him to keep her – they were terrified a headhunting firm would poach her. 'It's a *huge* offer,' he insisted, frustrated.

'It is.' Jane smiled again. They had begged, and pleaded, and in the end just thrown money at her. The final offer was nearly double her salary. Three hundred and fifty thousand dollars. A fortune for a twenty year old – the top young stars in investment banking, plucked straight from the Ivy League, didn't make as much.

'I don't want it,' Jane explained.

'You'll make *more* than if you ran a sales division.'

'I don't care. I want the training.'

'Training?' He blinked. 'For what?'

'For when I own this company.'

Turnbull Scott laughed. Jane didn't.

'I'm serious. Are you going to switch me into a front-line job?' she demanded.

'No!' he almost shouted.

'Then I quit.' Jane reached into her jacket, took out her letter of resignation and her car keys, and laid them on his desk. 'It's been nice working with you.'

With you. Not for you. These people weren't her boss. She held his gaze, defiant, icy cool.

Scott stared incredulously at her. The board was going to complain about this.

'You arrogant goddamned *bitch*!' he snarled. But she had already turned on her high heels and was walking her tight little butt out the door.

'There's a bit of a real estate slump,' said Marcy Wilkerson, her realtor. 'Places have been slow to move . . .'

Jane turned to her. 'Come on, Marcy. When I was buying, it was all jump on it now, you have to move fast. I read the property supplements every day.'

'The market's changed since you purchased this place.'

'No it hasn't. I want six fifty for this apartment.'

Marcy's eyes boggled. 'That's a profit of one hundred fifty in eight months.'

'It's eminently achievable,' Jane said crisply. 'Either you do it, within a month, or I'll find a better agent who can. Now excuse me please, I'm busy.'

Then she opened the door. Marcy walked out.

Bitch, she thought, as Jane shut the door firmly behind her. Hard as nails. Definitely needed to get laid.

But she went back to her office and listed the place for six fifty.

You didn't mess with Jane Morgan.

'I want a ticket to Los Angeles, please.'

'Certainly, ma'am.' The ticket agent looked curiously at the young girl standing in front of her. So pretty – slim and young, in a neat little designer dress, carrying a small holdall. She sounded intelligent – probably a student, looking for a last-minute deep discount. 'Let me see what comes up for you on the standby tracker . . .'

'No. First class.'

Her eyebrow lifted, but the girl produced a Prada wallet and coolly handed over a gold Amex.

'And when will you be returning?'

'I won't. One way.'

'That's three thousand dollars,' the older woman said tentatively, as if to ask, 'Are you sure?'

'That's fine. Ring it up, please.'

The ticket agent did as she was told, even more curious than before. Who *was* she? Turns up at the airport, flies first class? Why hadn't she booked? And strangest of all, there was no wedding ring. She could see this chick as some investment banker trophy wife, but there was nothing.

'The first-class lounge is upstairs.'

'Thank you.' She took her ticket and turned to go, cool and collected.

The agent sighed. She was forty-five, married to a welder and lived in a tract house in Queens. How she wished she could be like that English girl. There was something about her – not just that she was rich. She simply didn't give a damn.

Jane gave a little mental shrug as she walked into the first-class lounge. Let them stare. She knew how people thought about her, and she really didn't care. When she was a girl, who'd cared about her? Only her friends. She did not care about the rest of the world's opinion.

Turnbull Scott thought she was insane. A wild risk-taker. Junking her comfortable corporate life in favour of the wild blue yonder.

But that was only because he didn't understand.

To stay at Shop Smart now was to doom herself to failure. Jane had a clear idea of where her ladder headed, and if the top of it was resting against 'well-paid executive' then she wasn't bothering to climb.

She wanted security. What happened to Daddy would never happen to her. She wanted serious rich, Aaron Spelling rich, Paulie Lassiter rich. Rich enough to import a snow machine to your Los Angeles mansion at Christmas. Rich enough to hire out the city zoo for your kid's sixteenth.

And you didn't get that from a pay cheque. You got it from ownership.

She felt a little fear as she strode over to the bar and ordered a mineral water, choked with ice. This was new territory. And the business world had her pigeonholed into one box – Human Resources; stuff that does not count. It was why Shop Smart hadn't given her a shot.

And now somebody else would have to.

'Can I buy you a drink?'

It was a relaxed, confident masculine voice. American – certainly nothing like Jude.

'No.' Jane didn't look round.

'That's correct. Well done.'

Now, she looked at him – annoyed.

'Excuse me?'

The speaker inclined his head. Fifteen years older than her, still young, around thirty-five, she guessed. Dark eyes with thick black lashes. A rather arrogant, cruel mouth; a strong jaw, and a tan.

'I can't *buy* you a drink – because they're free. But we could still have one together.'

'I'm already having one. By myself.'

Jane turned back to it. This game was for losers, and she wasn't playing. They started out all nice and flirty. And when it became clear she really wasn't interested in being some junior marketing prick's one-night lay, then they called her a dyke and a bitch.

Her father had been charming, too – to strangers. And she'd let herself fall for a charming man when she met Jude Ferrers and flung herself into his arms, dazzled by his easy manner and empty heart. And that, chasing after the ghost of her father's neglect, had only brought her more humiliation. More misery.

Just because this guy was strong and handsome, so what?

Jane had been hurt. Too recently. She walled herself off.

'A great idea.' The man was unfazed. 'I'll have one by myself too. Right next to you. And then we can both get on our respective planes and we'll never see each other again.'

She relented. 'Sorry if I was a little cold.'

'Cold? I don't think you need the ice with that drink.'

Jane's eyes sparked again. He was *laughing* at her, this arrogant bastard. His eyes were on her, and his body language was completely relaxed, confident and at ease with himself. Another man would have slunk away.

'Does that often work for you?' she asked.

'What?' He grinned, dark eyes holding hers.

'Insulting girls.'

The bar girl sauntered up to them and made goo-goo eyes at him. 'Mr Levin. What a *pleasure* to see you again, sir.'

Jane's mental Rolodex did a quick check. 'You're not Craig Levin are you?'

His eyes danced again, with pleasure. 'Yes, ma'am.'

Craig Levin. Craig Levin! To Jane, dedicated reader of *Fortune* magazine, a girl who idolized billionaires and entrepreneurs, the name was magic. He was the king of them all. She flushed, and adrenaline sent the tiny hairs prickling on the back of her arms.

'What can I get for you, sir? Your usual?' purred the bar girl.

'That's fine, and please call me Craig, Iris.'

Iris beamed, obviously thrilled that he remembered her name. 'Coming right up,' she promised, in a breathy Marilyn Monroe voice.

Craig Levin, as Jane knew perfectly well, was rich. Rich enough to import a snow machine to his Los Angeles mansion at Christmas. Rich enough to own an island. Or two.

Craig Levin. Wall Street wonder, except not on Wall Street. A genius investor, Jane had seen him described as the 'next Warren Buffet' more times than she cared to count. He had influence enough to swing a stock. Like Buffet, he never split shares in his index fund, and they now traded at eight thousand dollars a share.

Some of his original investors had made hundreds of millions from a tiny initial stake. And Levin had a myth about him. He never gave interviews. No cosy little chats with *Fortune* – which is why she'd never seen his picture. No vanity slots on CNBC with Marissa Bartimolo, the 'money honey', beaming on in approval.

Levin was young, independent, and loaded.

No wonder he was arrogant.

Jane shuddered a little at the thought of being so close to him. And Levin clearly realized the effect he was having. His penetrating eyes were watching her.

'Does knowing my name mean you'll be nicer to me?'

Jane was cold with fury, half at him, half at herself. He was still gazing at her with that amused regard. His power, and handsomeness, and total confidence was a heady mixture; there weren't many men who looked down on her.

And she was horrified to find herself starting to get aroused.

She stiffened.

'It certainly doesn't. I'm not for sale.' Jane couldn't help herself; she nodded at the bar girl who was fixing Levin a generous Scotch on the rocks. 'Maybe she is, though. You might get lucky after all.'

His smile abruptly vanished.

'You're sitting here in the first-class lounge because you've got a first-class ticket. I don't know anything else about you, but I know you're a woman of means. She's a waitress. Probably on a bit more than minimum wage. So you sitting here in that elegant suit and calling her a whore isn't cool.'

Jane flushed purple.

'I'm sorry,' she said, wrong-footed and ashamed of herself.

He replied coolly, 'Enjoy your drink,' and walked away to the other end of the bar, retrieving his whisky from the beaming waitress as he passed her.

Jane winced. Levin was right; she should have been better than that. And he'd immediately lost interest in her.

Not that she *cared*.

Levin had been bothering her. The pursuit annoyed her. So why was she more annoyed when it stopped?

'Can I get you anything else, ma'am?' The simpering waitress was back, oblivious to anything that had happened.

'No. That's OK. Thank you,' Jane added, guiltily.

'That Craig Levin – he's hot. So funny, too. Did you ever hear him joke? He cracks everybody up.'

'Is he in here a lot?' Curiosity filled her.

The waitress – Iris, right, that's what he called her – grinned.

'All the time. He has more air miles than Santa Claus. And remembers people's names . . .' She sighed. 'And so damn handsome. Don't you think?'

Jane shrugged. 'If you like that sort of thing.'

'Man! I would in a heartbeat. But the girls I see with him are mostly models. Socialites . . . you know.'

'How clichéd.'

'I guess he can have whatever he wants, and he takes advantage. I never saw the guy be rude to any woman, though. Saw a couple of his girlfriends crying when he leaves on a plane. None of them last too long.'

'Rich playboy. It's as old as the hills,' Jane said, glad to be able to dismiss Levin.

But she still wished he hadn't walked away.

Jane told herself that was all business. Levin was so rich he could have bought Shop Smart by writing a cheque. You didn't want to cross a man like that. Maybe it was good that he didn't know her name.

'Flight 961 to LAX is now boarding at Gate 33.'

Jane stood up, half relieved, half disappointed. 'That's me. Thanks, Iris.' She put down a crisp twenty on the bar as a tip, to relieve her guilty conscience. 'Have a nice day.'

Jane thought about him as she walked through the corridors and walkways of the airport. She tried not to, but it didn't work. She had actually studied Craig Levin's portfolio. She'd practically memorized his résumé. Jane had never seen a photo, never cared to; Levin was a hero to her. Jane had built him up in her mind, wanted to meet him – he was one of the giants, one of the people she most admired.

And now he'd asked her for a drink, and she'd told him to go to hell!

She was annoyed with herself for regretting it. Really, he'd been hitting on her. Hadn't taken no for an answer. And Iris said he had a string of gorgeous girls.

A distraction. Jane tried to wrestle her mind back to the business at hand. Finding Helen, and Sally. Starting her own Shop Smart.

'Good morning . . . second on the left . . .'

The air hostess was repeating her inane instructions; Jane ignored her and walked past. Why did they do that? How tough would it be to find seat 2B? Aisle, up front. She took her heavy holdall and struggled to lift it up to the hand baggage compartment. A strong pair of hands whisked it away from her and tucked it inside.

'Thank you.' Jane glanced round. It was Levin. She gasped in shock.

'We're sitting together.' He smiled easily at her. 'Hope you don't mind.'

'I – no.' Her mind raced, and she thought about apologizing for earlier. But the moment had passed, what could she say? 'That's fine.'

Jane slid into her seat. She blushed, again. He was extremely attractive. Very different from Jude – muscular, not skinny; tanned, masculine; a rich and powerful man, and not a trust fund brat. There was an air of complete command to him.

With Jude, she'd been infatuated. This was different. Levin annoyed and disturbed her, but it was her body responding, in a way it had never done with her starry-eyed fake romance with the Englishman.

Her skin thrilled to be so close to him. She felt herself moisten, tighten. Her clothes suddenly felt insubstantial, as though he were Superman, and that penetrating gaze could see right through them.

Jane tried to cover her confusion. She busied herself with the pocket of the seat in front of her and took refuge in the free magazine, pretending to read it.

'Yes,' Levin said. 'That article on the strawberry growers of the Midwest is certainly fascinating stuff. I heard two of their journalists are up for a Pulitzer.'

Jane's eyes glittered. 'So the billionaire is laughing at the impoverished writers, is he?'

He grinned. 'Touché.'

Jane felt an unreasonable elation that she had scored with him. She forced herself to look away.

'Miss Morgan, can I get you some champagne, or freshly squeezed orange juice?'

'Orange juice. Thank you.'

'I'll have the same. One's my limit.' Levin passed Jane her glass. 'Are you teetotal, Ms Morgan?'

'For another three months. I'm not yet twenty-one.'

'Don't I feel old,' he said, with a grin that said he didn't.

'You don't need to worry about me; I'm an adult.' She lifted her head, defiantly.

'Glad to hear it,' he answered, with a soft, predatory intent that sent a tingle down her spine.

Jane chided herself. What the hell was she doing? Months – years – of brushing men off, and she was all but ready to start flirting with Craig Levin just because he was an alpha male?

'So let me see.' Levin's eyes focused on a point some way in front of him; it was unnerving. 'Morgan – female, twenty, British. That makes you Jane Morgan. Senior Vice President of Human Resources, Shop Smart Corporation.'

She blinked. 'How the hell did you know that?'

'I have a photographic memory. It's a big help when assessing stocks. So I'm right?'

'All except the last part. I quit Shop Smart yesterday.'

'Excuse me a second.'

'Of course,' Jane said, but she was disappointed. She had just started to enjoy herself. Levin turned from her, and swiped a black Amex through his Skyphone, punching in the numbers.

'Anna? Craig. Dump Shop Smart. Everything, the whole half-million. Tell the brokers to feed it out slow. See ya, babe.' He turned back to Jane. 'Tell me the rest of your story.'

She struggled with the unexpected wave of desire that rocked through her body. On two words from her, he'd just sold over ten million dollars' worth of Shop Smart stock. She'd watched him trade half a million shares.

The power. The decisiveness. The unutterably sexy, casual way he did it, and then turned back to her, as though he'd done nothing more important than check his watch.

'Why did you sell those shares?' she almost whispered. Jane was frightened her voice would come out husky. Don't stare at him, she pleaded with herself.

'Jane Morgan,' he replied, and his eyes flickered across her face, noting the dilated pupils, the flushed skin. It almost made her want to run away from him – except that they were in the air, and there was nowhere to go. 'Junior VP. Promoted from the shop floor. In her first year, cut costs in one store by thirty per cent and increased productivity twenty-seven per cent, all through personnel changes. Promoted to central management, applied techniques across the United States; immediate savings of fifteen per cent on salaries, management redundancies saving another eight per cent. Productivity data increase not yet in. You see, in such a low-cost store, staffing costs are about half the overhead. You had something. If they've let you go, they're nuts.'

He knew all about her. Jane struggled against her arousal. So what? It was a photographic memory, a trick of the mind.

She was used to being smarter, more driven, and higher achieving than every man she ever met. Not this time.

She tried to concentrate on business.

'I'm not interested in being a VP of Personnel,' she said. 'I'm interested in being a CEO. Of my own wholly owned business.'

'Why?'

Jane hadn't expected that question.

'I don't like being dependent,' she said, after a pause.

'I could help you.'

'You could buy me Saks and give it to me for a birthday present.' Jane spoke strongly, on more certain ground now. 'But I'm not interested in being a kept woman. I want to make it on my own.'

His smile deepened. 'Impressive.'

'And you should know a couple of things, Mr Levin,' Jane said bravely, challenging him. 'The first is – let's get this out the way – that I know all about you, and I admire you. Like everybody else working in business, I guess. The second is that I am *not* going to be one of your trophy girlfriends. Your throw-away identikit supermodel arm candy.'

'My *what*?'

'Remember Iris the waitress? She and I had a good talk.' Jane smiled triumphantly. 'And I'm not really interested in taking a number with any man, no matter how rich and . . . powerful.' Saying it sent little trawls of electricity across her stomach; Jane ignored them. 'So I hope we'll have a pleasant flight, and I'll admit it's been exciting to meet you. But you should know that all this flirtation is just a waste of time. I'm a busy woman, and I'm not interested.'

He lifted an eyebrow, and grinned at her.

'Intriguing,' he said. 'You like to say things straight out. Most women wouldn't dare. Yes, of course I'm flirting with you. And I understand your feelings.'

'My feelings?'

'It's all they are.' He smiled unapologetically at her. 'You have a perfect right to express all these things, and I have a right not to accept them. But don't worry, Miss Morgan. I'm not going to stalk you. I've never had to pester a girl yet. When you decide you'd like to date me – and you will – it'll be entirely of your own volition.'

'You're very cocksure.'

'I've earned that right.'

'Not with women,' she said, outraged.

'Certainly with women. Ask any of my ex-girlfriends.'

'*Ex*,' Jane retorted, with emphasis.

Levin inclined his head. 'I'm afraid so. They weren't enough of a challenge.'

'You date beauties, and yet you want to be challenged? Give me a break.'

'That's about it. I want everything in a woman. Brains, beauty, strength, humour – a certain style.' He shrugged. 'If we're expected to spend the rest of our lives with only one person, then I think we should be allowed as long a shopping list as we like. I start with beauty, yes.'

'Why?'

'It's the only quality that can be instantly assessed,' he replied calmly. 'To see if they are intelligent, or spirited, requires dating.'

'Has anybody ever told you you're a sexist pig?'

'Am I? So what do you require in a man?' he asked. 'How many poor, ugly, underachieving, diffident males have you gone out with recently?'

Jane was silent. She didn't want to tell him there had been nobody except one lousy English loser. This was America, where everybody was a shrink. She didn't want be psychoanalysed. Especially not by Craig Levin.

'So what are you doing in LA? Business?' Jane changed the subject.

'Yes, but I can't tell you what.'

She understood. The market watched Craig Levin's every move. For her to know what businesses he was looking at would equal insider trading.

'I'm going to start my business there. Buy a house. And find some old schoolfriends.'

He grinned. 'You make that sound easy.'

'Why shouldn't it be?' Jane said. 'People over-complicate life.'

*

As they touched down, she turned to him and briskly offered her hand.

'It's been nice to meet you, Mr Levin.'

'Craig,' he said, eyes dancing.

'I don't think we should. We might do business in the future.'

'Oh, we never will,' he said, at once.

'How do you know?'

'I'm attracted to you. And you're attracted to me. That's two complications too many for any kind of financial dealings.'

The plane halted and shuddered to a stop. Levin was up, instantly, retrieving his briefcase and handing her the holdall. Jane felt a huge sense of aggravation and loss; the flight was done, he was gone; she had been a pretty distraction, and now she would never see him again.

Her pride would not let her say a word.

'You have no idea whether I'm attracted to you or not,' she hissed in a low voice.

Levin leaned down, in to her, where she was sitting in her seat. He placed his mouth to her ear, so none of the businessmen milling around them could hear.

'Of course I do. There are certain physiological signs; you only need a basic understanding of biology.'

Jane bit her lip. She had never come across a man like Levin. God help her, his masculinity was arousing. She knit her hands in her lap.

'Here.' He offered her a business card. 'Goodbye, Jane Morgan.'

She took the card. Of course, she ought to have shredded it to confetti in front of him. But instead she slipped it into a jacket pocket.

Levin's hand reached out, and a calloused fingertip casually, secretively, traced a line across the back of her neck to the top of her spine.

It was electric. Jane, helplessly, reacted; her body shuddered, and she had to grip the sides of her seat to prevent anybody else from seeing her reaction. She blushed, hot with shame and wanting him, and waited it out.

And in a few seconds he was gone. Front of the queue; he left the plane without looking back. Jane had returned to Los Angeles the way she had left it. On her own.

Chapter Twenty-Nine

Haya stood up, gingerly. She was only two months gone, but her feet were still swelling. She walked into her garden, her embroidered slippers flip-flopping carefully, the *L.A. Citizen* clutched in her fingers.

Her stomach was churning – and it wasn't the baby. That was Sally, her Sally, in the papers!

She was in turmoil. First, the simple shock. After all this time, Sally's face. Staring out at her, older, calmer somehow, but unmistakably the golden girl. The aching loneliness Haya had felt since Ahmed's death had momentarily been pierced. Haya had almost forgotten what simple happiness was. And seeing Sally, alive, well, thriving – that gave her joy.

But then she read the article. Sally talked about her father, the pain, the shunning she had received. And Haya was flooded with guilt; when Sally needed her, Haya hadn't been there; she was half a world away, sweating out her pleasure in the grip of Ahmed's arms.

What had Jane and Sally thought? When they found her gone, with no notice? They must have felt it as a betrayal. And in a way, she knew, it was. She hadn't tried hard enough to find them, even when she got back to America. She had been so lost in Ahmed, in what they were building together – and after he died, just lost.

And now – here was Sally. Scandalous pieces, Haya thought, but with definite flair. Instant style. And Sally looked so beautiful! Even more so than at the party, Haya thought. Tragedy had burned some determination into her face, made her all-American good looks that little bit deeper.

The clothes looked good on her body. There was fit, elegance, a bit of sassiness that squeezed at Haya's heart – all Sally, big-hearted, optimistic, golden Sally. And she hadn't given up, she was just clawing her way back in. The *Citizen* gave her designs a rave review. The girl was doing well.

Haya's heart beat a little faster, with pure nerves. But she steeled herself. She would go to see Sally. If her old friend was furious, damned her to hell for not being there, Haya would understand. How must it look? As if she had dumped Sally as soon as she lost her money.

But there were few people, now, Haya liked in this world. Of course she still loved Baba, and Mama; but for what they had done to her . . . right now, she didn't *like* them very much. And maybe there were others she could have forged a relationship with, but she'd kept her distance. Hadn't wanted to tell anybody about Ahmed's child.

Sally Lassiter was different. Haya picked up the paper again, and committed the address to her memory. Melrose – right.

'Thank you so much.'

'Really – it's fabulous. And I'll take twenty in each colour. Just mail them to my billing address.'

'I will, ma'am, thank you.' Sally gave her the patented smile.

'Your stuff is just terrific,' the fat lady said, and sailed magnificently out of the room, like a galleon under full sail.

Sally sighed with relief. That was it; the society wife was the last customer. Not that she minded sales, but her heels, dizzy five-inch Manolos, were *painful*.

With the first little bit of money, Sally had bought herself a killer wardrobe.

That was even more important than a new house, because it was business. They'd all read the *Citizen* article. Half of her customers were rubber-neckers – come to see *her*. The golden girl down at heel. Paulie Lassiter's daughter, starting over.

Fuck it. Sally played the cards she was dealt. If they came to see her, then *she* was the product. Everything she sold reflected her. And that meant being one hundred per cent glamorous, at all times.

She added platinum highlights to her butterscotch hair. She deepened her tan with lotions. She wore Manolos on her feet – nothing else. Only her own line of jewellery – her necklace read: SURVIVOR – and her own designer clothes. Sally got her teeth whitened, and wore perfume at all times, even to bed. Glamour, she reminded herself, was a state of mind.

Beauty and style were like athleticism. They required practice and endless conditioning. If there was one thing Sally Lassiter knew, it was how to be a star.

And the customers drooled over it.

She nodded to Koko to lock up and gratefully slid her stockinged feet out of her narrow-toed shoes.

There was a knock on the door. And as she rubbed at the aching ball of her left foot, Sally heard a familiar voice.

'Are you still open?'

'Sorry, missy. No. Tomorrow, nine a.m.,' Koko said.

'I wanted to see Sally Lassiter.'

'Wait – Koko, wait.' Sally froze. 'Helen? Is that you?'

'Yes . . .'

'My God! Koko, let her in.'

Sally jumped up in her stockinged feet as Haya walked in. She was lovely, wearing a long dress, a little shapeless, with gold embroidery stitched across the azure blue cloth; her hair curled softly just to her shoulders, and her skin was luminous.

'Sally . . .' she began.

Sally was so happy, she actually squealed.

'Helen!' she cried. 'Helen, oh, oh my God! I never thought I'd see you again. Is it really you?'

Haya's eyes brimmed with tears, and she smiled.

'It's me.'

'Wait just a second. Koko, can you shut up the store and bank the cash for me? I'm going to take my friend to dinner.'

'Sure thing, Miz Sally.'

Sally grabbed her shoes in her hand and raced over to Haya, enveloping her in a crushing bear hug. She stared at her, as though she might evaporate.

'Look at you. You're amazing. Come out the back.' She wanted Helen all to herself.

'Nice to meet you,' Haya said politely to Koko.

'Can you eat dinner?' Sally found herself nervous, hurried. 'There's a great Thai place around the corner.'

'Sounds good. Thanks.'

Sally ushered her out of the back door. Sunset was sinking over the Hills, the smog settling into a spectacular light show. Sally kept staring at her friend; it felt like she was on a first date. Helen – so stately, now; a million miles from the diffident schoolgirl she'd been on the night of their party. Back when Sally used to protect her.

'Table for two.'

'Yes, Miss Sally. I seen you in the papers again,' the hostess gushed. 'Everybody said you looked great. Where you want to sit?'

'In the back – somewhere quiet.'

'You got it.' She ushered them through the packed, noisy restaurant to a dark corner booth, lit dimly by a red lamp. It was a kind light, but Sally could see Helen was crying – and that she had a ring on her left hand.

A ring! Then that marriage story was true.

Sally didn't know where to start. What to say. She plunged in.

'Helen! God, girl, I missed you.' There were tears in her eyes. 'I missed you so much. You and Jane. I looked so hard for y'all.' She grabbed Helen's hand. 'So. Tell me all about you. You disappeared so fast . . .'

Haya shook her head. 'I'm sorry I didn't call right away.' She couldn't bear to tell Sally the truth, not yet. 'When I first got to Egypt, I – I was sorting some things out. I just assumed you'd both be there when I got back.' She blushed. 'I did call, a few weeks later. And that's when I found out what happened to you, and Jane had disappeared. And after that, I couldn't find you.'

'Same here, exactly the same. Well, you're back now.' Sally smiled, so happy to see her. 'Thank God.'

'Definitely. Do you know where Jane is? Did you call her after you left LA?'

Sally shook her head. 'No. I was kind of the same as you. My mom and I went to Texas, and it was hard. We had no money. Stuff like that.' She blushed. 'I didn't want to call, I guess I was embarrassed. When I reached out for Jane, she'd moved.'

'We have to find her.'

'Oh, we do,' Sally said, her own eyes suddenly moist. 'We do and we will. Now you're back I feel like I could do anything. We'll hire detectives if we have to. Oh, it's so *good* to see you again, Helen!' She reached across the table and squeezed her friend's hand till it hurt.

'It is! It's so good. Oh, *mash'Allah*,' Haya exclaimed. 'Just . . . I knew people, but nobody who understood me. Nobody's who's been through things with me.'

'I know,' Sally said, excitedly. 'I feel that too. I just missed both of y'all.'

'But I warn you, I tried detectives already. Didn't get anywhere. And Sally – I changed my first name. After my marriage.' Haya sighed. 'It's Haya – Haya is my birth name, and my husband preferred it to the American version, so Haya, if you don't mind.'

'Not at all. It's beautiful. Haya,' Sally said, rolling it around with her tongue. 'Haya. Yeah, gorgeous. It suits you. Now, tell me everything. And I mean everything.'

'I don't know where to start,' Haya said honestly. 'Well, basic facts. I'm pregnant, and I'm widowed . . .'

'Oh, Hel— Haya.' Sally pressed her hand again.

'I was in Egypt.' Haya blinked back tears and now, putting away her pride, she told her friend the story, as fast as she could. It poured out; it was good, so good, to talk to somebody at last who would understand her. 'And you,' she said, at the end, as Sally was dabbing away tears. 'I had no idea what happened – when we came back here you were gone.'

Sally filled her in; it didn't take long. She told Haya everything, almost everything, stuff she had never confessed to another human soul: Mona's drunken binges, the pit of poverty and public disgrace.

And how she'd climbed over it all.

'Anyway.' Sally wiped away more tears; it was dark in here, after all, and it felt good to let the tears flow, let the emotion out. Sally trusted Haya. In the end, that was what mattered. 'It seems to have paid off. The customers are here . . . and they're buying. They want a little glamour in their lives.'

'I can understand it.'

'And the baby? What about that?'

'At least Ahmed left me something,' Haya said, blankly. 'It's what I live for.'

'And now you have a friend, too.'

'Yes,' Haya said, and they smiled at each other, gladly.

Jane glanced around the bungalow. It was warm, and different to her last place. A view over the Malibu ocean, if only in the distance. Driftwood and seaweed motifs throughout the house; clean modern lines, all in sands, greys, greens and whites; a decent little pool in the back.

'Good. I'll take it.'

The realtor beamed, and Jane told her to hold on; her bank would wire the money. It was a savvy purchase, the neighbourhood hip but not too expensive, the house tucked away up a sandbank far from the water's edge yet near the coast road.

'How much for the furniture?'

'That's not included.'

'Give me the number for the sellers,' Jane said. 'If you negotiate right, everything's included.'

LA was all about the new and the shiny. She was sure that if she talked them into it, they'd be happy to dump used sofas and last year's TV for newer models. Jane would get a discount, they'd get a blank slate, and everybody would be happy.

'I don't think I can do that.'

'You can and you will.' Jane smiled warmly at her, and the older woman grinned back. Jane's enthusiasm was infectious.

'Here you go.' She scribbled the number down on a piece of paper. 'Good luck, miss.'

'Thanks,' Jane said, picking up the phone and dialling.

Within fifteen minutes she had her house. Fully furnished.

Yes, she thought, with a blissful sense of triumph. She *owned* a house in Malibu. Very like the one the bailiffs had hustled her out of.

Jane Morgan was back!

She took care of the basics first. It was good to have something to do; that meant she didn't have to face her major problem – how the hell to start.

Also, she didn't think about Craig as much – when she was busy.

She called a cab into Beverly Hills and bought herself a car. Something hot and successful – the right look for the young female entrepreneur on the move. A small silver Porsche, chic and flashy; Ray-Ban shades on top of her head, and a bright red leather briefcase by Coach.

When all *that* was done, she bought a load of groceries and stocked the fridge.

And when that was done, it was time to go clothes shopping. Jane had donated her New York wardrobe to charity. She hadn't wanted to be held up at the airport with cases and, more importantly, the right look mattered. When she was raising finance with banks, she needed to look like she didn't need their help, that she was already rolling in cash and understood the hip, hot, LA scene. Subliminally, Jane needed to project that she knew exactly what kind of goods would sell best.

Money – and style.

She had a plan. Mix high-end goods with a fresh Angeleno look. Designer jeans, an eye-poppingly expensive Chanel jacket, and a hot little T-shirt underneath it. Something that said rich *and* trendy. A million miles from New York Jane's muted palette of creams and greys, a look to appeal to Wall Street. Here, she wanted to be something else: a maverick entrepreneur on a mission.

The rich girl purses, jackets and coats were easy to pick up. A quick trip to Rodeo and she was done. The stylish, newest T-shirts and jeans were harder. You couldn't use the convenient shorthand that luxury offered. You needed to prove your sense of style. Jane planned her wardrobe like a military attack. It was a key selling tool. If she wanted to pitch herself as a buyer of goods, then she had to buy the right stuff now.

She asked around; not the snooty senior sales assistants

in the expensive boutiques, but young girls, stylish Latinas and African-Americans or tanned Anglo surfer chicks with tattoos that she saw waiting at the bus stops or queuing to get into a rock gig.

One name kept coming up – Wave, on Melrose. It was the hot new place in town for low-end glamour. Even some celebrities shopped there, they told her, their drivers pulling up outside and waiting while they dashed in and bought Ts by the armload.

Jane thanked them and got the address. Perfect. A Wave shirt under a Chanel jacket. That would impress her investors. And she'd also look good in it; something that was starting to matter to her, despite herself.

There it was. Jane parked across the street and slid her sunglasses down her nose, watching the place for a couple of minutes. Damn, it was packed. And she could see why. The storefront stood out in a row of dingy shops; painted bright white, with a pale blue wave design all over it – unmissable. It was brightly lit, not dark or dingy. The doors were flung open and covered in seagrass matting. A little slice of the beach, right here on the boulevard, a unique look.

And the girls – the women. They were everywhere, almost fighting to get inside. Blondes with bright red nails, curvy little brunettes. Jane noted shoppers from every price bracket, skinny girls and heavy ones. She hated to think what the changing rooms were like. Forget that – she was a size six. She'd just buy up some basics, pieces with the Wave brand easily visible, and get out of the scrum.

Jane wondered about the owners of the store. Definitely had their fingers on the moment. Could she make them an offer? Produce designs for her? Once she had the financing for a superstore . . . why not?

She locked the Porsche and crossed the street, clutching

her new Prada handbag closely to her. It really was crowded in there.

The store was beautiful, though. It was just as bright inside, with mirrors on two walls to take pressure off the changing rooms, and a sand-and-sea motif. The signature T-shirts were brilliantly laid out. Instead of racking by style, forcing the shoppers to riffle through them hunting for the right fit, Wave had laid out the racks by size – 6 through 14. Once you found your size, anything you liked on that rack you knew you could wear. Brilliant! Jane was impressed. Even she hadn't thought of that.

She pushed her way up to the size six and took ten T-shirts up to the counter. It was a long queue; Jane took a moment to observe the sales staff. They were smiling despite the press; mostly immigrant women, she thought, all dressed in a semi-formal uniform – pale blue pants and sandy-coloured tops of various kinds. They looked good; busy but exhilarated. It was how she wanted her staff to look.

The queue moved up a little, giving Jane a sight of the counter. She gasped with shock.

Standing behind it, ringing up purchases, chatting and smiling, was Sally Lassiter.

'Oh, my God,' Sally said. 'Jane, it's really you. It's you!'

All Jane's thoughts of business evaporated like morning mist.

She managed to say, 'Sally . . . Oh, God, Sally . . .'

And then there were spots in front of her eyes, Jane swayed lightly on her feet, and fainted.

Chapter Thirty

Jane came round a few moments later, in Sally's back office; her friend was splashing water on her face.

'OK, OK!' Jane laughed. 'Enough. I'm back.' She stared at Sal as if she'd seen a ghost. 'I can't believe it, I thought you were gone for good. Do you have any idea of the money I spent trying to find you?' She grabbed at Sally's arm. 'Do you have a clue as to where Helen went?'

'I found her!' Sally said, bubbling up like a hot spring. 'Last week. She came into the store too – it's the best damn thing I ever did!'

Jane grinned foolishly. 'This is incredible. How is she?'

'She's called Haya now.'

'What?'

'Let her tell you.' Sally ran to open the door. 'Li-Soon, I'm taking the rest of the day off.'

'I have a car parked out front. Oh Sal, Sal!' Jane scrambled to her feet and clutched her closest, dearest friend in a bear hug. 'You have no idea what this means to me! No idea how long I've waited just to see you. I missed you, so much. Why didn't you call me?'

'I did. You don't exactly let the grass grow, honey. You'd skipped town. No forwarding address, no nothing.'

'Can we call Helen?' Jane asked hopefully. 'Where is she?'

'This way.' Sally showed her out back. 'Let's drive out there right now. She has a place near the Hollywood Hills.'

'That's my car,' Jane said, nodding across the street.

'Wow.' Sally's blue eyes widened. 'I guess you've done pretty damn well for yourself. Haya and I are getting along, but . . .'

'Money isn't everything. In fact without you two, it hasn't been all that much fun.'

Sally smiled, a touch of the old fire back in her eyes.

'Honey, that is about to *change*.'

'Aaaaaah!' Haya squealed for joy, and the plate she was scrubbing smashed in the sink. She ran out to her yard and flung her arms around Jane as she stepped from the car. 'It can't be!'

'You're pregnant?' Jane kissed her, and patted her round belly. She grabbed Haya's left hand. 'I heard about the marriage, about Ahmed. I'm so sorry.'

'Yes – my heart is broken. But this helps,' Haya said, full of an overwhelming gladness. 'It helps so much. I thought you were lost forever, Jane. Sally told me about your father – I'm sorry too. I never had a chance to tell you.'

Jane shrugged. 'You two were always my real family. Being away from you taught me that.'

'I tried a detective,' Haya blurted out. 'I looked really hard.'

'Sounds like we all did,' Sally said. 'One day we'll swap war stories.'

They stood in Haya's driveway, each reluctant to move an inch, to break the spell, as though their friends would evaporate again if they so much as tried it.

'Do you have a back yard?' Jane asked eventually. 'A pregnant woman shouldn't stand out in the sun . . .'

'Yes! Come inside, come inside. I'll fix some lemonade.' Haya could hardly stop herself from jumping up and down. 'I am so, so happy to see you, Jane. It's been far too long. It's been horrible,' she said, simply, and Sally laughed.

'Amen to that.'

They ate a hastily contrived picnic on the lawn, with tall iced glasses of lemonade, and Jane thought no fancy restaurant dinner had ever tasted quite so good.

'And so what happened to you?' Sally demanded.

'I lied about going to Washington,' Jane admitted. 'You'd lost your pa, and I didn't want you stressed over me. I had to pull myself out of the pit, you know. Get something of my own. When that bastard died, he took everything with him.'

She described her life, briefly; the scuzzy walk-up flat, the roaches, the sixteen-hour days, the bitchy girls from school . . .

'I can't believe they would do that,' Haya said, her mouth open. 'Even for them, that was pretty low.'

'It worked out OK,' Jane shrugged. 'That was how I met Rhodri.'

She gave the others a brief sketch of her rise to the top, leaving most of it out. Glancing round, she could see instantly that Haya, and to a lesser extent Sally, had managed to do OK – everybody was comfortable, and Sally had a thriving little store, but only she was now rich. And she didn't want to rub that success in their faces.

'And you? Tell me, Sal. How was Texas? Tell me everything.'

Sally hesitated. Even with Haya, she hadn't wanted to mention the rape. But now they were all there, she felt obliged, somehow. The girls were her closest friends, and friends shared everything, even the ugliest, bleakest wounds. Perhaps especially that.

'I was shunned by the extended family and Mom's friends dropped her. Worked in a beauty salon, made a little money. Mom was – is – an alcoholic. But it was worse back then. Sometimes you felt you were running as fast as you could just to stay still.'

Haya was a sensitive girl; her eyes pricked with tears.

'And then there was this jerk. I went to high school with him down there before I dropped out. He was the son of the owner of the store, and he drove me out of town one night and raped me. That's how I lost my virginity.'

Jane shuddered. 'My God. Sally, I am so, so sorry. If only I had been able to find you.'

'I couldn't tell you before,' Sally said to Haya. 'Couldn't find the words.' She stuck up her chin. 'But I'm telling y'all now because I'm not ashamed of it. It was his to be ashamed of, not me.'

'But are you OK? Have you had counselling?' Haya asked.

'Haven't had time. Somebody had to fix Momma.'

Haya took a deep breath. 'I also was too embarrassed to say, but the reason I went to Egypt was my parents tricked me. They shoved me into an arranged marriage with Ahmed. Against my will. When I was over there, I was looking for a way to stick around for a little while, save face and then come back. But I was afraid of him.'

'I bet,' Jane said.

'I ran,' Haya said simply. 'But I knew nothing of Cairo, couldn't speak the language. I was mugged . . . Ahmed followed me, saved me. They got my passport. While we waited to get me another one, he was the perfect gentleman, he showed more respect for me than my own parents. I fell in love with him. And thus it became a true marriage.' She sighed. 'It feels good to say it. I just . . . I didn't want to look stupid.'

'I don't have anything that bad to tell you,' Jane said.

'Thankfully.' Sally grinned wrily. 'It ain't a competition.'

'I did lose my virginity to a total asshole, but that pales in comparison.' She told them anyway, and told them what she'd worked out about Thomas. 'I'm good at money.' Jane shrugged. 'Not so good at men.'

'Nobody?' Haya asked.

She thought of Craig. 'There was this one guy . . .' She shrugged. 'Nothing's gonna happen there, though.'

Haya lifted her glass of lemonade. 'We found each other, and we're never going to be split up again.'

'Amen!' Sally said.

'To the future,' Haya proposed. 'To us.'

'To us,' the other two girls agreed, and they chinked their glasses and drank.

'I got to get back to the store,' Sally said, with a sigh.

'Come to my place tonight,' Jane suggested immediately, giving them the address. 'We've got so much to talk about. I feel like we only just started.'

The three of them met for dinner that night in Jane's back yard. She picked up some dishes from the Farmers' Market and laid out a spread: roast chicken, ham, strawberries, melons, French bread, wine and juices, a pitcher of sparkling water and crushed ice. It was an arid garden, but somebody had planted it cleverly: rosemary and lavender, palm trees and cacti; drought-resistant roses next to beds of Provençal herbs. Jane lit candles everywhere, soft light amidst the gathering LA dusk, she remembered leaving this city, a house just like this one, stripped down to nothing, poor and lonely. Her friends gone, her so-called nanny off as fast as her car could take her.

Jane allowed herself to revel in the moment; she was back, and now she had her friends, she had everything.

After all the horrors, and the struggle, and the sorrow, they were back together. And at this moment, Jane thought, she was with the closest family she'd ever had.

She vowed she'd never let them go again.

No matter what.

'Do you like it?' Jane asked. She'd finished giving the other girls the tour; it didn't last long, but she could be proud of the house. It was more than she'd ever had under her father.

'Fantastic. You did the best of us,' Sally said, with a touch of wistfulness.

'If you like, I'll give you a carpet – a house-warming gift,' Haya suggested. 'I have a silk Kashmiri rug that would go perfectly in your bedroom.'

'I couldn't accept something like that.'

'I want you to have it. Ahmed would have hated to see his things gathering dust in some warehouse in Laguna Beach.'

'You should sell them . . .'

'I can't. I have no store,' Haya said. 'And I won't dump them wholesale on some dealer. They are precious and deserve better.' She shrugged. 'Maybe sometime after my baby's born, I can deal with it. I'd like to find all his things good homes – the way Ahmed wanted them sold. With respect.'

'My crowd is only into fashion,' Sally said.

'How is that going?' Jane asked, curious.

Sally smiled. 'It's wild. I'm hiring new seamstresses every day. Can't keep up with the demand. And doing interviews. All the local press want to talk to me, and I have to say yes to everyone. You know,' she blushed, 'give them a little razzmatazz. They love that all-American look. So what about you? Why did you quit that cushy number back East?'

Jane told them, leaving Craig Levin out of it.

'So now I want to start a store. Tomorrow I'm going to the banks. I have thirteen appointments.' She shrugged. 'It'll be a tough sell, but I think I could follow the Wal-Mart/Shop Smart model and find some savings. At least I do have a record there. I'll need money to lease out the warehouse and buy the stock lines, computers, staff. It's a major amount of cash.' She tried to look confident. 'Somebody'll spring for it, though.'

Haya carefully sliced into a ripe nectarine.

'Why don't you *not* do that?'

'I told you, I'm not interested in taking a salary.'

'No, why don't you do it another way? All of us have problems. Sally needs space for her stock and a manufacturer – she can't rely on housewives sewing in back rooms forever. I don't want to run a shop by myself but I know about the business, and I have stock – beautiful stock. And you have training in the mechanics of selling.'

Sally blinked. 'You're suggesting we form a company?'

'A store. Yes. Why not?' Haya warmed to her theme. She looked at her two friends and realized it was the first time in ages she'd been excited about her career.

'Look at this great house Jane's got, and her car . . .'

Jane blushed.

'You said you were good with money. Well, I'd like some of my own. Not my father's or husband's, but *mine*.'

'Me too,' Sally exclaimed. 'I feel like I'm stuck at the starting gate, still.'

'So we all have talents. What would it be like if we combined them?' Haya suggested. 'Start our own store. And not just any store. A *great* store. Like Harrods or Saks.' She turned to Jane. 'I know you were thinking of mass volume and deep discount, but that field is packed. Why not turn it on its head? Designer goods. Low volume, high price. Each one sold like a jewel. The way Ahmed wanted our rugs to be sold. Like art. We had the right idea with the gallery, I think; we just didn't know the mechanics.'

Jane shivered with excitement. Man! Why not? Instead of trying to clamber up the mountainside all by herself, why not harness these two? Sally knew glitz like nobody else – she'd seen that. And from what she had heard of Haya, the woman had grown up, grown through her tragedy. She had that serene beauty, the depth, that Sally's sizzle lacked. Why not start a store that sold treasures for the discerning –

glorious Eastern carpets, objets d'art, hot fashion, the best make-up? There were so many rich women in LA. And it had worked as a concept all over the world.

The *superstore itself* as star. In Los Angeles, as Jane well knew, the upmarket stores were just malls – big, soulless malls where you rode escalators and walked down corridors of luxury shops. Do it this way, and Jane could provide those women with a single destination.

She got into the spirit.

'And beauty – we must have make-up.'

'I can design a range of cosmetics,' Sally said at once.

'And I can go home – back to Jordan. Source your moisturizers from the Dead Sea. Those muds have properties all the laboratories in Paris can't replicate.'

'What about a location?' Jane chewed on that. 'It will be our biggest capital expense.'

'But I already own a gallery,' Haya cried. 'It's empty now, but it's about ten thousand square feet. And it has a good size parking lot.'

'We'll need a lawyer.' Jane wanted to move, immediately; she couldn't hear a perfect idea and sit still. 'Form a company. What do you say, ladies, a third each way?'

'Sounds good . . .' Sally was nervous. 'Look, you girls both got money. I'm just starting to sell, I don't have any yet.'

'The company will loan you what you need.' Jane waved that aside. 'Sal, you have style we never will. That's what we need from you, interior design, fashion purchasing. Not just clothes. Haya can take care of the exotic stuff, but you need to find us the bread and butter – fabulous handbags, hot accessories, electronic gadgets, beauty therapists. It needs to be full of juicy, perfect little things. Toys for girls. The store has to be talked about – half of good retail is promotion. It has to be packed from the word go. Just like your little store on Melrose.'

'So that's what we'll call it?' Haya asked. 'Wave?'

'No,' Sally said, enthusiastically. 'This is brand new. This is ours. We need a new name. Something that sells what the store is all about. Something that sells what *we're* all about.'

Sally thought for a moment, then smiled.

'Glamour,' she said.

Chapter Thirty-One

'No.'

'I'm sorry – not for us.'

'I don't think so.'

'You have to be kidding me – you chicks are barely legal.'

It was the same story wherever they went. Only the degree of rudeness varied. Managers shaking their heads. Laughing at them. *Leering* at them.

'I wish Ahmed was here.' Haya bit her lip. 'He'd have smacked that guy in the face. Did you see how he looked at me?'

'It's your boobs,' Sally said, insouciantly. 'You have those big pregnancy boobs, Haya. Some men go nuts for that, especially since your belly doesn't show.'

'My dress isn't low-cut . . .'

'They can still see.'

It was true. Haya was wearing a modest, long cream dress with an empire waist that Sally had selected for her; Jane was in a Chanel suit – no need to go half funky any more, she had Sally for that now – and Sally wore a signature Wave cut-off, a flippy short skirt, and beads of her own design.

'They wouldn't treat men like this.' Haya glowered.

'Well, they wouldn't ogle them, I guess,' Sally said wisely. 'But they might kick them out. We have some experience, but it's not a lot.'

Jane frowned. 'You guys go on home – Sally, you get back to Wave, sell some skirts. We need the cash.'

'And what are you going to do?' Haya asked.

'I'm going to get us some capital.' Jane shrugged. 'From . . . another source.'

'Hope you're not gambling your house on a racehorse,' Sally said.

'No.' Jane grimaced. 'This is nothing that sensible.'

When the others had gone, Jane got back into her car, and shut the door. Her feet ached; she was exhausted. But she was focused on what she had to do.

Had to do – not what she wanted to do.

She took out her heavy cell phone and dialled.

'Levin Corporation. Craig Levin's office.'

Even though she was all by herself, Jane blushed. Deeply.

'May I speak to Mr Levin, please?'

'He's not in the office today, ma'am.' The smooth response kicked at Jane's guts; she couldn't believe how disappointed she felt. 'May I tell him who called?'

'Certainly. This is Jane Morgan.'

'From which company?'

'From GLAMOUR Stores.' It was sort of true. 'My number is 555–9856.'

'I'll pass on the message,' the assistant said blandly. 'Thank you for calling.'

Jane hung up, and gently rested her head on the steering wheel. Why? Why had she done that? He wasn't going to call her back. Craig Levin had bigger fish to fry.

No, she was just going to have to start over. Find some independent banks. Some venture capitalists—

Her phone rang. She jumped out of her skin.

'Jane Morgan.'

'Craig Levin,' he said, and she felt the warmth spread from her face all through her chest and curl its tendrils down into her belly. 'I'm disappointed, Jane.'

'Why?'

'You didn't call me at home. Or on my cell. Which means you want to talk business, or at least that's the excuse you're giving to yourself.'

Since he couldn't see her, she smiled.

'You got me.'

'Then come see me. At home. Hollywood Hills.' He gave her the address. 'I'm free right now.'

'Do you promise not to hit on me?' Jane demanded, fighting for some control.

She could hear his grin down her phone.

'I certainly do not. On the contrary, I promise to hit on you hard. Come see me – at your own risk, baby.'

Levin hung up. Jane immediately started the car and pulled into the traffic. What choice did she have? She had to go.

So it shouldn't matter that she also wanted to.

'Good afternoon. Miss Morgan?'

'Yes,' Jane said, dry-mouthed.

The butler smiled at her. 'Please follow me, miss.'

Jane's father had taken her into quite a few grand mansions. But never in her life had she seen anything like this.

The house was huge. Even the entrance hall, clad in marble, and full of pillars. Interior designed, with modern art and old masters jostling side by side; internal fountains, and lush greenery. As she followed the servant, Jane was led through peristyles and garden squares, caught a glimpse of a vast library, a home cinema, an internal swimming pool complex. It was a staggering, vulgar display of wealth. Nothing understated; Levin, she saw, was from the Sally Lassiter school of style. He made Sally's dad's estate look like a cottage in Virginia.

'He's sitting in the walled garden, madam.'

'Like there are more,' Jane joked.

'The house has six separate gardens,' said the butler, unsmilingly. 'Would you come this way?'

Meekly, she followed him.

'Jane.' He was sitting on a lounger by an Olympic-sized pool carved out of the hillside; smooth and glassy, it perched on the edge of the estate, so that you appeared to be swimming into the sky. There were Bali-style carved daybeds, hung with silk, a full poolside bar, and topiary hedges interspersed with frangipani flowers. 'Good to see you.' He got up and came over, kissing her on both cheeks, as his butler melted away. 'I took the liberty of fixing you a Bellini – fresh peach juice.'

Jane took the cocktail. It seemed the safest thing to do. That way she could concentrate on sipping the chilled champagne and not have to stare at his body. Levin was working on his tan: oversized shorts, casual flip-flops, shades – and nothing else. His chest was thickly muscled – this was a guy who lifted weights – and oiled with sunscreen.

She had a visceral reaction to that kind of strength. It did not help that she was here, now, as a suppliant, effectively flinging herself before him to ask for help. It charged the whole thing erotically.

And she was, she realized, already turned on.

'Thank you for seeing me . . .'

'If you say "Mr Levin" I'll throw you out.'

She blushed; she had indeed been going to try that.

'Craig.' She surrendered.

'You want finance, and the banks won't help.'

Jane blinked. 'How the hell do you know that?'

Damn. It was like he could read her mind. She instinctively knew that he understood her, in a way Jude Ferrers never had.

'If that weren't the case, you would not be here.' He grinned, lazily. 'It would have taken you two or three more months to come find me. You wanted to start a discount chain; no commercial lender's gonna fund you. And you could have taken a few more weeks, exhausted all the bankers and venture houses. But I know you. You're impatient. You want the world, yesterday.' His eyes fixed upon her, and Jane felt her knees weaken. 'So you came to me, because I can give it to you. Correct?'

Her throat was dry. 'Correct.' She took a sip of her Bellini. It was delicious, the scent of an Italian peach orchard.

'I told you I would not do business with you.'

Jane's confusion deepened. 'I see.' She tried to gather the shreds of her dignity. Maybe this had been crazy. Why would the guy sanction a multimillion dollar deal on the strength of one plane ride? 'Well, thank you for seeing me.'

'But I'll *give* you the money,' he said. 'A gift. No strings. A million dollars.'

She didn't ask if he meant it; that much was obvious.

'I can't.'

'You're an adult, like you told me. You can do whatever you want.'

'I can't – can't be dependent on a man. If you give me a million dollars, I'll be like Marie Antoinette playing at being a shepherdess.' She gripped the stem of her champagne flute. 'Mr Levin – Craig. Give me the million, not as a gift but as a commercial loan. You won't be doing business with *me*. You'll be doing it with GLAMOUR – and that's a company. Not just me. There's Sally Lassiter. She's our fashion buyer.'

'I know her.' He nodded. 'Big spread in the *Citizen*, hot shop on Melrose. I was considering making her a finance offer in exchange for a stake.'

'And Haya al-Yanna. My friend from school. She married an Egyptian – she has an eye, I've seen her stock. Haya brings us the physical building with a great lot, and some glorious Islamic art and antique rugs. And she will source other stuff for us too, exclusive cosmetics you can't get in the United States.' Jane wanted to be the evangelist. He would give her the money anyway; now she wanted to convince him.

She desperately wanted to impress Craig Levin. And she didn't examine her motivations too closely.

'Haya and I had a talk last night. Haya wants something special for GLAMOUR. She wants us to be at the forefront of ethical business – and I want to do it because it sells. Like the Body Shop. Like Anita Roddick. Haya will set up a worldwide operation for us sourcing handmade goods from indigent women, in Jordan, in the Middle East, where she has contacts – Egypt – everywhere. Later on in Africa and Asia too, once we have the money for scouts.' Jane rushed on, aware she was gabbling. 'Women will like it, the press will cover it. And Haya is determined. It's the way she is – if you could meet her, you'd know.'

'Perhaps I would.' His eyes danced over her, amused, as she pressed on with her case.

'So. Consider us as an investor. You know something of my track record with staff and costs. You said you might have approached Sally anyway. And as for Haya, OK, that is my say-so. But you can't deny that she brings us the store and the parking. So our company has physical assets.'

Levin inclined his head. 'Good pitch. Done.'

'No.' Jane stood strong. 'I want *two* million. For this store to work we need the best. Staff, uniforms, valet parking, stock. I'm ahead of the game because I have the real estate. But I need it to be *rich*, Craig. We're selling the all-American dream, with a little exotic flavour thrown in. And that has to be good.'

'Three million,' he said. 'And I take ten per cent of the company.'

'Four,' she countered.

Levin grinned. 'Three, sugar, or I'll walk away, and believe me, I know just how to do that.'

'I have to run it by my partners.' Jane smiled in the flush of victory. 'But I'm pretty sure they'll be OK with it.'

'Good.' He walked up to her, towering over her; his face above hers, his mouth close, too close. 'That's done. Can we move on?'

She struggled, fought with herself; the heat was spreading through her. Jane longed for him to kiss her, so much it made her weak.

'I'm not for sale,' she whispered.

Levin's eyes bore down on her, his mouth inched closer to hers; Jane's lips, moistened, parted. Just before the kiss, he pulled back.

Jane swallowed a gasp; she was left aching for him, frustrated.

'I don't want a girl I can buy.' His eyes flickered across her face, assessingly. 'I'm going to have those papers signed and the money in your corporate account by tomorrow. Once my lawyers have reviewed the share agreement. After that, you'll have what you needed from me, and I won't be able to take it back.' He reached out, and ran a fingertip down the side of her face; unable to stop herself now, Jane shivered at his touch. Instantly reminded of how he'd turned her on in the plane.

'After that, I'll come to you. And we'll see what happens.'

She forced herself to take a step back.

'My lawyers will be in touch.' She had to add, 'Thank you.'

'Tomorrow,' he said, with soft intent. 'See you, Jane Morgan.'

She turned on her heels and fled.

'I don't wanna go,' Mona whined.

'You have to.' Sally was firm. 'Mom, you have to. Here are your sneakers. You want me to lace them up for you?'

'I can dress myself,' Mona snapped.

Sally was glad to hear it; lately, she'd been wondering. Mona's room did not smell too pretty. Sally had stripped the sweaty sheets from the bed but the stale odour of too much sleep, and dissipation, still permeated the room.

No more. She wasn't going to give up on her momma. The company was formed, they had financing; for the first time in years, Sally believed good things, *really* good things, were about to happen.

'Here. I got you a new tracksuit. Nike – the best. We'll jog along Venice, next to the beach.' Because none of Mona's old friends would be there. 'After that I'm giving you a makeover, and you can come and see our new store.'

'What store?'

'GLAMOUR,' Sally said. 'You'll love it.'

If she could change style in LA, she could change her mom. Couldn't she?

Mona was an addict. Sally had faced that, as calmly as she could. You couldn't get an addict to just stop the addiction. It had to be replaced by something else. A positive addiction.

Sally decided on fitness. Mom would become a fitness freak. If that meant Sal had to jog an unnecessary three miles a day, then so be it. She was going to make her mother wash her hair, get a manicure and a wax, put make-up on daily and run to the beach. Mona had lost all pride, all self-esteem, and her mom had a pretty face, for an older woman. It shouldn't be this way. Crawling into a bottle or a box of pills.

Mona was sitting sullenly in her oversize pink tracksuit, and Sal, her long blond hair swept back in a neat ponytail, was wearing the same, only half the size. She was painfully aware how pretty she looked and how wrecked her mother was, Mona's once-thin thighs and bright complexion dulled by alcohol, ruining her skin and fattening her up.

But Mona could change. Everybody could. Sal had – she was a company director now.

She *believed* in the GLAMOUR philosophy. Beauty was more than skin deep, it was a matter of pride. Not everybody could fit the golden girl ideal like she could, but everybody could look their best. And Momma's best was better than this.

'Come on.' She forcibly grabbed her mother by the elbow; she smelled bad, of stale sweat, but Sally stuck with it. 'Let's go, Momma. Come with me.'

Every morning and evening, for a week, Sally forced Mona to jog. At first it was little more than walking pace, and her mother could only manage a mile. The second day, Mona occasionally broke into a trot before slipping back to walking. Sally didn't care. It was progress.

She tried to make her mom feel proud. Day one was the best – forcing her into a long shower, making her shave her legs, wax her lips, and get her hair washed and styled. Sally washed all the bedlinen and filled her room with lavender and roses. On day two, after the post-jog shower, Sally took time off work to give Mona a makeover. On day three, she took her to the shell of GLAMOUR and helped her pick out a couple of dresses – forgiving, beautifully worked Arab gowns from Ghada and Egypt, flown in the day before from one of Haya's suppliers.

And it was working. Sally could see the glimmer of interest that came back to her mother's face, the basic stirrings of self-esteem; Mona started showering, combing her hair, getting up without being nagged.

At the end of the first week, Sally came back from the store to find her mom had been shopping – all by herself. She'd bought some cushions and candle holders, and she had rearranged the décor in their little apartment.

At the end of the first month Mona fitted back into her old jeans. She hadn't touched a drop of alcohol – not even in mouthwash – for almost half a year. And there were other encouraging signs. She asked Sally if she could go to the dentist and get her teeth whitened – taking new pride in her appearance. Mona even joined a gym – she added weights to the running, morning and evening. Sally signed her up to a yoga class, where for the first time since Paulie died, Mona started to make friends.

Sally had tears in her eyes the first day she waved her mom off for coffee with a girlfriend. Fitness had done that – fitness, and self-esteem, and feeling good about life. Sometimes lipstick and a good dress really mattered. It wasn't too much of an exaggeration to say that style had saved her momma.

While Jane did her wheeler-dealing, hiring staff and meeting accountants and bankers, inking deals with suppliers, and planning store layout and infrastructure, and Haya took her pregnant body off on weekly flights to the Middle East, sourcing amazing lamps, rugs, mosaics and jewellery, Sally instructed her team of designers. She drew sketches, she placed factory orders, she did deals with other unknown talents. Anything to get GLAMOUR hung with the hottest new styles and the simplest classic pieces. Nothing cheap; nothing skimpy. Sally designed flaws away, she didn't want clothes that required a perfect body. All skirts and dresses were made of heavy material, and lined. And she started out with colour palettes that could be worn together.

There was a working woman's corner, too. Why sacrifice your femininity at the office? Sally paid for rich fabrics, silks, satins, velvet and heavy cotton – no linen, it wrinkled – and worked exclusively in black, white, sand, and navy; every piece went with every other piece. Classic cuts but with feminine tailoring. The blouses had cuffs and little shell buttons, but they were tapered at the waist and had a silky effect; the skirts swung to the bias and hovered on the knee, or fishtailed at the floor; the pantsuits had narrower waists but wider thighs, a little help where most women needed it.

Add a pair of Sally's own design slightly stacked heels and you got height, comfort, style – immediate weight loss of five pounds.

But Sally knew GLAMOUR had to be more than that. It needed to be a destination, an experience. Great clothes and cool rugs and pretty mosaics were nice, but Sally understood why women shopped. It was for a sense of Aladdin's cave, of being surrounded by pretty, gorgeous things.

Sally started work on the smaller stock: independent cosmetic houses, organic cruelty-free cosmetics, brands that didn't do business with the bigger stores. And she only went for gorgeous. Lipsticks with jewel-studded cases, faked-out rubies and diamonds. Soft make-up brushes, straight from the East, that used real hair. Perfume spritzers in dazzling cut glass. Little charm bracelets with pick-your-own gems to hang off them – you'd scoop them up with a mother-of-pearl spoon, like caviar, and pay per scoop. Delicate necklaces worked in Frisco by an artist she admired, glossy leaves sculpted from copper and gold, that jangled when you walked. Ankle bracelets, with bells on them. Little eyeshadows from a joint in Venice that packed them cleverly into seashells. Essential oils, in droppers, that could give fragrance to a whole room. Candles twisted into slogans – *HOTSTUFF* was her favourite, with a wick on each letter.

And so, slowly, the stock took shape. A lacy Parisian fan. A pair of tangerine leather strappy heels with cute white roses worked into the straps. Floris bath oils from Europe. Charbonnel and Walker chocolates. Scottish cashmere and Irish linens. Austrian silver coffee pots. It was the ultimate shopping destination, she thought, delighting when she found an original Black Forest craftsman who'd sell her a line of ornate cuckoo clocks, complete with dancing peasants, foxes and squirrels, or a real Roman gelato maker that would fly the original stuff in to serve in GLAMOUR's café. The store would be like a vacation for rich Americans who didn't feel like grabbing their passports. It was paradise. Little, irresistible, gorgeous things that just called out to your wallet . . .

She worked like hell. She worked like an obsessive, like Jane or Haya. All Jane thought about was getting that Levin guy his money back. Haya was into finding a legacy for her kid and helping poorer women who had been dependent on a man; profit meant little to her. Sally, on the other hand, thought about her mom, her dad, style and pride. She wasn't selfless, not some plaster saint. She wasn't Mother Teresa, forget *that*. Her sense of style had got her this far. If she could help other women, then *she* would get rich. She would get her whole life back.

While Mona worked out, sinking herself into her new fitness craze, Sally Lassiter got lost at the office. She dived into fashion, and she loved it.

Sally never thought about anything except her new job and keeping an eye on Mom, making sure she didn't relapse. There was no time for anything else.

Certainly not for men.

Chapter Thirty-Two

'And here's the ocean, right on the left.'

Sally nodded, conserving her breath. Great. Mom was fitter than she was, now. Showing her the new route she was taking, out to the highway and then cutting down to the beach.

'We'll go half a mile and hit the canyons.'

'Perfect.' Sally didn't want to talk. She was still slim and tanned, but her endurance had gone to hell.

'We'll cut through here, through the woods.' Mona was turning left, and Sally saw her legs moving efficiently down the sandy path. Damn, that woman had got some musculature going . . .

'Come on, honey!' her mom urged.

Sally blew out her cheeks. 'Coming . . .'

'Aaah!' Her mother slipped. It was so quick, Sally barely saw it coming. Mona's ankle twisted and cracked – Sally heard her groan, heard the nasty thud as she dropped to the ground – and she plummeted off the cliff-top path, slicing through the scrubby plants and crumbling, sandy earth, her manicured nails futilely scrabbling for a hold, down the side of the rock.

Sally grabbed for her mother's arms and missed. She screamed, and rushed to the side of the rock face. Mona was slipping and tumbling down the almost sheer hill, crashing and veering. Sally could make out patches of blood on her arms and legs. She shrieked, almost hysterical, calling wildly for help, but they were out here on their own . . .

Mona groaned and thudded and fell awkwardly on to an outcrop of rock; she didn't move. She was clearly unconscious. Sally felt a wash of dizziness surge through her body; black spots floated in front of her eyes; she was red and panting from the run. But she could not afford to black out now. She clutched at a tree trunk.

'Oh God! Help me!' she screamed.

'Hey.'

Sally jumped – it was the voice of a man, further down the path.

'You need help?'

'Yes! Please come! It's my mom.'

'I'm coming,' he shouted. 'Hold on.'

There was the sound of running feet and he appeared on the path, a tanned, strong-looking man with mirrored shades, a shirt and a Dodgers baseball cap; an enthusiastic Labrador bounded along at his heels.

'What's the problem?'

She grabbed his arm, babbling. 'Oh, thank God. My mom – her ankle gave out. She went over. She's down there . . .'

He took one look and straightened up. 'Stay right there. I have a car phone, I'll call 911.'

'Thank you . . .'

He ran back down the path. Sally looked over; her mother did not stir. She wondered wildly if she were dead. The seconds dragged on horribly.

Eventually he came back. 'Highway Patrol is sending a cruiser. I argued with them, looks like you need the coastguard and a chopper. They said it shouldn't be long . . .'

There was a shiver in the rocks; some stones, dislodged by Mona's fall, tumbled onto her prostrate body. One of them struck her ankle. Without regaining consciousness, she shifted, and hung further off the edge of the lip of stone, a dead weight pointing down.

Sally sobbed. 'Mom, oh God, Mom. They won't be here in time. She's gonna fall. She's gonna die.'

She clutched at the stranger. Ever since Leo, Sally had avoided men. She had never wanted to touch them. But right now she couldn't care less. She clung to this man.

Mona slipped a couple more inches. She was in a bad position. They could both see what gravity was doing.

'Wait there,' he said

'Don't leave me,' Sally wept. But he was gone. She inched closer to the edge herself. Her mom, her mom was all she had in this world, really. When you came down to it, what did a career mean? Without Mona, Sally was lost. Had she saved her from addiction just to watch with her own eyes as her mother plunged into the sea?

But she saw no way she could climb down. The ledge was too small to support them both. And since Mona was unconscious, Sally knew she couldn't lift her. If she climbed down the rock, they would *both* die . . .

'OK. Watch my dog.'

The man was back. He had a length of rope coiled round his waist and a pair of spiked shoes on. He ran up to the nearest tree, an elm a few feet to the right of her mother, looped the rope round, and hastily knotted it; then he tied another loop, and another, round himself.

'What are you doing?' Sally asked, hesitantly.

'No harness. I'm gonna get her.'

She bit her lip. This man didn't have the right equipment. He could slip – die. But Sally could not warn him. It was her mother.

'Watch Felix,' he said again, and slipped a length of rope between his hands.

Sally crammed her knuckles into her mouth. The elm tree did not have a wide trunk. It bent forward, leaning with his weight. He was tall, a strong, heavy guy, lean but bulky with muscle. She could see the strong muscles of his back working as he moved, quickly and with purpose, down the rock face; stones and plants gave way under his footing, but he just shifted his weight. It was impressive, if she had been in a mood to be impressed.

Mona slipped a little further.

'Hurry, please,' Sally shouted. He ignored her, and kept abseiling; lower, lower . ... almost there . . .

There was a loud crack; the small stone ledge shifted, tilted. Mona Lassiter's unconscious form slid inexorably forward . . .

And his thick, weightlifter's arm reached out and grabbed her by the elbow.

Sally watched in horror as the elm tree buckled and doubled over, the rope fraying. The man gasped and grunted, his feet losing their grip, scrabbling to get it back as he heaved, with brute strength, her mother's unconscious form over his back.

She ran to the tree and put her arms round it, desperately trying to hold it back. But her strength was as nothing – she couldn't stop it bending forward.

Sally looked over the cliff. He was climbing, slowly, agonizingly so, in contrast to the way he'd dropped down, fleet and surefooted. She could hear the grunts of pain; her mother's weight was being supported by a single hand as he used the other one to climb. Oh God! She was not a religious woman, but she prayed. Please let him be strong. Please let him not drop her . . .

After an eternity he was at the top, his face puce with effort, sweat pouring down his forehead.

'Take her,' he gasped.

Crying and laughing, half hysterical, Sally tugged and pulled at Mona's arms. Her mother slipped off her rescuer's shoulders and flopped forward on to the grass. She was bruised and bleeding, cut in several places, obviously concussed, but still breathing. As Sally examined her breathing, trying to loosen her shirt, wake her, the man hauled himself on to the grass and fell on to his back, panting, struggling to regain his breath.

Sally looked at him with pathetic gratitude and then winced. His palms were raw, cut and bleeding from the rope burns. His barrel of a chest was heaving, trying to get his breath, to recover from the monstrous effort.

'You saved her life,' she said. It was obvious, but she had to say it. 'Thank you – thank you so much, mister.'

He opened his eyes. 'Where's my dog?'

Sally's stomach flipped; she'd forgotten about the dog. This guy asked one thing and she'd lost his damn dog. She looked around wildly; the dog was sitting calmly behind her, wagging his tail, as though his owner had been engaged in a shopping errand.

'Right here,' she mumbled, guiltily.

He closed his eyes again. 'You forgot. It's OK. Felix is trained.'

There was a wail of a siren in the distance, getting closer. He struggled to sit up.

'Thank God for that.' Sally was in tears from the relief. 'The police are coming. They'll get you both to a hospital – you need the paramedics.'

He looked at her for the first time. She couldn't see the eyes behind the sunglasses, but she did register how his gaze travelled over her face, flickered over her body. A man who had looked at a lot of women.

She hated, detested being ogled. But this was different. His look had desire in it, but not contempt. And Sally, to her amazement, found her own body answering.

A shiver of wanting ran through her, and she dropped her gaze. An instinctive reaction, Sally told herself. The guy had just saved Mom. But all the same, she suddenly, fervently, wished she didn't look quite such a mess; hair sweaty from the run, eyes red with tears, no make-up, unwashed morning hair scraped back in a jogger's ponytail.

'I'm not staying.' He stood up. 'Your mom will be OK, once she's checked out.'

'Are you a doctor?' She didn't know why she asked him that; she just wanted him to stay.

'No. But I see a lot of sports injuries.' Finally, he took off the shades; and Sally, already red, blushed scarlet.

Along with the muscled body and square jaw, she now saw, was a pair of light grey eyes, unusually pale, like wolf eyes in the dark skin.

'Now you recognize me,' he said, without false modesty.

'I – yes.' Sally tried to cover her confusion. 'You – on the cover of that magazine.' Why was it coming out so stuttery? She felt like a moronic sports fan.

'*Sports Illustrated*.' He grinned. 'You really had no idea, did you?'

'I didn't. You're Chris Nelson. The baseball player.'

Sally wasn't a fan, but she knew about Chris Nelson, the shortstop for the Dodgers. Single-handedly turning the team around. An All-Star. A mega star, in this city; even Hollywood types sucked up to him.

'Yeah, well, do me a favour. Don't tell anybody about this. I don't need the publicity, the press will just hound me for weeks.'

'I won't.'

'I would stay to check on your mom, but I'm sure she'll be fine.'

'Thank you, again.' Sally bit her lip. She couldn't ask anything more of the guy. To do so now would look like she was just another one of the girls that tried to crash practice wearing the shortest skirts. 'We'll be good once the cops get here. And . . . you know, you're a hero – Mr Nelson.' It had to be said. Her blush deepened.

'That's cute.' He winked at her, and Sally's stomach flipped over. 'Long time since I've seen a girl blush.'

'Your hands are all messed up.'

'Yeah, well. My shoulder's practically dislocated.'

'I think your physio is going to put a hit on me,' Sally joked.

'John Tepes will, if I miss the series against the Yankees,' he said. Tepes was their manager. 'But don't worry. I'll come round and save you.'

The siren sounded closer. He stood up, and Sally was ashamed of herself for caring that he was leaving, while her mom lay a few feet away, knocked out.

'Your name is Sally Lassiter, right?'

She jumped out of her skin. 'How the hell do you know that?'

He was amused by her saltiness. 'Papers. My girlfriend showed me a picture. She bought some T-shirts in your store; looked hot on her.'

Girlfriend. Right. Of course. Like a hot superstar athlete like him was going to be single.

'Thanks, Mr Nelson.'

'I think it's Chris, after all that. Goodbye, sugar. Felix!'

He whistled, and the dog sprang from his sitting position and followed him, bounding, down the hill.

Sally was still staring into space when the troopers arrived; a couple of burly men, but with guts that would have done credit to Santa Claus. They would have been zero help.

'She's OK – we'll get her to Malibu Memorial Hospital. What happened here, ma'am? How did you get her back?'

Sally told the story, leaving out Nelson's name. They whistled as they grabbed her mother by the shoulders and ankles and staggered down the path with her.

'Some story,' the other one said. 'Some guy.'

Yeah, Sally thought, regretfully. Some guy.

Mona had suffered little more than concussion, a broken arm and some bad bruising; it was almost a guilty relief for

Sally to have her tucked away in hospital for a few days. She tried to fling herself into her work. The baseball player had disturbed her, profoundly, and she woke in the mornings restless from half-forgotten erotic dreams.

Sally tried to forget Chris Nelson. He wasn't a real person; he was an icon. With a girlfriend. And maybe she was just dealing with puberty hormones, or something. Since Leo, she'd never even wanted to kiss a man. She knew she was a normal, straight woman; maybe Chris was only the first man she'd had a chance to want. Pure coincidence, she decided.

But now Sally was aware of him, she was reminded of him everywhere – on the news, flicking through the channels, whenever she saw a fan in a Dodgers shirt. And a few days later, the news came through. An undisclosed 'injury' had put him on the disabled list for a month's recuperation. Nelson on the DL was the talk of LA.

Sally waited fearfully for something to happen, for the story to break; if the cops had traced his cell call or something . . . Half the sports fans in LA would be picketing their new store.

It didn't happen. He went into physiotherapy (the radio told her) and the rescue remained a secret.

So Sally got on with her job. Designing. Buying. Making GLAMOUR a statement. Over the top, fabulous, rich, a sumptuous experience from the second a buyer put their car in the lot. When you shopped here, Sally was determined, you wouldn't just be buying a dress or a pot of night cream; you'd be buying a little slice of the Hollywood dream.

She had a vision, and the other two girls let her go with it. GLAMOUR. The name said it all. Every shopping trip would be a vacation. Something to justify their sky-high prices.

Maybe Laetitia Berry would come and shop here, Sally thought. Chris Nelson's girlfriend.

Laetitia, or Letty, as the press called her. Former Miss Minnesota and now sitcom star. Tall, slim, African-American, with flawless ebony skin, a retroussé nose and blindingly white teeth. She shopped at only the best stores, drove a Ferrari and, as Sally was finding out, had been dating Chris Nelson for about a year. There was a pregnancy rumour. The gossip rags said they were getting married.

But of course. For Nelson to be unattached would have been fantasy. Sally was truly grateful he'd saved her mom, so she tried to be happy for Letty. And Chris.

It didn't work.

Sally told herself there were plenty more fish, and all that. Now she was interested in men . . . Now she'd saved her mom . . . Now she felt she could breathe . . . There were plenty of places a pretty young woman could meet men in this town.

That didn't work, either.

Well, Sally thought. Put it this way. Chris Nelson had warmed her blood, stirred something in her she thought she might never feel again.

Desire. Lust.

After the rape, she had closed herself off, become almost like Jane; a robot, obsessed with work, her career, saving her mother, climbing out of the pit of poverty. It was safer and simpler to think solely about that. When a man ogled her, she felt contempt, sometimes fear. Never desire.

Chris Nelson had risked his life to save a stranger's. He was no puffed-up millionaire. He was a man's man, as selfless and masculine as Leo Fisk had been bullying and weak. He used his strength for protection, not for bullying. And Sally's playful, flirtatious nature responded. She wanted him, she thought about being with him, making love to him. In her fantasies they got married and raised little softball-playing kids.

Of course, in her fantasies there was no other woman.

But Sally's bubbly, womanly nature, stunted by Leo's abuse, opened up now like a snowdrop breaking through frozen ground. And when she turned to her work, it was to distract her from wanting a man, not, at last, from her loathing of all men.

Sally was busy. Like it or not, pining or not, the store was rolling towards the grand opening. Now she had a PR campaign to organize. She got the hell on with it. What else could she do?

Chapter Thirty-Three

Haya stepped into the limo with relief.

It was air conditioned, a blessed change after the baking heat outside. She was an Arab, and she'd thought she could handle this weather, but the further along her pregnancy got, the less she liked it.

'Take me to Bar-al-Yanni, please,' she said to the driver.

'Of course, ma'am.' He spun the car directly into traffic with practised ease and Haya struggled to stay awake. Jet lag was bad, but she really wanted to get this trip over with. After that she could go back to the hotel, unplug the phone, hang the little sign on her door, and she'd be done.

It was vital to buy enough. She had to be four times as good on this trip, because her baby was getting too big, too restless in her belly. There would be no more sourcing from the Middle East after this. Haya needed enough goods to last in the stockroom for at least five months; she wasn't getting on a plane until her child was six months old and weaned, and it would take her four months to train another woman to her exacting standards.

At least she knew, now, that she couldn't do it all herself.

Choosing the precious objects had been a big deal for Haya. Sally took care of the Western fashion and the store design, Haya added the exotic flavour and the ethical dimension. She knew she had to live up to both ideals. Sourcing art, jewellery, fabric, lamps and rugs from the Islamic world, and not from dealers; from individual

women, or from the nascent collectives that had sprung up
– widows, unmarried women, women whose meagre
income from the glorious things they worked was keeping
flesh on the bones of their children. Haya had big ambitions
there. She wanted those rich Americans to get addicted to
this beauty, and pay top dollar. Everybody would win – the
buyers would get something unique, not mass-produced,
something that would look great in their houses for
generations. The women who made these things would
finally receive a fair price, even a generous one by local
standards. Haya had no doubt it would transform lives. And,
of course, GLAMOUR would take a hefty slice out of the
middle.

Haya wanted to make money, anyway. For her own
independence, and her child's – Ahmed's child. Profit and
principles. If she could combine them, Haya thought, she
could be happy; she could salvage something from her
husband's death, make a difference in the world.

Ghada was her last stop on the tour. She had already
shipped enough Jordanian mosaics, Moroccan carpets,
Egyptian lamps and carvings, and Palestinian cushions to
fill the holds of a small ship. This remote kingdom was the
final destination. Haya wanted to invest in a line of
traditional jewellery from Ghada. The desert tribeswomen
in the north crafted elegant necklaces and bracelets dripping with small metal discs, a variant on the coin jewellery
in other Arab countries. Haya thought they looked
feminine and delicate, good on any woman, and when she
had shown Sally Lassiter a sample, Sally had gone wild. The
intricate pieces would be the centre of the opening
GLAMOUR jewellery collection. The traditional metal was
silver; Haya wanted to negotiate for a commune of women
to work them for her in copper. Americans didn't like silver,
too much trouble to maintain, because it tarnished.
Jangling, luxe bracelets of fiery red-gold would knock the

Hollywood ladies out. They'd buy them by the armful, sexy trophies for women.

'We may have some delays on the road north of the city,' her driver said, lapsing into the Egyptian Arabic that was a lingua franca in the Middle East.

Haya sighed. 'Why is that?'

She didn't want to be late. They were waiting for her at the small oasis town and she had had some difficulty in securing this meeting; these women did not trust Americans, even Arab-Americans.

'There is a visit there from one of the sheikhas. Sheikha Aisha, the daughter of the King's half-uncle. They will have security.'

'Of course.' Haya didn't want to be rude, so she chewed on her lip. The royal family of Ghada, highly wealthy from a combination of oil and booming real estate in the metropolitan cities on the coasts, was large and well funded. There was the King, old and tired, an absolute ruler. His many brothers and sons, daughters and sisters, all princes and princesses. A few degrees removed from that, the royalty had lesser titles like Sheikh and Sheikha. Just in case, Haya reviewed her protocols. Prince, or Emir, Royal Highness; Sheikha, simply Highness.

'Why is she going there? Is there some function?'

'The royal women often patronize the markets and bazaars there. They support the traditional crafts.'

'Ah.' Haya smiled. 'Do they indeed?'

Perhaps, who knew, perhaps she could get something out of this. She thought of the Western love of titles. If they could market the Ghadan necklaces 'as worn by royalty', they would sell even better. Would the Sheikha agree to be photographed in a necklace? There would be some samples waiting for Haya today. She got excited, she could see the advertising campaign now. Even better, maybe there would be another lady, somebody further up the tree, one of the King's daughters or granddaughters, a true princess.

'If you can get me there half an hour faster, I will pay you a bonus,' she said. 'Especially if you take me as close as you can to where this visit is happening.'

It was a triumph. Firstly, Haya had the pleasure of having the work presented to her by Begum Ghida al-Ali, the widow of a former chief. She had organized this group of abandoned or poor women, many of them widows or former street children, who had lived in grinding poverty. They worked the tiny metal discs into the most delicate, exquisite pieces. They deserved to be treated as works of art, and Haya saw no problem in selling them as such, as her husband had planned to do. She signed a deal, the women toasted it with mint tea, and she left money behind, just as down payment. The joy with which it was received made her day.

And secondly, with great determination and a couple of sample necklaces in her hand, Haya had approached a woman in the Sheikha's retinue, an efficient-looking matronly sort in a Western suit with a neat scarf tied around her hair, and sunglasses. The lady would not see her now, she was told, but she took a number, and said somebody from the palace would be in touch. Yes, they liked to support the work of traditional craftswomen, and yes, they were looking for trade opportunities with the States. If the Sheikah could be sure that the deal the women were getting was fair . . .

Haya had no doubts on that score. She left a card with the protocol officer, and took a cab back to the hotel. There she took a long bath, washed her hair, and went to lie down on the bed, wrapped in a soft white towelling robe. Her room was air conditioned, and all she wanted to do was sleep well, then rise and get on the plane.

Job done. Nothing more to do than to wait for the birth of her child . . .

The phone rang. Sighing deeply, she rolled on her side to answer it.

'Hello?'

'May I speak to Haya al-Yanna, please?'

The voice was modulated; Arab with an English accent, she thought, educated abroad; she couldn't tell how old.

'Speaking.'

'Ms al-Yanna, my name is Jaber Ibn Mohammed, I work for the palace and the government of Ghada.'

Haya closed her eyes briefly. Damn it, a call she couldn't ignore.

'It's good of you to call,' she lied.

'I understand you are to fly back to the States first thing tomorrow. Do you have time for a meeting this evening? I can come to the Radisson.'

'Of course, I'd be delighted.'

'If the palace is going to approve any project like this, involving a sharifa, we have to vet it.'

'I quite understand,' Haya said, mentally relinquishing her night off. 'Is six o'clock convenient? We could meet in the lobby, or have dinner.'

'Wonderful. See you then.'

'Wonderful,' Haya echoed, and hung up. Damnation. She set her mobile phone to alarm; at least she'd have half an hour, and anything was better than nothing.

He was waiting in the lobby. Haya was surprised to see he was a young man, maybe a little older than herself, and tall, with an aquiline nose and aristocratic, searching eyes. Olive-skinned, with a tan from the sun, and a beautifully cut suit; a strong body, she thought, not bulky.

'Ms al-Yanna. Thank you for seeing me.'

'Thank you for coming.'

His eyes swept over her, appreciatively, she thought, and then blinked; his gaze had come to rest on her belly.

'You're pregnant,' he blurted out.

She smiled. 'Yes, *Mash'Allah*.'

'Excuse me, I didn't mean to be rude. I was just surprised. Is your husband with you?'

'I'm a widow,' she replied, coolly.

He flushed, embarrassed. 'I'm sorry.'

'You weren't to know.'

'Shall we eat?' Initially confident, Haya could see he'd been thoroughly fazed. 'Uh, a pregnant woman shouldn't go too long without dinner. They have some good cuisine here, even though it's a chain; some local dishes on the menu.'

'That sounds good.' Haya was pleased; he was thoughtful, she was hungry, and now he'd be trapped with her for as long as it took to eat a meal – long enough to pitch him her plan.

'Then come this way.' And to her surprise, he offered her his arm.

Beautiful manners, she thought. And a handsome face. And then felt instantly disloyal to Ahmed. She was seven months pregnant, even if it did not show too much on her body, except for the gentle swell of her stomach. What was she doing thinking about another man like that?

They ordered a perfectly reasonable meal, some local specialities, vine leaves wrapped round spiced meats, tiny roasted birds, a Ghadan version of *tabbouleh*, and a lemony whole goat's cheese in oils and herbs. She discovered Jaber had been educated at Cambridge – St John's College, he said – and had served a military apprenticeship in the US, at West Point.

Haya told him some of her story. Just a little, though; she did not want to drag Ahmed too far into it.

'I must ask you about your store,' he said eventually, getting down to business.

'It's going to be prestigious and luxurious, and will charge high prices. We have backing from a senior financier – Craig Levin.'

'Levin,' he responded, clearly impressed.

'I am a full partner; the site is my husband's former gallery. My further role is to source art, jewels and cosmetics from the Middle East. We are hoping to engage in ethical commerce, to buy from women, and to pay them fair prices.'

'And to make a profit.'

Haya was unabashed. 'Yes, this is a for-profit enterprise. In the end, you know, these women don't need handouts, they need long-term commercial partners. That can only be sustained if the buyers are making a profit.'

He smiled slightly, appreciatively. 'You sound like a woman who knows her own mind.'

'I am.' Haya inclined her head. 'And we must be perfectly honest with you, since we want the participation of a sheikha or a princess.'

'That is true.'

'The photograph of that lady in the jewellery will help our cause; it will make our company richer – come to that, it will make *me* richer.' Haya blushed a little. 'Although I have no doubt these pieces are of sufficient quality to sell without it.' Haya smiled. 'So you see, Mr Ibn Mohammed, I'm trying to be honest; it's a business proposition, though, in the end.'

'And a sound one.' He paused, his eyes travelling across her. 'As long as you can prove you will be paying a fair market price to the Ghadan women who are supplying you.'

'As soon as I get home, I'll fax the documents to the palace.'

'Very good.' He smiled, lightly, and his eyes moved, again, across her face; Haya was embarrassed, and looked away. 'Then we may be able to do business. I suppose you will not be back here for some time.'

'Not until after the birth of my child.'

'Of course.' He paused, and looked at her again. 'If I may say so, Ms al-Yanna, you're a very unusual woman.'

'Is that a compliment?'

Jaber grinned. 'It is. I assure you. I like to see a fellow Arab succeeding in the United States. Perhaps it's even better that you are a woman – and a widow, and mother-to-be, *insh'Allah*. That will – what do the Americans say – "set the cat among the pigeons".'

'That's right,' Haya said, and chuckled, liking him. 'You're pretty unusual yourself. I would expect a diplomat to be stuffy.'

'Thank you.' He inclined his aristocratic head to her, then returned to business. 'I can see Sheikha Aisha consenting to the photographs. If you do well with sales, and our women are benefiting, a more senior lady from the royal family, a princess, might become involved. The King does want trade.'

'Wonderful news,' Haya said, thrilled.

'But we would want a bigger shift of your buying to Ghada – including carpets and lamps and so forth.'

'I would hope we will open more than one store,' Haya replied confidently. 'But I wouldn't come back to you unless it happened. And we could order a lot more from Ghada.'

'Then I'm sure we can make a deal.' He lifted his glass of mineral water to her in a toast.

'I'm glad to hear it, Mr Ibn Mohammed.'

'Please call me Jaber.'

'Then Haya.' She smiled.

'And . . .' he hesitated. 'Not that it matters, but when you communicate with the palace, it isn't Mr . . . as it happens. I take a close interest in the affairs of Sheikha Aisha, you see, because she's my mother.'

Haya's water went down the wrong way; she spluttered in surprise. And then blushed richly, deeply embarrassed.

'You mean . . .'

He said nothing.

'I'm sorry, Highness,' Haya said, wanting to run off and hide.

'Nothing to be sorry for. I led you to believe otherwise. I should apologize. It's just that I hold a government position, and I'd rather be dealt with that way than as a member of the family.'

Haya saw he hadn't said *royal* family – he hadn't had to.

'I understand. Highness,' she added, again.

'I'd much prefer Jaber.' He signalled for the waiter, and spoke to him in the Ghadan dialect, too fast for Haya to follow. 'I should be leaving. I hope you have a pleasant flight, Ms al-Yanna.'

'Haya.'

'Haya.' He grinned. 'And we'll be in touch.'

She wondered if she should stand and curtsy, but it was too late. He bowed briefly to her, turned and left.

'I'd like to check out, please.'

'Certainly, madam.'

'Room 406.' Haya slid across her key and her credit card. 'There were some phone calls to the States, and two bottles of mineral water . . .'

'It's quite all right, madam; there's no charge.'

'Excuse me?'

'Your bill has been settled by the Kingdom of Ghada. Orders of His Highness Sheikh Jaber.'

'Dinner, perhaps . . .'

'The entire bill, madam.'

'I see.' Haya bit back a smile. 'How generous of His Highness. Could you possibly arrange for a taxi to take me to the airport?'

'That won't be necessary, ma'am. His Highness has sent a government limo for you. It's been waiting outside for an hour.'

All the way home Haya told herself it was just a courtly gesture. She had done some important business, maybe secured a PR coup. That was what mattered.

Jaber was a sheikh, and a government minister. He was probably married already. A man in his position was not going to be interested in a pregnant widow the size of a cow. It was important to keep her feet on the ground – even in the first-class section of Royal Ghadanian Airlines. When she got to the airport, Haya had found that Sheikh Jaber had ordered her business-class ticket upgraded.

When she got home, she immediately had one of Jane's assistants fax the business details to Jaber's office.

She was now getting really heavy, and she was exhausted. Haya chose to leave the grand opening to Jane and Sally. She'd walked through the store, seen the beautiful displays of the things she had sourced; together with Sally's exuberant fashions, they would be the heart and soul of GLAMOUR.

Right now, though, Haya had a child to attend to. It was foolish to hope for romance, and she didn't want her heart broken twice. She made no attempt to contact Ghada other than through the office. She decorated the nursery instead, a nice neutral yellow. No man was going to want to raise another's child.

Once the baby was born, she'd forget about any romantic possibilities. Right?

Chapter Thirty-Four

'Well?' Sally stood back, and just looked at it. 'Are you girls ready?'

She had her arm linked through the other two's. Jane on her right, Haya, almost ready to pop, on her left. They were standing in the parking lot, looking at the store.

It was six thirty, and the sun was sinking over the horizon, streaking the LA sky with a spectacular show of golds and reds. The building, gleaming white in the sun, was hung with banners of gold and silver silk, and pennants of scarlet and blue flying from every corner; it looked like a ticker tape parade.

'Tomorrow,' Haya said. 'I can't wait.'

'Nor me.' Jane agreed.

Tomorrow they would open. The big day; the climax of months of grindingly hard work, of forcing themselves to act like a team, even when it got annoying. Exquisitely appointed, staffed by experts, and laid out, as Sally said, 'like Christmas morning', they thought it was the hottest, richest, most luxurious store in the world.

The full service beauty parlour. The roving reflexologists, ready to offer manicures and hand massages to tired shoppers. The fabulous goods, the soft lighting and dove-grey carpeting, the mood music and attentive staff, the valet parking, the gift-wrap service . . .

It was a dream.

'They're all coming.' The other two knew Sally was

talking about the press. 'The *Times*, the *Observer*, the *Citizen*, *Variety*, the *Hollywood Reporter* – everybody.'

'Tough crowd,' Jane observed.

'Let's hope it works,' Haya said.

'It will.' Sally was determined. 'It has to.' She looked at her friends, all three of them, in this moment, young, beautiful, and determined.

'You girls want dinner?'

Jane shook her head. 'Let's go get some sleep. We have to be ready for tomorrow.'

They had determined they would take the press together, at lunchtime. Jane told the others there was a story; human interest. The three of them, touched by tragedy. An unlikely friendship.

And now a comeback?

'I agree.' Sally pursed her lips. 'Get your rest in, ladies. We have to look *good*.'

'Jane! What does it feel like for the store to be this mobbed?'

'Sally! Are you taking the offer from Chanel?'

'No,' she shouted, trying to be heard.

Behind them, in the store, it was pandemonium. Jane had told them to be calm; her staff were wonderful, they had everything under control.

'Haya! When is the baby due? Boy or girl?'

The flashbulbs popped around them; reporters shouted questions. As word of the frenzy at the store got out, more and more journalists had shown up. Right now it resembled a movie premiere.

'GLAMOUR by name, glamour by nature,' Sally whispered, nudging Jane.

Haya squeezed her hand. 'I don't feel so good. It's crowded in here.'

'I'll get rid of them,' Jane whispered back. Her friend looked bad, her face pale, and her breathing was laboured.

They'd done more than enough questions; Sally was brilliant with the media.

Whatever happened now, opening day was a triumph.

Jane stood up. 'Ladies and gentlemen—'

'Uuuh,' Haya whispered, slightly.

Jane looked down at her friend, but Haya just shook her head.

'Ladies and gentlemen, we're so glad you could come. GLAMOUR was a dream of three friends. Today it's a reality. I won't bore you with a long speech, since I think you'll find this store speaks for itself.' Jane smiled; at the back, behind the wall of press, she saw Craig Levin. And she looked right into his eyes; today was her triumph, but he had made it possible. Her lips parted, she paid tribute to him.

'Please,' Jane said, softly. 'Enjoy.'

The flashbulbs popped, and Levin, unobserved, winked at her. She shivered with pleasure, and admitted to herself how much she wanted him.

Haya squeezed her hand; Jane glanced down and saw her friend wincing. She sat down and put her head near Haya's.

'What's up?'

'I think I'm in labour,' Haya whispered. 'Can we get out of here?'

'Right. Come on,' Sally said. She stood up, subtly lifting Haya to her feet.

'Thanks very much, y'all,' Sally said brightly, her Texan drawl like melted honey. 'Have fun!'

The two girls took Haya out, smiling and waving so nobody noticed her grimacing in pain, and a second forest of lightbulbs popped and flashed as they passed.

'Ms al-Yanna, your mother is here,' said the midwife. 'Shall I send her in?'

Haya screamed.

'Send her in!' Jane said.

'I need Ms al-Yanna's permission,' the woman fussed.

Jane turned to her with an icy-cold face. 'She's a little busy right now. And I heard her say yes.'

'So did I,' Sally chimed in.

'Send her mother in.' Jane's voice brooked no argument, and the woman obeyed.

The baby was close now, very close. Jane could see the head crowning. She gripped Haya's hand, sweaty and hot, to encourage her; Sally was hooking her legs back.

'Here it comes,' Haya gasped. The door swung open and her mother bustled in, saying something rapid in Arabic Jane didn't understand. She let go of Haya's hand.

'No!' Haya said. 'Stay! All of you stay!'

The older woman grabbed her other hand, leaned over and whispered something to her daughter; Haya screamed again, and the baby popped out of the womb in a wet, slithery rush, into the waiting arms of the doctor, who took the child, rubbed a towel all over it, and cut the cord.

'Let me see!' Haya cried.

The doctor brought the baby across, wrapped in a striped cotton blanket. She said, 'Here, Ms al-Yanna, a beautiful daughter.'

Haya's mother's face fell.

'A girl,' Haya said wonderingly.

Sally cooed, 'How precious – she's so tiny.'

'She's perfect, absolutely perfect.' Haya's face was a picture of joy, and Jane did not need to ask if she was disappointed. She bent down and kissed the baby on the forehead. 'Praise be to God,' she said. 'I love her. Her name is Noor. Light. Because she's the light of my life.'

Mrs al-Yanna started to smile, leaned over and kissed her daughter and granddaughter.

'Congratulations,' Sally said, with tears in her eyes.

'She's adorable. We'll see you later,' Jane said. But Haya was already lost in her baby.

'Come on, Sal.' Jane wiped away a little tear from her own eye; she thought briefly of the mother she barely remembered. 'It's been a long day. Let's go get some dinner.'

They sat in the front of Jane's Porsche, the top rolled up, at a discreet distance from the store, eating thin-cut roast beef sandwiches and drinking iced Diet Cokes, watching the parking lot.

'I can't quite believe it,' Jane said, wonderingly. 'I watch it, and I still don't believe it. When you think what happened to us.'

Sally sighed with sheer pleasure. 'I know. We did it. We made it.'

The girls hugged.

'And Haya's a mom.'

'Right. That's nuts.' Sally sipped her Diet Coke and glanced across at her friend. 'You know what makes this better than before? I mean – if I could have Daddy back. But better than being at Green Gables? It's that that was all Daddy's, and this, this store, it's *mine*.'

'Ours,' Jane said, laughing.

'Sure.' Sally grinned. 'Good job you got that loan from Mr Moneybags.'

'It was, wasn't it?' Jane said, thinking of Craig. 'I know what you mean. Not too long ago I was cleaning dead roaches out of my refrigerator.'

'And I was buying my groceries late at night to get discounts.'

'Look at them,' Jane said. 'I love it.'

'We did good,' Sally agreed. 'Real, real good.'

She offered her best friend one manicured hand, and they smiled at each other, and shook.

There was a constant queue to get in and out; women swarmed around the lot like well-dressed ants, weighed down with GLAMOUR's signature glossy navy and gold bags. Several times every few minutes, male attendants in crisp navy GLAMOUR uniforms appeared carrying rolled-up carpets, more bags, or heavy items of furniture, and transported them to waiting SUVs.

'I guess those articles that came out last week really helped,' Sally observed.

Jane licked a spot of mustard off her lower lip. 'It's only the first day. We can't get carried away. Lots of PR. We have to see if it's sustained.'

'But this is good,' Sally insisted. 'At Wave, we had something a bit like this. And it stayed that way until I quit for GLAMOUR.'

'Yeah.' She could not deny it. 'It's good.' Her brow furrowed a little. 'I hope we have enough stock . . .'

Sally hit her. 'Cheer up.'

They grinned at each other, companionably.

'I'm going back to the office. Field some more press queries, do a debrief of the staff at the end of the day.' Jane sucked up the last of her Diet Coke. 'Call our bankers.'

'You mean Craig Levin,' Sally suggested slyly.

Jane blushed. 'Last time I looked, he was our banker.'

'You won't be able to hold him off forever,' Sally said. 'I'm going into the store. I'm gonna serve behind the counter, like at Wave.'

'You'll be mobbed. You know you're getting quite the following. The press seems to love you, Sally. You're turning into a star.'

'Honey, please.' Sally opened the door of the Porsche and tossed her long, blond hair. 'I have *always* been a star.'

It was only half a joke. In reality, Sally was starting to think of herself that way. The press had a story – little orphan Annie makes good – and they adored how she combined all-American good looks with design savvy. Maybe she wasn't brilliant, but in Jane Morgan, Sally had found a woman who was; and Haya added soul to their project that got them ten times the coverage.

Together they were way more than three times what they could have been singly. And Sally was the butterfly, the star in the middle. The fashion was designed by her – it was her.

She was it. She was back. She was GLAMOUR.

Maybe she wasn't as smart as the other two, but Sally was starting to believe in herself. And her talent. She brought something to the table. Let Jane go do the wheeler-dealing; Sally was there to *sell*.

She glanced back at Jane's gorgeous car as she went inside. By the end of this week, Sally promised herself, she'd have a sports car too. A better one – a Ferrari. And a home in the Hollywood Hills, like any aspiring star too small, at least for now, for a Beverly Hills mansion.

'Hi,' Sally said, for the fiftieth time.

She had ducked into the staff bathroom, fixed her make-up, brushed her hair out and whitened her teeth, and now here she was, smiling at the customers. The *fans*, as she was starting to think of them.

'Hi! You're Sally Lassiter. I saw you in the *Citizen*. Oh, I just love your stuff, it's simply too darling.'

'Why thank you, ma'am.'

'And those fabulous little moisturizers from the Dead Sea. I tried one on my hand, and it was so soft and luxurious . . . And the gift wrap was great. We bought a rug, didn't we, Hyam? And they're shipping it.'

'Satisfaction guaranteed,' Sally said, smiling broadly. 'It's been an honour serving you, ma'am.'

The fat woman clutched her husband. 'Isn't she amazing?'

'Amazing,' he said, looking Sally over with a mixture of lust and resignation.

'You know, sir,' she said, deftly wrapping the woman's

Ghadan disc bracelet, 'we have an electronics area on the third floor. It sells gadgets and the TV screens are permanently tuned to sports. We also provide armchairs and couches to sit in, if you'd like to wait while the lady shops . . .'

'Get out of here,' he said, blinking. 'Really?'

'Yes, sir. And there are waiters serving pretzels and ice-cold beer.'

The wife looked hopefully at her husband. 'Kitty,' he said, 'you enjoy yourself, honey, charge whatever you like. This is a hell of a store.'

He lumbered upstairs and Sally rang up the wife's purchase.

'You see, ma'am,' she stage-whispered, 'that was my idea. That area – it's like a crèche for husbands.'

The fat wife giggled. 'Wonderful! Fabulous. What a brilliant idea. I shall tell all my friends.'

'Please do. And keep shopping.' Sally winked at her, and the customer waddled away satisfied.

'So tell me,' said a low voice, one she recognized. 'Do those TV screens also show baseball?'

Chris Nelson was standing in front of her. Today, he wore a nondescript blue shirt and khakis.

'I – yes, sir. They do,' Sally murmured. She rested herself on the counter, so he couldn't see her knees buckle.

He leaned in a little closer, his eyes moving across her body. Sally felt acutely aware of the button that was open at the top of her blouse; her lips moistened, and parted.

'Don't call me sir,' he said, his voice low. 'Got that, sugar?'

'Yes . . .' she wanted to say 'Mr Nelson' but dared not give him away. '. . . Chris.'

'Better.' He gave her a lazy smile. 'Pretty busy place you got here.'

'It's just the first day.' Oh God! He was so handsome. Sally stiffened her back and lifted her head. She had to fight this. 'Maybe you could get Letty to come here and shop. We have some special cosmetic ranges for ethnic skin. Or she might like our perfume section, or a hand-crafted mosaic from Jordan.'

'How's your mom doing?' he asked, ignoring her response.

Sally blushed.

'Well. Thank you.' She lowered her head. 'Sorry, that was uncalled for, I – I know you didn't mean to hit on me, or anything.'

'Sure I did.'

Her head lifted. 'What? I don't fool around with other women's men.'

'Even me?'

Arrogant bastard!

'Yes, even you,' she snapped. 'But I'll send Ms Berry an engagement gift to your office, no charge.'

'It wouldn't reach her.' He looked at her, amused. Toying with her, Sally thought, with a fresh rush of heat. 'We're not engaged. So send any gifts to her own office.'

Sally opened her mouth, but Chris cut her off. 'And to clarify, we're not going out either. We've split up.'

'Why?'

'We just drifted apart,' he said, easily enough. 'She's a wonderful woman.'

Not that damn wonderful, Sally thought, annoyed.

'So what time do you get off work?'

'Whenever I want to. It's my store.'

'Then maybe you can buy me a cup of coffee,' he suggested. 'Apologize for forgetting my dog.'

'You want me to ask you on a date?'

'What's the matter? Not a modern woman?'

Sally tossed her hair. 'I don't beg.'

'We'll see about that,' he said, softly, and she felt her stomach turn inside out. 'But for now . . . coffee?'

Sally's throat went dry. She turned to the sales assistant, a bright Korean woman whose smile never failed. 'You can finish up here, right?'

'Yes, Miss Lassiter. Of course.'

'Thanks.' Sally came out from behind the counter, feeling naked now she was so close to him. To distract him, she asked, 'How come you haven't been mobbed?'

'In here? You got to be kidding, this is oestrogen central. Maybe if I went upstairs. To the husbands' crèche.' He grinned. 'Now that *is* a smart idea.'

'Where are you parked?'

'Right outside. And I left Felix at home. Come on, I know a great place we can get something.'

Sally followed him, meekly, her head down; she didn't want to be stopped either. Not right now. The store, her success, none of it seemed to matter. He was all she could think about. She hoped to hell it didn't show.

'You might want to be quick in the parking lot, though. More men out there.' As they left the store, he slipped his shades back on, and put one arm possessively round her shoulders; as a couple maybe they'd attract less attention.

'Hey!' They were almost at his car – she recognized it, a large Jeep, top of the range. 'Aren't you Chris? Chris Nelson?'

'Not today, pal.'

'That's Chris Nelson,' somebody else shouted.

'Oh my God!' a woman squealed. 'I love him!'

'What now?' Sally asked, dismayed.

He chuckled. 'Run!'

They made it to the car with moments to spare. Nelson opened the passenger door, Sally jumped in, and he wound up her tinted window; within seconds they were inside. She watched as he wound down his own window, where a thick little knot of fans was banging on the glass, and smiled broadly.

'Hey, it's good to see you folks.' They cheered wildly. 'Enjoy shopping at GLAMOUR?'

'We love you!'

'Thanks for all your support.' He reached out his hand and brushed at various grasping fingertips. 'I better get to practice, we have to whup those Cardinals Monday, right?' They cheered again. 'See you guys here again, maybe. It's a great store.'

Then he pressed the button, the window wound up, and he put the Jeep into gear. The crowd scattered, obediently, waving, and he spun the wheel and deftly took the Jeep into the anonymity of the LA traffic.

'You're very good at that,' she said.

He smiled. 'I've had quite a bit of practice.'

'So where is this place?'

'Malibu. Out on the coast, not too far. It's tucked away and they know me there. Nobody bothers you, plus, they have an open-air terrace overlooking the ocean.' He glanced at her. 'We won't get too near the edge.'

Sally laughed. 'OK, then.'

Suddenly he turned the car and pulled into a layby.

'You made a wrong turning?'

'No.' He looked across at her, pale eyes hot. 'I just want to introduce myself properly.'

Sally blushed, her skin tensing, and Nelson reached across the car, put one large, calloused hand behind the soft skin of her neck, and tugged her to him. His mouth crushed hers, his tongue probing deeply across her teeth, the roof of her mouth. His left hand brushed lightly, teasing, across her breasts. Sally felt desire rock through her, so intense that she could hardly contain herself; she kissed him back with helpless passion . . .

And then hated herself for it. Why? Why had she done *that*? What girl didn't melt in the arms of the big superstar? She fought, and reluctantly broke away from him. Thank

God her bra was padded, and he couldn't see exactly how turned on she was.

'Why did you do that?'

'I had to,' he said simply. 'Been thinking about you for weeks. Even when I was still together with Letty. Once we broke up . . .' He shrugged. 'Your picture's been in the paper an awful lot. I said to myself I'd come find you, check you out. For sure, you wouldn't be as cute as I remembered – not the big entrepreneur that you are. Except when I saw you behind that counter, you didn't look cute. You looked hotter than hell. And there's no way to test a woman out without kissing her.' He grinned. 'Some girls are pretty, but there's no fire. That's not you. You're hotter than hell, baby.'

Then, without giving her time to think, Chris started up the car again, put his shades back on, and concentrated on the road.

Sally was grateful; she turned her head aside and looked out of the window. Hoping he could not see her smile. Hoping he could not smell her desire. Oh God! She had to be careful now. Going out with somebody like Nelson was fun, but it could never last. Too many girls, everywhere, too much competition.

She had to be careful not to fall in love.

Chapter Thirty-Five

'Good to see you again, Mr Nelson. And Miss Lassiter, welcome.'

Sally's eyes widened; she slipped her hand into Chris's nervously.

'I've got everything ready, sir, just as you ordered. This way, please.'

The maître d' conducted them through the expensive looking restaurant – Sally recognized two movie stars and a senator – out to a terrace at the back, a manicured lawn surrounded by topiary hedges and climbing roses wound over trellises. There was a single table, directly overlooking the ocean, set with a crisp white cloth and beeswax candles in silver holders. A large silver bucket on a stand held a chilled magnum of champagne; from here Sally could see it was vintage Pol Roget. There was a bowl of crushed ice, filled with fruit – nectarines, plums, crisp-looking grapes; a luxurious arrangement of green and white flowers, and a series of small dishes set out across the table.

'Tapas,' Sally said, surprised. 'I love tapas.'

Nelson grinned. 'I know.'

The maître d' showed them to their table, uncorked and served the champagne, and then melted discreetly away.

'Here's to the start of something,' he suggested. And she drank, thankfully, in the hope that the wine would make her feel less nervous.

'How did you know I liked tapas? And how does he know my name?'

'After that day I did some research on you.' He shrugged. 'Read that article again. Asked around. Found your store on Melrose was closed, and had my assistants tell me what you were doing, with those other chicks. I thought it was pretty ballsy stuff.'

'You researched me?' she asked, outraged.

'That's right,' he said, easily. 'And I bet you researched me, too. Went and looked up my stats on ESPN. Didn't you?'

Sally blushed scarlet. She had. And more.

'But that waiter?'

'I told him I was coming here with you, as my date. No questions about Letty, we'd broken up.'

'You used to bring her here?'

'Of course.' He shrugged. 'It's my favourite restaurant. Have one of those spiced ham slices and you'll see why.'

'But . . .' Sally was trying to process it. It felt like Chris Nelson was three steps ahead of her. Maybe because he was, she thought, and found the idea totally erotic. 'That means you knew I'd say yes.'

'I did know it.'

'Isn't that arrogant?'

He gave her a lazy grin. 'Sally, I've known a lot of women. And I know how they look at you. You were interested, that day. You didn't say anything, but you didn't have to. I knew once I'd finished with Letty you'd see me.'

'Good job you were right, or you'd have lost your girlfriend for nothing,' Sally said acidly.

'It was.' He picked up a plate of vine leaves stuffed with rice. 'Try one. I ordered them specially for you.'

She bit into one. It was delicious; the herbed oils drizzled a little across her lips. She licked it away, and blushed again. Everything she did, here, seemed to be charged with sex.

'I don't have sex,' she blurted out.

His eyebrows lifted; the first time she had surprised him. 'You're not a teenager any more, are you?'

Sally shook her head.

'Then don't worry,' he said. 'We can fix that.'

'I had a bad experience,' Sally whispered.

His eyes clouded. 'How bad? Do you want to talk about it?'

Sally shook her head. 'No.' She felt herself almost dizzy with wanting him. 'I'm not – not going to sleep with you,' she said.

'And what's wrong with me?' Chris was leaning forward now, eating, but not concentrating; his eyes never seemed to leave her body.

'You're too much,' she said. 'You're too good-looking, and strong, and you saved my mom . . .'

'I hope that's not going to be a strike against me.'

'You're famous. Like, really famous. And rich. And you date supermodels.'

'One. Singular. Ever. And I told you, we drifted apart.' Chris was protesting, but gently. His eyes fixed on Sally's. He was serious, and she couldn't fault him.

'You're so . . .' She flailed, she wished she could be as cool as Jane or Haya, find some fancy words to finesse it, instead of saying what she meant. 'You're so damn hot.'

He grinned. 'So far, this doesn't sound like a list of crimes of the century.'

'Stop playing with me!' Sally said, passionately. 'You know what I mean. So I sleep with you, you get what you wanted, you dump me and I'm left pining after you like some bitch in heat. And you move on to the next chick. Some actress or another model . . .'

Nelson's face softened.

'I'm not that way,' he said. 'Really.'

'I wanted to be a virgin,' Sally blurted out. 'I was raped.'

There. It was out. She felt a weight slip from her shoulders, and she looked at him.

Chris reached out and took her hand.

'I'm real sorry some bastard did that to you,' he said, gently. 'Are you past it, do you think?'

Sally nodded. 'But I'm not a virgin. And I wanted . . .'

'Saving it up for marriage?'

She blushed, defensively. 'Maybe. Somebody special, anyway. Special to me.'

He sighed, defeated. 'Well, I guess nothing's gonna happen tonight. Although you would have enjoyed it.'

Sally could hardly deny it; he'd had her leaping and squirming in his arms, just from a kiss.

'Maybe tonight, yes. But what about tomorrow? I have to be careful.' Sally lifted her chin, defiantly. 'I know who you are, Chris Nelson. But I know who I am, too.'

Nelson's eyes lit up, and he grinned appreciatively.

'OK, then,' he replied, and gave her a warm smile. 'No more pushing. But I want to tell you something.'

'Go ahead.' Sally took her flute of champagne, drained it, and poured herself another.

'You want to accuse me of having laid a lot of girls. I'll tell you right now, guilty as charged. I started in school as the best batter in the team. Went up the minors. Got drafted in college. All the way through, I got raging hormones and I got the prettiest young girls throwing themselves at me. You do the math.'

She nodded, smiling slightly. At least Chris Nelson was honest.

'Only thing I *can* say is, I used a condom, because my elder brother wound up knocking up this chick he hated, marrying her and getting divorced after eight miserable years. Rough on the kid. Anyway, same time I hit the bigs, it starts to get old. Can't tell you why – just did. I looked down on the girls, started to look down on myself. Waking up in strange rooms with some random broad who might start crying, or stalking me. It was a headache.' He paused. 'And this may sound dumb, but I started thinking about my Aunt Esme, she raised me since my mom died when I was two. She's like a mom to me. Anyway, she's been married to Uncle Jake for twenty years and they have three kids apart from me. Didn't used to have much money but they were always happy. I wanted that.'

'They didn't *used* to have money?' Sally raised a brow.

He shrugged, admitting it. 'I bought them a house and some cars and gave them a bank account. My cousins too. They're all millionaires now. Anyway, I decided to cut out all the one-night stands, grow up and pick a girl. So I decided she had to be especially beautiful – like you, say. There's a lot of temptation. And also strong, because I don't want to be bored. When I met Letty, she seemed like a good fit. Also she was as rich as hell, so I knew she wasn't a gold-digger.'

'Makes sense,' Sally said, hating Letty Berry.

'It was never great, but it was pretty good. We went out for a year, I never cheated on her.'

'So what happened?'

He ate a chicken wing, and sat back from her, giving her space. Sally registered this; her body didn't like it. 'Told you, baby. We drifted apart. It happens. And right when the wheels were coming off, I went jogging. And I heard you. Like I say, you intrigued me. Just – I don't know what. You were brave. Polite and reserved. You carried yourself different from most girls when you knew who I was.' He shrugged. 'Even though I could see you wanted me. Of course I told myself it was only an intense moment, nothing to get worked up about.'

Sally smiled; she had thought the same.

'But then I started looking you up. Your guts. Your talent. How you looked after your mother, not just that day at the cliff. You and your two gutsy friends. They're cute, too.'

Sally frowned; she felt a stab of jealousy.

'Nothing like you, though, Sal. And you know, I started to think about you all the time. I used to take a detour and drive past your store and watch the trucks loading in the stock. It was really happening. What kind of a twenty-something chick does that shit? They're all wasting Daddy's money at college, working on their MRS degrees. And one night, I was with Letty, we'd already had a fight and I started thinking about you. Closest I ever came to cheating on her.' Sally blushed. 'I broke up with her the next day.'

'Was she upset?'

'Yes. I don't want to talk about it.'

'I'm sorry . . .'

'Are you?'

'Sorry she was hurt.'

'If I loved her for real, I wouldn't have been thinking about you.' Nelson shrugged and reached for his own wine, draining it, refilling his glass and topping hers up. 'I'm not going to say I love you, I hardly know you. You might be a psychopath. But if you want to wait to find out how serious we are before you slide into bed with me, that's cool. I can wait.' He paused. 'A little.'

Sally smiled. 'Thank you.'

'Do you like the food?'

'You're changing the subject.'

'Don't tempt me, girl. I'm only human,' he growled.

She felt the familiar hot press of wanting him and meekly bit down on a slice of chorizo.

'Yes. It's delicious,' she said.

Nelson stood up, leaned across the table, and kissed her on the lips, his mouth just brushing hers; a more modest kiss than the first but still Sally was on fire.

'Try a peach,' he said. 'They're sweet. They're cold.'

She couldn't help herself; a tiny moan escaped her lips.

'Good,' he said, pulling back. 'At least I won't be the only one to suffer. Want some mineral water?'

When he dropped her off at the apartment block, he kissed her again.

'I'm going to send you tickets to the game tomorrow night. There's a box for the players' wives and girlfriends. Starts at eight, so maybe you'll be done with the store.'

'The press will see me . . .'

'Honey, I lay you two to one they already know. You going to be there?'

'You know I am,' she said, surrendering to the fact that she was totally, insanely, passionately hot for him.

'Good. It'll help me wear down your resistance,' he said, and winked at her. Then he rolled up the window and drove off.

'So where have you been?'

Mona was sulking; her arm still in a cast, she was fussing at not having heard from Sally all night.

'Sorry, Mom. I'll call next time. Hey, that thing can come off tomorrow.'

'Yes, well. That's good.' Mona sniffed. 'I can't run for four weeks, but they have an Olympic pool at the gym, so I'm starting swimming.'

'Sounds like fun.'

'Sally! What man were you with?'

Sally started, guiltily. 'How do you know I was with a man?'

'That look on your face.'

'Just . . . a nice man. We're going out again tomorrow. He's the man that saved you, Mom.'

'Oh – well. I suppose it's OK, if you don't do anything stupid. Remember Daddy is watching over you.'

'I will,' said Sally, feeling the heat in her evaporate. How did Mom know exactly the right buttons to press? Maybe mothers did that by instinct.

'And Jane and Haya called. Haya said to tell you thanks and you can come by the hospital at two tomorrow.'

'OK.'

'There isn't going to be a problem with those two, is there, honey?'

'What do you mean?'

'I don't know.' Mona shrugged. 'Bothering you at home. That Jane, I know you always liked her but she has a bit of a hoity-toity way about her.'

Sally grinned. 'Mom, that's just her accent. Jane's been my best friend forever.'

'Well, honey, I hope it lasts,' Mona said, doubtfully. 'But I'm so proud of you, all this work you've put into the store. And I know it's nice to have some lotions from the Middle East and stuff—'

'Haya does a lot more than that, Mom.'

'And Jane runs the accounts for you, but that's not the main part of the job, is it? You're the one with all the glamour and style, baby, you're the one picking what they sell.'

'I know that. So do they.'

'It's *your store*,' Mona said protectively. 'You should be the boss. I don't want any stuck-up foreigners taking it away from you just because you all hung out at school.' Her mother's face was pink, and it was the longest speech Sally had heard her make in quite some time. 'I think you're going to be very rich, honey, and Daddy lost it all once. I'd just *die* if anybody tried to take it from you again. We've come too far.'

'Mom! I love those girls. They both know I'm GLAMOUR and they don't mind.' Sally patted Mona on the shoulder. 'We've been through so much together. We're not rivals.'

'Well, if you're sure,' Mona said slowly. 'Anyway, Jane

wanted you to know that the store opening broke some sort of record. She says you have a problem with enough stock and can you bring in anything extra from Wave?'

'OK!' Sally grinned. There it was, that glow of achievement. Chris Nelson wanted more than a pretty face, and she had no intention of being just that.

'And then lots of journalists called and asked if you were going out with a baseball player.'

She froze. 'What did you say?'

'I hung up on them.'

'Good job, Mom.'

'So are you?'

Sally surrendered. 'Yes. The man who saved you plays a little ball, yes.'

'He's an All-Star shortstop?' Mona asked, determinedly. 'For the Dodgers? Cover of *Sports Illustrated*? Future Hall of Famer?'

'I don't know why you're asking if you already know,' Sally sulked.

'I didn't. The journalists told me.' Mona smiled. 'If somebody famous was the man who saved me, I reckon he must be a good man. Those celebrities are usually pampered brats. He took a risk.'

Sally remembered the welts on his hands. 'He certainly did.'

'Just remember, honey, you only have one heart.'

Sally went over and kissed her mother on the forehead. 'Believe me, Mom,' she said. 'I'm trying.'

Chapter Thirty-Six

Jane was trying to keep her feet on the ground. It was only one week, one full week. There had been factors: curiosity, well-managed press. Additional coverage after that, from stuff you could never script: Haya in labour, Sally starting to date some famous athlete – boy, they'd loved that. Even Jane, who tried to stay in the background, was getting well known.

But you couldn't fool people forever. If the shoppers came back, it would be because of their excellent service, first-rate staff, and the whole experience she was selling.

Maybe she would wait and see if they did come back.

But damn, these numbers. Out of the park. Like a ball off the end of Sally's new boyfriend's bat. Home run stuff. Records.

She was now fielding new calls. Not just from the style sections. From Wall Street analysts.

She turned off her computer and flopped down on the bed, exhausted. These last three weeks had been mad. And with Haya gone, and Sally's eyes dazzled by Chris Nelson, all the stock rearrangement had fallen on Jane, as well as staff evals, billing, and the rest of it.

They needed to hire management, she thought. Vice presidents. Who could she steal from Saks? And that wasn't all. At this rate of cash flow – be honest, she knew it wasn't going to drop, in fact it was going to increase. The brand now had critical mass, and their foundations of quality were there. It was an out-of-the-gate success. Well, at this rate of money, they'd have to expand. Move into the East Coast. New York. Then Chicago. Then DC. Seattle. She ticked the cities off in order of importance. After that, they'd be looking for major new investment and some places abroad: Paris, London and, to be different, perhaps a boutique in Mauritius. GLAMOUR was just that. It had to be open in St Tropez and Milan . . .

The store was going to be a major success. Perhaps she should push to formalize her leadership of the company. Just to avoid any misunderstandings, later. Wouldn't everybody be happier if the roles were more clearly defined?

But there was so much to do. Maybe later.

Jane sensed exhaustion creeping up on her, and she couldn't have that. Burnout was what happened to other people. Bond traders . . . She had to be able to cover Haya for a couple of months. Resolutely, she peeled off her clothes, dumped them in the laundry hamper, and put on her swimsuit. The pool in the yard would do fine. It was a blisteringly hot day, and she would cool off and work out at the same time.

Tomorrow this house would go on the market. Sally and Haya were already moving. This place was cute, but far too small, and she could now afford to upgrade. Part of GLAMOUR was the fantasy, anyway; of course the owners had to live well. They were the brand, as Donald Trump had learned.

She plunged into the pool. Man, she loved exercise. It was the one time when she could totally focus on herself. The physical effort forced her to clear her head. Figures, money, deals just melted away. Without exercise, she thought she might crack. Jane swam twenty laps, revelling in the movement of the water against her body, then propelled herself lazily up to the steps in the shallow water, and slowly walked out of the pool, reaching for her towel—

'Good evening.'

She gave a little shriek. Craig Levin was sitting there, on her sun lounger, dressed in a lightweight summer suit. His gaze ran quickly across her body before she wrapped it in a towel.

'What the hell are you doing here?' Jane snapped.

'I called, I faxed, I emailed. No reply.' He grinned. 'Started to think you were ducking me, Miss Morgan.'

She had been. 'I was busy,' Jane extemporized. 'Opening week . . .'

'I noticed.' He inclined his head. 'I do have three million dollars in your store. And ten per cent of the company. Which I believe makes me the major non-owner shareholder.'

'The only one,' Jane conceded.

'And it appears I'll be getting a nice return on that ten per cent.'

He certainly would.

'I'll buy your shares,' she said. 'Four million dollars, and you've increased your money in six months.'

'Now why would I sell something for four that's worth five now and, I strongly suspect, twenty or thirty in a couple of years?' Levin asked coolly. 'If you were me, would you sell?'

Jane had to shake her head. 'No.'

'Then don't ask foolish questions.'

She stood there, dripping, water from her soaked hair streaming down her back, her feet naked on the hot tiles. Nothing but a towel between Levin and her nude thighs; her suit was high-cut, with a hole across the belly; she understood clearly that he had an excellent idea of her body, right now, down to the flat of her stomach and the swell of her breasts.

Levin was clothed; wearing a smart pair of shoes, and a paisley tie; they looked good on such a muscular man.

'I have to get dressed,' she muttered.

He spread his hands. 'Nobody's stopping you. But please don't bother on my account.'

Jane fled into her bedroom and whisked the curtains closed.

Five minutes later she was back out there, wet hair combed through, her feet in stacked mules, wearing the closest thing to hand – a sample of one of Sally's new summer dresses; it had spaghetti straps and a close-fitting bodice, with a light skirt that fluted prettily around her knees.

'Nice,' Levin said, making her wish she'd added a shawl. Only it was just too hot.

'Can I get you some iced tea?' Jane was flustered. 'I have a jug in the fridge.'

'Thank you,' he said, to her discomfiture. It meant that he was going to stay. And that she would have to fetch him the tea. A small act, but one he somehow imbued with meaning.

At least she was out of her swimsuit. Jane fetched him, and herself, a large glass of tea choked with ice and sliced a lime into it.

'Delicious,' he said. 'Unsweetened.'

'I'm watching my figure,' Jane confessed.

Levin shook his head. 'No need. Believe me.'

'So what can I do for you?' she asked, as briskly as she could, under the circumstances.

'I want daily accounts sent to my office.'

'You can't have them.'

'I own ten per cent. I want a seat on the board.'

'Can't have it. Talk to your lawyer.'

'If you want my money for expansion, you'll co-operate.'

Jane shrugged. 'I think the banks will be ready to talk to me, now.'

He grinned. 'I think so, too. But you won't be able to do the mom-and-pop thing forever, you know. Even Branson went public. And when you do, I'll be there with my chequebook.'

'And until that time, I'll send you a once-monthly summary,' Jane said. 'And we'll be repaying your loan early.'

Levin was still looking at her in that disturbing way.

'You do understand that you are an insect to me, right? That I could take anything I wanted from you. I could have City Hall ride you on parking or health and safety. I could buy out the contracts with your suppliers. I could hire away your staff by doubling their salaries and send them on fact-finding missions to Cancun.'

Jane squared her shoulders. 'We'd sue.'

'Whatever resources you have, throwing them at me would be like dropping a pebble into the ocean,' he replied, matter-of-factly. 'I have so much money that consortiums of commercial banks wouldn't take me on.'

She gritted her teeth. 'I will *not* let you sit on the board. I'd rather go under.'

'Don't worry,' he said, smiling at her. 'I wouldn't force you. But I want you to know that I can.'

'Does that usually work? Puffing out your chest like a pigeon in mating season?'

'You respect work. And success.' His eyes lingered on hers. 'I want to remind you of mine, so you stop fighting me so hard. We're supposed to be allies. I've been treated better by companies that were my takeover targets. No matter how much you came on to me in that press conference.'

Guilty. She knew it. He knew it.

'I know you, Jane Morgan,' Levin said suddenly. 'It's why you interest me so much. You're one of the most driven women I have ever met. You're brave; not fearless, it's not the same thing. Determined and gutsy. And you don't have time to waste on the wrong guy. But I'm not the wrong guy. I'm not Jude Ferrers.'

Jane stiffened. 'How the hell do you know about that?'

'It's nothing sinister. You didn't exactly have a lot of boyfriends in New York. When you went out with Jude, people noticed. Mostly to wonder if you'd totally lost your head.' Craig's eyes narrowed. 'Some rich playboy, weak in body, weak in mind. The guy wasn't good enough to fetch your coffee, let alone date you. But yeah, I asked. And I know you got burned.'

Jane didn't reply; she didn't think she had to. He wasn't mocking her. He was sympathetic.

'You need somebody stronger than you, not weaker than you. Why do you think you fascinate me? We are so alike, we too.'

'There's nobody stronger than me,' Jane said, dry-mouthed.

'You're not as tough as you think you are,' Craig said. 'And I want to prove that to you. I want to be the part of your life that you've been ignoring. Up to now. I see a very feminine woman. You're soft and responsive. And, of course, extremely lovely.'

Jane blushed richly. How did he know how to talk like that? To mirror everything she was feeling?

'So tell me,' he said, drawing the sentence out. Clearly enjoying himself. 'Do you treat all your benefactors this way?'

Jane tried, and failed, to think of a comeback.

'So why me? You know I could have been of greater assistance. More money. Contacts. An advertising budget. You should now have full pages in *Vogue* and *Elle*.'

'I apologize,' Jane said, blushing. 'I should have been more responsive.'

'My question is why you weren't.'

She tried, 'I've been so busy . . .'

'Making hundreds of business-related calls. Just not to me.'

'I—'

'Tell the truth,' he said, grinning. 'Admit it. You'll feel better.'

Oh man. Jane shook her head. He was too close to her, too strong. Too damn powerful. And so good-looking.

'I – I find you attractive.'

There. She had said it aloud. Jane lowered her head.

'Better,' he said. 'And you know, I think that's still legal in all fifty states.'

'And it's best not to get involved with a colleague!' she added, in a burst of inspiration.

'Now, Jane. You were doing so well. And then you relapsed.' Craig's confident, teasing tone was so arousing; Jane could hardly look at him. Colouring, she stared at her sandals. 'Shall I help you out? You're a tough woman – and you want to stay that way. You're frightened of me. Frightened of wanting me, frightened of my past girlfriends, frightened of being one of a list. Slightly ashamed of yourself for having used my attraction to you to get this deal. Determined that you'll return my money and never see me again. Scared of any romance, any man, maybe. Thinking that one day perhaps you'll marry a house-husband, a nice, unthreatening guy with self-esteem problems, who can give you a baby or two and then run a farm somewhere, while you bring home the bacon; somebody who'll never challenge you . . .'

Jane's eyes flashed. 'Cut that out!'

Levin put his face close to hers. 'Pretty near the knuckle, am I, baby?'

'I'll tell you this. I'm never going to be used by any man.'

'But you used your stunning beauty to get to me, didn't you?'

'No.'

'Oh yes, you did,' he said, softly. 'Oh yes, Jane, and you know it.'

She ran her tongue over her lips. Wanting to kiss him. Or run.

'You're hard,' Levin said. 'The hardest woman I've ever

met. I have no idea why I'm chasing you like this. And no idea why you're running.'

'I just—'

'And now I'm going to kiss you,' he said, and came forward, and she froze, couldn't move a single muscle, and then his lips were on hers, hardly touching them, just brushing lightly against the skin; she could smell the scent of him, feel the strength of his torso right in front of her . . .

Jane was unable to help herself. He was teasing her, not taking her. Daring her to resist. Or ask for more. She was moist and hot for him, her body, so focused and tensed, melted and warmed and she moaned under her breath and surrendered, her tongue thrusting back into Levin's mouth, her lips pressing against him, pleadingly . . .

He chuckled deep in his throat. Underneath her dress her body was leaping against him as he ran a hand slowly across it. Jane fell into his arms, feeling his jacket, his belt, the buttons of his shirt. Her senses felt unbelievably heightened. She wanted him so much. A voice in her head was telling her not to, to leave him alone. They hadn't even dated. But she would not listen. His strength, his assured touch, all over her, like he owned her . . . she wanted it, at that moment, more than anything.

Levin kissed her again, triumphantly, and swung her into his arms; her weight was nothing to him. Jane buried her hot face in his chest, pressed her breasts against him. As he carried her through the sliding glass doors and into the coolness of her bedroom, Levin was already unbuttoning the top of her dress.

She lay, naked, drained, against him. It was night now; they were both covered in sweat; Jane's body was relaxed, as though orgasm had unknotted every muscle under her skin. She wondered if she had the energy left to move.

'Craig . . .'

He dropped a slow kiss on the top of her shoulder. 'At least we've got rid of Mr Levin.'

Jane hung her head. 'What have I done?'

'I could remind you,' he said. 'If you have short-term memory problems.'

'Stop it,' she protested, smiling a little. Was it possible he could have her again? Three times, in rapid succession; he had the vitality of a teenager.

'I'm done,' he said, sighing. 'At least, I think I am. You're dangerous. It's a good job I keep in shape.' He pulled away from her. 'Let's shower. Together.'

But Jane looked down, knotting her fingers together in the bedlinen.

'Am I going to see you again?'

She was miserable, now; her body felt good, but her heart was sick. This was it, exactly what she had feared. She'd wanted him, craved him, for months, and as soon as he touched her, she'd fallen into his hand like a ripe peach.

And he had made her body leap, and dance, and finally satisfied her, made her yield herself so completely, that she was now helplessly and hopelessly in love with him.

But the chase was over, he'd got what he wanted. Now she was just another conquest.

'Do you think I'm that kind of man?'

'I don't know,' she said. 'That's the point. I hardly know anything about you.'

Just that I want you, she did not say. Just that I have to have you. Just that I think about you all the time.

'Let's get in that shower,' Levin said, his eyes flickering across her naked body, dappled by the moonlight, warm and blotchy from his touch. 'I won't promise not to molest you, though. And then get dressed. And come with me.'

'What do you mean?' Jane asked, ashamed to show that she was crying.

'You want to see me again?'

She nodded; he knew her intimately, knew the intensity of her response to him; there was no point trying to hide anything now.

'Then why wait? See me again now. Come home with me. Spend the night at my place.'

'We didn't even date,' Jane said.

'So this will be our first. Dinner. I could eat. Couldn't you? Then breakfast. And I'll pick you up for lunch. That makes three dates in what, eighteen hours?' He winked at her. 'I know how to play catch-up.'

She slid her long legs off the bed. Even now, when she was trying not to hope, not to get over-excited, he was leaving her no choice. Jane tried to come to terms with it; where there were two people, she could not have total control; and she was afraid of how much she liked that.

'OK,' she said. 'OK.'

'And you want me again.'

Levin came and sat down on the bed, and stretched his hand out. She gasped, again; pressed against him.

'You're hotter than hell,' he said. 'Hotter than I'd ever imagined. And I'd imagined plenty.' He shook his head and gave her his hand. 'Come on, Jane. Let me earn your trust.'

Chapter Thirty-Seven

It was strange how shy she was. After all that passion, after all her athleticism. Levin wore the marks of her nails raked across his inner thigh, the small of his back; her own skin was covered in small, delicate bruises from his lips and teeth. Yet they were now dressed, and sitting in his dining room – or one of his dining rooms. Over the dinner table. It was a romantic setting: candlelight, Sèvres porcelain dishes, fresh flowers. But Jane felt as nervous as a teenager.

'Come on. Eat something.' Levin gestured at the slices of roast partridge, delicately fanned out in front of her, next to buttery parsnips and spinach. 'If you don't like that, the chefs can get you something else.'

'You've got more than one?' Jane joked.

'I've got five.'

Damn. She moistened her lips.

'I'm not hungry.'

'After that, you must be.' He forked up a floury roast potato, crisp and browned around the edges, and wolfed it. 'I chose this because I thought it was British. But they can get you anything you like.'

'I'm . . . I'm embarrassed,' she murmured, and lowered her head. Levin watched her, and to his amazement found himself stirring again. What a woman. Why was she like this? So reserved, and so beautiful?

'Because you don't know me? Other than in the Biblical sense?'

'And the pages of *Fortune*,' Jane admitted.

'Ah, yes. I recall you saying you admired me.' He grinned. 'I hear that a lot. From you, it was a turn-on, though. Tell you what, I'll make a deal.'

'A deal?'

'Eat your food. Drink some water, some juice. A glass of champagne. I don't want you passing out on me, later.'

'Later?'

'If you're good; no promises.' She had to smile. 'You eat, and I'll talk. The unofficial version of my life. Then you'll know me. Anything to get you to relax.'

'All right,' Jane said, softly.

Levin was unlike any man she'd ever known; he didn't buckle to her, or crumple in the face of her coldness. He stood firm against her. And he directed things. She took a bite of the partridge; it was good, and she found she wanted to eat it. To please him.

'I don't have a rags to riches story. I grew up an only child, and that's about all the bad things you can say of my early life. Dad worked in the Sanitation Department as an administrator, Mom was a court reporter. We had a little tract house in a decent part of Queens, back in New York, a nice car, took a vacation to the Jersey shore most summers. I had two working parents and a big extended Jewish family; we weren't religious, but there were still plenty of weddings, bar mitzvahs, you know. Most of my friends were Jews, too.' He grinned. 'I hated my life. Does that sound awful? Loved my folks, hated my life. It was so suburban. I felt so trapped. And at school, I was the weeny little Jew. There were bigger kids there who used to kick my ass on a regular basis. Dad wouldn't let me quit, said I had to be tough. Good girl – now drink some wine.'

Jane took a sip. Warmth started to spread through her again, and she didn't think it was just the alcohol.

'There had to be more. I knew it. Every time I took a

subway into the city – it was the seventies, it was full of crime, and dirty, but it was so exciting. Those skyscrapers – electric. Wall Street. The big theatres, Times Square, Fifth Avenue. Manhattan was life and Queens was nothing. It was like you had your nose permanently pressed up against life's shop window, and they wanted me to get a good union job. At the most, to get into real estate or become a school principal. I was brighter than most kids they knew. Partly because of my memory, with a photographic memory you ace most multi-choice tests. But mainly because I was good at math. Better than good. School bored the hell out of me.'

'So what did you do?'

Now she had started eating, she was ravenous; Jane devoured her vegetables and helped herself to a slice of the raspberry cheesecake set on a silver platter in front of her.

'First, I joined the Y and started lifting weights, till I was big enough to kick a little ass myself. They say violence never solved anything. Bullshit.'

Jane grinned.

'Next I sat down and figured it out. If I wanted to get into Wall Street other than on the subway, I'd need to be a broker. So I started buying the *Wall Street Journal* with my allowance. Next I started figuring out the numbers, and the charts. Seeing patterns. Looking at stocks. I quit school early and my parents cut me off, but by that time I had a job as a gofer in a brokerage house. I used to give them tips – and they worked. They thought I had insider info.' He smiled. 'Nothing they couldn't have figured out if they were paying attention. But at eighteen I was a trader. Before I could drink, I owned my own apartment. Sound familiar?'

'So far,' Jane said, inclining her head. 'But I'll never be as successful as you.'

'That's true,' he said, cool as you like, and she thrilled to it. 'You never will.'

'Your parents forgave you?'

'Soon as they knew I'd be OK. I was a senior broker at twenty, VP at twenty-one. Had a nice little brownstone in the Village at twenty-three, drove a Spider. At twenty-four I quit. Started to put together a fund. You know most of the rest.'

'I heard you were a workaholic.'

'I don't see it as work.' His eyes lit up, and she responded to his passion. 'I love business, I love numbers. I can just . . . I *see* stocks. I don't know how else to explain it. For me, trading is like a computer game. Winning is fun. Money is fun. Five chefs – I always wanted this, I wanted to live like my house was a hotel. Got lots of staff and I pay them outrageous wages. Give lots to charity. My parents are in Florida now, in a mansion with a private beach. I keep my head down, I don't talk to the press, I just play the game. And I win, nineteen times out of twenty.'

'And the twentieth?'

'Maybe I sabotage myself sometimes. Just to make it interesting.'

'So.' She spooned up the last of the cheesecake, meltingly sweet, the tartness of the raspberries a perfect contrast. 'Tell me about your personal life.'

'I thought I just did. Oh – you mean women?'

'I mean women,' Jane said, her eyes narrowing.

Levin smiled. 'There have been a few girls. I like beautiful women. I never promised any of them anything serious, unless I meant it. I've had three proper girlfriends – one for six months, one for two years, another for a year. It just didn't work out in those cases.'

'Why not?'

'If I knew that I never would have asked them out,' he said, reasonably.

'And me?'

'You're different. Incredibly so.'

'Tell me why.'

'Let's go to bed.'

'Before bed.'

'Don't trust yourself, in my arms, to be objective?' Jane blushed scarlet, and Levin grinned. 'Very well. You are more intelligent and more independent. I never dated fluff – maybe when I was younger there were a couple of trophy dates, cheerleaders for the New York Giants, that sort of girl. Later on models, but always smart ones. One of my long-term girlfriends was a lecturer at Vassar.' His eyes flickered across her. 'None of them were like you. In business, a self-made woman. One who came back from a tragedy – an orphan. What you did with Shop Smart was amazing. And leaving your job was pretty great, too. Maybe it's vanity; I saw something of myself in you. You didn't want that comfort trap. A house in the suburbs or a vice-president's salary, it's all bull if you know you can do better. And of course there just aren't that many women who do well in business.'

'Sexist pig.'

'It's the truth, and you know it. You and your girlfriends have something here. But I warn you, I don't think it's gonna work. Not long term.'

Jane froze. 'What do you mean by that?'

She had been worrying about the same thing. But it stung to hear him say it.

'Three women, all strong personalities. Completely different from each other. Different responsibilities. But all joint chief execs?' He shook his head. 'Power-sharing never works, honey, just ask the United Nations. Somebody has to be the boss. And you'll want that somebody to be you.'

Jane shrugged. 'I take all the business decisions, Sally does the styling and Haya adds the ethics. No reason for us to tread on each other's toes. And anyway, we're *friends*.'

'You are now. But for how long?'

'I organize the company,' Jane said, firmly. 'And you don't know us.'

'We'll see. I admit you have a good model. Excitement. Achievement. You're more than beautiful, and sexy, with that British accent—'

'English.'

'Whatever. You're like me. You're in this game. You're . . .' he paused, then smiled. 'Not a civilian.'

She smiled back, and stood up from the table.

'Not to mention that you're smokin'.' Levin grinned.

Jane held out her hands to him. She sensed she was in great danger, that he already had her heart, and she had surrendered every part of herself. Because she wanted so badly to believe that she was the one, she was the woman who could take him out of this life.

He'd told her his life story. But it wasn't just about knowing him. Jane wanted far more than that. She wanted to be his girl, his only girl. Yes, it was a womanly desire as old as the hills and the air; Jane knew already that she wished for marriage.

But her body was a traitor; it wanted him. Now.

Craig came over to her, leaving the rest of his food untouched.

'I thought you just wanted to sleep,' he murmured, whispering into her neck, kissing it, his tongue tracing the line of the caress.

'That was then,' Jane said. 'And at least now we've had the first date.'

Chapter Thirty-Eight

'You can trust me.' Mrs Doughty, Emily, was firm. 'She'll be fine. Won't you, princess? Who's a clever girl?'

Noor waved her little clenched fist and gurgled happily. She gave a gummy smile to her mother and her nanny.

'Do you know about warming the bottle? And don't use those commercial wipes. Just tissues in warm water, or she gets a rash . . .'

'Ma'am, I've brought up four of my own.' The Scotswoman shook her head. 'Now get in the cab. The sooner you go and do your trading, or whatever it is, the sooner you can come back to her.' She gave Haya a shove. 'It's been four months. They need you at work, too. Now go.'

The limo driver honked his horn, and Noor scrunched up her face. She started to wail, and Haya wanted to as well.

'Go,' Emily Doughty insisted.

Haya did as she was told, and as the limo door shut behind her, she watched the nanny put her baby comfortingly over her shoulder.

'LAX?'

'Just drive,' Haya snapped. She turned her face to the window, so that he would not see her tears.

Everybody in LA knew who Haya al-Yanna was now. He said a quick, 'Yes, ma'am,' and stepped on it. Suited her fine.

She knew she had to do this, of course. Noor was four months old, and Haya couldn't stay home forever. Not with the way GLAMOUR was going. They had queues at the store daily, just to get in. Jane was negotiating with some defunct American chains, trying to buy up real estate, looking for a good lease on Fifth or Avenue of the Americas, jetting off to Paris and London. Sally, when she took an evening off from the ball park, was turning into a bona fide star; her days were spent designing, her nights at glittering premieres, jetting off to talk shows, or giving interviews for magazines. They called her 'fashion's Martha Stewart' and, more cruelly, 'Business Barbie'. But Sally rode it all like a pro, and every single item she wore in public was sourced from the GLAMOUR store.

Their next opening was to be New York, and Jane and Sally had personally begged Haya to come back. Ethical business was a money-spinner – the women's magazines loved what they were doing with local craftswomen, and when Sally posed in *Women's Wear Daily* wearing her own new trademark, a floor-length red velvet sheath, with one of the Ghadan necklaces draped round her long neck, orders had just gone wild.

'We have only a few hundred carpets – we're on a waiting list.'

'The jewellery sold out weeks ago. We've got empty sections of the store.'

'Haya,' Jane insisted. 'You can't just go on buying trips, what you have to do is find staff – buyers – people you trust. They can purchase the ethical trade in bulk as long as it's up to standard. We can't jeopardize the brand.'

'Jane found a spot in Venice, too. We have to have enough for six new stores. By year's end it'll be twelve.' Sally grinned. 'Say hello to GLAMOUR Tokyo.'

'I suppose you're right. There's just no way I can fulfil that number of orders.' Haya was excited. 'Is it really that busy?'

Sally groaned. 'Please come back.'

Of course she adored Noor, her little sunshine, but . . . it was time to get back to adulthood; Haya had missed her friends, missed her business. She was too driven to spend every single day in the nursery.

'So, recruit buyers?'

'At least twenty. I can give you a salary structure, please don't deviate from it,' Jane said.

Haya spread her hands. 'Staffing is your baby. They have to be the right women, though, people I trust not to buy any old junk, and only to pick the right suppliers . . .'

'You could hire male buyers. As long as we maintain the policy of sourcing from poor women,' Sally said. 'Our customers want that. It's a little bit of sisterhood in with the designer jeans.'

'OK, then.' Haya nodded; she would need the help. With a baby, no way could she go back to full-time jet-setting. 'I think I'll pick buyers in every country, you know, somebody in Egypt, in Morocco . . . to look for the different goods.'

'It's your turf,' Jane said. 'Handle it however you want.'

Haya agreed. The frazzled faces of her girlfriends had added the coda, *but handle it.*

And, frankly, she didn't want to lose her position. GLAMOUR was her idea, she had been the one to suggest it, that night at Jane's new house. Without her putting some soul into the company, they would just be another Saks or Harrods, nothing to write home about. Women's magazines and TV channels were eager to cover them because of the good they did in the developing world. Haya felt GLAMOUR truly was hers. If she dropped out, she would take the heart of the thing with her.

That could not happen. This store was in her soul now. It was her own thing, and she would fight like a tigress to protect it. And to protect herself at its heart.

Fair enough. And so now she was on her way back, to Amman, Jordan. Leaving Noor behind for four whole, brutal days.

It had to be done; but she didn't have to like it.

*

Jaber shook his head and tried to concentrate. The computer screen before him was thick with facts and figures, a spreadsheet showing the progress of public works in Ghada City. Important stuff; costings for the schools and the hospitals he had persuaded the King to invest in.

A project that was dear to his heart.

And he knew he should focus on this. The fact was, his star was rising in the kingdom. There were plenty of advisers, from bankers to generals, and an assorted gaggle of princelings and relatives clustered around the King. But he had never been one of them. He had merely excelled at his job, quietly and methodically, and the ruler of Ghada had noticed.

First there came more responsibility. The dam project, in the south. Investment in a desalination plant, to gain fresh water from the sea and irrigate the desert plains of the west. Bringing modern technology companies to Ghada City. There was no increased compensation and no honours, at court or elsewhere. A lesser man would have complained. Jaber welcomed the new workload. He was driven to change things. And soon he was formally promoted, and the King raised his mother and himself in rank.

It was exhilarating. Jaber was on his way. Other courtiers were angry, some of the advisers bitched. He ignored them all. He was sunk in his work. And on the rare occasions he sent advice to the King, it was listened to.

Jaber was only human. He perceived that the King saw something in him, a combination of Western efficiency and local values, a lack of desire to flatter and scrape. The wine of power was heady. His wish to succeed in government intensified. There was a chance, a real chance he might make the inner circle, and have a say in how the kingdom was governed. His stamp could be on reform, on progress, all across the country.

He started to work much longer hours. He became almost

robotic. And he continued to have influence, and get things done.

Surely it was time to consolidate his position; to marry a suitable woman from inside the royal family, produce some sons, play his part in the social life of the court, as well as the government offices . . .

But then he had met Haya al-Yanna.

And everything changed.

What was he thinking? Jaber rubbed his dark fingers, calloused from so much typing, against his temples. Surely she was *completely* unsuitable. A Muslim, yes, but that was about it. An American citizen, educated in Los Angeles. No virgin – a widow with a child, and a knowing sensuality about her that he found utterly intoxicating. He would be raising another man's daughter, and a merchant's daughter at that, in the villas and gardens of the Royal Palace enclosure. And she was the antithesis of the women his cousins married: slender, of aristocratic family, with no ambitions other than to give the right parties, wear the correct gowns, and win the favour of the queen of the day. Maybe shop a little in Dubai or Paris. And, of course, to give birth to gaggles of privileged children.

Haya al-Yanna was different. She was – how to put it? A player. She was a combatant on the great stage of life, like him. A child bride who had succeeded in two businesses, a global success, a single mother, a champion of the underclass. But not in the usual way of monied women, throwing charity parties and writing cheques. Haya got out there and empowered poor communities; she helped them to start micro-businesses, she gave them a market to sell to, she paid them a fair price for their goods, and the knock-on effects were huge. A prosperous woman, she spread prosperity, and not through charity. Through cold, hard, cash. Through trade. He had seen it, first hand – how she treated everybody as an equal.

Her stunning face and her lush beauty were only matched by her drive and her brains. In the brief time he had spent with her, and in the phone conversations they had sometimes had since, Jaber had never for one moment been bored.

And although he had told himself, repeatedly, that this fixation was nuts, he had never stopped thinking about Haya since the day she left Ghada. The other women he forced himself to dine with were as dull as hell in comparison. She was an itch, and he could not get her off his mind.

And now – now, Haya al-Yanna was coming back here. And Jaber was going to see her.

He had no idea what was going to happen.

'Welcome, Ms al-Yanna.' The desk clerk was all smiles. 'It's good to have you back, ma'am. I hope you enjoy your stay in Ghada.'

'Thank you.'

'Your meetings have been arranged in the Roosevelt Conference Room for nine a.m. tomorrow, as requested.'

'Great. If I could just get my room key . . .'

Haya was very tired; it had been a long day, and she was looking forward to a quick TV supper and then bed.

'Here you are. The Presidential Suite. Take the penthouse elevator, second on the left.'

'I didn't book that suite,' Haya said, wearily. She hoped that this wouldn't delay her all that long; tomorrow's work started early.

'No, ma'am. It is a complimentary upgrade. And we have a message to deliver to you,' the receptionist said with a coy smile, 'from His Highness Sheikh Jaber.'

Haya blinked with shock. He remembered her?

They had negotiated with the Ghadan palace through the office, and over the phone; Haya had sent documents via one of Jane's assistants. She had never expected to hear from Jaber again.

'Here.' The receptionist handed her an envelope; thick vellum, with a small gold crest, a stylized palm tree, on the back. 'Shall I have a bellhop show you to the suite?'

'No, I'll manage.'

Haya walked into the elevator, barely noticing her surroundings; her case was compact, neatly packed with lightweight, long dresses. She rode up to the Presidential Suite; it was incredibly luxurious, with tinted windows on four sides looking out over Ghada City. Haya gave it a cursory glance, dumped her suitcase on the bed, and ripped open the note.

Dear Ms al-Yanna,

Congratulations on the birth of your daughter. The Office of Protocol has kept me up to date with developments with your company; His Majesty's Government is quite satisfied with the funds that have flowed in to our citizens thus far. We are willing to consider further involvement of the royal family in exchange for more significant orders worldwide.

I would, however, prefer to discuss such matters with you personally. Could you call the palace and confirm if you are free for lunch on Saturday at one o'clock?

Wa-es salaam,
Jaber

Stop it, Haya told herself. You're reading way too much into this. He is a young handsome sharif, not a man to be tempted by a widowed single mother. And anyway, what if he was? She was a partner at GLAMOUR Inc. and he worked for the government here. It would never work.

But it was no good; her heart pounded as she dialled the

number on the stationery. Well, hell, it *was* exciting. She'd been stuck in a nursery with only Elmo videos and nappies for company for the last four months. She should just see it as a business success.

Whatever. It was thrilling. Haya gave herself permission to enjoy that. She thought of Ahmed, her love. He was in Paradise – he would not mind, not if anything was to happen. Before, she had felt guilty; now that she had his Noor to love and cherish, she felt, instead, an overwhelming peace.

Haya looked round the suite properly. She understood at once why she had been given the best room in the hotel. As hot as GLAMOUR was, there were other rich businessmen here. No, this came from the favour of His Highness. And she took every lavish inch of it as a compliment.

'Good afternoon,' said a voice in Arabic.

'Hello. My name is Haya al-Yanna—'

'Oh yes, thank you for calling, madam. Will you be able to join His Highness for lunch?'

'Yes, I will,' Haya said, taken aback that the operator knew so fast.

'That's wonderful news. We will send a government car to your hotel at twenty to one, if convenient. If you could bring your passport for identification.'

'Thank you,' Haya said. A government car! She couldn't believe it. Why was he laying out the red carpet again?

'We'll see you tomorrow, madam, *insh'Allah*. Have a wonderful day.'

She hung up and went into the suite's sumptuous bathroom; a stand-alone tub made of pure copper that you could almost swim in. Tomorrow morning she had interviews, eighteen candidates for six positions, and they would have to be done by twelve forty.

Haya could manage it. She had learned to trust her instincts. Those with a love of beauty and of Ghada would stand out. The important thing was to get them hired, fast, lose the dead wood, and then come back here. Whether she was right about Jaber's interest or not, she had to look fabulous. If she could get a true princess of this country involved . . . Forget it. GLAMOUR's PR and marketing would explode just as Jane was opening the new stores.

Haya had been out of commission for a while. She wanted to contribute, to be as much a part of this as Sally and Jane. Originally, they had been the two friends; Haya had come in late. She did not want to be an outsider, the third wheel, in GLAMOUR.

If she could bring more sizzle than Sally then nobody could accuse her of being some kind of afterthought.

'Here we are, ma'am. Passport, please.'

Haya meekly handed it over. The chauffeur – or was he a soldier, in his Ghadan uniform with the palm trees on his epaulettes – passed it across to the guard at the gate. Haya leaned forward, out of the window, and looked down the drive to the palace complex.

It was exquisitely beautiful. Vast, and covered with blue and gold tiles, like the decoration on a pharaoh's headdress. It glittered in the sun like jewellery, and the gardens stretched ahead of her, lush and beautifully stocked. There were fountains playing in the courtyards, and Haya noted the brickwork, old and red. There was something of the Alhambra about this place. She shivered with tension. Did she look good enough? She had selected a traditional Jordanian kaftan, red silk, embroidered with gold thread, antique, stretching down to her ankles and flowing beautifully about the body; almost no make-up, just a touch of foundation and some lipgloss and mascara, and a delicate scent, Chanel No. 19, one Haya had always favoured; fresher and greener than the more famous blend. Round her neck she wore a jangling, original Ghadan coin necklace, one from GLAMOUR's own stock; it was disturbingly sensual, she thought, like bells on her when she moved.

'Thank you.' Her passport was returned to her, and the limo pulled through the ornate carved gates, covered in Moroccan-style mosaic work. Haya tried not to stare as the driver took her round the left wing of the palace, past marching guards, into a small courtyard, and parked in a spot they were waved to by a saluting guard, who came round to open the door.

'Greetings, madam,' he said, in thick accented English.

'Thank you,' Haya responded in Arabic. The soldier smiled, and lapsed into his native tongue.

'*Sidi* Jaber is waiting in his office. If you'll come this way.'

Haya nodded, and was led through marble corridors of unimaginable opulence, set about with wooden panels carved in an intricate Islamic design, to a small, modern room – part of a cleverly designed extension – where Jaber was sitting.

He jumped to his feet.

'Your guest, Highness,' the soldier said, bowed slightly, and withdrew.

'Haya.' He came forward, and clasped her shoulders warmly, kissing her on both cheeks in the Arab fashion; Haya, feeling awkward, clumsily dropped a low curtsy.

Jaber raised an eyebrow. 'You do not have to curtsy to me. Although your manners are as beautiful as your face.'

She blushed, deeply; hopefully she was tanned enough that he would not notice.

'I was delighted to get your letter, sir,' she began, formally.

'Good. And it's Jaber. I won't have to spend the afternoon calling you Ms al-Yanna, will I?'

She shook her head. 'Haya.'

'Then come.' He extended a hand. 'I have had them cook for us in my mother's apartments – she is at an Arab children's conference in Dubai.'

*

Haya tried to eat, if only to be polite; she was a guest, it was rude to refuse hospitality. But she was intimidated. Stroppy American businessmen, rude suppliers, government customs officials who enjoyed demonstrating their power – none of them had made her feel like this. She respected Ghada, and Jaber; it was a beautiful country, a rich country, and yet they cared about the nomads, the tribeswomen, the indigent widows she was trying to help.

And here she was, in a small corner of the centre of power. And he was across the table, as deferential servants attended him, and then her; incredibly handsome, as she thought; charming, and powerful – not so much in the abstract way one describes a banker or a newspaper magnate, as one having influence, but absolutely, in his own right. As a government official, and a member of a ruling family that still ruled.

Jaber took his time. He made small talk with her, about the store, the candidates she had interviewed, the GLAMOUR expansion programme.

'And you?' he asked, at length, when she was picking through a delicate pastry of roasted chicken and raisins. 'You are taking a full part in this? You look to me as though you were never pregnant at all, although of course I know differently.'

'This is my first major contribution since Noor was born.'

'And it will be major,' he said, with calm assurance. 'I wonder, have you been following events here in Ghada?'

Haya was embarrassed. 'I haven't – I have hardly listened to any news since she was born. I was nursing . . .' Her voice trailed off. Was that too intimate a detail to have shared with him? Why was she starting to think of him as a friend, rather than who he was? 'Anyway,' she added hastily, 'I think the *New York Times* on the plane on the way over was the first paper I've really read in months. Please excuse my ignorance, High—' She caught a sight of his face. 'Jaber.'

'Much better,' he said. 'And don't worry. I find it refreshing. Anyway, His Majesty has decided to honour my mother, his cousin, who is widowed, and has raised her to the rank of a princess here, with the title Royal Highness. Under our law, these things are at his absolute discretion.'

'That's wonderful,' Haya responded automatically, trying to work out what that meant for her company. She already had photos of the sharifa – now princess – wearing GLAMOUR jewels. Was her work here done, then? They could start a whole new ad campaign on that.

'And me,' he said, matter-of-factly. 'I have been involved in government, as you know. A little more than protocol; there was a dispute with Dubai over some oil pipelines. We managed to reconcile it. I was directly involved with the King in the matter.'

Haya was confused. 'And he moved you out of the protocol section?'

'I am now Foreign Minister,' Jaber said. He shrugged. 'And my rank has been raised to emir, prince.'

Haya digested this. 'You are a Royal Highness now?'

'Yes.'

'I can't go on just calling you Jaber.'

'Since I've asked you to, to do otherwise would be most discourteous,' he said.

The servant arrived with a service of mint tea and sweetmeats to round off the meal; Haya thanked him profusely, glad of any distraction. Jaber waved a hand, dismissively; at once the waiter and the other servants melted away.

'You do not need to court us,' he said brusquely. 'I, and my mother, are convinced of your bona fides. My mother will work to promote the Ghadan goods you sell. You can arrange it through my successors in protocol.'

'Thank you.' Haya nodded; that would be a real coup. It was what she had come for. But now, should she leave? Her business was concluded.

'I was wondering if you would consider spending the afternoon with me,' he said, his words suddenly coming out in a rush, uncharacteristically fast. 'Not for business – on a date.'

Haya half jumped in her carved chair. He had asked her – he had actually asked!

'You know . . . I am widowed . . . and I have a daughter?'

'You told me. And congratulations.' Jaber smiled, his pale grey eyes ranging over her; Haya, unused to scrutiny, dropped her eyes at once.

'You must know that you are very beautiful,' he said, 'and you have fascinated me since we met. I have followed your enterprise, and your success. And hoped you would return here. A date is just a date – if you are comfortable with it, Haya.'

'I – yes, thank you,' she said shyly.

'That's good news.' He grinned back, as though tension had been released. 'There are some wonderful Persian ruins outside the city. I thought you might like to go and see them. No chauffeurs – I have my own car.'

She walked with him around the glorious, crumbling ancient walls of Shirah, marvelling at the winged lions with the heads of bearded men, the carved vulture gods and cuneiform writing littered around the streets, half-tumbled pillars lying amidst scrubby desert grass while lizards and butterflies played around them.

'It's truly magnificent.'

'We want to promote this as a tourist destination.' Jaber smiled at her. 'I'm glad you like it. My house is near here.'

'You have a villa in the royal complex?'

'I do now.'

Haya nodded. He had told her something of his life; father dead at three, his mother fighting to give him as much normality as possible; education in Britain, with a stint in the army as an officer in the Desert Rats; trying to find a place for himself in government, wanting to be useful. And he had probed Haya, gently but efficiently, about Ahmed, about her parents, America, Noor, every part of her life. When she told him about Miss Milton's, Jaber smiled wrily; he too had been bullied at school in the West.

She found herself trying for reserve. He was so intelligent, so charming, and yet so sharp; and obviously, there was no future for her with him. Nice to go on this date, Haya was telling herself. But you'd be a moron to get those hopes up.

'The King promoting your family must have been a great joy.'

'I'd be lying if I said Mama wasn't thrilled,' Jaber admitted frankly. 'Not so much at the rank, although that's nice for her. But over what it meant for me. King Nazir trusts me. And he's old; there's jockeying amongst his sons over the succession. So for a while I can do things – change things. We're building schools in every district, establishing a court system. Eventually I'd like the monarchy to be nothing more than decorative, like the Brits. But it will take time. At least now I can make a start.'

'And I suppose the King will select a princess for you?' Haya teased.

He stopped, and looked deeply into her eyes; surprised, she could not hold his gaze.

'I'm old-fashioned. I don't believe in divorce. I don't want a succession of wives. The woman must be right – she must be perfect. I have made it clear I will not accept an arranged marriage.'

'I understand.' Haya would not look up at him. She tried to change the subject. 'Look at that amphitheatre . . . amazing.'

Jaber was having none of it.

'Let's sit,' he said. 'I want to say something to you.'

Haya allowed herself to be led to a shady spot. They sat together on the white limestone benches, thousands of years old, with a view of the arena; she wondered if men had died here. It was an old land, beautiful, and full of ghosts.

'I'd like to see you,' he said. 'A lot. I think you're beautiful. You're modest, and a lady, but you have something else. A steel spine. You started this amazing business, you flew round the world building it up, you found a way to make money and to help others. I admire how you work with your friends from the West. Yet you are a believer. Your daughter has a Muslim name.'

Haya smiled. 'Her father insisted I change my own. He never liked Anglicization.'

'And you have guts; you're not afraid to talk of your husband to me. I would not have admired a woman who could abandon his memory.'

'I loved him.'

'That is clear.' Jaber put it to her with that directness she liked. 'Tell me now, before I fall too deeply. Could you ever love again?'

'It is possible,' Haya said. 'I only loved Ahmed when I got to know him . . . I don't want to rush marriage again, Jaber.'

'No. Of course.' He was eager. 'And you have a child. And an enterprise of your own. I see that you are not about to be mine for the asking, Haya. So I have a proposal. Not of marriage,' he added, with a grin, and she smiled. 'Yet. Why do you not establish yourself in Ghada for six months? You can have offices here, you can go on short trips, by car, with your child; I will have the palace provide a nanny, or two. You can buy locally and send your deputies further afield, to Europe. We have all the major technologies you would need – email, faxes. Running water.' He winked. 'In essence, you could establish a department here, a buying division. Which you could head. That would consolidate your position in the stores more than a few one-off purchasing jaunts. Meanwhile, your child can grow here, where she will hear Arabic spoken every day.'

'And I can see you?'

'I never said I had no ulterior motives.' Jaber shrugged. 'Let us see if we like each other, really. Whether or not you do, you will have my protection. In the end, if you can't stand me, what have you lost? Nothing. Your career will be advanced.' His eyes searched hers. 'I told you I had thought about you. Tell me the truth. Did you ever think about me?'

'I did. I just didn't believe . . .'

'Believe it,' he said. 'So. Will you come? Spend time here?'

She thought about it. She did love Ghada. And she did want to be the equal of Sally, and Jane. It would mean leaving them behind, of course. She would be breaking up the trio, for the second time . . .

But GLAMOUR was big now. Bigger than all of them. It could no longer be run by three friends making it up as they went along. Haya had tasted power, and influence, and she liked it. Anita Roddick had managed her own global empire in ethical commerce and become a billionaire in her own right. Why not Haya al-Yanna?

'It is a brilliant idea,' she said. 'Of course I will have to discuss it with my friends.'

'And if they say no?'

She looked at him, and at the beauties of the Persian ruins, with the desert horizon stretching out westwards in a shimmering haze of heat.

'I will still come,' Haya said. She smiled. 'I have got used to making my own decisions.'

Chapter Thirty-Nine

They discussed it over dinner, two days after she got back. She found Noor thriving and not particularly overwhelmed to see her; the baby was engrossed in loud banging on a tin drum Emily Doughty had bought her.

Haya grimaced. 'What did I ever do to you?'

'Hurrrr,' said Noor, happily, smashing her wooden spoon down.

'Ah, let her enjoy herself. I'll be putting her down in a minute.' Emily cluck-clucked over the baby, who gurgled and buried her chubby cheeks in Haya's skirt. 'You have a bath and go to your meeting. You can see she survived.'

'All right,' Haya said, looking at her daughter. Wondering how she would cope in the desert. And how she herself would cope without her two friends.

They dressed up for the meal. Nobody suggested it; all three women knew they had to. At this point, they were minor celebrities, and Sally was turning into a major one. Haya chose a floor-length, sweeping gown of Egyptian cotton in bright yellow, embroidered with green thread; a Chanel purse, and one of the jangling Ghadan bracelets, her feet encased in buttercup-yellow leather Manolo strappy sandals with a high heel. Sally wore her own red dress, with a GLAMOUR necklace of rubies by Montfort Jewels; Jane chose a cream silk suit, with pearls, Wolford tights and Christian Louboutin shoes in dove grey.

They met at the Ivy, and posed for pictures outside; arms

around each other, smiling and laughing; all three knew the snap would make the business press the next day, Sally in the middle, the golden girl sheathed in in-your-face scarlet; Haya, ethnic, elegant, and stunning, the creamy yellows bright against her clear olive skin; Jane, English and reserved, the picture of the sexy businesswoman.

The business press loved the shot. They were as glamorous as their company. Three sexy friends; three powerful women.

Nobody knew the tensions behind the smiles.

Work had become strained. Very strained. Jane was exasperated when the other two could not follow her financing. Sally took offence when Haya and Jane didn't dig a new line of hers, a hot new dress, a jeweller she'd taken on; Haya seemed to think these were Western baubles, beneath her, and simply refused to get involved with anything short or low cut, while Jane only had eyes for boring-ass figures. And Haya resented being pushed to the side; she loved her friends, but they weren't making enough of an effort, showing an interest in what she'd sourced or the ethics programmes she set up. They were a team, but increasingly each girl did her own thing. And each of them was convinced she did most of the work.

This dinner had an inevitability to it.

'I know what this is about,' Sally said glumly, as soon as the waiter had departed. 'It's Noor, isn't it, Haya? You're quitting, right? You've hired those buyers, and you're quitting. You want to stay home.'

Jane looked at her quizzically.

'I'm not quitting.' Haya was a little annoyed Sally would even suggest such a thing. 'But I am leaving. I need to be in the Middle East.'

She explained, leaving out the part with Jaber; that was too precious, new, and fragile a thing to talk about just now.

Jane listened in silence and then looked over at Sally.

'You can't leave!' Sally was saying. 'We'll never manage—'

'But we will,' Jane said. 'And actually; I think I should go, too.'

Sally blinked. 'What?'

'To New York.'

'I don't get it. Who's gonna train the staff?' Sally was angry. 'And what are you talking about? I can't manage the damn store by myself.'

'I have VPs there now who can train the staff. Ari Gabriel, he's brilliant. Lillian Kovac. I trust them. You have to delegate. Even you, Sal.'

'Salads, ladies!'

The waiter put down their salads with the fried soft-shell crabs, wittered on about the wine list, and mercifully, eventually, vanished.

'We're too big,' Jane said, simply. 'You guys have to decide what you want. The company can't go on like this, with us in LA. I need to be in New York. I'll do the banking, the real estate, the distribution deals. All the major work.'

'That's not the major work, now is it?' Sally said, reasonably. But Jane ploughed on.

'Sally, you're the designer and the public face; you *are* GLAMOUR – what every little girl wants to be,' she said, mollifying her friend. 'We don't need you stuck in a back office in LA, we need you out there, on magazine covers. And if you're the face, Haya is the soul. So yes, she can do that properly in the region, not here. She's wasted in LA. So am I. But it's where you should be – you're the *star*.'

Haya told them about Jaber's mother.

'I love it!' Sally momentarily forgot her anger. 'Get a princess to a photo shoot? I'll do it with her. That'll make *Elle*. Maybe *Vanity Fair*, if we do it right.'

'You're the glitz, Sal; now we have some royal gravitas. That'll help in New York. All they talk about is the American

Queen of Jordan.' Jane grinned. 'My goodness, girls, this is really going to be big.'

'And it means we can't stay together?' Sally asked glumly.

'It's not like we won't be friends,' Haya replied. 'We still will. This time you'll have my phone number.' She smiled.

'I know it has to happen.' Sally sounded heartbroken. 'I just . . . I didn't think it would be this soon.'

'It's just life,' Haya said, and examined Jane. 'There's a man, isn't there? Your Craig Levin. *He* lives in New York.'

'He has a house here,' Jane said, defensively.

'But he mainly lives there.'

She couldn't deny it. 'It may have something to do with this, yes.'

Sally clapped her hands. 'The ice maiden melts?'

Jane blushed. 'God help me, I love him,' she said; and her girlfriends thought she sounded a little despairing. 'No man I've ever met understands me the way he does. And nobody else is strong enough for me. But that's why you can stay here, Sally, isn't it? You're practically living with Chris Nelson.'

Sally blushed. 'Actually, I am living with him. I moved in yesterday.'

'What about your mom?'

'She's in a guest cottage at his estate in Malibu, but she's talking about getting her own apartment. There's a luxury block in Century City.' Sally smiled. 'She likes Chris – doesn't want to put him off. And she doesn't need me any more.'

Haya felt a pang of loss – Mona might not, but she wasn't sure she didn't. Sally had been her first protector. And now she was going to be all on her own.

'And you?' Sally flicked her fountain of glossy blond hair. 'Haya, you've been very quiet on the subject. But I know you. There's something in your eyes. Is there a man?'

'Possibly.' She wouldn't say any more. 'In Ghada . . . But I don't know; we haven't really started going out yet . . .'

'Well, you'll need to be back here in six months,' Sally said, firmly. 'With or without your date.'

'And why is that?'

'We weren't going to announce it, but since you two are skipping town . . .' Sally lowered her voice. 'Chris and I are getting married.'

'Sally!'

'Sally Lassiter! Over here!'

'Give us a smile, baby! Let's see that rock!'

Sally turned and waved, and gave them a dazzling smile. 'There you go.' She extended her finger, to display the princess-cut natural pink diamond, three carats, a million dollars.

'I have to go shopping,' she informed the crowd of photographers, blinking her long lashes at them.

'Sal! Gonna get your wedding dress in the store?' somebody shouted.

She practically purred. 'Of *course*. What do you think inspired me to open GLAMOUR's bridal boutique? And I'm getting my wedding day scent specially blended for me in GLAMOUR Paris. Chris and I are going there on honeymoon.'

They loved it. The flashbulbs popped, again. She was now almost as famous as he was. But Sally was quick on her feet; she turned and dashed into the store, waving to shoppers who were dizzy with excitement, while security guards escorted her to the staff elevator. Make them wait outside; the press always had to be left hungry, wanting more. Sally was shopping at GLAMOUR for the sports wedding of the year. That was what they needed to know.

'Great stuff out there.' Maxi, her assistant and PR booker, rushed to greet her, bearing Sally's usual tall glass of fizzy water and crushed ice with lime.

'You watched?'

'From a window. You work them like you were born to it.'

Oh, I was, Sally thought.

'And the *New York Times* called. They want to do a Style section feature on you and GLAMOUR.'

'Say yes.'

'Access Hollywood wants to film the wedding.'

'No, but they can do a short bit at the reception.'

'Ma'am, it's Mr Nelson on line one,' said one of the secretaries.

'What are you doing, baby?'

'I'm at the store. Getting the gown. So don't pick me up, it's bad luck.'

'At the store?' There was incredulity in his tone. 'Damn, girl, you are such a salesman. Even with our wedding.'

'They watch me, you know that.'

'Don't I just,' Nelson said darkly.

'Don't be mad. I'm running out the back door, I'll be with you soon.' She wanted to tell him about all the new magazine covers, the TV slots, the offer from Hollywood that she was turning down – business was the star, and she, Sally Lassiter, *was* GLAMOUR. 'I'll make it up to you, baby,' she promised.

Sally could hear his grin down the phone. 'You certainly will.'

'Mark Cohen on two.' She punched the line to hang up on Chris and pick up Mark. Wow! This store was a rocket. If she didn't physically leave the building, her phones would never stop ringing. Mark was Jane's latest hire, shipped in from New York; the general manager of GLAMOUR LA, their original, flagship store. Jane had insisted they run them like a first-class hotel.

'We got the extension from the city.'

'Fabulous.' Haya and Ahmed's place was way too small,

they had discovered that months ago. Now she could concentrate on building something glorious. Lots of smoked glass, she thought, and an indoor garden, with fully grown trees, like they had in the lobby of CAA . . .

'And the monthly sales figures have *trebled*. We're selling stock as fast as we can ship it in.' Cohen was ecstatic. 'Ms Morgan called and told me to pass on to you that three more consortiums have made offers. She also wants a meeting to consider going public.' He paused. 'Ms Lassiter, what with the amazing figures from the opens in New York and London, do you understand how rich you are now?'

'Doesn't matter. We've only just started,' Sally said coolly. 'And tell Ms Morgan's assistant I'll call her back.'

She hung up, told Maxi to deal with her messages, and got ready to sneak out the back door.

She had an important appointment. With a realtor, and her fiancé. Let's face it, Sally thought. Life is pretty damn sweet.

Chris whistled a little, as soon as the pushy broker had left them to themselves.

'This is quite a house,' he said. 'Are you sure we need this much space?'

'Think of the fun you'll have christening every room.'

He kissed her, one of those slow, lingering kisses that got her squirming and impatient.

'If you like the place, folks, ask is ten,' said the agent, bustling back in after half a minute. Sally pulled away from her fiancé, annoyed.

'We need much more time to think about it. Please give us some privacy.'

'Oh, certainly,' the woman said, in a snooty manner. 'But I have another viewing at five o'clock.'

'If you don't leave right now, I'll call the owners and tell them you personally cost them a sale.'

The agent bolted.

'Tough cookie,' Chris said, admiringly, feeling her ass; Sally shifted under her dress, wanting him, right there on the kitchen floor. 'But baby, ten mil. I'm not *that* rich. Sorry.'

'We'll bid five,' Sally said. 'They'll take it. I have to have this house.'

'There are lots of other good ones—'

'You're not that rich, but I am,' she interrupted, kissing him back, stretching up on her toes to do it. 'GLAMOUR . . . it's doing well. More than well.' She summarized for him.

'Man.' He blew out his cheeks. 'When I met you, you were living in a scummy walk-up apartment. Is the store really that hot?'

Sally nodded, proudly. 'Hey, at least I know you're not marrying me for my money!'

Chris slapped her. 'Just for that, when I get you home, I'm gonna make you work out naked.'

'Promises, promises,' Sally teased back; but she was turned on, and he could see it.

Chris took her hand. 'Let's go. I want to see you on that exercise bike.' He whistled loudly, and the realtor came running back in, like a well-trained puppy.

'Seven and a half mil. Not a cent over,' he said firmly. 'Call me back if you have a signed contract. Come on, sweetness.'

And he ushered her out, back to the car.

They hadn't driven more than half a mile before the car phone rang.

'Chris? It's Jemma.'

'Hi, Jemma.'

'They've accepted!' she trilled. 'I'm having a signed contract messengered over to Malibu. Congratulations! I'm sure you'll enjoy Beverly Hills.'

'Good. You'll get the money wired by tomorrow.' He punched the button and hung up. 'Looks like you got it, baby.' Nelson shook his head. 'Man, that house is so big, it's like owning my own country. It's a long way from the Bronx.' He casually lifted her skirt with his left hand, and felt her inner thigh. 'So why did that place appeal to you so much? There are lots of other mansions . . . Bel Air . . .'

'You don't understand,' Sally said. 'That was my home. My dad's place. The one they threw us out of.' Her face was bright with a fierce pride. 'And now it's mine again. Mom can live in the guest cottage. Maybe one day I'll give her the whole house.'

He was shocked. 'Seven point five million?'

'The way things are going, we'll soon be able to afford six of them,' Sally told him.

'Man, what am I doing in practice all day?'

'Getting ready to win the World Series?'

'There is that, I guess.' His hand went higher. 'You're still gonna be working out naked. Somebody has to keep you under control.'

Chapter Forty

'Have you seen the latest consignment?' Haya was angry. 'I expect quality control, Suri. You can't assume honesty.'

'Nine times out of ten—'

'Ninety-nine out of a hundred,' Haya interrupted. 'But we serve an amazingly expensive, luxurious chain. I need the quality to be there *one hundred times* out of one hundred. When I made a surprise inspection at the Cairo docks I found four machine-woven carpets. Machine woven! Do you know the scandal that would cause if we misrepresented them? Furthermore, do you understand what that means?'

The older woman hung her head. 'That the suppliers did not buy them from the artisans?'

'Exactly. So not only are we being cheated, some poor woman who depends on us for her survival is too.'

'It won't happen again, *Siti* Haya.'

'It better not. Or you're fired. And don't call me *Siti*,' Haya snapped. They were always doing that. She hated it, all the assumptions, the idea that Jaber would marry her in due course, make her his.

The more she was seen at the palace, the more they said it was a done deal. And only Haya knew differently.

When she talked with him, she was free to be herself. He was intelligent, strong and masculine, and yet respectful of her, interested in her business, and how she was shaping it. Jaber relaxed her, and she knew that however hard she tried, she was falling for him.

Yet in the last month, he had withdrawn from her. They had met for dinner only twice, and he was moody and distracted. The only time he seemed like his old self was when he played with Noor, ten months old and delicately taking her first steps.

There was some other woman, Haya was sure of it. And her heart ached at the thought. She loved Ghada now with a passion, but she couldn't stay here; couldn't turn on the TV, read the local papers and see the Emir, the favoured Foreign Minister, accompanied by a new princess, his chosen bride. Jaber worked hard for charity; he would attend every benefit, every concert Haya got involved with. And as one of the world's most success-ful Muslim businesswomen, that would be quite a few. Haya and GLAMOUR were famous in Ghada. Famous across the Middle East. She had insisted on sticking to her principles – ethics *and* profit – and people loved her for it. Haya only talked to the regional press. The company had its strategy; let golden Sally be the face of GLAMOUR in the West.

So she would have to move. And Haya had already decided she would go back to Amman, live in a villa, somewhere secluded and safe for Noor to grow up in; the country her father had left for America. With her, it would come full circle. She would always love the States. But she would live with her heritage.

'I understand,' Suri said, chastened. 'I'll check them all personally, Ms al-Yanna.'

There was a hard rap on the door.

'Come in,' Haya called.

A soldier opened the door; he wore the epaulets of the royal house and had a gun at his belt. Suri shrank back, towards Haya, who instinctively put her arms around her employee.

'What do you want?' Haya asked, fighting to stay calm.

'Madam, you must come with me,' he said, in guttural English. 'It is His Royal Highness who orders it.'

'I'm not going anywhere.'

He looked at her, his eyes expressionless. 'I have orders to take you by force if necessary. It is for your own protection.' He lifted the gun. 'Please come.'

Haya was terrified; her palms started to sweat. 'What's going on?' she cried. 'Where is Noor? *Where is Noor?*'

'There is trouble at the palace. Your baby and her nanny have already been collected – they are at His Highness' compound.' He moved forward, to grab her, but Haya was already ahead of him.

'Take me to my daughter,' she said, firmly. 'At once. Do you hear me?'

Startled, the soldier gave a small bow.

'Yes, *Siti*,' he said.

This time, she did not object.

'You're here.' He walked over to her, and kissed her on both cheeks. '*Mash'Allah*, you are safe.'

'And Noor?' They were standing in his private apartments, and Haya was still shaking; the ride through the streets, her car, armoured, flanked by five riders with guns, had taken fire; screaming, she had dropped to the floor. The centre of Ghada City was on fire. People in the streets were running, yelling, throwing rocks. Even inside the royal compound, it was all different; rows of the palace guard, no longer ceremonial, AK-47s at their side, dressed for battle.

'She is upstairs. One of my servants will show you to a guest room. We have supplies, baby formula. You are too well-known as my companion – they would have come for you.'

'What's going on?'

'The sons of the Crown Prince are impatient; they have prepared a revolt. There are mercenaries here, and they

404

intend to kill the King. I am to fight them. If I fail, take this.' He looked behind him and withdrew some papers and money from a cabinet. 'Passports in a false name for you and the child, money to take you across the border. My personal bodyguard will see you out of the palace.'

Haya wept – she wanted to hold him, to kiss him. But they were not even engaged.

'Be careful,' she blurted out. 'Come back to me, come back safe. I pray you will come home!'

'It will be quick,' he said, grimly, and then, to her astonishment, leaned forward and kissed her lightly on the lips.

'Haya, I love you. Maybe this is not the time or the place, but I have no choice. If we survive this, will you marry me?'

She opened her mouth to consent, but Jaber stopped her.

'I knew this was coming. It is why I did not ask you. But Haya, know this. If you are my wife, you cannot be directly involved in GLAMOUR any more. You will be a princess. You will have to be merely a partner, and instead of commerce, perform other duties with me.' He pressed her hand. 'And they *are* duties, Haya, and there is no time off. So choose.'

There was gunfire in the distance. She looked at him; now her heart was on the line, there was no choice. Not really, not when he might die.

'I accept,' she said, and kissed his hand. 'Go with God!'

He looked back at her, briefly, then picked up his gun, lying on the table, and rushed from the room.

A nursemaid, in palace uniform, crept into the apartments and gave Haya a small half-curtsy.

'I will take you to your daughter,' she said.

'Yes, let me see her.' Haya's heart was full. Terror, and joy, and loss mingled together. Oh God! She loved him now, loved him so completely.

She had no idea what the night would bring. She

clutched the papers to her. Of course, if she had to flee, she would flee. Noor's safety came first. But she didn't want to go. She never wanted to leave Jaber.

The baby was crawling around the bedroom, with a frightened Emily Doughty manfully trying to play with her; she laughed with delight at seeing Haya. There was another burst of gunfire outside the windows, closer this time.

Haya picked Noor up and covered her with kisses, slinging her over her shoulder.

'What are those?' Mrs Doughty asked, looking at Haya's papers.

'Safe conduct to get out. If you want to go, Emily, you can get an armed escort to the border. I'll see to it.'

'I've grandchildren of my own.' The older woman wrung her hands. 'Oh God! What shall we do?'

'It's absolutely fine if you want to leave, but I believe if there's unrest here, they'll be at the airport too. Prince Jaber has an armed force to protect us. I'm staying here,' Haya said. She was cool and, the nanny thought, regal. 'You must make your own decisions. There's plenty of money here, and a passport for you.'

Mrs Doughty looked at her friend and employer, Haya's shoulders squared, the kaftan swirling around her feet.

'If you think we should stay, we'll stay,' she replied. 'You've a smart head on your shoulders for a lass who's not even Scottish.'

Haya took control. She arranged calls for Emily Doughty and herself to their worried families on a secure line; she dictated a will, and faxed it off to her father. She tried to distract the anxious staff in the villa by organizing the cooking of a meal on the single working gas ring in Jaber's kitchen. When the violence was close, so close you could hear the shots outside the gardens, less than a mile away,

Haya sang nursery rhymes to Noor, loudly, so that the bangs and crashes would not frighten her.

By the time the baby was sleeping soundly – Haya had had her cot moved into the centre of the villa, into Jaber's own bathroom, as far away from the sounds of violence as possible – the fighting had died down. Into the night there were occasional bursts of gunfire, or a flare arcing overhead. Haya remained awake, with her papers at her side. Ready to run, at any moment. Her bags for Noor packed, by her feet.

At half past three he finally returned; there was blood on his shirt, and some more that had dried in his beard. Exhausted, he slumped on a couch in the reception hall; his servants gathered around, and he muttered a few words in the Ghadan dialect. They smiled and clapped.

Haya leaned forward, anxiously. 'It's OK? What happened?'

'They put down the coup attempt. The ringleaders are in custody. Nobody liked them coming here with a foreign force. In the end the men of the city took to the streets and destroyed their vehicles. Then it was over.'

'*Mash'Allah*. And you? Are you injured?'

'A knife wound. Don't worry,' as she darted forward. 'A doctor has dressed it. There was hand-to-hand fighting at one point. They came within feet of the King.'

'The man who wounded you?'

His eyes darkened. 'I killed him.' Jaber looked away. 'I didn't want to tell you of this, when I had my suspicions. But I should have spoken up, warned you. Instead, I was too confident of their loyalty. I put you in danger. Is the baby OK?'

'Fast asleep.' She pointed.

'I have to sleep,' he said, apologetically. 'I'm sorry, I am dropping. But call your parents, have them fly out here, first class on the first plane, and anybody else you wish to be here. The palace will reimburse them. We will sign the *nikkah* the day after tomorrow.' He squeezed her hands. 'That is, if you still wish it?'

'I do,' Haya said, her heart full.

'And you will even give up your enterprise?'

'I will still own it,' she said, with a touch of stubbornness. 'But otherwise, yes, I can see that I must give up the day-to-day business.'

'Good.' Jaber sighed. 'That will certainly make things a little easier. He'll be pleased, at least, I persuaded you to do that.'

'He?'

'The King. He did not want me to marry you.'

Despite the desperate circumstances, Haya felt a moment of shock and annoyance. 'Why not?'

'You are a believer, but you are also an American. That's tricky. And not a virgin – and there is already a child.'

Haya frowned. 'That's backward thinking, Jaber.'

'I know it.' He shrugged. 'But it is protocol. I have been trying to persuade the King for some months, now, my love. It wasn't good to be seen with you.'

'And if you had not been able to persuade him?'

'Then we would have left Ghada together.' Jaber looked into her eyes. 'You are not the only one who can fight for what she wants.'

Haya was bold; she leaned forward, and kissed him on the lips.

'You sleep,' she said, 'my love. I will make some calls.'

Jane Morgan tossed on her bed. It was an Indian summer in New York, blisteringly hot and muggy. Her apartment was a ten-million-dollar penthouse on Fifth, overlooking the museum, a real palace; triplex, with eight bedrooms and four bathrooms. All her own. And now the air conditioning had broken down.

There wouldn't be an engineer available till tomorrow,

and who knew what time. She would be taking four cold showers a day just to keep from getting sweaty.

She bet the air con was working just fine at Craig's place, in the Village.

Her body ached for him. Levin was like an addiction. Big, strong, thick, the perfect antidote to her softness – in body at least. And too much for Jane. She was struggling with her feelings. Trying, and failing, to give him up.

Craig wouldn't marry her.

They had been together now for six months. Well, if you could call it together. Dating, and sleeping together, minus the sleep. Sex that was hotter than hell. His touch was certain, and inexorable. She couldn't fight it, in any way that mattered. Levin turned her inside out. Jane would get aroused now, whenever she so much as read his name in the papers. If she saw a clip of him – they were always brief – on TV, she would be useless for business for the next half hour; her unruly, frustrated body crying out for him.

It was so much more than just hot sex, too. Jane loved every moment she spent talking with him. Craig discussed his business, her business, the world, the markets. They spoke the same language. He wasn't frivolous, and he never treated her like a robot, the caricature that the business press loved to slap on her. Craig Levin made Jane laugh; he fascinated her, he was her mirror. They were two halves, she sometimes thought. They could finish each other's sentences. He was, now, as much her best friend as Sally or Haya had ever been.

Craig could always surprise her; he was thoughtful, he was imaginative; life with him was the perfect adventure. All Jane wanted in this world was for their love to go on forever.

And yet, and yet. Craig would not marry her. He had not asked. Jane had followed him to New York – but GLAMOUR needed her. Proud, she had purchased her own, fabulous apartment; full daily maid service, a concierge and a gardener for her rooftop oasis; Levin shrugged, and kept his own townhouse in the Village, four thousand square feet of Victorian brownstone, right next to his fellow billionaire Magnus Soren. He would have this relationship on his own terms. Jane wanted it on hers. Not that she said anything explicit; Levin kept seeing her, she would not beg to be loved.

They both continued with their business. Jane worked like she never had before. Haya was sending excellent articles, and generating lots of goodwill; Jane traded on it expertly. Sally Lassiter – now, there was a superstar. Jane did not mind every time she saw Sally's golden prettiness beaming out at her from the cover of *In Style* or *Women's Wear Daily*. Jane had a different following: smaller articles, fewer pictures, but ones that mattered to her; her peers, those that read things other than fashion magazines, knew all about her.

For the girl on the subway, Sally was GLAMOUR. For the broker reading the *Wall Street Journal*, it was Jane Morgan. At a ridiculously young age, shaping up to be one of America's most notable businesswomen. There were others ahead of her, but Jane wanted to change all that.

She didn't see her competition as Sally. She saw it as Craig Levin.

He played in another league. Fact. Jane didn't want to compete in the girls' division. She wanted the championship. Yes, OK, she admitted it to herself, as the sweat drenched her skin. When Craig used to tell her, his hands moving capably across her arching body, that he could buy and sell her ten times over, it was a turn-on. But in the morning, she tried to fight.

All her rage, all her frustration, she poured into her business. Expand. Invest. Supervise. Hire. Repeat. As the GLAMOUR empire spread – her empire, her baby – Jane's plans got bigger. Turn it into the Wal-Mart of luxe. Own the sector. They thought retail was dead until Sam Walton came along. Why not her?

Maybe one day she could compete with Craig, on his own terms . . . There were days when Jane didn't know if she loved him or hated him.

Sally was getting married. And her blithe, bubbly love of Chris Nelson grated on Jane. Whenever she saw Nelson on TV – and as the Dodgers were 2–1 up in the series against the Red Sox, that was quite a bit – she had the opposite reaction to when she saw Craig. Loss. Anger. Frustration. Because Chris was *marrying* Sally. He'd asked, she'd accepted, and it was to be just like the old days – a party at Sally's former house, with eight hundred of their closest friends.

Jane couldn't bear Craig to come with her. Couldn't bear the jokes.

'So when is it *your* turn?'

'Gonna catch that bouquet, Jane?'

She was rich, beautiful, aristocratic, and a self-made woman, and yet here she was, a slave to love. Sick with desire. Shamed to be so much Levin's, and know that he was not hers.

She thought, too often, about that first night, that long, intense night by the pool.

If only he had not come over. If only she had not had sex with him. Those fires, once lit in her belly, apparently could not be put out. And all Jane wanted to do was to cry out why – to ask him why he would not marry her.

But there could only be one answer, one she did not want to hear.

He didn't love her.

Craig liked her, cared for her, was best friends with her, desired her. Saw himself in her, as he told her again and again. They understood each other better than anybody else in the world.

But it must be that he did not *love* her. Not the way she loved him.

That was it. Wasn't it?

Jane felt tears, private tears, wetting her cheeks, and let them fall; this was her sanctuary, after all. Nobody could see her here. She was completely alone.

Her cell phone rang.

Jane blinked. It was three in the morning. Who could be calling? Almost nobody had this number. She prayed it was not Craig. Nope; that wasn't him on the caller ID.

'Jane Morgan.'

A brief pause. 'I've woken you – I wanted to leave you a message, I'm sorry. I thought the phone would be off.'

'Hey, Haya. It's never off. But don't worry about that, I was awake anyway.' Jane dashed the tears off her face. She could do with a little business talk – refocus. 'What's up?'

'I know it's short notice, but could you get a flight to Ghada City tomorrow?'

Her stomach squeezed. 'Are you OK?'

A laugh. 'I'm fine. Actually . . . I'm getting married.'

Jane blinked. 'Huh?'

'Well, it's the *nikkah* ceremony, there will be another formal wedding later, but once the *nikkah* happens, you are married. Just my parents, you and Craig, and Sally and Chris. If you can come.'

'Who is he?'

'Jaber.' Jane could almost hear her friend blushing. 'I think I might have mentioned him to you.'

'A little.' Jane blinked, disbelievingly. 'You don't mean *Prince* Jaber, do you?'

'Yes. We've been seeing each other . . . I didn't want to talk about it until I was certain.' Haya paused. 'There was some political stuff here.'

Jane ran the details through her mental processor. 'But

Prince Jaber is the Foreign Minister of Ghada. How can you—'

'Jane, I can't,' Haya said, knowing what Jane was about to say. 'I can't. I have to retire – just from active management, of course,' she added hastily. 'But I've trained up some excellent people and the systems are in place . . . I've got to be a blind partner now. Devote myself to charity works and do-gooding,' she said, self-deprecatingly.

Jane's stomach churned so hard she thought she might pass out. Emotions washed through her, one after the other, so strongly she could hardly believe it. Haya! Haya too. Married . . . *twice*. A damn *princess*. An actual princess with an actual crown. Sally, in her way, American royalty. And she, Jane, rejected by the only man she had ever loved. Or ever would love.

'Sally and Chris will be there,' Haya went on, oblivious to Jane's torment. 'Can you and Craig make it?'

'I – no.' Her and Craig? Last time she'd seen him he'd shut the door of his office and bent her over his desk. He had a meeting in Stockholm tomorrow, the chances of cancelling it for a social trip to the Middle East were nil. And to go by herself? No way. 'We can't. I'm sorry, it's too short notice.' Her tone was cool, that practised formality she used against all pain. 'I'll come to the real wedding.'

'This is the real wedding.' Haya was a little distant now herself. 'But of course it is hugely short notice . . . we just want to be married.'

'I understand.' What woman in love didn't? Jane thought for a few moments. 'If you are retiring from business, Haya, will you sell me your shares? I'll happily give you market price, or a premium, even.'

There was silence.

'Haya? Are you still there?'

'Yes; no thank you, Jane, I won't be selling. The business of GLAMOUR is key to Ghada and the region, and I've built it up quite carefully. I'll just be leaving day-to-day management to you and Sally.' Her tone now was as crisp as Jane's.

'I see – that's fine,' Jane lied. She was angry, now, she couldn't immediately fathom why. But this was out of her control, the whole thing. Her business. Her life. She wondered if Haya would sell to Sally – those two had always been closer. 'Congratulations on your wedding, Haya, I'm sure you'll be extremely happy, and I'll come to the next ceremony. Can I send a gift to you?'

'Just donations to the Red Crescent,' Haya said.

Donations? How impersonal. Jane felt it as a rebuff. Was her friend already acting like a princess, and not the Haya she'd known, whose legs she'd held up as she squeezed out her daughter?

'I'll be glad to make a donation. A hundred thousand, first thing tomorrow.'

'That's very generous, Jane. Thank you. Goodnight then.'

'Goodnight, Haya,' Jane replied, hanging up.

She crawled back into her bed, tears welling up again. Tomorrow she would take a good cold shower and make herself up to look the best she possibly could. And she would go to see Craig, and once and for all she would finish it.

Chapter Forty-One

'I can't believe I'm doing this on our day off.' Chris was still pissed off; he took care to speak sotto voce, though. 'It's as hot as balls out here.'

'Ssh,' Sally hissed, angrily. 'You're here now, make the best of it! You can sleep on the plane on the way home.'

'Two days' rest before Boston, and I'm spending them thirty thousand feet in the air.'

'And how many other royal weddings are you going to get invited to?' Sally whispered back.

He squeezed her arm. 'True, but you'll always be my princess.'

In front of them, Haya was bending over the scroll; she lowered her head and signed it.

Sally stared at her friend with something close to awe. She felt loss, too; envy, a touch of anger. With that signature, Haya, as she knew her, had gone, and not like the first time; she had vanished forever.

Vanished from the company. Surely vanished from their friendship. There she stood, robed head to toe in fluttering golden silks, a long kaftan-like dress, studded with seed pearls and embroidered with crystals; there was some kind of headdress on her head, like a storybook princess from Sally's childhood, square, with delicate chiffon scarves of pale gold floating behind it. What a dress! Haya did not look real to Sally. Her husband wore a traditional, embroidered coat; it was white satin, and appeared to her to be encrusted with diamonds.

He had signed first. The imam said something in Arabic. The assembled guards presented their guns in a salute, pointed them out at an angle, and fired.

Chris instinctively moved to cover Sally, with his body.

'It's OK. It's ceremonial.'

He grinned. 'Jumped out of my skin.'

But she was watching her friend. There were women in the same sort of robes, just less ornate; Sally guessed they were maids of honour, and they were coming forward. They leaned closer, and removed the square headdress from Haya, and a sort of round white cap from Jaber; and then they were led forward to two ornately carved chairs. As they passed the King, he bowed, she curtsied. He said something to them; then they sat down in the chairs.

Two soldiers came forward bearing silken white cushions.

'What's that?' Sally whispered.

Chris leaned forward, blinked, then put his mouth next to her ear.

'Crowns,' he said. 'Little crowns.'

Open-mouthed, Sally watched as they placed the glittering golden circlets first on Jaber's head, then on Haya's; her tiara, all gold and icy white diamonds, glittered in the sun.

There was a burst of trumpets from the assembled military guard; then Jaber and Haya stood, he offered her his arm, and they processed back down the red carpet, past the assembled Ghadan court; and Sally watched as everybody curtsied or bowed as Haya walked past them. Her parents' faces were a picture of ecstatic joy; as her daughter walked past, Mrs al-Yanna sank into a curtsy so low her knees practically scraped the ground.

The royal couple were approaching them now. Chris stood up straight; he smiled appreciatively at Haya as she walked past. Sally, blushing scarlet, aware she was Haya's only invited friend, dipped into an awkward bob.

It was amazing how much it stung. As she rose, looking now at Haya's extended train, Chris stared at her, amazed. And actually quite annoyed.

'You're a damn American,' he said, taking care to keep his voice low. 'What the hell did you do that for?'

'We're the only Western guests without some kind of title, I wanted to show respect. Not let her down.'

He shrugged. 'I don't bend the knee to no man. Never thought to see you do it, either.'

'Another reason why I love you,' Sally said, honestly.

She was jealous; it couldn't be denied. What all-American little girl didn't grow up wanting to be a princess? And Haya was a real one; nothing metaphorical about it.

The band struck up a Debussy waltz, and the ceremony was over. A uniformed officer from the palace approached them.

'Mr Nelson, Miss Lassiter?'

'Guilty,' Chris said. Sally dug him in the ribs.

'Her Royal Highness, Princess Haya al-Jaber, asks me to conduct you to the top table. May I take you to the Emira?'

'Why, certainly,' Sally said.

Damn! What a moment. If her mom could see her now. If her *dad* could see her . . .

Then it struck her, like lightning, that Haya would definitely, absolutely, not be coming back to GLAMOUR. What if she could take her shares? Then maybe she'd have a chance, for once, not to feel like this – inadequate, the dumbest of the three of them. Jane charged ahead, and never took or asked her advice. Haya had been out of touch for months. Yet she, Sally Lassiter, had been the driving force behind the store – who'd launched it, who inspired its fashion, who was on magazine covers the world over?

Haya had won the lottery here. Good for Haya, Sally

wished her joy – and no doubt she was going to get it. GLAMOUR would be little more than a toy to her now. But the store had been Sally's redemption.

'I would love to sit next to the Princess,' she said confidently.

Haya ran to the back door of the villa to check on Noor, and found Mrs Doughty waiting for her.

'She's fine. Just went down for her nap,' the older woman said, then smiled and curtsied. 'And congratulations to you, Your Royal Highness.'

Haya was horrified. 'Don't do that!'

'Oh, I have to. People are watching. You might as well get used to it, at least in public – *ma'am*. You can't put Prince Jaber under the microscope. He chose an unconventional wife, don't make him look bad. My two penn'orth.'

Haya twisted uncomfortably. 'You're absolutely right. I just feel funny about it.'

'There's gossip amongst the other nannies,' Mrs Doughty said, lowering her voice. 'About your husband's position. They say he's in high favour right now. I wouldn't ruin it. Don't let anybody see you not observing the correct protocol.'

'OK.' Haya had heard some of that gossip herself. She blushed. 'I'm not good at politics.'

'Just be a princess. Remember that you are one. Be as good at it as you were at business. All right, I'm done. And congratulations again, my dear.' Emily Doughty kissed her on the cheek. 'You'll have a very happy life.'

On her way back to the marquee, Haya did not run. She walked, slowly and elegantly; cooks and waitresses bowed, curtsied as she passed; soldiers saluted her.

She knew what her nanny meant. Of course she did. There was speculation that Jaber would be raised, made Prime Minister; second in Ghada only to the King. And if that happened, what an opportunity!

Whatever she had been able to do with ethical trade would be nothing, absolutely nothing. If her husband had the King's ear, what could be done with the vast oil wealth of a country like this? Schools for the poor, cultural festivals, introducing democracy, improved relations with the West, promotion of arts and crafts on a global scale. She could actually make a difference, improve the lives of hundreds of thousands.

And she had always respected Jaber, and his rank. Jaber had rejected a royal cousin, one born to this, in her favour. She had to prove to the court that he had not made a mistake with the boorish American girl.

A uniformed servant held back the doors of the marquee; the entire crowd dipped down as she walked to the high table.

Haya lifted her head, feeling the coronet upon it, and smiled graciously. As she passed the gold thrones on which the old King and his wife were sitting, she herself sank into a profound curtsy, her wedding robes billowing about her. Jaber smiled at her, and extended a hand to lift her up.

'Your friends are here,' he said. 'Mr Nelson and Miss Lassiter.'

'Great,' Haya murmured. She walked round to Chris and Sally, suddenly feeling the eyes of the entire court, the Queen in particular, boring down on her.

'Hello,' she said. 'It's so wonderful you could come.'

Chris Nelson was wearing a lightweight suit, and looked ill at ease; he shook her hand briskly. 'Hey, Haya, it's great to be here,' he said, and smiled warmly at her.

She suppressed a wince. Haya? Couldn't he suck it up and be just a little formal in public? They'd never once met before. And the guy didn't even have a carnation on.

'Sally, you look beautiful.' She turned to her friend. Sally did bob a curtsy, her golden head down, but when she came up her face was flaming. Why did she have to look so uncomfortable? Haya did a quick inventory: Sally was wearing a long evening gown, very pretty, in azure blue velvet, but it had shoulder straps, and was cut to display the tops of her impressive bosom. It would knock them out at any ball in California, but Ghada was a little more conservative. 'I'm so glad you're here,' she said quickly and urgently.

'Congratulations,' Sally said, giving her an awkward hug.

'You must be cold,' Haya said, diplomatically. 'I'll have somebody bring you a shawl, it gets chilly in the desert at nights.'

'Thank you, but I'm fine,' Sally replied.

Haya hesitated. Should she whisper something about the shoulders? But people were watching, including the boyfriend, very possessively. So she just squeezed her friend's hand. 'I hope we'll get to talk . . . the guard will show you to your seats.'

'Am I next to you? I don't know a soul,' Sally whispered.

'My dad's on my other side, but you're right opposite me, how's that?'

'Fine,' Sally said, nervously. 'As long as I have Chris next to me. Somebody to talk to!'

As they were led away, Haya beckoned a serving woman.

'Get my friend a large shawl and arrange it around her shoulders. Quickly, please.'

'Yes, Highness,' the woman said, throwing a scandalized glance at Sally's gown.

Chris pulled his fiancée to him, hugging her tight. Concerned for her.

'You OK? You two didn't seem to be getting on like old friends, just then.'

Sally sighed, admitting the stiffness, the awkwardness between them.

'She's been away from the States for a while now.' She

wanted to excuse Haya. 'And you know, there are cultural differences, plus this is a royal wedding, lots of customs, lots of traditions . . .'

'Making your friends feel welcome is a pretty universal tradition,' Chris said, unimpressed, and Sally couldn't help but see Haya through the cold light of his disapproving eyes. 'She barely said two words to me. Looked down her nose because I used her first name. Does she even understand what the World Series is, what we gave up to come here?'

Sally flushed with embarrassment and guilt. She was having serious misgivings about having dragged Chris from his practice.

'Look, it's probably just nerves. She's sat us at her table, Chris. I'm sure she'll make me feel just as welcome as she can. Haya would never embarrass me. We've been through too much.'

As she said it, she wanted to believe it. But the long green sweep of the lawn, covered with candles, the darkening, starry sky, the uniformed guard, the trumpeters, the robed guests, the looming walls of the palace . . .

They all said different.

Haya is a princess now. You've lost her. She's gone.

The guards ushered Chris and Sally to their places, opposite Haya and Jaber. Jaber, deep in conversation with an emir to his right, nodded and smiled at them, but said nothing. Chris, in a valiant attempt at good manners, introduced himself to his other neighbour, a plump woman with her hair in a stylish bun set with jewels.

She shrugged and responded to him in Arabic.

Chris exchanged annoyed glances with Sally. The thoughtlessness stung her; her fiancé couldn't have been found a place next to somebody who spoke English? He'd be left speaking only to her all night.

Desperately, Sally addressed Haya. Trying to get her away from fussy protocols and onto a subject they both knew.

'So, Haya. You're quitting the company?'

'Day to day, yes. I'll be a silent partner. So, how are your wedding preparations coming?' Haya tried to change the subject – she didn't want all Jaber's relatives listening to her talk business on the day of her *nikkah*. His mother, Princess Aisha, was already looking her over with a narrowed glance of disapproval. Mentally she tried to signal to Sally. Damn! Why were *her* friends so tone deaf when it came to culture?

She knew Jaber secretly considered Sally some sort of bimbo, riding on the success of herself and Jane. Of course she knew better. But *why* did Sally pick that dress?

'Just fine. Y'all will enjoy it,' Sally promised, smiling broadly at Jaber. 'It's going to be a lot like this, but different food. Hope you don't mind American!'

'Not in the least,' he said, with a broad smile.

'We'll get you cooking on the barbecue,' Chris Nelson promised the Prince. 'I make my own marinade. It's famous in the locker room.'

Haya died a thousand deaths.

'So, Haya.' Sally came right to the point. 'If you're going to do the Princess thing full time, you should let me buy you out.'

Haya lost her temper; this was too much, really. On her wedding day.

'Funny, Jane asked me the same thing. I'm not selling. Surprised she didn't tell you that, Sally.'

Sally recoiled, shocked. *Jane* had asked to buy the shares? Jane Morgan? Didn't she already have enough, with all her stock deals on the side and her billionaire date? GLAMOUR was Sally's baby, it was all she had.

And – Jane hadn't told her. Was she trying to force her out? Take the whole thing?

'But why? You know you don't need that company now.'

'Because it's mine,' Haya said, shortly.

Sally's eyes flashed. If Haya's thoughtless unconcern for her friends was bad enough, this was different. This selfishness was extending to Sally's life now, to Sally's whole business. Haya was being a real dog in the manger about it. Didn't she *see* that pretty gold crown sitting on top of her head?

'And we won't talk business on my wedding day, if you don't mind.' Haya decided hinting was no good. 'That's not the custom here.'

'Madam . . .' The servant woman came forward, holding out the shawl, and a little officiously tried to tie it around Sally's shoulders.

Sally was now properly angry; she'd moved heaven and earth to be there, taken Chris away on his two days' rest in the middle of the biggest event of his damn life, the World Series. And Haya – get a title, and suddenly her friend had turned into some kind of mega-snob.

Sally untied the shawl and firmly handed it back.

'No, sorry,' she said. 'I'm not cold. I don't think I will, thanks.'

The woman muttered something in Arabic and nodded at Haya; Sally caught the word *emira*; that one she knew – Princess.

'It's all right,' Haya said, in both Arabic and English. But her face had flushed red with embarrassment.

Haya hadn't been ashamed of Sally back when Sal was protecting her from the playground bullies. Chris squeezed her hand, sensing her anger; slow to spark, but deadly once it had ignited.

'Wanna split?' he whispered.

She shook her head, biting her lip. Haya, with a frown, had turned aside to speak to her father.

'I need Ghada for the company,' she whispered back.

There would be no scene. Sally made small talk with

Chris, and sat through the first course of *tabbouleh* and the second of spiced beef. After that she gave her fiancé the smallest look; he cleared his throat.

'Haya, it's been great. But Sally and I are feeling kind of beat, and we have to get back to the airport – I can't skip practice tomorrow, facing the top of the Red Sox rotation Monday. Jaber, many congratulations. We wish you guys all the best.'

He offered his arm to Sally, and she took it, thankful that she had a man who wasn't fazed by anyone or anything.

'Haya, congratulations to you both. Hope to see you in the States before too long. It was a wonderful wedding,' Sally said, forcing herself to draw on her reserves of Southern politeness. 'Enjoy the rest of your special day.'

Haya blinked – they were actually *walking out* of her wedding, leaving two empty places at the top table, where the whole of the royal family were sitting.

'Have a safe flight,' she said, icy cold.

Sally nodded, gave her a brisk smile and left.

Tears of embarrassment and anger were prickling the eyes of both women.

Jaber leaned over, kissed his wife on the cheek.

'Not your fault,' he said. He turned aside and beckoned sharply, murmuring softly to one of his bodyguards; the man nodded, and within moments a sharif from the protocol office, and his wife, overjoyed at the honour, had been shown to the empty seats.

Chris waited while Sally packed her case – in her current mood, she threw everything in there, and was done in five minutes – and arranged with the hotel for a limo to take them to the airport. He took charge, as Sally fumed; pulled out his credit card, and had them safely ensconced in a first-class seat on Royal Jordanian, winging their way home to New York.

He was the first to speak. 'Don't let her bother you, honey. She was beyond rude. Princess? I've seen barmaids with better manners. No idea about making guests feel welcome.'

'I don't know.' Sally shook her blond head. 'Ever since she first went out to Ghada, before Noor was born even, she's been drifting away from us. She was so serious about her damn carpets and lamps. Made me feel bad about having a little fun.'

'But that's not it, is it?' Chris, like Sally, was sharp. He respected his girlfriend's mind. Just because it came encased in a hella bodacious body didn't mean she was dumb. He wouldn't have fallen for her if she had been. Sally had proved her intelligence to him a thousand times over. And right now he could see the wheels ticking.

'No.' Sally chewed her lip, the way she always did when seething. 'She wouldn't sell me her shares. And she told me Jane already asked. Jane didn't tell me.'

'Did you tell Jane?'

'I only just decided to ask. Anyway, I would have done.' Sally wasn't a hundred per cent sure that was true; she glossed over it in her mind. 'The *point* is that neither of them are being fair. Haya's a princess now, she's richer than any of us will ever be. What the hell does she need to hang on to GLAMOUR for? GLAMOUR is my deal.'

'And Jane?'

'Same thing. She doesn't care about the store, to her it's just a business deal. She doesn't design anything, she doesn't care about the stock or the shopping experience. To her GLAMOUR could be a baked bean factory. She just wants the money. Why can't she get it trading shares? I *live* GLAMOUR, Chris. I design all the fashion, I do worldwide press and interviews for it twelve hours a day. I've got *fans*.'

'Starting with me,' he said. Wanting to take her into the airplane bathroom and do that mile-high thing.

But Sally was absorbed in her anger.

'When the customers go into the store they aren't going there because Jane bloody Morgan knows how to get a good deal on a fleet of distribution trucks, or because Haya al-Yanna found them some great carpets. They're going there for the *sizzle*. For the *style*. For *me*.' Her small fist clenched. 'You know, those girls will always be my friends – I hope.' He didn't think she sounded certain. 'But I have to make sure that GLAMOUR is mine. It matters more to me than anybody. And when we get home I'm gonna find a way to take control.'

Chapter Forty-Two

Jane checked herself out in the mirror. Yes; she looked good. Fresh and rested, for one thing. Maybe it was a good job she hadn't been able to get a meeting with Craig yesterday; his plane, stuck in a Scandinavian storm-bound airport, had saved her from herself.

Yesterday, with no sleep and a broken heart, she'd had a drawn look no concealer could disguise. Bags under her eyebrows the size of the new Hermès Kelly. Circles so dark you could suck a star into them, Jane thought. Her own personal black holes.

She wanted to look good every time she dated Craig.

For breaking up with him, though, she wanted to look perfect.

She switched on the TV. It was Sunday morning, no need to rush to his place before the morning coffee had brewed.

'Thanks, John. We'll be catching up with the weather every thirty minutes here on *Good Day America*. And now for a little light relief.' The co-anchor turned her head to the man on the couch, tossing her chestnut-brown bob and giving him a glossy smile. 'Did you hear this one, Ken?'

'What's that, Molly?'

'America has a new princess!' Jane stared as the TV cut to footage of a sumptuous marquee, in the desert; there were uniformed soldiers and ladies in ballgowns, and there in the middle, sitting on a damned throne, next to a handsome man in white, wearing a real crown, was Haya. 'That's Haya

427

al-Yanna, better known to America's women as one of the fashionable trio of ladies who run the GLAMOUR superstores. And now she's Her *Royal* Highness, Princess Haya of Ghada! Princess Haya grew up in LA and was the daughter of a local auto trader.'

'Hey, GLAMOUR by name, GLAMOUR by nature, I guess,' said the male anchor, turning a bland white smile to camera.

'Sally Lassiter, America's sweetheart, the *hottest* designer coast to coast, who founded the stores with the Princess, was in attendance with superstar fiancé Chris Nelson.'

The screen flashed to a shot of Sally sitting next to Chris; he had her hand in his.

'Definitely the royal wedding of the year. Two amazing couples there. I expect this will bring even more shoppers through the GLAMOUR doors.'

Jane waited for them to mention her.

'And now we jump to Richard for the traffic. Rich? What you got for us?'

Bitter, Jane flicked her remote at the TV. Turn that bloody thing off. It wasn't just the States; everywhere was like that. Part of a couple, glamorous, then you got attention, then you got credit.

She, Jane, was not as beautiful as her friends. She had no princely coronet and no va-va-voom figure. And she didn't muck around with dress designs or picking out tasteful objects for sale. Hers was the business of business. She was the one whose brain had come up with this store. She had financed it, single-handedly. And, as it turned out, at the cost of her heart.

Who had found sites for twenty more stores? Who had managed every aspect of the corporation from staffing to invoicing? Who had bought the ad buys that Sally Lassiter's pretty face featured in, in billboards across America?

Jane Morgan. De facto CEO – but on paper, sharing that

title. Multimillionairess, sure, but sharing it with two friends who had ridden to the top on her coat-tails.

And Haya had blown her off when it came to the shares.

Jane was almost grateful. She didn't begrudge Haya and Sally their fame, their celebrity status. But she wanted the business side of things, her own project, to herself. Had either of them lived in a roach-infested apartment, or worked eighteen-hour days? No. She thought not. She had done fine by her friends, she'd given them wealth and position beyond dreaming. It was time to take control for herself.

A blessing. Something to focus on. Something to get her mind off her inner pain.

She went into the kitchen and, mechanically, made herself a pot of coffee and toasted half a bagel. She wasn't hungry, but she didn't want her stomach to rumble, or to get dizzy from lack of blood sugar. Besides, she had got into the habit of looking after herself.

When she was done, she brushed her teeth again to lose the coffee breath, spritzed on a little scent, and headed for Craig Levin's house.

'Jane? That you?'

There were no staff at his place Sunday mornings – Craig gave them the day off. And Jane had the code to his keypad entry gates. Another excellent reason to do this today.

'Take all your clothes off except your jacket,' he called from the bedroom, 'and your high heels, and come upstairs.'

Man. She loved that thick-throated, sexy voice. Craig Levin was as funny and as raunchy as hell. And she loved how he knew she was wearing a jacket.

'I'll be right there,' she shouted out, and went to the refrigerator. Before leaving last night, the chefs had prepared various things for breakfast. Jane selected the large, ice-cold pitcher of freshly squeezed orange and peach juice, poured out two tumblers, and took them up with her.

He was lying sprawled under the Pratesi sheets on his designer Swedish sleigh bed; the sheets cut off, very sexily, at the thick line of hair right above the flat of his groin.

Jane wanted him instantly. She wished to hell she didn't have to do this. They could spend a normal day together, making love, eating a long, leisurely brunch somewhere, laughing together, having one of those talks that could last for five hours at a stretch and you always wanted more. Craig got under her skin and into her head, so many more ways than sexually.

Man, how she loved him.

Jane took refuge in a long pull on the chilled, delicious juice.

'Here's yours.' She handed him the tumbler.

'You're not naked,' he observed, taking it in. 'That's not good, honey.'

Slowly – Levin let himself sleep long and solidly on Sundays, and he was still groggy – he raised himself to a sitting position; the silk sheet slipped dangerously, but Jane didn't look.

'Here,' she said. She opened her Chanel purse and handed him two sets of keys. 'The spares to your place in Hollywood. And the flat in Rome.'

'I don't want to know what this is about, do I?'

Jane shook her head; she was already fighting down the tears. 'I'm finishing it.'

'You've said that before.' He caught her round the waist. 'And I remember how I talked you out of it.'

'I love you, and you don't love me.' She dashed the back of her hand against her eyes and forced a smile. 'Not a good position to make a trade.'

'I do love you,' Levin insisted. The 'but' hung in the air.

'Both my friends have got engaged or got married.'

There. She had dared to say it. The M-word.

'But they're not us. What's right for them is not right for us.'

'Says you.' Jane sighed. 'I never should have slept with you, Craig.'

He shook his head, annoyed. 'What is that? Are you some kind of Catholic now? No sex before marriage?'

'You tell me,' Jane responded wearily. It was over, she didn't have to watch her words any more. 'You have what you want. Sex and friendship, no strings, no commitment. Why should you change that?'

Levin winced, just slightly; perhaps she was too near the knuckle, after all.

'I've never cheated on you, Jane. I gave them all up for you.'

'Your trouble is you want a gold medal for doing the right thing. You're an amazing man, Craig. You're brilliant; you're funny; you're driven; you're a dominant male.'

'Exactly what you're looking for,' he said, quite serious. 'Jane, if you make the perfect the enemy of the good, just because I'm not ready—'

'I told you,' she said. 'I love you. I can't be with you and give myself to you when you hold yourself apart from me. I always wanted you, from the first conversation we ever had. But since I slept with you, it's like an addiction. There's no reason not to get married, not to have kids. Unless you haven't decided I'm the one for you. On some level, you're keeping your options open.'

'I'm just not ready,' he repeated. Levin had no wisecrack. Not this time.

'Unfortunately I am. So. This is it. I'm going to take over GLAMOUR. I want your ten per cent. Please give it to me, Craig; I'm asking you, as a favour.'

'Jane—'

'Don't. Just don't,' she said, crying in earnest now. 'I never tried to force you into anything, and I'm not now. I just won't settle, Craig. Not with you. Either you choose me or you choose your freedom.'

'I've never felt about anybody the way I feel about you.'

She flinched; the soft words hit her heart with a physical stab of loss.

'It isn't enough,' Jane said. 'Will you sell me your stock?'

'My broker will call tomorrow and sell them to you at market,' he said, a touch bitterly.

'Thank you.' She paused. 'Goodbye, Craig Levin. I love you.'

'I love you too,' he responded. Her heels were already clattering down the stairs.

Levin flopped back onto his bed; it was a sunny day, and he could see the leaves of an elm tree, golden in the autumn sunlight, waving gently outside his skylight; but his world had gone dark.

No. He would not marry her. Even though she was young, and beautiful, and intelligent, and feisty, and the hottest damn lay he'd ever had in his life. Not because she was skilled, like some high-class hooker, but because of her intense, shuddering responsiveness.

Was she the kind of woman a man married? Everything that drew him to her shouted no. So hot, so strong, so driven. Passionate and independent. Would she settle with him? Mother his children, look after them?

He could not tell if Jane would ever stop looking, ever stop being hungry.

She said she wanted to be married. Levin thought that would ruin it. What if she did stop? Would he want her if she was there all the time, available, not having to be chased? Would he want her after a morning of picking out drapes or talking to some boring interior designer?

He loved his freedom. And Jane was freedom.

But he did not want to let her go.

Ruefully he stared at the ceiling. It was so, so like her. To confess her pain and love so matter-of-factly – as if he hadn't known, of course he had – and then ask for his shares. At the one time he could not deny her.

She was moving on. Moving up. He thought she was just tremendously impressive. Burying herself in work was exactly what he would do himself.

God, how he loved her; they were partners in crime.

Levin, a man's man, never cried. He tried to ignore the fact that as he rolled over on to his pillow, his eyes were wet.

Top of the eleventh. Sally breathed in, deeply. She couldn't take the tension. If the Dodgers struck out again, she was going in search of some alcohol – the real stuff in the VIP boxes, not that useless beer the vendors carted round the stands. Anyway, they'd run out hours ago.

It was a bitterly cold autumn night in Boston, but nobody felt that. The electricity in this stadium could have powered the national grid.

Game seven. The World Series. Tiebreaker. This was it – win, or go home. Baseball's biggest prize, eternal glory or ignominy, on the cards. Every player on the field had been dreaming of this moment since he was knee high. For half of them, that lifelong dream was about to turn into a nightmare.

Just to up the pressure, the game was in overtime.

It hadn't been Chris Nelson's finest hour. He'd scored a useless single in the third, got a walk in the seventh, apart from that he was oh-for-eight. This from a guy with a post-season average of .376.

Sally didn't need to have a radio with her to imagine what the commentators were telling America.

'He's exhausted.'

'What was Nelson thinking, spending two days off in the air?'

'Manager Thomas Kent should have put his foot down.'

'His fiancée dragged him to a fancy Middle Eastern wedding. Hope that slice of cake was good, Chris! Looks like that's the only trophy you'll be picking up *this* season.'

The guilt boiled up inside her. They'd all be right, too. What the hell had she been thinking? Lost Chris his dream so that he could get snubbed in the desert, thousands of miles from here.

The World Series, the Championship, was more than just one match. It was life. It was the ring you wore forever. It was the Hall of Fame. Lose it, and you might sink into alcoholism or despair. Would that happen to Chris? Would their relationship even survive?

She bit her knuckles. Every inning he failed to connect was a new chance the manager would pull him. In Thomas's place, *she'd* have pulled him!

Leo Olsen – first up. Single. Thank God. Sally clapped wildly. Even if Chris couldn't do it, it wouldn't matter as long as the Dodgers won. His performance thus far would make him man of the series – even with a terrible last game.

Next, Rick Angelo. Swing and a miss. Ball. The crack of the bat, connecting – she could hardly look. No – no good, no good! He popped it up, and the Boston shortstop caught it with ease.

Another Dodger came up to the plate – hit a flyout, just shy of that magic wall that would have added two runs to their total.

That meant Chris was next. Sally shut her eyes tight. Then she opened them. She couldn't miss this, she had to share his pain. That was her punishment.

And she thanked God she did, because a second later the in-ground cameraman found her and flashed her face up on the jumbotron screen, next to a still shot of Chris's face.

The crowd booed. Sally wanted to shrink in her seat. As far as the fans were concerned, she was public enemy number one.

Then the cameraman found Chris, at the mound. He was listening to them booing Sally. His face, his handsome, square-jawed face, looked monumentally angry. The Dodgers fans shut the hell up. The Red Sox fans cheered even louder.

Holding his hand up to the pitcher, Chris turned round, looked up in Sally's general direction, and blew her a kiss.

The knot in her stomach melted; his protection, his salute, was like a shot of hot buttered rum against the cold.

The umpire shouted something. The pitcher, eyes cold, wound up and swung forth with a deadly fastball—

– and Chris connected, not off pitch like the other two, dead in the middle of the bat. She could hear the crack in the stands. The ball was soaring, higher, deeper; Chris's bat had shattered, he flung it from him and raced to first base, Olsen was already at second . . .

But the ball wasn't stopping . . . It arced high, long, and into the stands at left field.

Home run!

Sally blinked, hyperventilating. Home run! Two run home run! And Boston had already replaced most of their hitters, slicing through the roster in a desperate search for firepower. Olsen and Nelson raced round the bases. The Boston fans stopped cheering; the Dodger fans went nuts.

The jumbotron had fixed on Sally again. She waved, she smiled – she blew a kiss back down to Chris.

The crowd went wild.

The fight trailed out of Boston. They gave up another run off a double and single before striking out the side. When the Dodgers' closer, Ramiro Sanchez, came up to the plate, it was a foregone conclusion. Two strikeouts.

And just to add a little sugar to the cake, Chris unerringly caught the final out; a pop-up direct to the shortstop.

Boston was silent; another dream in ruins. The Dodgers fans went completely crazy; Sally could not stop shrieking.

She raced down the stairs, down through the tunnels reserved for the players, and rushed out onto the field, mixing with the other wives, the children, the girlfriends; Chris was just being lowered to the grass by his teammates who had hoisted him around; he caught sight of her, ignored the forest of microphones shoved in his face, put his arms round the small of her back, and bent her into a slow, powerful kiss that had every housewife in America fanning herself.

Chapter Forty-Three

'Don't you think you should sleep?' Sally asked, as they settled into the small private jet, parked on the tarmac at Logan Airport. They had just come from a riotous post-game dinner, yet Chris had refused more than a single glass of champagne, and had told Sally not to have anything either. 'We had a suite at the Victrix. We could just go back, make love all night . . .'

'I don't want you listed as my girlfriend for one more minute.' Nelson shook his head. 'This has been the most spectacular day of my life and I don't want it to end.'

'But going back to LA now—'

'We're not going to LA. We're going to Vegas. We're getting married. At the Bellagio. I have it all arranged.'

Sally gasped. 'Married?'

He bent forward, kissed her lightly on the lips. 'I decided that in the seventh inning stretch, win or lose. Called the owner on my cell; this is his jet. Screw the party, we can do that too, but I want to elope. Just you and me. No damn guests. No protocol. It's the fairytale night, baby. Anything's possible.'

'Oh God!' Sally burst into tears. 'I love you, Chris!'

'Glad to hear that,' he said. 'I love you too, honey. And it's a good thing, because I have nothing else to do with myself now except make love to you and bring up the rugrats.'

She blinked. 'Why?'

'I'm quitting baseball. I'm thirty-five, at the top of the game . . .' He grinned. 'World Champ. Hit the winning homer. Caught the final out. You know what every last athlete does? They hang on, they try to repeat, one more season. They wind up getting less and less dough, watching their stats slip, being booed off the field and playing in the minors or retiring from injury after a losing season with the damn Detroit Tigers.' He shook his head. 'Not for me. I don't need the cash or the back problems. You be the star now, 'cause I'm looking forward to a long, anonymous retirement, as rich as Midas and getting laid every day.'

Sally wiped away the tears and started to laugh. 'You know you're crazy as hell.'

'Not gonna try to talk me out of it?'

'Hell no. I want to be Sally Nelson. And I want you there, not halfway around the country.'

She moved closer to him, feeling his warmth, slipping one hand inside his shirt; he was aroused, she could tell just by looking at him.

'No,' he growled, batting her away. 'Insatiable little minx. If I can wait, so can you.'

He'd done it perfectly: the honeymoon suite, an enormous bed covered with rose petals, white, her favourites; no tacky Elvis chapel, just a black-robed Justice of the Peace, with an off-duty cop as a witness; fruit juices, bagels, crisped bacon laid out in their suite, so they didn't have to interrupt themselves to get the door for room service. The management, sensing a coup, had somehow managed to obtain some World Series Champion memorabilia, and decorated the suite; the TV was replaying the game when they walked into the room.

After they were legally wed, Chris politely shook hands with the judge and the cop, then half shoved Sally into the nearest elevator. He rode it in silence to their suite, and unlocked the door. Then in one strong motion, he swept her, squealing, into his arms and hoisted her unceremoniously over his shoulder, head down, long hair streaming, as if she was nothing, as if her weight didn't bother him in the slightest. He carried her into the suite and flung her down on the bed.

'Evening, Mrs Nelson,' Chris said, straddling her and pinning her down with a kiss.

Sally moaned; it was four in the morning, but she had never felt so alive. She reached down, fumbling, for the buttons of her shirt.

'No time,' he said, yanking down her jeans.

Eventually, three hours later, sweating in each other's arms, they surrendered to sleep as the sun came up over the desert.

'I've got to call Mom,' Sally said, when they woke at noon.

'That can wait. You'll be just as married tonight,' Chris said. 'Come here.'

They stayed in the honeymoon suite for three days, ordering room service, leaving only for a dip in the rooftop pool. Sally sent orders via the bellhop, and fresh clothes were delivered to the suite; they had packed nothing. It was pure bliss. Mona, once told, didn't even mind; Chris's parents were mad, but managed to swallow it for the sake of family harmony, especially when he reassured them the big wedding party was still on.

Sally was bruised in the best way; she decided she loved it. Chris couldn't get enough of her. And to hell with protection. If she got pregnant now, all the better. There was a Governor of Kansas who did the job while carrying twins.

Finally, even Chris wanted to go home; it was fun being cheered every time he set foot outside his rooms, but even poolside they wanted his autograph.

'That eighty-acre plot in Beverly Hills is starting to look real good.'

'Told you,' Sally said smugly.

He patted her on the ass. 'Watch yourself, Mrs Nelson.'

'And I want to get back to work, as well. Jane Morgan's left several messages on my voicemail. She's flying down for a meeting.' Sally looked at him out of the corner of her eye to check if he was annoyed, but Chris just shrugged.

'Like I said, knock yourself out. I'll be the one taking laps in the pool. And lying on the couch with the remote.'

Sally beamed. Haya could eat her heart out; he was the *perfect* man!

The GLAMOUR boardroom was a beautiful thing. Architect designed, in the new extension, it said that the company was owned by women. Sally had been meticulous. A long table and chairs, Scandinavian blond woods. Some of Haya's finest tapestries framed on the walls; a few select magazine covers – Sally on the cover of *Time*, Jane on the cover of *Fortune*. Fresh flowers, daily, just in case. Soft Aubusson carpets. The latest in audio/visual. And a terrific view of the Pacific from the huge windows, tinted against the ferocity of the sun.

Not that they needed all that space. Jane had insisted that nobody be there except Sally and herself. No secretaries. No lawyers.

'But if it's a board meeting, don't we have to notify Haya?' Sally had asked.

'It's not a board meeting. I just want to talk to you.'

'Fine.'

Sally had hung up, intending to be there. She still liked Jane, but she no longer trusted her.

And now here they were. Adults; beautiful women. Jane would never be as sexy as Sally, but she definitely had something – fiery New York chic. That hard casing, though, it would put men off – all but the toughest. Sally wondered what Jane had to prove. She had a suspicion she was about to find out.

'I want to take the company public,' Jane said.

Damn, Sally thought. No chitchat. No pleasantries. Jane meant business.

'Why? Financing?'

Jane nodded. 'We can go global. And we can still retain enough shares to have a controlling interest.'

Sally nodded, slowly. 'You asked Haya if you could buy her shares.'

Jane flushed. How did Sally know that? She saw the flicker of anger in her partner's spine, and stiffened. Jane had underestimated Sally, perhaps. But it didn't make any difference. What she was doing was just.

'She wouldn't sell them to me.'

'But why didn't you tell me?'

Jane's dark eyes narrowed. 'Did you ask her the same thing, Sally?'

Sally nodded, slowly.

'For the same reason you didn't tell me, I suppose.' Jane gave a great sigh; she was glad, cards on the table. 'I know both of you have made a huge contribution, and I'd never force you out, and you're both rich. But GLAMOUR is mine. I'm at the stage where I want to control it. I think it would be best for me and the company, and you guys too. Haya can get on with being a princess, you can be a star. I'll take care of the dollars and cents.'

Sally was furious. What blatant contempt!

'Um, excuse me, Jane, but GLAMOUR is mine. *My* designs, *my* image. Being a star, as you put it, is what sells this store. I could get anybody to do the financials, any damn firm in New York. That's backroom stuff.'

There was a long pause.

'Don't let's fight over this.'

'I think that ship has sailed,' Sally responded.

Jane twisted her fingers. 'Do you have the other shares, then? Did Haya give them to you?'

'No. And I think she's being a total dog in the manger about it. She doesn't even want to stay involved. At least you and me both live it.'

Jane nodded, hugely relieved. There was still a chance, then.

'We can force her to go public. You and I, together, can vote for that with two-thirds of the shares. That way things are on the open market. If you can get control, good for you. You know I'm going to try to. I value our friendship, Sally, you know I do. But this is apart from that and it's my life. You've got Chris, Haya's got a whole new life . . .'

'So what's Craig Levin? Chopped liver?'

Jane had to smile at the New York expression. 'My ex-boyfriend,' she said, simply. 'We broke up.' She blushed, and admitted, 'He sold me his shares.'

'God*damn* you!' Sally shouted, jumping to her feet. 'You never even told me!'

'Less of the histrionics,' Jane responded sharply. 'Same way you never told me after asking Haya. We both think our way is best. Let's not make this personal.'

'It's always been personal. GLAMOUR is me. Not some random brand. Me. In a store. It's what America loves.'

'If we go public, you have a chance to compete for those shares. So do I. I want to form my own company now, aimed at taking over GLAMOUR. Morgana, Inc. It'll have financial offices everywhere. And no partners.'

Sally sat down again, slowly. 'I want to make Nelson a company, too. My own brand cosmetics, as well as the GLAMOUR own brand. And I want to mop up whatever's out there. You can do just as well with any stock, Jane, to you it's just money.'

Jane swallowed the insult. Tempers were high. If she said what she was thinking, she could lose Sally's friendship for good.

'If we don't go public, it'll be eternal stalemate. You and I on each other's nerves. Both of us resenting Haya. No good for us or the company.'

'I agree with that.'

'I'll never sell up to you, nor you to me.'

'And Haya's sitting tight. No – it's the only way. I see that.' Sally nodded. 'I'll call our lawyers and vote my stock with yours. So long as we have seats on the board and a controlling stake.'

'Of course. You want to tell Haya?'

Sally thought of the wedding, of Haya's haughty attitude, the waitress thrusting a shawl over her carefully chosen dress.

'You better do it.

'You two fallen out?'

'Not fatally. We seem to have drifted apart a little.' Sally felt a pang; anger, relief, regret, she wasn't sure. 'Same as you and me. Same as all three of us.'

Jane was silent then, her dark head bowed.

'I'll make you a very generous offer for your shares, Sal. I can get the money. Then this wouldn't come between us.'

Sally stood up. 'At the end of the day we are friends, not sisters. Things happen. Life happens. I want GLAMOUR, Jane. I hope you get even richer any which way, but I want this store.'

Jane nodded, sadly. 'I'll call Haya. And I'll be in touch. We should do it fast. I'm looking to float in six months. In the meantime, I can still work with you?'

Sally laughed. 'You kidding? I'll be tripling the promo. We want this to be the biggest launch ever. When GLAMOUR floats, I want it to be a proper global chain.'

Jane reached across the table and offered Sally her hand;

after a second's hesitation, the blonde girl shook it. She gave Jane a knowing smile.

'I think you Brits might say, "May the best girl win".'

'It's beautiful,' Haya said. 'Thank you.'

She gave the little Moroccan girl a hug and a kiss. Her parents looked on, beaming with pride; they called down God's blessings on Her Royal Highness.

Haya lifted up the little picture, clumsily drawn on paper in bright felt-tip pen, showing Haya standing beside a GLAMOUR store that resembled a large bazaar. Appropriate really, that's what it was. The girl, Salma, was twelve, but had Down's; the drawing was as garish as a five year old's. Salma grinned toothily, pleased with her hug and kiss.

The special school was a new one in Casablanca. Haya was making a whistlestop tour of charitable schools in the region; she'd planned out a full schedule with Jaber, and started on it the day after their honeymoon.

'But you've got an event every day.' He shook his head. 'Four tours a year, not counting my state visits . . .'

'I can't sit on my hands, you know that,' Haya told him. 'If I'm going to do the charity thing, I want to *do* it. Full time. Use the title, use the position. I've been a company director for years now, I need that buzz. Noor will come with me. And they're mostly in Ghada, I'll only be apart from you a couple of weeks a year, at most.'

'And when our children come, *insh'Allah*?'

'Then I'll stick to Ghada. But hey, princesses here travel in style,' Haya teased him. She wondered if she'd ever get used to it, the enormous limos, the outriders, the crazy jewels and exquisite robes. First-class, air-conditioned comfort wherever she set foot. Being the Prince's favoured girl had been one thing; this was a whole new ball game. But Haya was determined to earn her keep. She refused to be one of those spoilt young ladies who spent their lives at polo matches or shopping in Dubai. 'Up until the end of the pregnancy, it shouldn't be a problem at all.'

'If it happens, you'll travel with the royal physician.'

'Well, yes, sir.' Haya kissed him on the lips.

'I'm proud of you.' Jaber ran his hands possessively over her body, tugging her towards the bed. 'The people love you. Everybody is noticing. Even the Queen is starting to approve.'

'After that wedding . . .'

'Never mind that.' He brushed his thumbs across her breasts, feeling her shudder, then slipped the robes from her shoulders, gently biting down upon them. 'Come here, Princess, come and get the seal of *my* approval.'

Haya grinned, remembering it. She felt guiltily pleased that today was her last day in North Africa and the royal flight would be taking her home tomorrow. She hated to be away from Jaber. She loved him, and she wanted him.

Her aide, a Miss Aisha al-Akhtam, was giving her that discreet little wave. Haya stood up, gave an enthusiastic little speech about Salma and the wonderful work being done at the school, shook hands with the bowing and curtsying staff, and allowed herself to be escorted out by her bodyguards.

'You have some calls, Highness.'

'Thanks, Aisha. Give me the mobile.'

Aisha shook her head, emphatically. 'No, ma'am. We must get you to a secure place.'

'There's trouble?' Haya demanded, instantly alert. She beckoned the new nanny to come over with Noor and cuddled the toddler, who was already half asleep. Emily Doughty had long since tired of the heat and gone home to Scotland; Haya still missed her. She had presented her friend with a fabulous diamond brooch in the shape of the Ghadan palm tree; it was worth more than a chic flat in Edinburgh, but Haya doubted Mrs Doughty would ever be parted from it.

'Yes – no – please get into the car, *Siti* Haya.'

She obeyed. A face like that was not to be argued with. But as soon as the driver had pulled onto the streets – miraculously cleared by her omnipresent outriders – and they were safely heading to the airport, Haya demanded to know what the problem was.

'His Majesty is gravely ill.'

'The King?' Haya shook her head. 'Poor man, God spare him! Where is my husband?'

'That is just it, Highness. The Prince asks you to come home at once. He says things are happening and you must be there. Your appointments for this afternoon have been cancelled.'

Haya did not like that. 'On whose orders? I never cancelled them.'

'Prince Jaber's,' Aisha said firmly.

Haya bit her lip. Her husband outranked her, of course, and could do what he liked. She found it slightly sexy that he was ordering her schedule around. On the other hand, Jaber would never do that unless something was up.

'Is there any danger?'

'No, Highness.'

'Then let's get going,' Haya said.

'And one more thing, your friend rang from the United States. Miss Morgan. She said it was important.'

What now? This was exactly the wrong time for Jane to be calling her. 'That can wait.'

Aisha nodded. 'She said if you said that, to tell you they are selling the company.'

A rush of adrenaline poured through Haya; her palms started to sweat; she felt the soft hairs on the back of her neck start to prickle and rise.

'Get me on that airplane!' she said to her driver.

'Yes, Highness,' he replied, and stepped on the gas.

Chapter Forty-Four

While Noor was settled, eating her lunch of puréed fruit and soft cheese, Haya retreated into her private cabin to call from the Skyphone. They had in-flight TV, and although the national station was censored, she could pick up what was going on; the King, suddenly ill with a stroke, and now recovered, was tinkering with the succession. His eldest son, who had tried to kill him, had long been exiled; the younger brother was a playboy, and was apparently being removed. That meant it was wide open. He had five other boys, a half-brother and a vast array of cousins.

Would the new Crown Prince favour Jaber? Would he be finished as Prime Minister? Almost certainly. A new administration would put its own man in . . .

She wanted to get back there, to be with her husband. When she got through to him, he was calm. Talked about the King's health and said it was all in God's hands; Haya thought the palace lines might be bugged; if he was anxious, he wouldn't discuss things over the phone.

That left Jane. What the hell? Haya wanted this nonsense out the way, and fast.

She dialled the number Jane had left.

'Morgana, Inc. How may I direct your call?'

'I'm sorry, I was looking for GLAMOUR,' Haya said, confused.

'Were you looking for Miz Morgan, ma'am? This is her

new company. Any queries about the stores can go directly to her office. Who shall I say is calling?'

Haya felt an icy chill. What the *hell*?

'This is Haya al-Yanna,' she said, angrily. 'Put me through to her at once.'

'Yes, certainly, Your Royal Highness.' Haya was impressed; typical Jane to hire the best staff around, right from the get-go, she thought; even the operators were capable of putting two and two together. 'One moment, ma'am.'

There was a pause, and Jane came on directly. Haya supposed she should be grateful for not being put on hold.

'Haya?'

'I got some crazy message, and believe me, Jane, this isn't the time,' Haya said, crisply. 'We're not doing anything dramatic with GLAMOUR right now. My husband—'

'Yes, it's on the news. I know you'll want to focus on him, Haya.'

'If that's another pitch for my shares . . .'

'Not directly. Look, I've known you too long to soft-soap it, and I can see you have your hands full, so here goes. Sally and I are determined to take GLAMOUR public. We're holding a board meeting on Monday, and this is your notification. You don't need to be there, because we form a quorum without you, and we are going to instruct banks to put the company on the market.'

Haya gasped. 'You wouldn't.'

'It has to be, Haya. It's got too big. And we all have different visions.' Jane sounded slightly wistful, but she was ploughing on. 'The fact is both Sally and I want to own the company, and the only way out of the stalemate is to float the shares and compete with the stockholders. We'll be holding back enough of a personal stake to make sure the three of us still sit on the board – that is, if you still want to.'

'Damn right I do!' Haya was shouting, and she didn't care who heard her. 'Are you two using this crisis to shove me out of the picture? I'm the *soul* of our store, it's *mine*. I provide half the stock and ninety per cent of the vision. Without me you wouldn't bother with one ethical sale—'

'When you're a public company, ethical is making money for the pension funds who own your shares. Families have their savings in you.'

'But we're not public!'

'We're going to be.' Jane was clearly amused by Haya's claim, and that drove her to a white-hot fury. 'It seems all three of us think we made the biggest contribution here.'

'So much for friendship.'

'We could argue that since you are now a bona fide royal with no intention of working again, you would have been a friend to sell your shares to Sally and me. It's a bit selfish, Haya. You're being a dog in the manger about this.'

'I could never trust anybody else with my regional operation. You know how much sweat I put into that thing?'

'Haya, face it.' Jane was blunt. 'You're done. You're finished. Princesses and boardrooms don't mix, at least you got that right. You could at least let your co-founders run with the ball.'

'We'll see if I'm finished,' Haya shouted. 'I don't want to be just somebody's wife. Ahmed had his business and Jaber has his politics, but GLAMOUR was my thing. My own. My store, my stock, my damn business model!' She was enraged. 'Have you forgotten who suggested the idea of this store in the first place? It was me! I'll be there on Monday, Jane Morgan. And if you start that meeting without me I'll sue your asses off!'

She slammed down the phone and jumped to her feet, pacing around the cabin, seething with rage.

There was an urgent knock on the door, and Aisha, her face shiny with excitement, poked her head inside.

'Highness!'

'Did I say come in?' Haya was simmering with rage, and her unfortunate aide was in the line of fire.

'Excuse me, Highness!' Aisha said. She bowed her head low, and sank into a very deep curtsy, which brought Haya up short. Aisha and she had been working together for a while now. Except in public, Aisha never curtsied. 'But you must come in here, you must come and see the television!'

Haya hurried out into the main cabin. Everybody was staring at the wall-mounted TV, which was tuned in to CNN via satellite; as she entered, they all turned to look at her.

'Mama!' Noor said, oblivious.

The screen showed her husband, dressed in a dark Western suit, sunglasses on, surrounded by soldiers, exiting from the Queen Fizouleh hospital in Ghada City; Haya's mouth dropped open as she saw the caption scrolling across the bottom of the screen.

'And regional sources confirm, I repeat, we have confirmation,' the red-headed anchor was saying, 'that King Ali has appointed his Prime Minister, Prince Jaber Ibn Mohammed, as the new Crown Prince of Ghada. Prince Jaber's wife is Princess Haya –' her own face, smiling with Sally and Jane, an old PR shot, flashed up – 'an American citizen and a founder of the wildly successful GLAMOUR chain of luxury stores. So we could wind up with two American queens in the Middle East, Jack!'

'Prince Jaber is known for his moderate attitude towards the West and a strong commitment to social justice and democracy,' the co-anchor said. 'But Ghadan officials were keen to stress that the King's health remains good . . .'

Haya paled, and steadied herself against a seat.

'Turn it off,' she said quietly.

A soldier leaped to obey her.

'We will all pray for the health of the King,' she added. And as they were staring at her, she covered her face and turned towards Mecca.

Oh God . . . please spare him!

She didn't want to be Queen. She hadn't signed up to be Queen!

Haya thought of her daughter, her husband, her new country, her parents. And she thought of the news item she had just seen. If her life was to shift again, in this cataclysmic way, the palace would definitely want her to stay the hell out of the boardroom.

Haya did not care. Jane and Sally would be counting on that. But the one thing Haya was damn sure of was that she was going to save her company.

She hoped Jaber would understand why it mattered. But come hell or high water, Sunday night she was getting on a plane to LA.

'Great doing business with you.' Rose Rothstein shook hands briskly with Jane. 'It's a great space, I think you'll be very happy. If we can assist you with anything more, get in touch.'

'I will. Thanks.' Jane liked Rose, one half of the dynamic J.R. Realty team; with her husband Jacob she was battling to take over his family's company, Rothstein Realty. Jacob was rich, but Rose had started with nothing. They offered the best value business leases in town. She had just stolen five thousand square feet on the Lower East Side. And even better, it came fully carpeted and equipped; Jane wouldn't have to waste time.

She walked around her new offices. Great views of lower Broadway, looking up to the World Trade Center; perfect for a Wall Street newcomer.

Jane would employ fifteen brokers, two analysts and fifteen assistants. As she expanded, she hoped it'd be more.

Maybe she could never be another Craig Levin, but she was sure as hell going to try. Until GLAMOUR was hers, that meant trading in currencies and stocks; Jane intended to take buy-and-hold positions, maybe start a retail hedge fund. Her track record there was golden. Plus, she thought she might dabble in real estate. Buying and leasing sites for the stores had taught her about commercial property.

She didn't want to be another woman executive. To persuade stockholders to sell their GLAMOUR shares to her, she needed to be playing in the mixed divisions.

The thought of Haya, shouting and raging, crossed her mind; of Sally, telling her any broker could handle the finances.

And of Craig, her man, her love, lying there, not stopping her, not holding her.

Her father; the last time she had seen him, clutching ineffectually at him as he got into his diplomatic car.

Friends. Lovers. Family. In the end, you could trust only yourself.

Let Monday come. When she sat down in that boardroom, her offices would be fully staffed, fully funded, and trading.

She walked out. Time to get her hair and nails done. The press would be there, Monday. Haya was an almost-queen, and Sally was a star. She, the single girl, didn't want to look bad.

Jane thought of Craig, and winced from the sheer physical ache of it. She wanted him so badly. Wanted his body driving into hers, his strong, bearish frame on her slight one, her fingers clutching at his back.

But she wanted so much more than that, too. And he wasn't going to give it to her.

Love – whatever kind of love – was always dangerous, a bad risk. She'd never got away with her heart intact. Now she was just playing to win.

But as she locked the office door behind her, there were tears in her eyes.

Jane despised her own weakness.

*

Sally glanced down at the little stick. She'd had the pregnancy test included in her grocery deliveries; that way it could be anonymous. She got her shopping with a credit card in the name of her assistant, to stop the tabloids raking through her trash. Didn't want to read about it in the *Enquirer*.

The little blue flush crept up to the window. Sally held her breath . . .

But no; there was only the one line. She waited. Nothing. Not pregnant.

Sally sighed. Of course, it wasn't gonna happen right away. She was just gonna have to be patient. Oh yeah – and practise a lot.

She was fitter than she'd ever been. Chris loved to play around while working her out. Talk about an incentive! He made her watch while he lifted weights with his shirt off. Got her so worked up, watching his strong muscles slide around under that tanned skin, his biceps straining, that Sally could scarely keep from jumping on him as soon as he was done.

Before, it had been good. Now they were married, it was perfect. Every time she looked down at the thick band of white diamonds – there was enough ice on her left hand to satisfy a polar bear – Sally felt a rush of deep, profound pleasure. He was hers – signed, sealed, delivered. She relaxed in bed in a way she hadn't thought possible. All she wanted now was to have his babies . . .

And to run her company.

Hey. This wasn't a once for all thing, she consoled herself as she looked at the single, lonely little line. They got an infinite number of attempts.

With GLAMOUR, not so much. Sally threw out the stick, washed her hands, and went downstairs to call her lawyers again. She might not be the world's biggest brain, but she was smart. And there were brains around for hire.

Sally hadn't gone through it in Texas for nothing. She was her daddy's daughter to this day. Let Haya and Jane pit their bookish minds against her street smarts. Sally knew who was going to win.

'But aren't you under contract? To GLAMOUR?'

The grey men in suits were sitting behind the table in the Chicago office, trying not to ogle Sally. She knew how she appeared to them: a butterfly among moths; her tight, short dress displaying her perfectly toned figure; her long, blond hair shimmering with fresh white platinum highlights shot through a buttercup base, like liquid strands of sunshine; a ruby and diamond necklace, another gift from Chris, lying against the creamy hollows of her throat.

'Yes. The Lassiter brand is theirs. Which is why I'm proposing to start a new one.' She dazzled them with a smile.

'But what could be more recognizable than Lassiter?'

'*Sally*,' she said, and winked.

The chemists and marketing executives sighed. *Sally*. Of course. It was perfect. One word. One name. America's sweetheart.

'I'll want the highest quality and on-time delivery; we'd be talking to America's premiere outlets, not just GLAMOUR. This would be on sale at Harrods, at Saks Fifth Avenue, at Scruples in LA. And that means zero mistakes. I'm thinking Crème de la Mer – but bigger. A little less expensive, too. Affordable luxury, like a Chanel lipstick.'

They nodded frantically, as similar execs had done in every cosmetic house she'd visited.

'And the marketing?'

'I have it out to five top Madison Avenue firms.'

'It's been a very impressive presentation, Mrs Nelson,' said their chairman, standing up and all but rubbing his hands together in glee. 'And we'd love to be in business with you. We'll messenger our costings to your people later today.'

'Total creative control,' Sally repeated firmly. 'It's my brand, you'll be supplying the raw materials – that's going to be in the contract.'

'Mrs Nelson, you *are* the brand,' he replied, looking surprised. 'Why would we go anywhere else?'

Sally shook hands, delighted. Yeah, they got it. If only her two former best friends could see things the way the marketing men of America did!

On the limo ride back to O'Hare Airport she mulled things over. She could get this going by the end of next week. Samples on her desk, packaging included . . .

She'd intended to use it purely as blackmail. But now another idea was forming. Two companies – one public, one her own. Why not? If Jane could branch out, why not her? Showing she was competent, showing she could run things – that would sweet-talk the shareholders into selling GLAMOUR back to her.

Yeah. It was a great idea. She took out her mobile and dialled the direct line to her chief lawyer. He was head of a big firm in LA, and available to her whenever needed.

'Tony? Sal. Listen, I'm going ahead. Can you draw everything up, get it registered in my name? Sally Lassiter Cosmetics. Thanks, doll. Have the papers waiting when I get home.'

She listened as he gave her a report. Perfect. Everything was going fine.

Jaber sighed with pleasure and rolled off Haya, panting; drained, he lay on the bed and stared at the mosaics in the ceiling.

She was exhausted herself. But man, was he good. Patient, exacting, knowledgeable . . . Jaber applied all his considerable intelligence to handling her body, and Haya leaped in his arms like a salmon swimming upstream. Plus, when the solid brass doors to their bedchamber had shut, he reverted to the desert warrior, uncompromising and masterful; she responded, intensely, unable to help herself.

'I couldn't handle this without you. None of it.'

'You couldn't have refused?' Haya asked, timidly.

'Refused?' Jaber propped himself up on his elbows and stared down at her, her glorious dark hair pooled out over the white Egyptian cotton sheets. 'You can't refuse your destiny when it calls. That way lies eternal regret.'

She turned onto her belly to meet him, and nuzzled kisses into his ear and throat.

'Which is exactly why I have to go.'

'Haya.' He sighed. 'The King isn't doing as well now. He could die any minute. While you're out there. You would be the Queen of Ghada, and sitting in some boardroom in Los Angeles! How would it look?'

'Like you aren't a man who compromises his principles,' she said. 'You took a risk when you married me, Jaber. You know what a woman I am – a businesswoman, a professional. Yes, I set it aside. But not so that they can destroy everything I've built up. Let me save the company. One day. It's all I ask.'

He shook his head. 'Haya, I cannot deny you. But make it as quick as you can, and be back on the jet the second you get out of there.' Jaber sighed. 'Women. You'd think as King I might have it easier.'

She hit him on the chest, grinning. 'No chance.'

'I should have married that distant cousin,' Jaber said, darkly. He reached for his wife, yanking her to him; Haya was amazed at his inexhaustible energy.

'Never mind.' He kissed her lightly, deliberately. 'I'm going to give you a chance to make it up to me.'

*

'The press is coming,' Sally told Jane, bluntly. 'They got word of what we're doing – and the fight.'

'You told them?'

'No,' Sally replied, coldly. 'There are three sets of lawyers' offices involved now, Jane.'

Jane pursed her lips. Damnation.

'Then I suppose the answer is dress well and act civilly. If the analysts think we're at each other's throats, the IPO will be disappointing. They need to understand we remain a team – you and I, at least. Haya's out of the game.'

'Agreed. See you Monday,' Sally said crisply, and hung up.

Jane was listening to a dial tone. Slowly, she replaced the receiver. She had no doubt that Monday afternoon, Pacific, she would be making the deals with institutions that would give her control. So why did she feel so down?

Her phone rang again, and Jane jumped. But it was only the double tone that meant the concierge was calling.

'Yes, Ortiz?'

'Miz Morgan, we got a delivery here. Boy, do we ever.' The fat old man was chuckling. 'Flowers, from Mr Levin.'

She shivered. Why would he do this? Hadn't she been clear? She wanted a clean break.

'You can bring them up.'

'No, ma'am, *I* can't. But the delivery men will.'

'What do you mean?'

'He sent you flowers – like, a *truck* load. There has to be about a hundred arrangements. In pots. There's even a flowering orange tree. Smells pretty good down here, ma'am.'

'Is the truck still there?'

'Unloading now.'

'No,' Jane said. The pain was as bright and sharp as a diamond now. 'Ortiz, refuse delivery, OK? I don't want them. Tell the men to take them back.'

There was a pause, but he knew not to argue with her.

'Yes, ma'am. Any message?'

She thought about it.

'Yes. Tell him "All or nothing".'

She replaced the receiver again and fled into her rooftop garden. Somewhere with no phone, high enough so that nobody overlooked her, where she could lie on a recliner, by her Japanese fountain, look at the sky and have a little peace.

My heart can't take this, Jane thought. I know they all think I'm made of stone. But it hurts to love him, it hurts so deeply.

She decided she would check into a hotel, the Victrix on Central Park. Nice and anonymous, strictly no incoming calls, and stay there until the flight left on Monday.

Craig would get the message. She loved him far too much to act like his personal hooker. And perhaps her rebellious heart would get the message, too. Grief is there so you can move on.

Chapter Forty-Five

Craig Levin sat in front of his desk and tried to concentrate. Behind him, a sheer wall of glass looked out over Wall Street. It was an office for a master of the universe. His playground, too. He'd had it modelled on Gordon Gekko's pad in the movie; a cautionary tale, but Levin used it as a motivational tool.

Last night he'd dated a model. Very smart girl, Israeli, dark and doe-eyed, a pre-med student before she quit for the catwalk. Just a date; just dinner. Even though she was obviously willing, and her body had been rounder and lusher than Jane's ever was, he'd stopped at dinner; feeling sick, feeling like he was cheating on Jane.

Dumb. They'd broken up.

He spent a poor night thinking of his ex. Angry with her. Make that furious. Why had she taken the hottest thing in his life, the best thing, and messed with it? Stupid, conventional notions of love. He *did* love her – passionately. What the hell difference did a ring make?

Lots of folks had told Levin it was their way or the highway. He'd never failed to take the highway, and it had worked out well enough.

Not this time.

He knew Jane, though. Younger than he was, not quite as smart, and he enjoyed that, enjoyed making her feel it in bed, enjoyed forcing deeper and higher orgasms from her. It was better because she always fought it. She was so damn hot, an ongoing challenge.

He knew every inch of her. Knew just how she was pining for him.

What was he thinking? He had got Jane in the first place with a planned campaign, patient months of waiting, letting her longing do the work. Now all he had to do was get her back. He lifted the phone and called the all-night florist, delivery first thing in the morning.

Just now, his chief assistant had called with the news. And Jane's message.

It was so – so strong. So classy. She was everything the model hadn't been. She fascinated him. Levin felt himself start to weaken, to surrender. For once in their relationship, he thought, she was going to triumph.

He called her building.

'She's gone, Mr Levin,' the doorman told him, with, Craig thought, a touch of pride. 'She said to tell you to please stop chasing her. She won't be back until after her meeting, and she doesn't want you to call even then.'

'Thanks for telling me, Ortiz.'

He hung up as his assistant buzzed him.

'Craig, your nine a.m. from Bank of America's in the outer lobby and the nine twenty from KKR are waiting in reception . . .'

'Emily, apologize to them, cancel all my appointments.'

'All of them?' she protested.

'All of them. For the week.'

'Are you feeling OK, Craig?'

'No. I'm sick. And I'm going home. Tell Peter to deal with everything.' His deputy in the firm. 'And don't call me.'

'You got it,' she said. The light disappeared. Secretaries who argued the toss with him didn't get to keep their jobs very long.

He called one of his personal PAs, back at the house.

'Claudette, send the limo to the office. We're going to

JFK. I want to be on the first flight to LA. Call the people at the Hollywood house and get it ready.'

He had no idea what he was going to say to Jane, but he was going to see her. And she couldn't hide forever. She'd be in LA, Monday morning, going to that meeting at GLAMOUR. And Craig Levin was gonna be waiting.

By Thursday, the story had broken.

And boy, had it broken.

In a suite at the Victrix, in the vast master bedroom in Bel Air, in the palace of the Crown Prince in Ghada City, the three young women opened their papers, logged on to their computers. Nobody liked what they saw.

It was ugly; a bloodbath.

The dry, dull pages of the business press had something juicy, for once. A scandal involving pretty girls, billions of dollars, athletes, financiers and kings.

The *Wall Street Journal* said it all: the single-word headline was *Catfight*.

Haya – in both robes and coronet, and a T-shirt and jeans, figured prominently. The Yank princess. Anita Roddick, or an obsessive putting her cash before her country?

Jane – a workaholic boss from hell. Laid off thousands of Shop Smart workers. Loner, anti-social, not a feminine bone in her body. Why should shareholders trust her? A fluky career, too young, no real track record . . .

Sally. Business Barbie, or brainless bimbo? The dull grey suits in the business press had been waiting to tear her down. Daughter of the disgraced Paulie Lassiter. Athlete's wife. Good to design clothes and get her picture taken – hardly the stuff of corporate governance.

Put together, the news hacks reluctantly concluded, these women had something. But it couldn't last. After years of explosive growth and more cash than most male CEOs made in a lifetime, they were already at each other's throats.

When GLAMOUR went public, it was a great opportunity for some *true* retailers to come swooping in.

On Monday, the shares were out there for the grabbing. It was time, the consensus said, for the market to clean up the mess.

There was a little speculation as to which shark could mop up most of Jane Morgan's shares the first. Surely she'd be most easily elbowed aside. Her expertise could be replicated.

But what about Haya? Ethical business? What was the point of that? Even the Body Shop sold out to L'Oréal, they sneered. On the other hand, Haya had made, to say the least, a *very* good marriage. As Crown Prince, Jaber had sixteen palaces! What if he used his personal fortune to hoover up the shares before US brokers could get to him? Nobody could compete with that kind of firepower.

And Sally? Well, that was different. America just loved her. She was the Homecoming Queen, all grown up and sitting pretty at the boardroom table. Wife of the champ. Brand gold. The male writers agreed she'd have to be placated. The new corporate owners should pay her a very handsome premium, give her some placatory title, a non-exec directorship, anything to keep her there.

Whatever, it would be interesting. The shares went on sale right after the meeting; 10 a.m., Pacific. Of course, they'd all be rich: but one, or all, of these women would find their dream had been ruined.

'The Embassy is on the phone, Your Royal Highness.'

Jaber frowned. He did not need to ask which embassy. This was the third call this morning.

His Excellency began with the usual formalities, then got right down to business.

'The Princess cannot come, sir.'

'Haven't we had this conversation, Ambassador Rashman?'

'Yes, but Your Royal Highness has not seen the press . . .'

'Indeed I have,' he said, heavily. He did not want Haya there either. The King was sinking. The whole thing was disastrous.

'I mean the physical press. It's only Saturday, and they are already gathering near the store. It might as well be the Oscars. They are staking out positions. You must forbid this scandal, sir, you must—'

Jaber cut him off. He did not like Haya's plans, but she was her own woman. And he would not be dictated to by anybody.

'*Must* is an interesting word to use to your Crown Prince, *Excellency*.'

A long pause. 'Sir, forgive me. Your wife—'

'Her Royal Highness has decided to make the trip. That's all there is to it. You may send along a special adviser to accompany her.'

'But—'

'I strongly advise you not to cross my will, Rashman. If I find the Princess has been interfered with, you will be replaced within twenty-four hours. While His Majesty is sick, I am regent. Not to put too fine a point on it,' Jaber smiled, thinly, 'my word is law. Do I make myself clear?'

He heard the official swallowing. 'The Princess's wish stands. Yes, Your Royal Highness. Please do forgive my—'

'Goodbye, Excellency,' Jaber said firmly. He hung up.

Haya was standing there, in the archway to his private apartments.

'Excuse me – I heard most of that.'

'I hope you know what you're doing,' he said, heavily. 'The King is sinking, Haya.'

'When I go, I will go as a princess,' she promised him. 'No informality; I will wear the circlet. They will see a modern woman of Ghada who bears herself with dignity.'

'Hurry back,' he said. Uncomfortable, still. How much

dignity could she have with those dogs of photographers ready to tear her to shreds?

Jane wanted to be sick. Her hands physically shook when she read those papers. They were saying Sally was right. That anybody could manage the finances. That once they went public, she would shortly be replaced.

She had to perform at that meeting. She had to give the performance of her life. The only way to survive was to get her hands on one of the other girls' shares.

She wondered how Craig Levin, financial genius, would handle it, and then hated herself for her need, for her ache for him.

No, damn it, no! No Cinderella fantasies. There was no white knight ready to ride and save her this time. Craig had been there at the start. At the end, it was going to be up to her.

Sally stepped out of the shower and reached for a towelling robe. She had these brought in direct from GLAMOUR, and they were the softest, fluffiest things this side of the Regent Beverly Wilshire hotel. Perfect, in fact, for moments like this, when she barely had the energy to towel herself off.

Chris was out at the ballpark, playing catch with a bunch of disabled kids. She was so proud of him; the only work he did these days was for charity.

She hadn't complained to Chris. In fact, she'd ordered the maid to sweep away the papers and keep the TVs permanently tuned to ESPN. This fight was her deal, no need to involve her husband. Pay her off? Bribe her with a salary? Those male writers thought she was the bimbo, but they'd somehow failed to see that she had more money than God. And when GLAMOUR went public, forget it, she'd be able to buy her own country . . .

She didn't want money. Didn't they get that? It was all about control, about self-esteem.

Right now, she was gonna take care of herself. Go sit on the terrace, and watch the sun set over her lawn; that big lawn where the tents had been pitched for her party, all those years ago. Jane Morgan's social debut.

Sally found herself sighing, with nostalgia, and bitter regret. She glanced behind her at the long, spiralling staircase. The three of them had walked down that staircase, together, beautiful, *beyond* beautiful, sixteen years old and with the world at their feet.

At Sally's feet, anyway; she had spread the blanket of her popularity across them for protection; that dazzling night, it had worked.

Maybe those things didn't count for much now. Maybe it was time to grow up, to put the past behind her.

Jane and Haya evidently had.

She was walking out of the door when something caught her eye. There, in the bathroom trash basket. The little stick she had tossed.

No *way*.

But yes – there was something different about it, something half covered with a tissue, that had caught her peripheral vision . . .

Sally picked it up. She'd been too fast to throw it out. She hadn't waited the full three minutes.

There was a second line. Faint, but distinct. She reached out one manicured hand and steadied herself against the wall of her walk-in marble wet room.

She was pregnant.

There was no socializing. No small talk. None of the girls was up for it. They shook hands; their lawyers shook hands. Nobody curtsied to Haya; she had not been expecting it.

'The meeting will come to order,' Jane said, loudly.

The lawyers shut up. When Jane Morgan spoke, people tended to listen.

'We're here to sign off on the exact terms of the IPO. I take it you all have the documents?'

Haya raised her hand. 'Madam Chairman, if I may?'

Jane sat down immediately.

'Of course, Your Royal Highness,' she said, with studied politeness.

'The company has aggressively pursued ethical commerce. As you know, ethical trade in the Middle East, with a remit to expand into Europe and Asia, has been my focus as a director. What guarantees can you give me this will continue?'

'I can't. A public company can make no such arrangements.'

'That's unacceptable,' Haya said, instantly. 'We made commitments, and I intend to honour your word.'

That stung.

'May I say something?'

'Mrs Nelson has the floor,' Jane said crisply.

'My lawyers have discovered that Lassiter make-up and Lassiter designed clothes accounted for twenty-five per cent of total merchandise sales. Further to this, we estimate that at least a third of the goodwill value of the chain comes from my personal image.'

'You're hardly unbiased,' Jane said. 'Haya would contest that.'

'Princess Haya,' Haya snapped.

Jane inclined her head. 'Forgive me, ma'am. *Princess* Haya. I think you'll find that my figures for the total real estate, staffing, distribution, funding, inventory management, analyst presentations and general costs come to over fifty per cent of the total value of this company.'

There was a long silence. The three women around the table glared at each other.

'Well, ladies.' Kent Green, the head of the firm of Sally's lawyers, spoke up, a touch smugly. 'Perhaps it's time to let the professionals take over, otherwise this meeting could go on all day. And we *do* have a deadline.'

'Just a second.' Sally spoke up. 'I'd like y'all to give us the room, please. I want to speak to my partners alone.'

'I don't think that's wise, Sally,' Kent said, paternalistically.

'I can't allow Her Royal Highness to be unrepresented in the room,' piped up Ahmed al-Jamir, the special adviser. Babysitter, as Haya thought of him.

'I won't let my client go to bat by herself.' Jane's lawyer, Rachel Frohman, spoke clearly and authoritatively. 'Sorry, Miz Nelson, but we're staying.'

Jane was looking over at Sally; then she glanced at Haya.

'No, you're not. Give me the room, please, Rachel.'

'But Miz Morgan—'

'Now, please.'

'Mr al-Jamir, you too.' Haya nodded at the diplomat, then backed it up in Arabic.

There was a creak and a shift, and with great reluctance the small army of lawyers, assistants, advisers, and accountants left the room.

As soon as the door shut, Sally smiled.

'Girls, what the hell are we doing?' she said.

'What we have to,' Jane replied, with a heavy heart.

'Bull*shit*, girlfriend. We're doing what we think we have to. We're cornered into this. Nobody wants to be here.' Sally looked at her two friends – determined they would stay that way. 'Y'all want to know what happened to me today? I found out I was pregnant.'

Haya beamed, shocked out of her reserve. 'Get out of here, Sally!'

'Really.' She shook her head, tears in her eyes. 'You guys remember that day in the playground, the first day Haya turned up? Nobody wanted to talk to her. I figured we'd look out for her. Why? Because I was pretty and Jane was smart. We filled the gaps with each other. Don't see why life has to get complicated. Don't see why we still can't do that.'

'But GLAMOUR is everything we've worked for,' Jane said. 'It's everything I am.'

'The hell it is. You were doing just fine before we started. And you'll do great after this. I want the company. We all do. But I was an only child, you two were practically my sisters.' Sally passed one hand over her belly. 'I've started *Sally* make-up. Jane's got Morgana now. Haya, looks like that crown you're wearing's gonna get a bit bigger, no? *This is just a store.*'

Jane jumped up from the table and went to the window; not before they saw the tears streaming down her face.

She had lost Craig. And now she would lose these two?

'You're a hundred per cent right.' She turned round. 'But we have different ideas. This store is something special. Let's not put it on the market and let men chew it up. Let's just decide who's going to run it.'

Haya said, 'I owe you both an apology. I've got caught up in my husband. I haven't talked enough to you.' She blushed, richly. 'Sally, I dumped you in my wedding without bothering to explain a damn thing. I'm sorry.'

'Me too, Haya.' Sally came over and gave her a hug. Haya stood up and went and rubbed Jane's back.

'You guys will guarantee the livelihoods of all the poor women supplying us, right?'

Sally and Jane both nodded.

'Then you can have my shares. Fifty-fifty. I'll give the money to charity.'

As soon as she said it, a smile broke out on her face; something lifted, almost physically, from her heart.

'What a relief,' she said. 'It's been great, you know? But nobody needs this kind of pressure.' Haya cocked her head, looked at Sally. 'You're going to have a baby. If you want my two cents, let Jane have it. She's been the most driven of all of us.'

Sally exhaled, then shrugged. 'Yes. All right, then. Jane.'

'No.' Jane turned around; her eyes were red, but, like Haya, she was smiling; she rubbed the tears away. 'Sally, you said it. All these years, I've been fighting the fact I had nobody to love me. No father, no mother. But that was wrong. I had you two. I just couldn't see it.' She paused. 'I have succeeded in everything I've done. Why does it have to be the thing I started out in? Maybe I'll go into real estate. It hardly matters. But GLAMOUR, GLAMOUR is special. There can only be one choice. It's you, Sally. You who looked after both of us. You who taught us how to use being beautiful. There are a lot of sceptics out there, a lot of analysts sneering. But I never thought you were dumb. Street smarts count for a lot in this world. You take it, and you show them all that being a woman isn't some kind of choice between beauty and brains.' She grinned. 'Besides, I want to trade stocks. I could use all that liquid cash.'

Sally could hardly believe it. She clapped her hands, like a kid at a birthday party. 'Really? It's mine?'

'It's all yours,' Jane replied, and shook her hand.

The three girls came together and gave each other a hug.

'Shall we let them back in?' Haya asked, with a wink. 'There are gonna be some pretty sad lawyers. All those billable hours, down the drain.'

'Let's.' Jane grinned. 'Can't wait to see the press when we announce this. The media loves it when women fight. What are they going to say now?'

Sally nodded, and Jane flung open the doors. The large knot of hangers-on raced back in and sat around the table.

'Don't get too comfortable,' Jane said, smiling. 'The deal's off. No public stock.'

There was uproar.

'We have arranged a private sale. Ladies and gentlemen, I give you the new Chairman and CEO of GLAMOUR. Ms Sally Nelson.'

Jane got up from the head of the table and surrendered her position to her friend; as she went and sat at Sally's seat, she felt no pain, no regret; just an open sense of joy and possibility. The future was hers; no limits, no ties.

She looked across at Haya, and saw that she felt the same way.

Sally shook out her long, glossy hair, in a delicious shimmer of gold, leaned back confidently in her chair, and glanced over the table full of dumbstruck investment advisers.

'I'm in charge, gentlemen,' she said. 'So let's get to work.'

Epilogue

King Nazir died a day after Haya touched down in Ghada City. Jaber led the mourning, and Haya found herself Queen, mingling with royalty and heads of state at the funeral. She didn't have much time to stand around and wonder; a week later, just before the coronation, she discovered she, too, was pregnant.

She decided to make her role her full-time job. Haya never let a day go past without visiting some charity, and the people loved her. She founded girls' schools across the kingdom, and worked with Jaber as a full partner on drawing up new laws to promote democracy.

She and Noor were often seen, at weekends, dropping in to the new GLAMOUR being built in Ghada City. It became the hottest store in the country.

Sally continued work up until one day before her wedding party, which was the social event of the year, and two days before she gave birth. Queen Haya attended the wedding, and was Sally's matron of honour; Jane preferred to sit quietly in the front row. But at the birth, Jane was there, holding Sally's hand as Chris Junior came shrieking into the world. His dad, the toughest guy in sports, had refused to come in and watch Sally moaning a pain he could do nothing to spare her from.

Sally took two months off. When she came back, she instituted flexible working and staffed crèches at every GLAMOUR store around the world. Women loved it, and the global sales soared.

*

'See? It's always the good guys who finish first,' Haya told her friend.

Jane Morgan had believed that. She left the meeting at GLAMOUR smiling; for the first time in her life, it felt good to lose. She posed for pictures with Haya and Sally, Sally in the middle, the boss, the winner, and Jane didn't mind at all.

She had other things to think about. Like starting over. And mending her heart.

When the press finally melted away, Jane headed back to her limo. She got in the back seat, slipped her sunglasses on, and sighed, a deep, personal sigh of release.

'LAX, please.'

The driver tipped his cap. 'Yes, ma'am.'

She checked in, in no particular hurry. First class meant you could take the first flight that became available.

'I'm afraid we only have seat 1B available, miss. Is that OK for you?'

'That's fine,' said Jane, even though she usually chose her own seat. She shrugged. 'Everything's fine.'

'Great,' said the flight attendant, glancing at her colleague with a sly look. 'Then you're all set. Have a great flight.'

When she boarded, Jane looked around the first-class cabin; it was empty. She spoke to the stewardess.

'I was told there was only seat 1B.'

'That's right, ma'am, all these seats are booked. Can I show you to your . . .'

But Jane was already marching up the cabin. Great, they were going to be really late, all these last-minute boarders. But she wouldn't let something like that spoil her mood. Not now; not today.

At least there was one passenger – the back of a man's head in seat 1A. So much for a peaceful flight. Jane grabbed her case and lifted it.

'Let me get that,' he said, standing and walking into the aisle.

Jane gasped; it was Craig Levin.

He took it from her, just like that first day, and hoisted it easily into the overhead rack.

'I'm not sitting here,' she said, looking wildly around for the stewardess. But the woman had melted away, smiling discreetly.

'You are if you want to fly in this cabin. There are no more seats.'

'Look around you.'

'I bought all of them.'

Jane blinked. 'What? You bought an entire first-class cabin?'

'Just so you had to sit next to me. I think you'll agree that a gesture like that is worthy of respect, at least. Sit down.'

'Craig—'

'I said sit.'

She sat.

He leaned over and kissed her, softly, possessively, on the lips.

'I saw what you did today. That was brave, Jane. That was good.'

'She's right for it.'

'And you're right for me,' he said. 'I want to see if I can soften you up a little more.' Jane stared as he reached into his pocket and drew out a ring case. She put her hands over her mouth. He flipped it open, showed her the small circlet of gold, set with emeralds. 'It was my mother's.' He took her trembling hand, and gently slipped the ring onto it. 'It's a simple fact; you were made to be my woman, nobody else's. I can't sleep without you. And the thought of another man so much as touching you is more than I can bear. So there's only one way to get you to myself. Pre-emptive strike.' Levin kissed her again, much harder, wanting her urgently, hating that they had to wait five hours.

'That's a hell of a proposal.'

'I'm not asking you. I'm claiming you. You're mine; my woman. My wife.'

'Yes,' she said, melting with happiness, and lust, and the sheer exhilaration of it. 'Your wife.'

They kissed, hard; then slower; then his arms snaked around her.

'Damn,' Jane said, grinning, when she came up for air. 'This is going to be fun.'